"A magnificent thriller . . . superbly executed . . . the artfully compulsive storytelling of a master. The hinting at dark mysteries . . . the flawless technique of tantalizing with promised depths beyond the latest revelation—this is story in all its grandeur."

—*The New York Times Book Review*

"THE SCAPEGOAT is the most thrilling of all the famous Du Maurier novels."

—*Wings* (The Literary Guild Review)

"Never has she written a stranger, more tense tale, or one more certain to fill the reader's mind with speculation."

—*Chicago Sunday Tribune*

"Daphne du Maurier, who excels in mystification, has found herself a wholly fascinating situation to explore in her new novel. With wizardry Miss du Maurier makes the book believable and compelling."

—*The Atlantic Monthly*

THE SCAPEGOAT
was originally published by
Doubleday & Company, Inc.

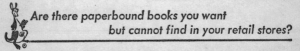

Are there paperbound books you want but cannot find in your retail stores?

Daphne du Maurier

THE SCAPEGOAT

PUBLISHED BY POCKET BOOKS NEW YORK

THE SCAPEGOAT

Doubleday edition published February, 1957

A *Pocket Book* edition
1st printing........February, 1958
6th printing...........June, 1969

This *Pocket Book* edition includes every word
contained in the original, higher-priced edition. It is printed
from brand-new plates made from completely reset, clear, easy-to-read
type. *Pocket Book* editions are published by Pocket Books, a division
of Simon & Schuster, Inc., 630 Fifth Avenue, New York, N.Y. 10020.
Trademarks registered in the United States and other countries.

L

THE
SCAPEGOAT

Chapter 1

I left the car by the side of the cathedral, and then walked down the steps into the Place des Jacobins. It was still raining hard. It had not once let up since Tours, and all I had seen of the countryside I loved was the gleaming surface of the *route nationale*, rhythmically cut by the monotonous swing of the windscreen wiper.

Outside Le Mans, the depression that had grown upon me during the past twenty-four hours had intensified. It was inevitable, always, during the last days of holiday; but this time, more than ever before, I was aware of time having passed too swiftly, not because the days had been overfull but because I had achieved nothing. The notes I had written for the lectures I was to give during the coming autumn were scholarly, precise, with dates and facts that I should afterwards dress up in language designed to strike a spark in the dull minds of inattentive students. But even if I held their flagging interest for a brief half hour, I should know, when I had finished, that nothing I had said to them was of any value, that I had only given them images of history brightly coloured—waxwork models, puppet figures strutting through a charade. The real meaning of history would have escaped me, because I had never been close enough to people.

It was all too easy to lose oneself in a past half real, half imaginary, and so be blind to the present. In the cities that I knew best, Tours, Blois, Orléans, I lost myself in fantasy, seeing other walls, older streets, the crumbling corners of once glittering façades, and they were more live to me than any real structure before my eyes, for in their shadows lay security; but in the hard light of reality there was only doubt and apprehension.

In Blois, in the château, feeling the smoke-blackened walls with my hands, a thousand people might ache and suffer a few hundred yards away but I saw none of them. For there

1

beside me would be Henri III, perfumed and bejewelled, touching my shoulder with a velvet glove, a lap dog in the crook of his arm as though he nursed a child; and the false charm of his crafty feminine face was plainer to me than the mask of the gaping tourist at my side, fumbling for a sweet in a paper bag, while I waited for a footstep, for a cry, and for the Duc de Guise to die. In Orléans I rode beside the Maid, or, like the Bastard, held her stirrup when she mounted, hearing as he did the clamour and the shouting and the deep peal of the bells. Or I might even kneel with her in prayer, awaiting the Voices that sometimes hovered within the fringe of my experience but never came. And I would stumble from the cathedral, watching my half-boy with her pure, fanatic's eyes, close to her unseen world, and then be jolted out of time into the present, where she was nothing but a statue, and I an indifferent historian, and the France she had died to save a country filled with living men and women whom I had never even tried to understand.

As I drove out of Tours, on the last morning, my dissatisfaction with the lectures I should give in London, and my realisation that all I had ever done in life, not only in France but in England also, was to watch people, never to partake in their happiness or pain, brought such a sense of overwhelming depression, deepened by the rain stinging the windows of the car, that when I came to Le Mans, although I had not intended to stop there and lunch, I changed my mind, hoping to change my mood.

It was market day, and in the Place des Jacobins lorries and carts with green tarpaulins stood parked close to the steps below the cathedral, and the rows of stalls were crowded one beside another. It must have been one of the big market days, for the Place was full of country people, and there was an unmistakable smell in the air, half vegetable, half beast, that could come only from the soil, muddied, ruddy-brown and wet, and from the steaming pens where huddled cattle moved in uneasy comradeship. Three men were prodding a bullock towards the lorry beside me. The poor brute bellowed, turning his roped head from side to side, backing away from the lorry, which was already packed with his snorting, frightened

2

fellows. I could see the red flecks in his bewildered eyes as one of the men pricked his flanks with a hayfork.

Two black-shawled women argued beside an open cart, one of them holding by the feet a squawking hen, whose fluttering, protesting wings brushed the wide wicker basket, heaped with apples, on which the woman leant; while towards them came a great hulking fellow in a nut-brown velvet coat, his face purple with good cheer from a nearby bistro, his eyes blurred, his walk unsteady. He grumbled to himself as he peered down at the coins in his open hand, fewer than he had expected, too few—he must somehow have miscalculated in that vanished hour of heat and sweat and tobacco, whence he now came to quarrel with his mother and his wife. I could picture the farmstead which was his home and had been his father's before him, two kilometres from the road up a sand track full of potholes, the low house a pale lemon wash, the roof tiled, the farm and outbuildings a smudge amidst the flat brown fields heaped now with line upon line of pumpkins, lime green or salmon pink, rounded and firm, left to dry before they were fed to the beasts for winter fodder or to the farm people themselves as soup.

I walked past the lorry and across the Place to the brasserie at the corner, and suddenly the pale sun shone from the fitful sky, and the people thronging the Place, who had seemed black smudges in the rain, crowlike, bent, impersonal, became animated blobs of colour, smiling, gesticulating, strolling about their business with new leisure as the sky fell apart, turning the dull day to gold.

The brasserie was crowded, the atmosphere thick with the good smell of food, soupy and pungent—of cheese upon sauce-tipped knives, spilt wine, the bitter dregs of coffee—and rank, too, with the wet cloth of coats heavily rained upon, now drying, the whole scene framed in a blue smoke cloud of Gauloise cigarettes.

I found a seat in the far corner near the service door, and as I ate my omelette, the herb juice splaying the plate, satisfying, warm, the swing door kept bursting backwards, forwards, pushed impatiently by waiters heavily laden with trays piled high with food. At first the sight was an apéritif to my own hunger, but later, when my meal was over, it became some-

3

how a deterrent to digestion—too many fried potatoes, too many pork chops. The woman who ate beside me was still forking beans into her mouth as I called for coffee, and she expostulated to her sister upon the cost of living, ignoring the pallid little girl who sat on the husband's knee and demanded to be taken to the *toilette*. The conversation never ceased, and as I listened—for this sort of thing was my one relaxation when preoccupation with history left me free—my former depression returned to nag beneath the surface of enjoyment. I was an alien, I was not one of them. Years of study, years of training, the fluency with which I spoke their language, taught their history, described their culture, had never brought me closer to the people themselves. I was too diffident, too conscious of my own reserve. My knowledge was library knowledge, and my day-by-day experience no deeper than a tourist's gleanings. The urge to know was with me, and the ache. The smell of the soil, the gleam of the wet roads, the faded paint of shutters masking windows through which I should never look, the grey faces of houses whose doors I should never enter, were to me an everlasting reproach, a reminder of distance, of nationality. Others could force an entrance and break the barrier down: not I. I should never be a Frenchman, never be one of them.

The family sitting beside me got up and left, the clatter ceased, the smoke thinned, and the patron and his wife sat down to eat behind the counter. I paid, and went out, and walked aimlessly along the streets, my lack of purpose, my shifting gaze, my very clothes—grey flannel bags, tweed jacket too well worn over a span of years—betraying me as an Englishman in this jostling crowd of provincials on market day, who sought bargains among the nailed boots hanging upon strings, the aprons spotted black and white, the plaited slippers, the saucepans and umbrellas. Young girls laughing with linked arms, their hair newly frizzed from the coiffeur; old women pausing, reckoning, shaking their heads at the price of checked tablecloths, moving on, not buying; youths with blue-grey chins and purple suits, eyeing the girls, nudging one another, the inevitable cigarette dangling from their lips: all of them, when the day was done, would return to some familiar plot they knew as home. The silent fields were

4

theirs, and the lowing of cattle, the mist rising from the sodden ground, a flyblown kitchen, a cat lapping milk beside a cradle, while the scolding voice of the old grandmother went on and on and her son clumped out into the muddy yard swinging a pail.

Meanwhile I, time no object, would check in at yet another strange hotel, and be accepted as one of them until I produced my British passport; then the bow, the smile, the genuine show of politeness, and the little shrug of regret. "We have very few people at the moment. The season is over. Monsieur has the place to himself," the implication being that surely I must want to plunge into a bunch of hearty compatriots, carrying Kodaks, exchanging snapshots, lending Penguins, borrowing each other's *Daily Mail*. Nor would they ever know, these people of the hotel where I passed a night, any more than those whom I now jostled in the street, that I wanted neither my compatriots nor my own company, but instead the happiness, which could never be mine, of feeling myself one of them, bred and schooled amongst them, bound by some tie of family and blood that they would recognise and understand; so that, living with them, I might share their laughter, fathom their sorrow, eat their bread, no longer stranger's bread but mine and theirs.

I went on walking and the rain came spattering down again, sending the crowd to huddle in the shops, or to seek the shelter of cars and lorries. For no one promenades in the rain unless he is on business bent, like the serious men in broad-brimmed trilby hats who hurried into the Préfecture with brief cases under their arms, while I stood uncertainly on the corner of the Place Aristide Briand. I went into Notre-Dame-de-la-Couture beside the Préfecture. It was empty, save for an old woman praying, tears like pearls in each corner of her wide staring eyes, and later a girl with high pattering heels came briskly up the hollow aisle to burn a candle before a blue-washed statue. Then, like a gulf of darkness swamping reason, I knew that later on I must get drunk, or die. How much did failure matter? Not, perhaps, to my small outside world, not to the few friends who thought they knew me well, not to the persons who employed me nor the students who listened to my lectures, not to the officials at the British

5

Museum, who, benign and courteous, gave me good morning or good afternoon, not to the smooth, dull, kindly London shadows amongst whom I lived and breathed and had my being as a law-abiding, quiet, donnish individual of thirty-eight. But to the self who clamoured for release, the man within? How did my poor record seem to him?

Who he was and whence he sprang, what urges and what longings he might possess, I could not tell. I was so used to denying him expression that his ways were unknown to me; but he might have had a mocking laugh, a casual heart, a swift-roused temper and a ribald tongue. He did not inhabit a solitary book-lined apartment; he did not wake every morning to the certain knowledge of no family, no ties, no entanglements, no friends or interests infinitely precious to him, nothing to serve as goal and anchor save a preoccupation with French history and the French language which somehow, by good fortune, enabled him to earn his daily bread.

Perhaps, if I had not kept him locked within me, he might have laughed, roistered, fought and lied. Perhaps he suffered, perhaps he hated, perhaps he lived by cruelty alone. He might have murdered, stolen—or spent himself in lost causes, loved humanity, embraced a faith that believed in the divinity of both God and Man. Whatever his nature, he always hovered beneath the insignificant façade of that pale self who now sat in the church of Notre-Dame-de-la-Couture waiting for the rain to cease, for the day to fold, for the holiday to come to its appointed end, for autumn to set in, for the day-by-day routine of his normal, uneventful London life to close upon him for another year, another span of time. The question was, how to unlock the door? What lever would set the other free? There was no answer—except, of course, the blurred and temporary ease which a bottle of wine at a café might bring me before I climbed into the car again and drove north. Here, in the empty church, prayer was the alternative; but prayer for what? To complete the half-formed decision in my mind to go to the Abbaye and hope to discover there what to do with failure? I watched the old woman gather herself together and depart, thrusting her rosary into her skirts. Her tears had gone, but whether from consolation or because they had dried upon her cheek I could not tell. I thought of my *carte Michelin* back in the car, and the blue circle with which I had marked the Abbaye de la Grande-Trappe. Why had I done so? What did I expect to gain from going there? Should I have the courage to ring the bell of the building where they lodged their guests? They might have my answer, and the answer to the man within. . . .

I followed the old woman out of church. I had a sudden desire to ask her if she was ill, or lately widowed, or had a dying son, and whether she had new hope since she had prayed; but when I passed through the door and came upon her, still muttering, outside, she mistook my anxious glance for tourist charity, and with a little sidelong glance held out her hand for alms. I gave her two hundred francs, despising my own mean spirit, and fled from her, disenchanted.

It was no longer raining. Red ribbons spanned the sky and the wet streets glistened. People were going home from work on bicycles. The dark smoke from the factory chimneys of the industrial quarter looked black and sullen against the new-washed sky.

I lost any sense of direction, walking away from the shops and boulevards along streets that seemed to lead nowhere, converging upon themselves, frowned upon by factory walls and tall grey buildings, and I knew that what I was doing was without reason: I should either go and fetch the car and book a room for the night in one of the hotels in the centre of the town, or leave Le Mans altogether and drive through Mortagne to la Grande-Trappe. I was surprised to see the station ahead of me, and I remembered that the car and the cathedral were at the other end of the town. The obvious thing to do was to take a taxi back, but first of all I would have a drink at the station buffet, and come to some decision about la Grande-Trappe. I crossed the road, and a car swerved to avoid me and then stopped. The driver leant out of the window and shouted in French, "Hullo, Jean, when did you return?"

The fact that my own name was John confused me. I thought for a moment that he must be someone I had met somewhere, whom I ought to recognise, and I called back, also in French, "I'm only passing through—I go back tonight," wondering who the devil he was.

"A wasted visit, I suppose," he said, "but you'll bluff them all at home it's been a success."

The remark was offensive. What made him think my holiday had been wasted? And how on earth could he know about my own deep personal sense of failure?

Then I realised he was a stranger. I had never seen him before. I bowed politely, excusing myself. "I beg your pardon," I said, "I'm afraid we have both made a mistake."

To my astonishment he laughed, winked broadly, and said, "All right, pretend I haven't seen you. But why do here in Le Mans what could be better done in Paris? I'll ask you when we meet again next Sunday." He let in the clutch and, laughing, drove away.

I watched his car disappear, and turned into the station buffet. If he was drunk, and in a mellow mood, I saw his point. I might follow his example. The buffet was full. People were either boarding trains or leaving them. Chattering travellers elbowed me from the counter. Luggage barked my shins. Whistles blew, the deafening screech of an approaching express merged into the choking gasp of a local train, dogs on leashes yapped, a child wailed. I thought longingly of my car parked beside the cathedral, and how I would sit there in peace, and open my Michelin map, and smoke a cigarette.

Someone jolted my elbow as I drank and said, *"Je vous demande pardon,"* and as I moved to give him space he turned and stared at me and I at him, and I realised, with a strange sense of shock and fear and nausea all combined, that his face and voice were known to me too well.

I was looking at myself.

Chapter 2

We did not speak: we went on staring at one another. I had heard of these things happening, of people who meet casually and turn out to be long-lost cousins, or twins parted at birth; and the idea is amusing, or perhaps fraught with tragedy, like the Man in the Iron Mask.

This was not funny: nor was it tragic. The resemblance

made me slightly sick, reminding me of moments when, passing a shopwindow, I had suddenly seen my own reflection, and the man in the mirror had been a grotesque caricature of what, conceitedly, I had believed myself to be. Such incidents left me chastened, sore, with ego deflated, but they never gave me a chill down the spine, as this encounter did, nor the desire to turn and run.

He was the first to break the silence. "You don't happen to be the devil, by any chance?"

"I might ask you the same question," I replied.

"Here a moment . . ."

He took me by the arm and pulled me closer to the counter, and although the mirror behind the bar was steamy, and partly hidden by glasses and bottles, and confusing because of the many reflections of the other heads, it showed us plainly enough to be standing together, straining, anxious, searching the mirrored surface as though our lives depended upon what it had to tell. And the answer was no chance resemblance, no superficial likeness to be confounded by the different colour of hair or eyes, by the dissimilarity of feature, expression, height, or breadth of shoulder: it was as though one man stood there.

He said—and even the intonation sounded, in my ears, like my own—"I make it a rule never to be surprised by anything in life; there is no reason to make an exception now. What will you drink?"

I was too shaken to care. He asked for two *fines*, and we moved with one accord to the further end of the counter, where the mirror was less steamy and the pushing crowd less dense.

We might have been two actors studying our make-up as we glanced from the looking glass back to one another. He smiled and I smiled too; and then he frowned and I copied him, or rather copied myself; and he arranged his tie and I arranged mine; and we both drank our brandy at one gulp to see what we looked like drinking.

"Are you a man of fortune?" he asked.

"No," I said. "Why?"

"We might do an act at a circus, or make a million in a cabaret. If you haven't got to take a train immediately, I suggest we go on drinking." He ordered two more *fines*. Nobody seemed surprised at the resemblance. "They think you're my twin brother here at the station to meet me," he said. "Perhaps you are. Where are you from?"

"London," I told him.

"Are you in business there?"

"No, I live there. And I work there too."

"What I mean is, where is your home, what part of France do you come from?"

I realised then that he had taken me for a Frenchman like himself. "I'm English," I said. "I happen to have made a study of your language."

He raised his eyebrows. "My compliments," he said. "I wouldn't have known you for a foreigner. What are you doing in Le Mans?"

I explained that I was in the last few days of holiday, and gave him a brief account of my tour. I told him I was a historian and gave lectures in England about his country and its past.

He looked amused. "Is that how you earn a living?"

"Yes."

"Incredible," he said, and offered me a cigarette.

"You have historians over here doing the same thing," I argued. "In fact, your country takes learning much more seriously than mine. There are thousands of professors giving lectures on history all over France."

"Naturally," he said, "but they are all Frenchmen talking about France. They are not Frenchmen who cross the Channel to spend their holidays, and then return here to talk about England. I don't understand why you should be so interested in my country. Are you well paid?"

"Not particularly."

"Married?"

"No. I have no family at all. I live alone."

"You're lucky." He spoke with emphasis, and raised his glass. "To your most fortunate freedom," he said. "Long may it last."

"What about you?" I asked.

"Me?" he said. "Oh, I can call myself a family man. Very

much so, in fact. I was caught long ago. I might even say I have never escaped. Except during the war."

"Are you a man of business too?"

"I own some property. I live about thirty kilometres from here. Do you know Sarthe?"

"I know the country better south of the Loire. I should like to explore Sarthe too, but I'm on my way north. I'll have to leave it for another time."

"A pity. It might have been amusing . . ." He did not finish his sentence, but stared at his glass. "You have a car?"

"Yes, I left it at the cathedral. I lost my bearings, walking, that's why I'm here at the station."

"Are you stopping in Le Mans overnight?"

"I don't know. I haven't planned. As a matter of fact . . ." I paused. The brandy had given me a comfortable glow inside, and I had the impression that it would not matter what I said to this man; it would be like talking to myself. "As a matter of fact, I was thinking of spending a few days in la Grande-Trappe."

"La Grande-Trappe?" he said. "Do you mean the Cistercian monastery near Mortagne?"

"Yes," I said. "It can't be much more than eighty kilometres from here."

"For the love of God, why do you want to go there?"

His phrase was apt. The reason why men went to la Grande-Trappe was to find the love of God. Or so I supposed.

"I thought if I went," I said, "and stayed there before returning to England, I might find the courage to go on living."

He looked at me thoughtfully as he drank his *fine*.

"What's the trouble?" he asked. "A woman?"

"No," I said.

"Money?"

"No."

"You are in some sort of scrape?"

"No."

"You have cancer?"

"No."

He shrugged his shoulders. "Perhaps you're a drunkard," he said, "or a homosexual. Or enjoy discomfort for its own sake.

There must be something seriously wrong if you want to go to la Grande-Trappe."

I glanced beyond him to the mirror once again. And now, for the first time, I could see the difference between us. It was not the clothes, his dark travelling suit and my tweed jacket, which distinguished us; it was his ease of manner that made a contrast to my sober mood. He looked, and spoke, and smiled as I had never done.

"There's nothing wrong," I said. "It's just that, as an individual, I've failed in life."

"So have we all," he said, "you, I, all the people here in the station buffet. We are every one of us failures. The secret of life is to recognise the fact early on, and become reconciled. Then it no longer matters."

"It does matter," I said, "and I am not reconciled."

He finished his drink and glanced at the clock on the wall.

"There is no need," he observed, "to go to la Grande-Trappe immediately. The good monks are waiting upon eternity, they can wait a few more hours for you. Let us go where we can drink in greater comfort, and perhaps dine, because, being a family man, I am in no great hurry to go home."

It was then that I remembered the man in the car who had spoken to me outside. "Are you called Jean?" I asked.

"Yes," he said, "Jean de Gué. Why?"

"Someone mistook me for you, then, outside the station. Some fellow in a car shouted, 'Hullo, Jean,' and when I told him he was mistaken he seemed amused, and obviously thought I, or rather you, didn't want to be recognised."

"That wouldn't surprise me. What did you do?"

"I did nothing. He drove off laughing, calling out something about seeing me on Sunday."

"Oh yes. *La chasse* . . ."

My words must have started a new train of thought, for his expression changed, and I wished I could have read his mind. The blue eyes clouded, and I wondered if I looked as he did when a problem, not easy to solve, thrust its way to the surface of my mind.

He beckoned to a porter who was waiting patiently with a couple of valises outside the swing door of the buffet.

"Did you say you left your car by the cathedral?" he asked.

"Yes," I answered.

"Then if you don't mind giving room to my valises, we might fetch it and drive somewhere for dinner?"

"Certainly. Anywhere you say."

He tipped the porter, summoned a taxi and we drove away. It was odd, and like a dream. So often, dreaming, I was the shadow, watching myself take part in the action of the dream. Now it was happening, and I had the same lack of substance, the same lack of will.

"So he was quite deceived, then?"

"Who?"

His voice, almost like the voice of conscience, startled me, for we had not spoken since getting into the taxi.

"The man who hailed you outside the station," he said.

"Oh yes, completely. He will probably accuse you when you meet. I remember now—he knew you had been away, because he suggested your trip had been unsuccessful. Does that convey anything?"

"Only too well."

I did not pursue the subject. It was none of my business. After a moment I glanced at him, half furtively, and saw that he was looking as furtively at me. Our eyes met, and instead of smiling instinctively, because of the bond of likeness, the sensation was unpleasant, like contact with danger. I turned away from him to gaze out of the window, and as the taxi swerved and pulled up by the cathedral the deep, solemn bells sounded for the Angelus. It was a moment that never failed to move me. The summons was always unexpected, and in a strange way touched a nerve. Tonight the bells rang like a challenge, loud and compelling, as we climbed from the taxi. Then the clanging softened to a murmur, and the murmur to a sigh, and the sigh to a reproach. Two or three people passed through the doors into the cathedral. I went and unlocked the car. My companion waited, looking at the car with interest.

"A Ford Consul," he said. "What year is it?"

"I've had it two years. Done about fifteen thousand."

"You are satisfied with it?"

"Very. I don't get much use out of it except at weekends."

As I stowed away his two valises in the boot he asked me all sorts of questions about the car with the interest of a

13

schoolboy trying out a new machine. He fingered the switches, felt the seats to test the springs, fiddled with the gears and the indicators, and finally asked, with a burst of enthusiasm, whether he might drive her.

"Certainly," I said. "You know this town better than I do. Go ahead."

He settled himself with assurance behind the wheel and I climbed in beside him. As he turned the car away from the cathedral, and so out to the Rue Voltaire, he continued to enthuse in schoolboy fashion, murmuring, "Magnificent, excellent!" under his breath, obviously enjoying every moment of what soon turned out to be, from my own rather cautious standard, a hair-raising ride. When we had jumped one set of lights, and sent an old man leaping for his life, and forced a large Buick driven by an infuriated American into the side of the street, he proceeded to circle the town in order, so he explained, to try the car's pace. "You know," he said, "it amuses me enormously to use other people's possessions. It is one of life's greatest pleasures." I closed my eyes as we took a corner like a bobsleigh.

"Meanwhile," he said, "you are probably dying of hunger?"

"Not at all," I murmured. "I'm at your disposal." It struck me, as I spoke, that the French language was too fine, too polite.

"I was thinking of taking you to the only restaurant where it is possible to eat superbly," he said, "but I have changed my mind. I am known there, and somehow I feel that tonight I want to be without identity. It isn't every day that one comes face to face with oneself."

His words gave me the same sense of discomfort that I had experienced in the taxi. The likeness between us was not something that either of us wanted to show off in public. I realised suddenly that I did not wish to be seen with him. I did not want waiters to look at us. I felt in some way furtive and ashamed. The sensation was peculiar. He began to slow down as we approached the centre of the town.

"Possibly," he said, "I won't go home tonight after all, but take a room at a hotel." He seemed to be thinking aloud. I don't believe he expected a reply. "After all," he went on, "by the time we have dined, it would be rather late to telephone

14

for Gaston to bring in the car. And anyway, they are not expecting me."

I have made the same sort of excuses myself to put off facing something unpleasant. I wondered why he was not anxious to return.

"And you," he said, turning to me as we waited for the lights to change, "after all, you may decide you do not want to go to la Grande-Trappe. You, too, could stay in a hotel."

His voice was odd. It was as though he was feeling his way towards some sort of agreement between us, some sort of solution to a problem that neither of us fully understood, and as he looked at me the expression in his eye was probing and at the same time evasive, masked.

"Perhaps," I said. "I don't know."

He drove through the centre of the town, an enthusiast no longer but preoccupied, and he did not draw up before either of the main hotels that I had noticed earlier in the day, but came to a quarter where the buildings appeared greyer, drabber, closer to the factories and warehouses. In the meaner streets were cheap pensions, dingy lodging houses, and places for a night or an hour where passports were not demanded and questions never asked.

"It is quieter here," he said, and I still could not tell whether he spoke to me or uttered his thoughts aloud. But I did not think much of his choice as he stopped the car in front of a shabby house sandwiched between others equally drab, above whose half-open door the word "hotel," in dim blue electric light, gave warning of its nature.

"Sometimes," he said, "these places can be useful. One does not always want to run up against one's friends."

I said nothing. He switched off the engine and opened the door.

"Are you coming?" he said.

I had no desire to penetrate the mysteries of the *Tout Confort* that I saw advertised, in small letters, beneath the blue light, but I climbed out of the car and heaved his two valises from the boot.

"I don't think so," I said. "You go inside and book your room if you want to. I'd rather dine first and then decide what to do."

I was more inclined to my northern route—the drive to Mortagne, and then the side road to the Abbaye de la Grande-Trappe.

"As you like," he said, shrugging, and I lit a cigarette and watched him push through the door into the hotel. The drinks I had swallowed at the station buffet were beginning to take effect. Nothing that was happening had reality, and in a state of blurred confusion I asked myself what I was doing here in an unattractive side street in Le Mans, waiting for a companion who less than an hour ago had been quite unknown to me, who was still a stranger, but who, because of chance resemblance, had taken charge of my evening, directing its course for good or ill. I wondered whether I should slide into the car and drive away, and so be quit of the whole encounter, which, fascinating at first, now seemed menacing, even evil. I was reaching for the switch when he returned.

"That's fixed," he said. "Come and eat. No need to take the car. I know of a place just round the corner."

I couldn't summon an excuse to be quit of him, and, despising my own weakness, I followed him along the street like a shadow.

He led me to a place half restaurant, half bistro, in the next street. The entrance was stacked with bicycles—it must have been the headquarters of a cycling club—and the inside crowded with youths in coloured jerseys, singing and shouting, while a knot of older men, workmen, played some dice game at a table. He pushed his way with assurance through the turmoil, and we sat down at a table behind a battered screen, the strident voices of the youths half drowned by a crackling radio.

The patron, waiter and bartender in one thrust an indecipherable menu into my hands, and a glass of wine was before me and a plate of soup that I hadn't ordered; for the ceiling was now merging with the floor and time losing significance, and my companion was leaning across the table, his glass raised, saying, "To your sojourn at la Grande-Trappe." Sometimes a fourth drink can have the temporary effect of clearing the confusion caused by the previous three, and as I ate and drank the face in front of me swung back into focus, no longer uncanny or a threat, but benign and familiar as my own in the mirror, smiling when I smiled, frowning when I frowned; and his voice, which seemed to be an echo of my own, urged me into conversation, prodded me into confession, so that I found myself talking about loneliness, death, the empty shell of my personal world, the uncertainty of feeling, the absence of all emotion.

"And so," I heard my voice saying, "surely at la Grande-Trappe, where men live by silence, they must have an answer to this, they must know how to fill the vacuum, for they have deliberately gone into darkness to find light . . . whereas I . . ." I paused, trying to clarify my meaning, because what I was trying to tell him was vital to our two selves. "In other words," I continued, "at la Grande-Trappe they might not give the answer, but they could tell me where to look for it; for although we must each have an individual answer to our individual problems, just as every lock has its own key, yet might not their answer be universal, just as a master key opens every lock?"

His blue eyes, flippant and amused, were not the reflection of my drunken mood but the doubt that follows after it, the mockery on waking.

"No, my friend," he said. "If you knew as much about religion as I do you would run from it like the plague. I have a sister who thinks of nothing else. I have learnt one thing in life, which is that the only motive force in human nature is greed. Insects, animals, men, women, children, we live by greed alone. It is not very pretty, but what of it? The thing to do is to minister to the greed, and to give people what they want. The trouble is, they are never satisfied." He sighed, and poured himself another glass of wine. "You complain that your life is empty," he said. "To me it sounds like paradise. An apartment to yourself, no family ties, no business worries, the whole of London a playground, if you wish—though personally I did not find London gay when I was in exile there for a time in the war, but at any rate the city is vast and free. It does not hang about your neck like a rope."

His voice changed, becoming hard, and there was resentment in his eyes, and exasperation—it was the first sign he had given that he too had his personal problem which he did not wish to face—and he leant forward across the table and said, "You have all the luck in the world, and you are not content. Your parents died many years ago, you told me, and you have no one to make any claim upon you. You are a free man, to wake and eat and work and sleep alone. Count your blessings, and forget this nonsense of la Grande-Trappe."

Like all solitary people, I had become glib of tongue and indiscreet too soon, warming to sympathy. He knew all the little dullnesses of my life, and I knew nothing of his.

"Very well, then," I said, "now it's your turn for the confessional. What's your trouble?"

I thought for a moment that he might be going to tell me. Something wavered in his eyes, a flicker of uncertainty, then it was gone again and in its stead the tolerant smile, the lazy shrug.

"Oh, me!" he said. "My one trouble is that I have too many possessions. Human ones." And his gesture of dismissal as he lit a cigarette was a warning not to question further. I could be introspective if I liked, exploring my own black moods; but I must not probe his. We had finished eating, but we went on sitting there, smoking and drinking, and the chatter of the laughing boys with the bicycles came in great gusts above the tortured singing from the radio, with the scraping of chairs and the arguments of the workmen at their game of dice.

I fell silent, having suddenly no more to say, and I was aware of his eyes upon me all the time, bringing a strange discomfort. When he said he must telephone home, and got up and left the table, I was relieved, as if his absence made it easier to breathe. When he returned I said, "Well?" more as a comment than a question, and he answered briefly, "I told them to send the car in to fetch me tomorrow." Calling the patron, he paid the bill, brushing my feeble attempts aside, and then seized my arm and pushed me through the singing youths into the street.

It was dark, and raining once again. The street was empty. There is nothing gloomier than the fringe of a provincial town on a wet evening, and I murmured something about finding the car and going on my way and what an experience it had been to fall in with him, but he went on holding my

18

arm and said, "I can't let you go like this. It's too unusual, too bizarre." We came once more to the entrance of his shabby, dim hotel, and I looked through the still open door and saw there was no one behind the desk. He noticed it too, and looked over his shoulder and said quickly, "Come upstairs. Let's have one more drink before you go." His voice was urgent, insistent, as though we had little time to lose. I protested, but he half led me up the stairs and across a passage. He took a key out of his pocket, and opened the door, and switched on the light of the small drab single room. "Here," he said, "sit down, make yourself at home," and I sat on the bed because his open valise was on the chair. He had thrown out his pyjamas and hairbrushes and a pair of slippers, and now he brought out his flask and was pouring cognac into a tooth glass. Once again the ceiling hit the floor as it had done in the bistro, and it seemed to me that what was happening was fated, inevitable, that I should never be rid of him or he of me: he would follow me downstairs and come with me in the car, and I should never shake him off. He was my shadow or I was his, and we were bound to each other through eternity.

"What's the matter? Are you ill?" he said, and his eyes were peering into mine.

I stood up, torn between two desires—one to open the door and get away downstairs, and the other to stand beside him once again as we had done at the station buffet, and look into the mirror. I knew that the first was wisdom and the other somehow evil, and yet it had to be done, it had to be experienced once again. He must have guessed my intent, for we turned with one accord and stared, and here, in the small quiet room, the likeness was more uncanny and more horrible than it had been in the crowded buffet, with all the noise and smoke and sound of people, or in the bistro, where I had not thought about it. This wretched room with the patterned wallpaper and the creaking floor was like a tomb shutting out the world: we were here together and there was no escape. He thrust the tooth glass of cognac into my trembling hand and himself drank from the flask, and then he said, his voice unsteady as my own—or was it I who spoke and he who listened?—"Shall I put on your clothes and you wear mine?"

I remember that one of us laughed as I hit the floor.

Chapter 3

Someone was knocking on the door. The sound went on and on, breaking through a dream to consciousness, until finally I roused myself from heaven knows what depths of darkness and shouted *"Entrez!"* staring about me at the unfamiliar room, which gradually became known to me, and real. A man came in, wearing a faded, old-fashioned chauffeur's uniform, with buttoned coat, breeches and leggings, and holding his cap in his hands. His build was short and square, his eyes deep brown, and he looked at me from the doorway with compassion.

"Monsieur le Comte is awake at last?" he said.

I considered him a moment, frowning, and then I glanced once more about the room and saw one valise open on the chair, another on the floor, and the clothes of my late companion thrown over the end of the bed on which I lay. I was wearing a striped pyjama coat I did not recognise. On the washstand were the tooth glass and the flask of cognac. There was no sign of my own clothes, and I could not remember taking them off or putting them away. All I remembered was standing in front of the mirror with my companion by my side.

"Who are you?" I said to the chauffeur. "What do you want?"

He sighed, flashed a sympathetic eye at the disorder of the room, and said, "Monsieur le Comte would like to sleep a little longer?"

"Monsieur le Comte isn't here," I said. "He must have gone out. What's the time?"

The events of the night before became clearer in my mind, and I remembered how my companion had gone to the telephone, while we sat in the bistro, and had given orders for a car to come and fetch him the next day. This must be the chauffeur who had now arrived, and mistook me for his master. The man looked at his watch and told me it was five o'clock.

"What do you mean—five o'clock?" I said. I glanced at the window. It was broad daylight, and I could hear the sound of traffic outside.

"It is five o'clock in the evening," said the chauffeur. "Monsieur le Comte has slept very soundly all the day. I have been waiting here since eleven o'clock this morning."

His words held no reproach: they were merely a statement of fact. I put my hand to my head, which ached abominably. I could feel a swelling on the side of it which was agony to touch, but my head was not aching for this reason only. I thought of the drinks of the night before, and that last tooth glass of cognac. Perhaps it was not the last? I did not remember.

"I fell," I told the chauffeur, "and I think I must have been drugged as well."

"Very possibly," he said. "These things will happen."

His voice had the soothing quality of an old nurse speaking to a child. I swung my legs out of bed and gazed down at the unfamiliar pyjama trousers. They fitted, yet they were not mine, and I had no recollection of putting them on. I put out my hand and touched the vest and pants at the end of the bed, a different type and texture from my own, and I recognised the dark travelling suit of my companion.

"What happened to my clothes?" I asked.

The chauffeur came forward, and, taking the suit, hung the coat on the back of the chair and smoothed the trousers.

"Monsieur le Comte was no doubt thinking of other things when he undressed," he observed, and he glanced across at me and smiled.

"No," I said, "those things aren't mine. They belong to your master. Mine are probably in the wardrobe there."

He raised his eyebrows and pursed his lips, making the little grimace of someone who humours a child, and, crossing to the wardrobe, flung it open. There was nothing hanging there. "Open the drawers," I said. He did so, and they were empty. I got out of bed and rummaged in the two valises, the one on the chair and the other on the floor. They were filled with the possessions of my late companion. I realised then that we must have exchanged clothes in a fit of drunken folly, and somehow the thought of it was distasteful, beastly, and I brushed it aside because I did not want to remember anything else that might have happened.

I went to the window and looked down into the street. There was a Renault drawn up in front of the hotel, and my car had gone.

"Did you see my car when you arrived?" I asked the chauffeur.

The man looked puzzled. "Monsieur le Comte has bought a new car?" he asked. "There was no other car when I came this morning."

His continued self-deception irritated me. "No," I said impatiently, "my car, my Ford. I am not Monsieur le Comte. Monsieur le Comte has gone out wearing my clothes. See if he left a message with anyone below. He must have taken my car too. It's a joke on his part, but I am not particularly amused."

A new expression came into the chauffeur's eyes. He looked worried, upset. "There is no hurry," he said, "if Monsieur le Comte wishes to rest a little longer." He came to me, and very gently put out his hand and felt my head. "Would you like me to fetch something from the *pharmacie?*" he asked. "Does it hurt you when I touch it, like this?"

I knew I must be patient. "Would you ask whoever is at the reception desk to come upstairs?" I said.

He left me and went down the stairs, and when he had gone I looked about the bedroom once again, but nowhere, neither in the wardrobe, nor in the drawers of the dressing table, nor on the table, was there anything of mine by which I could prove my identity. My clothes had vanished, and with them my wallet, passport, money, notebook, key ring, pen, every personal thing I was in the habit of carrying. There was not a stud or a cuff link here that was mine: everything was his. There lay his brushes on the top of the open valise, with the initials J. de G.; there was another suit of clothes; there were shoes, shaving tackle, soap, a sponge, and on the dressing table a wallet with money, cards with "le Comte de Gué" printed upon them and "St. Gilles,

22

Sarthe," in the bottom left-hand corner. I tumbled out the things in the other valise in the vain hope of finding something that belonged to me, but there was nothing—only his clothes, a travelling clock, a small writing folder, a cheque book, various packages wrapped in paper that seemed to be presents.

I went and sat down again on the bed, my head in my hands. There was nothing I could do but wait. Presently he would come back. He must come back. He had taken my car, and I had only to go to the police, tell them the number, explain the loss of my wallet with money, traveller's cheques and passport, and they would find him. Meanwhile . . . meanwhile what?

The chauffeur came back into the room, and with him a greasy, furtive-looking man whom I took to be the reception clerk, or even the patron. He had a slip of paper in his hand which he handed to me, and I saw it was the bill—the price of the single room for a night and a day.

"You have some complaint, Monsieur?" he asked.

"Where is the gentleman I was with last night?" I asked. "Did anybody see him go out this morning?"

"You were alone when you took the room yesterday evening, Monsieur," replied the man. "Whether you were alone when you returned later in the evening I couldn't say. We are discreet here, we never question our clientèle."

Beneath the obsequious tone I caught the note of familiarity, of contempt. The chauffeur was staring at the floor. I saw the hotel clerk or patron glance at my tumbled bed, and from the bed to the brandy flask on the washstand.

"I must get on to the police," I said.

The man looked startled. "You have been robbed, Monsieur?" he asked.

The chauffeur raised his eyes from the floor, and, still clutching his cap in his hand, came and stood beside me, as though to protect me.

"It would be better not to have any trouble, Monsieur le Comte," he said in a low voice. "These things are not very pleasant. In an hour or two you will be feeling more like yourself. Let me help you to dress, and then we will drive

23

home as quickly as possible. Any argument in a place like this might be awkward, you know that very well."

Suddenly I became angry. I thought what a fool I must look, sitting on the bed in that sordid little room, wearing a pair of pyjamas that was not my own, my identity mistaken as if it were a music-hall farce, the victim of a practical joke that was no doubt funny to my late companion but was certainly not to me. All right. If he wished to make an idiot of me, I would do the same to him. I would put on his clothes, and drive his car to hell—as he was no doubt driving mine—and have myself arrested, and then wait for him to turn up and explain his senseless action as best he could.

"Very well. Clear out and leave me," I said to the chauffeur. He went, and the hotelkeeper with him, and with a strange distaste and fury mingled I reached for the vest and pants and began to dress.

When I was ready, and had shaved with his tackle and brushed my hair with his brushes, my reflection stared back at me from the mirror with a strange indefinable difference. My own self had become submerged. It *was* the man who called himself Jean de Gué who stood there now, just as I had seen him last night for the first time when he brushed against my shoulder in the station buffet. The change of clothes had brought a change of personality: my shoulders looked broader, I seemed to hold my head higher, even the expression in my eyes resembled his. I forced a smile, and the reflection in the mirror smiled back at me, a casual half-laugh that somehow went with the square padded shoulders of the coat and the bow tie so unlike any tie I had ever worn. Slowly I took his wallet and counted the notes. He had about twenty thousand francs, and some loose change that had been lying on the dressing table. I searched the wallet carefully in case he had left a word of explanation, some scrawl admitting the joke that he had played upon me. There was nothing, no word, no clue to prove that he had ever been in the room, ever come to the hotel.

My anger grew. I foresaw the string of explanations that was going to be forced upon me—the rambling, disjointed story to the police, their bored reluctance to come with me to the station buffet and the bistro where we had dined the

24

night before, and to hear confirmation of my evidence that two of us, identical in appearance, had been together there. How he must be laughing at me now, Jean de Gué, with nearly a whole day gone, at the wheel of my car, driving north, east, south or west, anywhere he pleased, with twenty-five pounds of traveller's cheques still uncashed and what other money I had, wearing my clothes, perhaps even sitting at some café reading my lecture notes, that look of lazy amusement on his face. He was free to enjoy his joke, to go where he pleased and return when the joke palled; while I sat in a police station or a consulate, trying to make the officials grasp my story, and very likely not even being believed.

I put the washing and shaving kit and pyjamas back into the valise, and then went downstairs and asked the furtive-looking fellow at the desk to fetch the things from the room. He still wore an expression half familiar, half amused, as though we shared some smutty understanding, and I wondered if this place was a haunt of Jean de Gué's, if he had been in the habit of coming here, in secret, to heaven only knew what rendezvous. And when I had paid the bill, and he had followed me out with the luggage to the ancient Renault and the waiting chauffeur, I realised that I had taken the first step in duplicity: by not protesting, by not at once demanding the police, by wearing the wrong clothes and passing myself off as Jean de Gué even for half an hour, I had put myself in the wrong. I was now the accomplice of the man who had driven away, and no longer his accuser.

The chauffeur had put the luggage in the car and now stood by the door, holding it open. "Monsieur le Comte is himself again?" he asked anxiously.

I could have answered, "I am not Monsieur le Comte. Drive me to the police station at once," but I did not. I took my second decisive step, and got into the driving seat of the Renault, which happened to be a make of car that I knew well; for in other years, if I had not brought my own car, I would generally hire one and drive to places of interest near the town or village where I was staying. The chauffeur sat in the passenger seat beside me. I started the car, filled with an intense desire to get away from that dingy, shabby hotel and never set eyes on it again, and, as my anger rose and self-disgust took possession of me, I followed the first road I saw that led out of Le Mans, away from the city and what had happened there the night before, and onto the *route nationale* to open country. Last evening he had let my poor Ford rip, indifferent to the consequences because it was not his; now I could return his carelessness with interest. I stepped on the accelerator, and the old car leapt in response. Whatever damage I do to her, I thought, it does not matter—she isn't mine. I am without responsibility, and the accident would be Jean de Gué's. If I turn the car deliberately into the side of the road it will be his action, not mine.

Suddenly I laughed, and the chauffeur beside me said, "That's better. Before we left Le Mans I was afraid that Monsieur le Comte was going to be ill, and it would never have done to be found there, in that hotel. I was upset last night when you told me to fetch you there. It was a good thing Monsieur Paul did not come instead of me, but luckily he had too much to do."

I let my third chance pass. I could have stopped the car and said to him, "This has gone far enough. Take me back to Le Mans. I have never heard of Monsieur Paul, and I will prove it to you and to the police." But instead I drove faster still, overtaking the cars ahead of me, possessed by a reckless feeling I had never known before, the sensation that I myself did not matter any more. I was wearing another man's clothes, driving another man's car, and no one could call me to account for any action. For the first time I was free.

I must have driven about twenty-five kilometres along the *route nationale* when an approaching village forced me to slow down. I saw the name of the village, but took no notice of it, and we were through and out again the other side before the chauffeur said, "You have missed the turning, Monsieur le Comte."

I knew then that I was committed. It was too late to retract. Some freak of fortune had brought me, at this day and hour and minute, to this place on the road, this spot on the map, to the heart of this unknown countryside, in a land to which I did not belong and which I had for years told myself I wanted to understand. For the first time I saw the

26

point of the joke, the irony of the situation as it must have struck Jean de Gué when he left me sleeping in the hotel in Le Mans.

"The only motive force in human nature is greed," he had said to me. "The thing to do is to minister to the greed, and to give people what they want." He had given me what I asked, the chance to be accepted. He had lent me his name, his possessions, his identity. I had told him my own life was empty: he had given me his. I had complained of failure: he had lifted the burden of failure when he took my clothes and my car and drove away as myself. Whatever I had to carry now, in his stead, could not matter to me because it was no longer mine. Just as an actor paints old lines upon a young face, or hides behind the part he must create, so the old anxious self that I knew too well could be submerged and forgotten, and the new self would be someone without a care, without responsibility, calling himself Jean de Gué; for whatever this false Jean de Gué did, whatever folly he committed, it could not hurt me, the living John.

Some intuition of these things flashed through my mind now as I slowed down. I had no future, except what other, unknown people made of it, beginning with the chauffeur at my side, who had just told me, perhaps prophetically, that I had missed the turning.

"All right," I said, stopping the car. "You drive the rest of the way."

He looked at me enquiringly but made no answer, and we exchanged places without a word. He turned the car back to the village we had passed and struck left, leaving the *route nationale* behind us.

Now that I no longer had the car like a live thing to direct I slouched in the passenger seat, a dummy figure without thought. The fever and excitement died away. Let them do their worst—but who "they" were I did not trouble to ask myself.

The setting sun dipped in our wake, and as we drove east the deep country folded upon us, forested and still. The lonely farmsteads lay oasis-like and misty, isolated patches amongst the soft red glow of fields. The acres of land were remote and beautiful as a vast ocean unexplored, and the golden asparagus fern like mermaids' hair, bordering the ribbon road that wound towards the trees. Nothing was real to me, nothing had substance. Everything I saw had the quality of a dream, from the pale stubble to the reedy stems of sunflowers long since picked and left to fall upon themselves with the first autumn frost. The solidity of haystacks, streaky white, usually hard and clear-cut on the horizon, merged to the soil, becoming part of it, and long avenues of poplars, with shivering, falling leaves, came out of nowhere and disappeared again. Ghost trees, tall and slim, closed in upon the lone figure of a peasant woman walking, head bowed, towards some unseen destination. A sudden impulse bade me tell the chauffeur to stop the car, and I stood for a moment, listening to silence, as the sun went down behind us dark and red, and the white mist rose. No traveller venturing for the first time in territory unmapped and unexplored could have felt more isolated than I did for that one moment upon the empty road. The stillness came from the land. Long centuries had moulded it, a million ages kneaded it, history had trampled upon it, men and women had fed themselves and lived and died upon it, and nothing of what we thought or said or did could trouble the brooding peace that was the soil. There beneath me and about me was the heart. I wondered how close I was, for one brief second, to an answer to my turmoil, doubt, distress; closer even amongst the patterned fields under the darkening sky than I might have been had I followed that first forgotten impulse and driven northward to la Grande-Trappe.

The chauffeur said, "Monsieur le Comte has no great longing to go home?"

I looked down at his kind, honest face, sympathy in the depths of his brown eyes, and irony too, the gentle mockery of one who must surely love his master well, who would fight for him and die for him, yet dare to tell him when he strayed. It occurred to me that never before had I sensed devotion in anybody's eyes. His warmth brought a smile from me in answer, until I remembered that it was not me he loved but Jean de Gué. I climbed back again into the car beside him.

"It isn't always easy," I said, "to be a family man," echoing the words that had been spoken to me the night before.

28

"Very true," replied the chauffeur with a shrug and a sigh. "There are always so many problems to solve in a household such as yours. Sometimes I wonder how Monsieur le Comte avoids disaster."

A household such as mine . . . The road topped the brow of a hill and I saw the warning sign of the approaching village of St. Gilles. We passed an ancient church, a little sandy square flanked with a few worn houses and a solitary grocer's shop, a tobacconist's and a petrol pump, and swung left down an avenue of limes over a narrow bridge. And now the enormity of what I was doing, of what I had already done, hit me like a violent blow. A surging wave of apprehension, and indeed of terror, engulfed me totally. I knew the meaning of the word "panic" in its full sense. I had but one desire— to run, to hide, to be concealed anywhere in some ditch or hole, not to be carried forward fatefully and inevitably to the château I saw looming ahead of me behind ivy-covered walls, the small windows in its two foremost towers aflame with the last dying whisper of the sun. The car jolted over a wooden bridgeway spanning a moat that had once perhaps held water but was now gone to grass and nettles, and, passing swiftly through the open gate, circled the gravel approach and came to a standstill before the waiting château. A narrow terrace ran beneath the windows, which were already shuttered against the evening, giving a lost, dead look to the façade, and as I hesitated, still humped in the seat of the car, the figure of a man came out of the one dark door between the windows and stood there on the terrace, waiting.

"There's Monsieur Paul," said the chauffeur. "If he questions me later I shall say you had business in Le Mans, and that I picked you up from the Hotel de Paris."

He got out of the car and I followed slowly.

"Gaston," called the man on the terrace, "don't put the car away. I shall be using it. There's something wrong with the Citroën." He looked down at me, leaning on the balustrade. "Well?" he said. "You've taken your time." And he did not smile.

My own forced greeting died on my lips, and like a criminal, hunted, snatching at any cover, I retreated to the back of the car for refuge. But the chauffeur—his name was Gaston, then—already had the two valises in his hand and barred the way. I went up the steps to the terrace, lifting my eyes to meet the first penetrating gaze, the man's use of the familiar "tu" proving him, surely, to be a relative. I saw that he was shorter, thinner, probably younger than myself, yet with a haggard appearance as if he were tired or his health bad, and the lines around his mouth were pinched and dissatisfied. I stood beside him, waiting for his move.

"You might have telephoned," he said. "They waited lunch. Françoise and Renée declared you had had an accident. I said it was extremely unlikely, and you were probably spending the day in the bar of the Hotel de Paris. We tried to get you there, but they told us you hadn't been seen. After that, of course, there were the usual lamentations."

Surprise that I had passed his near inspection kept me silent. I was not sure what it was that I had expected. Doubt, perhaps, a closer stare, an intuition on his part that I was not the man he knew. He looked me up and down, then laughed, the laugh of someone who is irritated, not amused.

"I tell you frankly, you look a wreck," he said.

When Gaston had smiled at me so short a while since, the unaccustomed warmth had been a benison unearned. Now, for the first time in my life, I recognised dislike. The effect was strange. I was angry for the sake of Jean de Gué. Whatever he might have done to incur hostility, I was on his side.

"Thank you," I said. "Your opinion doesn't worry me. As a matter of fact, I feel extremely well."

He turned on his heel, walking towards the door, and Gaston caught my eye and smiled. I realised with amazement that I had said what was expected of me, and the answering "tu," which I had never used before, had come naturally, without effort.

I followed the man named Paul into the house. The hall was small and surprisingly narrow, leading to another, wider passage whence I could see a twisting stairway going to the floors above. There was the clean, cold smell of polish, bearing no relation to the faded deck chairs stacked against the wall in odd juxtaposition to the Louis XVI chairs beside them. At the far end of the wider passage hall there was a great cabinet between two doors, the sort of graceful, fluted thing one sees roped off from the public in museums, and facing it, upon a stuccoed wall, a tortured, blackened picture of Christ crucified. The murmur of voices came from one of the half-open doors.

Paul crossed the passage and called through the first of them, "Here is Jean arrived at last," his voice betraying the exasperation he had already shown to me. "I'm off, I'm late already," he went on, and, glancing at me once again, "I can see you are in no fit state to tell me anything tonight. We can discuss things in the morning." He turned, and went out again by the door leading to the terrace.

Gaston, the two valises in his hand, was mounting the stairs. I wondered if I should follow him, when a woman's voice called from the room beyond, "Are you there, Jean?" the note in the voice high, complaining, and once again the chauffeur glanced down at me in sympathy. Slowly, with lagging steps, I passed through the open door into the room. I had one swift impression of vastness, heavy curtains, papered walls. Standard lamps, masked by ugly shades with beaded fringes, dimmed the light. An exquisite chandelier, glittering through a veil of dust, the candles broken, swung unlit from the high ceiling. One long window, still unshuttered, betrayed acres of tangled grassway disappearing into alleyways of trees, and cropping the grass, almost beneath the window itself, were black and white cattle, their shapes ghostly in the falling light.

Three women were sitting in the room. As I entered they looked up, and one of them, tall as myself, with hard, clearcut features and a narrow mouth, her hair strained back and twisted in a bun, immediately rose to her feet and left the room. A second, with dark hair and eyes, handsome, almost beautiful, yet marred by a sallow skin and a sullen mouth, watched me without expression from the sofa where she sat, some sewing or embroidery beside her, and when the first woman left the room she called over her shoulder without turning round, "If you must go, Blanche, please shut the door. I mind draughts, if nobody else does."

The third woman had faded, rather colourless blonde hair. She might have been pretty once, and perhaps was still, with small delicate features and blue eyes, but her expression of defeat, of petulance, destroyed the first impression of charm. She did not smile. She gave a little laugh of exasperation, as the man Paul had done, and then, rising to her feet, came towards me across the polished floor.

"Well," she said, "aren't you going to kiss either of us?"

Chapter 4

I bent my head and kissed her on both cheeks, and, still saying nothing, crossed the floor and kissed the other woman in the same fashion. The first, the fair, blue-eyed one—it was she who had called when I was in the hall, for I recognised the voice—then came and took my arm, leading me to the open hearth on which one log smouldered.

"You may well look ashamed of yourself," she said, using the familiar "tu" just as Paul had done. "We have been worried sick that you might have had an accident, but as usual you didn't give that a thought. What have you been doing all day, and why didn't you go to the Hotel de Paris? They told Paul on the telephone that they hadn't seen you at all. I begin to think you do this sort of thing on purpose, just to frighten us and make us imagine the worst."

"And what would that be, the worst?" I asked her.

My retort, coming so quickly, gave me confidence. The dream, or rather nightmare, was something completely out of my experience. I felt that it did not matter what I said or did: however outrageous, these people would have to accept it.

"You knew perfectly well we must have been anxious," the woman said, dropping my arm, giving me a little push. "When you are away from home you are capable of anything, and you never think of anybody but yourself. You talk too much, you drink too much, you drive too fast . . ."

"I do everything, in fact, to excess?" I interrupted.

"You do everything you can to make us miserable," she said.

"Oh, leave him alone," called the other woman. "It is obvious from his manner that he isn't going to tell you anything. You are just wasting your time."

"Thank you," I said.

She looked up from her work, flashing me a look of understanding. We were allies, perhaps? I wondered who she was. She bore no resemblance to Paul, though both were dark. The other woman sat down again and sighed. I realised now, from her figure, that she must be expecting a child.

"You could at least tell us what happened in Paris," she said. "Or is that to remain a mystery too?"

"I have no idea what happened in Paris," I said carelessly. "I'm suffering from loss of memory."

"You are suffering from too much to drink," she answered. "I can smell it on your breath. It would be a good idea if you went up to bed and slept it off. Don't go near Marie-Noel —she has some fever, and it might be catching. They have a case of measles in the village, and if I were to get that"—she paused and looked at both of us significantly—"you can imagine what might happen."

I went on standing with my back to the hearth, wondering how I could escape and find the right room. I should recognise the valises, of course, unless they had been unpacked. Even so, in one of the rooms I should be able to find the hairbrushes with the initials J. de G. Bed was at least a refuge, a place to think and plan. Or did I no longer want to think or plan? Laughter, uncontrolled, rose in my throat.

"What is it now?" asked the fair woman, resentful, complaining.

"It's an extraordinary situation," I said. "You neither of you know how extraordinary."

The freedom of saying this acted like a charm on my own lingering consciousness of self. It was like being invisible, or possessing a ventriloquist's voice.

"I see nothing funny in infection," said the fair woman, "and certainly not at the present moment. I have no desire to bring a blind or perhaps crippled child into the world, which can happen to someone in my condition who catches measles. Or do you mean the situation in Paris was extraordinary? I hope, for everyone's sake, that you came to some agreement, though I can hardly believe it."

33

I turned from her questioning, reproachful eyes to those of the other woman, but her expression had changed. A wave of colour had come into her sallow complexion, adding to her beauty, but she looked wary, and before she dropped her eyes again to her work she shook her head, imperceptibly, as if in warning. She and de Gué were undoubtedly allies, but in what cause? And what relationship were the three of them, one to the other? I decided suddenly to tell the truth as a test of my courage, and also because I was no longer sure of my own sanity.

"Actually," I said, "I am not Jean de Gué at all. I am someone else. We met in Le Mans last night, and changed clothes, and he has disappeared in my car, heaven knows where, and I am here in his place. You must admit it's an extraordinary situation."

I expected an outburst from the fair woman, but instead she sighed again, gazing a moment at the single smouldering log on the hearth. Ignoring me, she yawned, and, turning towards the other woman, said, "Was Paul going to be late this evening? He did not tell me."

"After a Rotary Club dinner of course he'll be late," the dark one replied. "Have you ever known Paul back early on those occasions?"

"He was not in much of a mood to enjoy himself," said the other, "and seeing Jean come home in this sort of condition won't have improved his temper."

Neither of them glanced in my direction. My remark, which they must have interpreted as some tasteless joke, had fallen so flat that they had not even thought it worth while to make a crushing retort. This surely proved that deception was complete. I could behave as I pleased, say anything, do anything: they would merely believe me to be drunk or mad. The sensation was indescribable. Driving the Renault had been the first moment of intoxication, but now that I had passed the test of speaking to de Gué's family, embracing them, even, and still they had sensed nothing unusual, the feeling of power was overwhelming. I could, if I chose, do incalculable harm to these people whom I did not know—injure them, upset their lives, put them at odds one with another—and it would not matter to me because they were dummies, strangers, they had nothing to do with my life. When Jean de Gué left me sleeping in the hotel in Le Mans, did he realise the danger? Was his action not the wild prank it appeared, but a deliberate desire that I might wreck the home which he said possessed him?

I was aware of the dark woman's eyes upon me, brooding, suspicious. "Why don't you go upstairs as Françoise suggests?" she said. Her manner was peculiar. It was as though she wanted to get me out of the room, afraid that I might say something out of place.

"Very well, I will," I said, and then I added, "You were both right. I drank much too much in Le Mans. I spent the day there senseless in a hotel."

The fact that it was true added flavour to deception. Both women stared. Neither said anything. I crossed the floor and went out of the half-open door into the hall beyond. I heard the one called Françoise break into a torrent of words as soon as I left the room.

The hall was empty. I listened at the other door, on the further side of the great cabinet, and could hear the distant sound of kitchen noises, running water, the clatter of plates. I decided to try the stairs. The first flight ended in a long corridor, leading left and right, and above me was a further flight to a second floor. I hesitated, then turned left along the corridor. It was dark, lighted by a single electric light bulb without a shade. The boards creaked under my feet. I was seized with a furtive excitement as I put out my hand and turned the handle of the door at the far end of the corridor. The room was dark. I felt for a switch. The light revealed a bleak high room, dark red curtains drawn across the windows, a high single bed also draped with red, above which hung a large reproduction of Guido Reni's *Ecce Homo*. I could see by its shape that this was a room in one of the towers, for the windows were circular, forming as it were an alcove, and this had been adapted as a place for prayer, with a prie-dieu, a crucifix, even a stoup for holy water. This little cell was bare but for its sparse religious trimmings, and the rest of the room was furnished with a bureau, chairs and a table, besides the heavy chest of drawers and wardrobe, suggesting its uncomfortable use as sitting room and bedroom combined. Another religious picture faced the bed, a tortured reproduction of the Scourging of Christ, and on the wall by the door near which I stood there was a third, of Christ falling with the Cross. The room struck chill, as though it were never heated. It even smelt forbidding, a mixture of polish and heavy hangings.

I switched off the light and went out. As I did so I saw that I had been observed. A woman had come down to the corridor from the floor above, and now stood watching me before descending further.

"*Bonsoir, Monsieur le Comte,*" she said. "Are you looking for Mademoiselle Blanche?"

"Yes," I lied quickly, "she's not in her room."

I felt myself obliged to go towards her. She was small, thin and elderly, and from her dress and the way she spoke I judged her to be a servant.

"Mademoiselle Blanche is with Madame la Comtesse," she said, and I wondered if she knew instinctively that there was something wrong, because the expression in her eyes was curious, even amazed, and she glanced over my shoulder towards the room I had just left.

"It doesn't matter," I said. "I can see her later."

"Is there anything wrong, Monsieur le Comte?" she asked, and behind her small eyes I could see still greater curiosity. Her voice was intimate, confiding, as though possibly I had a secret that we might share.

"No," I said. "Why should there be?"

She looked away from me again, down the corridor to the closed door.

"I beg pardon, Monsieur le Comte," she said. "I only thought there must be something wrong for you to go to Mademoiselle Blanche's room."

Her eyes flickered away from me. I sensed no affection there, no warmth, none of the trust that I had seen in Gaston; yet there was at the same time a suggestion of long familiarity, bringing some understanding between us of an unpleasant kind.

"I hope Monsieur le Comte's visit to Paris was successful?" she said, an inflection in her voice other than courtesy, as though she hinted that something might have gone amiss which would earn criticism.

"Perfectly," I replied, and was about to pass her when she said, "Madame la Comtesse knows you are home. I was just going down to the salon to tell you. It would be best to come up and see her now or I shall have no peace."

Madame la Comtesse . . . The words were ominous. If I were Monsieur le Comte, then who was she? Doubt began to return to me, the first faint brush of panic.

"I can go later," I said, "there's no great hurry."

"You know very well she won't wait, Monsieur le Comte," said the woman, her inquisitive black eyes fixed upon me. There was no escape.

"Very well," I said.

The servant turned towards the stairs and I went after her up the long, twisting flight. We came to another corridor like the one we had left below, which branched to a third, running parallel, and I caught a glimpse of a service staircase through an open baize door, whence the smell of food came floating from the depths. We passed through yet another door, and then stood before the last one in the corridor. The servant opened it, giving me first a little nod, like a signal, and as she went through she said to someone within, "I met Monsieur le Comte coming up the stairs. He was on his way to see you."

There were three persons in the room, which was large but so filled with furniture that there was hardly space to move between the tables and the chairs. Dominating the whole was a great double bed with curtained hangings. A stove, burning brightly with open doors, gave out an intense heat, so that walking into the atmosphere was enough to stifle anyone coming from the cold rooms below. Two small fox terriers, with bows and bells jangling from their collars, ran towards me barking shrilly.

I swung my eyes round the room to take in what I could, the dogs leaping at my legs, and I saw the tall, thin woman who had left the salon when I entered it, and close to her an ancient curé, white-haired, his small black cap on the back of his head, his pleasant round face pink and unlined. Beyond him, almost on top of the stove itself, seated in the depths of a great armchair, was a massive elderly woman, her flesh sagging in a hundred lines, but her eyes, her nose, her mouth so astonishingly and horribly like my own that for one wild moment I believed after all Jean de Gué had come up here before me and was masquerading as a final jest.

She held out her arms, and, drawn to her like a magnet, I went instinctively to kneel beside her chair, and was at once caught and smothered, lost in the mountain of flesh and woollen wraps, feeling momentarily like a fly trapped in a great spider's web, yet at the same time fascinated because of the likeness, another facet of the self, but elderly, female and grotesque. I thought of my own mother, dead long ago when I was a boy of ten, and she seemed dim and faded, lost to memory, bearing no resemblance to this swollen replica of all that might have been.

Her hands clung about me, reluctant to let me go yet pushing me at the same time, murmuring in my ear, "There, there, be off with you, great baby, great brute. You've been amusing yourself, I know." I drew away from her and looked into her eyes, half hidden by the heavy lids and the pouched skin beneath, and they were my own eyes, mocking, my own eyes buried and transformed.

"Everyone is upset as usual with your goings on," she said. "Françoise in hysterics, Marie-Noel with a fever, Renée sulking, Paul ill-tempered. Ouf! They make me sick, the whole collection. I was the only one not to worry. I knew you would turn up when you were ready to come home, and not before." She dragged me down again, chuckling in her throat, and then patted me on the shoulder and thrust me away. "I am the only one with faith in this house, isn't it true?" she said, looking up at the curé, who smiled at her, nodding his head, and as the nod continued intermittently I realised it was a nervous trick, a sort of spasm that he could not help, having nothing to do with assent. The effect was disconcerting and I withdrew my eyes from him, glancing instead at the thin woman, who had not once looked at me since I entered the room, but now closed the book she was holding.

"You don't wish me to go on reading any more, I suppose, Maman," she said, her voice dead, expressionless. I knew from what the servant had told me that she was the Mademoiselle Blanche in whose bedroom I had just trespassed, and guessed that she must therefore be an elder sister to my masquerading self. The countess turned to the curé.

"Since Jean has come home, Monsieur le Curé," she said, her voice altered from the chuckle in my ear when she embraced me to one of courtesy and respect, "would you think it very rude of me if I asked to be excused this evening from our usual little session? He will have so much to tell me."

"Naturally, Madame la Comtesse," said the curé, the smile and the nodding head giving him so great an appearance of benevolent acquiescence that surely a refusal or a denial, coming from his lips, would never bring conviction. "I know very well how much you have missed him, even for so short a time, and it must be a great relief for you to have him back again. I hope," he went on, turning to me, "all went well for you in Paris? They tell me the traffic nowadays is quite impossible, and that it takes an hour to get to Notre-Dame from la Concorde. I should not care for it at all, but that does not worry you young people."

"It depends," I said, "whether one is in Paris for business or for pleasure." To engage him in conversation meant safety. I did not want to be left trapped with my supposed mother, who surely, instinctively, would know that something was amiss.

"That is true," said the curé, "and I expect for you it was a little of both. Well, I won't keep you any longer. . . ." And without warning he slipped from his chair onto his knees, closed his eyes, folded his hands and began to pray with great rapidity, followed by Mademoiselle Blanche, while the mother, clasping her hands likewise, bowed her massive head upon her chest. I knelt also, shielding my eyes with my hands, and the two fox terriers came sniffing and pawing at my pockets. I glanced out of the corner of my eye and saw that the servant who had brought me to the room was also kneeling, eyes fast shut, echoing in singsong fashion the responses to the curé's prayers. He came to the end of his intercession, and, lifting his hands, made the sign of the Cross upon us all and scrambled to his feet.

"*Bonsoir, Madame la Comtesse, bonsoir, Monsieur le Comte, bonsoir, Mademoiselle Blanche, bonsoir, Charlotte,*" he said, bowing and nodding in turn, his pink face wreathed in smiles. There was a little commotion by the door as he and the daughter of the house each held back for the other, neither yielding in courtesy, until finally the curé passed first, closely followed by Mademoiselle Blanche, head bent low like an acolyte.

The servant Charlotte began mixing something from a bottle in the corner of the room, and as she came towards us with a medicine glass she said, "Monsieur le Comte will have a tray up here as well?"

"Naturally, idiot," said the comtesse, "and I'm not going to take any of that stuff. Throw it away. Go and fetch the trays. Get out!" Impatiently she gestured with her hand to the door, the flesh on her face puckering to annoyance. "Come here, come close," she said, beckoning me to sit beside her, while the two fox terriers leapt upon her lap and settled there. "Well now, did you do it, did you settle with Carvalet?"

It was the first direct question put to me since I had come to the château which I could not evade with some jest or careless remark.

I swallowed. "Did I do what?" I asked.

"Renew the contract," she said.

Jean de Gué had gone to Paris, then, on business. I remembered there had been envelopes and folders in the writing case in the valise. His friend outside the station had suggested the visit was wasted. The matter was evidently important, and the expression in her eyes brought back to me once again those words of Jean de Gué about human greed. "Minister to it . . . give people what they want . . ." This being his creed, doubtless he would satisfy his mother now. "Don't worry," I told her, "everything is arranged."

"Ah!" She gave a little grunt of satisfaction. "You actually came to terms with them after all?"

"I did."

"Paul is such a fool," she said, relaxing in her chair, "always grumbling, always looking upon the worse. Anyone would think we were completely ruined from the way he talks, and obliged to close down tomorrow. You have seen him already?"

"He was just going out," I said, "when I arrived home."

"But you told him your news?"

"No. No, there wasn't time."

"I should have thought he would have waited long enough to hear that at least," she said. "What's the matter with you? You look ill."

"I drank too much in Le Mans."

"In Le Mans? Why drink in Le Mans? Couldn't you have stayed in Paris if you wanted to celebrate?"

"I did the same in Paris."

"Ah . . . !" This time the exclamation was not a grunt, but a sigh of sympathy. "Poor boy," she said. "It's difficult for you, isn't it? You should have stayed longer for your fun. Come, kiss me again." She pulled me to her, and once more I was buried in the massive folds of her flesh. "You amused yourself well, I hope," she murmured. "Did you, did you?"

The insinuation in her voice was unmistakable. Instead of being repelled I found myself amused, intrigued even, that this great creature, with her monstrous likeness to myself, who had just been praying with the curé, should wish to share the secrets of her son.

"Naturally I amused myself, Maman," I said, realising, as I drew away from her, that I had called her Maman without effort. Oddly, this shocked me more than anything that she herself had said.

"Then you brought me the little present you promised?" Her eyes went small, her body stiff with expectation. The atmosphere suddenly became taut and strange. I did not know how to answer her.

"Did I promise you a present?" I asked.

Her great mouth sagged. Her eyes pleaded with a tense, frightened look I would not have believed possible a moment ago.

"You didn't forget?" she said.

I was spared the impossibility of replying by the reappearance of Blanche. A change of expression came like a mask over the mother's face. She bent to the terriers on her lap and began to pet them. "There, there, Jou-Jou, stop biting your tail, will you, and behave. Give him some room, Fifi, you take up the whole of my lap. Here, go to your uncle."

She forced the dog, which I did not want, into my hands and it wriggled and squirmed until it was free, and then ran and hid under her chair. "What is the matter with Fifi?" she said, astonished. "She has never run away from you before. Has she gone mad?"

"Let her alone," I said. "She smells the train on me."

The animal was not deceived. The point was interesting. In what did my physical difference from Jean de Gué lie? His mother had sunk back in her chair, and was staring morosely at her daughter. Blanche stood stiff and straight, her hands resting on the back of a chair, her eyes fixed upon her mother.

"Am I to understand there will be two trays here for dinner?" she asked.

"Yes," rapped the mother. "It is more amusing for Jean to dine upstairs with me."

"Don't you think you have had enough excitement as it is?"

"I am not excited. I am perfectly calm, as you can see for yourself. You only say that because you want to spoil our fun."

"I don't wish to spoil anything. I'm thinking of your good. If you become too excited you won't sleep, and then you will have one of your bad days tomorrow."

"I shall have a worse day, and a worse night, if Jean does not stay with me now."

"Very well." The acceptance was calm, the matter shelved. The daughter proceeded to tidy books and papers about the room, and I was struck by the complete tonelessness and absence of emotion in her voice, and by the fact that she never looked in my direction. I might not have been there, for all the notice that she took of me. I guessed her age to be about forty-two or -three, yet she could have been older or younger. The cross and chain which she wore over the dark jumper and skirt were her only concession to adornment. She brought a table beside her mother's chair in preparation for dinner.

"Has Charlotte given you your medicine?" she asked.

"Yes," replied her mother.

The daughter sat down some distance from the roaring stove and took up knitting from a table. I could see a missal on the table, leather-bound prayer books and a Bible.

"Why don't you leave us?" said her mother in sudden savagery.

"I am waiting until Charlotte brings the trays," was the reply.

The passage of words between them had the immediate effect of making me a partisan of the mother. Why, I could not tell. Her manner was deplorable, and yet I found her sympathetic and the daughter the reverse. I wondered if I was drawn to the mother merely because of her likeness to myself.

"Marie-Noel has been seeing visions again," said the comtesse.

Marie-Noel . . . Someone below had talked of Marie-Noel having a fever. Was she another religious sister? I felt some comment was required of me.

"It's probably due to her fever," I said.

"She hasn't a fever. There's nothing wrong with her," said the comtesse. "She likes everyone to notice her, that's all. What did you say to her before you went to Paris that upset her?"

"I didn't say anything," I answered.

"You must have done. She kept telling Françoise and Renée that you were not coming back. It was not only you who told her, but the Sainte Vierge as well. Isn't that so, Blanche?"

I glanced at the uncommunicative sister. She raised her pale eyes from the clicking needles, but to her mother, not to me.

"If Marie-Noel has visions," she said, "and I for one believe her, then it is time that somebody in this house took them seriously. I have said so for a long time. The curé agrees with me."

"Nonsense," retorted the mother. "I was speaking to the curé about it this evening. He says it is a very common thing, especially among the poor. Marie-Noel has probably got ideas from Germaine. I will ask Charlotte. Charlotte knows everything."

No emotion showed itself on Blanche's face, but I saw her lips tighten. "We have to remember that the curé is getting old," she said. "He becomes forgetful when too many people talk to him at once. If these visions continue, I shall write to the bishop. He will know the best thing to advise, and I am very sure what his advice will be."

"What then?" asked her mother.

"That Marie-Noel should live amongst people where she cannot possibly be corrupted," came the answer, "and where she can offer her gifts to the greater glory of God."

I expected an outburst from the comtesse, but instead she patted the dog on her knee, and, fumbling at her side for a paper packet, took a chocolate-coated sweet and thrust it between the dog's teeth.

"There," she said, "it's good, isn't it? Where's Fifi? Fifi, do you want one too?" The other terrier scrambled from under the chair and leapt onto her lap, nosing at the paper bag. "You are a fool, Blanche," she continued. "If we are to have a saint in the family, let us keep her at home. There are possibilities in the idea. We might turn St. Gilles into a place of pilgrimage. Naturally, it would have to be done with the approval of the bishop and the Church, but it would be worth considering. Money might be found at last to repair the roof of the church. The Beaux-Arts will never do anything."

"Marie-Noel's soul is of greater importance than the roof of the church," said Blanche. "If I had my way she would leave the château tomorrow."

"You're jealous, that's your trouble," said her mother, "jealous of her pretty face and her big eyes. One of these days Marie-Noel won't bother about visions any more—she'll want a husband." She dug her elbow in my side. I was not surprised that her daughter made no answer. "Isn't that so, Jean?" the mother persisted.

"Probably," I said.

"Pray God I live long enough to see the wedding. He'll have to be rich . . ."

Charlotte came in with a tray, closely followed by a little red-cheeked *femme de chambre* of about eighteen, who at sight of me blushed and giggled and said, "*Bonsoir, Monsieur le Comte.*" I wished her good evening, and she arranged a tray for me on another table. Blanche rose to her feet and put aside her knitting.

"Do you want to see Françoise or Renée before you settle for the night?" she asked.

44

"No," replied her mother. "I saw them both for tea. I shall sleep well tonight, now that Jean is home, and I don't want to be bothered by anyone else, least of all by you."

Blanche crossed to her chair and kissed her mother, bidding her good night. Then she left the room, without having once spoken to me or looked at me. I wondered what Jean de Gué had done to offend her. I uncovered the bowl of soup on the tray beside me. It smelt good and I was hungry. The little *femme de chambre*, whom Charlotte addressed as Germaine, followed Blanche from the room, but Charlotte still hovered in the background, watching us eat.

Curiosity made me venture a question to the mother. "What was the matter with Blanche?" I asked.

"Nothing particular," she answered. "If anything, she's irritated me less than usual. Did you notice, she didn't jump on me when I said that having a saint in the family opened up possibilities?"

"She was shocked, wasn't she?" I asked.

"Shocked? You mean delighted. You watch—she'll work on the idea. If Marie-Noel seeing visions could bring some reflected glory to herself and to St. Gilles, no one would be better pleased than Blanche. She'd have something to live for. Charlotte, are you there? Take this away, I've had enough. And give Monsieur Jean his wine. Why don't you tell me more about Paris? You have told me nothing yet."

I searched my imagination. I had not been to Paris during my past holiday, and what I knew and loved of it was too full of museums and historical buildings for her ear. I talked of eating, which she understood, and the expense, which pleased her even better, and with sudden inspiration invented visits to the theatre, a meeting with wartime friends—she even supplied their names for me, which helped. By the time we had finished eating—and we had eaten well—and the trays had been removed, I felt more at my ease with her than I had ever done with anyone in my life. The reason for this was simple: there was no reserve on her part. She accepted me, believed me, loved me, trusted me; I held a position that had never been mine before. Had she encountered me as a stranger we should have had nothing to say to one another. As her son I risked no disapproval in anything I said.

45

I laughed, I joked, I chatted, and the unaccustomed ease was a delight to me—until suddenly, when Charlotte had left the room, and she said to me, "Jean, you didn't really forget my little present, did you? You were joking."

Once again the sagging mouth, the pleading eyes. The change in her was startling. Gone was the wicked humour, the twinkle in the eye, the rollicking impression of warmth and savagery combined. She had changed into a pitiable, trembling creature, hands clawing at mine. I did not know what to do or what to say. I rose and went to the door and called, "Charlotte, are you there?" The terriers, wakened by my voice, jumped from her knee to the ground and barked furiously.

Charlotte came quickly from some room nearby, and I said, "Madame la Comtesse is unwell. You had better go to her."

She looked at me and asked, "Haven't you brought it?"

"Brought what?" I asked, and the woman stared at me, eyes narrowing.

"You know, Monsieur le Comte, what you promised to bring from Paris."

I tried to think of the contents of the valise, and remembered the packages that looked like presents. What they were I did not know, nor where the things had been unpacked.

Charlotte said to me swiftly, "Go and find it at once, Monsieur le Comte. She will suffer if you don't."

I went down the corridor and the first flight of stairs, and then hesitated again, not knowing which way to turn. I heard bath water running from some room to the left of the first-floor corridor, and I went along it, uncertain, until I saw a half-open door next to the one which must be a bathroom. I paused in the doorway, but there was someone moving inside it, so I went on again past the bathroom to the room beyond. The door was wide open and the room empty. I threw a quick glance round it, and to my relief I had struck lucky. It was a small dressing room, and I recognised the brushes on the table and a dressing gown thrown over one of the chairs. Someone had unpacked for me and the two valises had been removed, but there on the table were the packages I had seen in one of the valises, neatly piled alongside each other like presents on a Christmas tree. I remem-

bered how there had been notes thrust through the string of
each one, which had conveyed nothing when I looked at them
in the hotel room, but now they made sense, with F, and R,
and B, and P, and M-N, and, thank God, here was one
addressed to "Maman," with no fancy wrapping but in
strong brown paper, sealed. I took it and went out of the
room, and up the stairs again.

Charlotte was waiting for me at the head of the stairs.
"Have you got it?" she said.

"Yes," I answered. "Does she want me to give it to her?"

She stared at me and answered, "No, no . . ." as though
shocked, outraged even. Taking the package from me, she
said, "Good night, Monsieur le Comte." Then she walked
quickly away along the corridor.

The dismissal must mean that I was not needed any more,
and I went slowly down again to the dressing room, wondering what to make of the abrupt end to the evening. It must
have been some sort of seizure, some mental disturbance,
understood by Charlotte and Jean de Gué but not necessarily
by the rest of the family. I hoped that whatever was in the
package from Paris would bring relief. She had seemed so
sane, so perfectly in control, apart from temper. She had
not given me the impression of someone mentally sick.

I went and stood in the dressing room, suddenly tired and
depressed. I could not forget the change in the mother's face.
As I stood there, wondering what to do, I heard a voice
calling to me from the bathroom, "Have you said good night
to Maman?"

I recognised it as the voice of Françoise, the fair, faded
woman, and I noticed for the first time that leading into
the bathroom was a door which had been screened from me
by a large wardrobe. She must have heard me come into the
dressing room. A new thought struck me. There was no bed
in the dressing room. Where did Jean de Gué sleep?

"Are you there, Jean?" the voice called again. "I thought
you might want a bath, so I ran the water for you." The
voice sounded more distant now, as though she had passed
into the further room.

I went to the bathroom. It had all the signs of being used
by two persons. Sponges, tooth powders, towels . . . I

recognised the shaving kit, but there was a bathing cap too, and a pair of woman's slippers, and a woman's bathrobe hanging on the door.

I stood quite still, fearing I might be heard from the room beyond. I heard the click of a light, and a sigh, and then the voice called, complaining, "Why don't you answer me when I speak to you?" I braced myself for the effort and went through the door. I was looking into a large bedroom, the same shape and size as the one belonging to the sister Blanche, but brighter, with lightly figured wallpaper and no religious pictures. The tower alcove here held no prie-dieu, but a dressing table, lights and a looking glass. A large double bed, without hangings, faced the alcove. The woman called Françoise was sitting up in it, her hair pinned in curlers, a fluffy pink bed jacket round her shoulders. She seemed suddenly shrunken, and smaller than she had appeared downstairs.

She said to me, still plaintive, still aggrieved, "Of course you had to stay the whole evening upstairs with Maman. Don't you ever for one moment stop to consider me? Even Renée, who is generally on your side, said you are becoming quite impossible."

I glanced away from her weary, complaining face to the empty pillow on the other side. I recognised the travelling clock on the small table, and a carton of cigarettes. Even the striped pyjamas that I had worn at the hotel were folded neatly on the turned-down sheet.

I had thought, in my stupidity, that Françoise was married to Paul, and was the sister of Jean de Gué. I realised, with a sinking heart, that on the contrary she was his wife.

Chapter 5

My first instinct, absurd and automatic, was to retrieve the pyjamas from the bed, and I went and fetched them, not glancing at Françoise, and turned back again towards the bathroom. To my dismay she started to cry, saying something about not caring for her, and being miserable, and how

Maman had always come between us. I waited in the bathroom for the sounds to cease. Presently there was a blowing of the nose, and those little sniffs and coughs that accompany the aftermath of crying and the attempt at self-control. The idea that she might get out of bed and follow me to the bathroom unnerved me, and I slammed the door and locked it, realising, as I did so, that I was probably playing my character aright. This would be the action of Jean de Gué if he was ashamed or bored or both. Once again I became angry, as I had been in the hotel when I was forced to put on his clothes. How he would laugh if he could see me now, a farcical figure with the pyjamas over my arm, hiding in a bathroom, with his wife in bed in the room next door. This was a situation that evoked screams of delight in the theatre, and I thought how very close to humour must disgust and horror always be. We laugh to stave off fear, or we are attracted because we are repulsed; in a bedroom farce it is disgust at what might happen—disgust mingled with a furtive excitement—that makes the audience scream. I wondered if Jean de Gué had foreseen this moment, or whether he had thought, as I had in the car driving to the château, that after an hour or two the game would be played out, the masquerade be over. It might be that never for an instant had he considered I would do what I had done. And yet, how definite our conversation of the preceding night, my wail at the emptiness of life, the lack of ties. What a chance for him to laugh and say, "Try mine!"

If he really intended to slip away himself and make me his scapegoat, then it clearly proved that he cared for no one at the château. The mother and the wife who loved him well counted for nothing. He did not mind what happened to them, or to any of the others: I could do with them as I pleased. Considered coldly, the masquerade was so cruel as to be inhuman. I turned off the dripping bath tap and went back to the dressing room. The elation and ease I had experienced when having dinner with the mother had changed to depression with her change of mood. Instead of dismissing the ravaged face as just another incident in a fantastic evening, I had wanted to placate her, to find the package quickly and hand it over to Charlotte. Now, with the realisation

49

that the complaining Françoise was de Gué's wife, I wanted to placate her too: her tears distressed me. Downstairs in the salon they had been unreal to me, yet here, in the privacy of their rooms, these people were without defence, betraying me into emotion. The fact that they were unconscious victims of a practical joke was no longer funny. Besides, I was not so sure that it was a joke. In a curious way it was a trial of strength, a test of endurance, as though Jean de Gué had said to me, "Right. I have allowed myself to be possessed by my family. Could you do better in my place?"

I went to the table and picked up the package marked F. It had a fancy wrapping and was small and hard. I stood a moment, weighing it in my hand, then I went deliberately through the bathroom once again and opened the bedroom door. The room was in darkness.

"Are you awake?" I said.

I heard a movement from the bed, and then the light was switched on and she sat up, looking at me. The curlers were now concealed by a cap made of net, tied under the chin with a pink bow, and the fluffy bed jacket had been exchanged for a shawl. The effect was incongruous against the pale tired face. She yawned, and blinked at me.

"What is it?" she said.

I went over to her. "Listen," I said, "you must forgive me if I was abrupt just now. Maman seemed suddenly unwell, and I was worried. I would have come down earlier, but you know how she can be. Look, I bought you this in Paris."

She stared doubtfully at the package which I put into her hand. She let it drop on the coverlet, and sighed. "I wouldn't mind if it was just once in a while," she said, "but it happens so often, every day, always. Sometimes I think that Maman hates me, and not only Maman but all of you, Paul, Renée, Blanche. Even Marie-Noel has no feeling for me." She did not seem to expect an answer, and I was thankful, for I had no words. "When we were first married it was different," she went on. "We were both younger, the country was free again after the Occupation, life was full of hope. I felt so happy. Then little by little it all seemed to slip away, the happy feeling. I don't know if it's my fault or yours."

The wan face under the ugly net cap stared up at me without hope.

"It happens to everyone, sooner or later," I said slowly. "Married people become used to one another, take each other for granted. It's inevitable. That's no reason to be unhappy."

"Oh, it's not that," she said. "I know we take each other for granted. I wouldn't care if I had you to myself. But here everyone is on top of us. I have to share you with so many people, and the terrible thing about it is that you don't notice, you don't mind."

The evening with the mother had been too easy. This was different. I did not know what to say to her.

"Everything's closing in on me," she said, "the château, the family, the whole countryside. It's like being suffocated. I long ago gave up trying to do anything in the château, giving orders, altering things: your family made it quite plain that they considered it interference. What happens here has always happened. Do you realise that the one interest I have had in the past months has been to order new stuff for the curtains here in the bedroom, and the flounce for the dressing table, and even that was thought extravagant?"

She stared up at me, and I knew some sort of apology was expected of me.

"I'm sorry," I said, "but you must know how it is. In the country we get set in our ways. Everything is a matter of habit."

"Habit?" she repeated. "That comes well from you, of all people. You go off whenever you feel like it on pretence of business. No question of you being set, or a man of routine, leading the same life day in, day out, as I have to do. Never for a moment have you suggested taking me with you. It's always a question of 'one of these days' or 'next time,' and now I'm used to your excuses and don't even ask. Besides, at this particular moment it wouldn't be possible—I've been feeling too unwell."

She fingered the package, which she had not opened, and I felt there must be something a husband should say under the circumstances, a word of comfort or sympathy, but her particular condition was one I knew little about.

Suddenly she said quite simply, without complaint or grievance, "Jean, I'm frightened." I did not know how to answer her. I took the package from her and began to open it. "You know what Dr. Lebrun said when I lost the last. It isn't easy for me."

I felt inadequate and useless. I undid the string and paper and drew out a box, and from the box a small velvet case which I opened. Inside was a locket, framed in pearls, which, when the release was sprung, revealed a miniature of myself, or rather him. It could be worn either as a clip or as a brooch, for there was a gold pin at the back to fix it. The workmanship was very fine, the idea ingenious, and it must have cost the purchaser no mean sum of money.

She uttered an exclamation of wonder and delight. "Oh, how beautiful!" she said. "How very lovely! And how dear of you to think of it. I have been grumbling, complaining . . . and you bring me this. Forgive me." She put her hand up to my face. I forced a smile. "You are good to put up with me," she said. "Let's hope it won't be much longer, and then I shall feel more like myself again. When I talk to you I hear words coming out of my mouth that I don't really mean, and I hate myself for it, but I can't prevent it."

She closed the locket, then opened it again two or three times, smiling at the trick of it. Then she pinned it on her shawl.

"Look," she said, "I wear my husband on my heart. If anyone says to me in future, 'Where is Jean?' I shall only have to open the locket. It's a very good likeness, you know. It must have been copied from the photo in your old identity card that I used to like so much. Did you have it specially done for me in Paris?"

"Yes," I said. It was probably true, yet my own lie sounded shabby to my ears.

"Paul will never get over it when he sees it," she said. "But I suppose it means that everything was all right and the visit was successful after all. How exactly like you to celebrate by doing something extravagant. You know, I feel so helpless when I hear Paul talking about the impossibility of carrying on at the foundry, and I feel he is hinting at my own money all tied up in that ridiculous way. However, if we have a boy . . ." She lay back, still touching the locket pinned on her shawl. "I shall sleep now," she said. "Don't be long. You must be tired if you have been talking business to Maman all the evening."

She switched off her light, and I heard her sigh and settle herself once more against the pillow.

I went back to the dressing room, threw open the window, and leant out. It was a bright moonlit night, cold and clear. Beneath me was the tangled grass of the moat, and the rough stone ivy-covered walls surrounding it, and beyond stretched what might once have been formal garden but was now given to grass too, where the cattle wandered, this in turn forming rides and avenues that became lost in the dusky trees. A small rounded building, like the twin towers guarding the bridgeway across the moat, stood isolated amid the grass in front of me, and I realised from its shape that it must be a *colombier*—an old dovecot for pigeons—and beside it was a child's swing, with the rope broken.

An indefinable melancholy brooded upon the hushed scene, as though once there had been laughter here, and life, and now there was none, and the people who looked out of the château windows, as I did, gave themselves to regret and malcontent. The deep silence was broken now and then by a single plopping sound, like the drip of water from a wellhead tumbling to the depths below, and I leant out and craned my head to try and trace it, but could not, for no water came from the grinning gargoyle face that stared down at me from the coping of the tower above.

The church clock in the village behind the château struck eleven, a high, reedy note which for all its lack of depth held the same warning as the Angelus bell from the cathedral in Le Mans, and when the last note had sounded and died away the feeling of oppression and distress increased within me, and the voice of reason seemed to say, "What are you doing in this place? Get out, before it's too late."

I opened the door to the corridor and listened. Everything was quiet. I wondered if the mother was now sleeping, pacified by the mysterious package I had given to Charlotte,

53

or if she still sat huddled in her chair. Was the sister Blanche kneeling at her prie-dieu, or watching the scourged Christ facing her from her bed? I could not forget the intimate, touching words of Françoise, "Jean, I'm frightened." They were not meant for me. Nothing here was mine. I was an alien. I had no part in their life.

I went along the corridor and down the stairs. I had turned the handle of the door leading to the terrace, through which I had made my first entrance to the château, when I was aware of a footstep on the stair behind me, and, looking up, I saw the dark woman, Renée, in wrapper and slippers, with the hair which she had worn high now loose on her shoulders.

"Where are you going?" she whispered.

"Outside, for some air," I lied swiftly. "I couldn't sleep."

"What is it?" she asked. "I knew you weren't really tired or sick—that was just an excuse for Françoise. I heard you come down from Maman, and then I waited for you, leaving my door open. Didn't you notice it?"

"No," I said.

She looked incredulous. "You must have realised I urged Paul to go out to the dinner on purpose, as soon as I knew you would be home. Now the evening is wasted. He'll be back any moment."

"I'm sorry," I said. "Maman had a lot to say to me—it was impossible to get away. Surely we can talk tomorrow?"

"Tomorrow?" she echoed, her manner abrupt and queer. "Tomorrow is soon enough for you, is it, after ten days in Paris? I might have known it. I suppose that's why you didn't bother to answer my letters."

I wondered if I looked as dumb and ineffectual as I felt, standing there with my hand on the door. Earlier in the evening this woman had seemed an ally and a friend. Now she was a confidante turned sour, and I had the feeling that in some way she was deeply angered. I wished uneasily that I knew her relationship to the rest of the family, and what the matter was that she had wanted to discuss with Jean so privately and urgently.

"I can only say I am sorry," I repeated. "I hadn't understood that you wanted to see me especially. Why didn't you send word upstairs, when I was with Maman? I would have come down."

"Is that meant for sarcasm," she said, "or are you truly drunk?"

Her anger irritated me. The mother's mood had touched me, and the wife's too, for a different reason. I had no time for this one, who so suddenly thrust herself between me and escape.

"You'll catch cold," I said to her. "Why don't you go to bed?"

She stared at me, and then, catching her breath, she said, "*Mon Dieu*, how I hate you at times!" Turning her back on me, she went away upstairs.

I opened the door to the terrace and stepped outside. The air felt clean and good after the atmosphere within, musty yet chill behind the fastened shutters. The gravel terrace crunched under my feet, and I walked softly down the steps and onto the driveway where the car had turned. I was making my way to the left of this, towards outbuildings in the thickness of the wall beside the moat, which I judged to be stables and a garage, when the lights of a car flashed in the lime avenue descending the hill, and came straight towards the bridge and the gateway to the château. It must be Paul returning. I took cover under the dark cedar tree close beside me, wondering if his lights had picked me up, and in a moment he was over the bridge and through the gate and had swung right, making for the outbuildings. I heard him slam the door of the Renault, and this was followed by the dragging noise of garage doors sliding in a groove. In a moment or two there was the sound of footsteps, and he came towards the terrace, passing close to my hiding place. He went up the steps and into the château, closing the door behind him.

I waited a few minutes. Then I came out of my shelter and walked softly towards the wall of the moat. I was within a few feet of the archway through which Paul had come when I heard a muttered growl. I saw then that beside the archway was an enclosure, and within it a great retriever, who at sight of me barked furiously. I murmured to him, but it was useless. The sound of my voice drove him to greater fury, and I turned back to the shelter of the cedar, where he could not see me, and waited for him to quieten before deciding upon my further move. The barking continued intermittently, then settled to a muttering, and finally to silence, and once again I ventured forth and looked about me, and up at the massive walls of the château, forbidding, pale, yet strangely beautiful in the clear light beneath the moon. A door in the terraced wall led to the grounds beyond, and some impulse made me pass through it, and stand looking over the sunken moat to the verdure where the cattle had wandered, to the ghostly alleyways bordering the forest, and the silent dovecot, and the broken swing.

Somewhere the author of the joke in which we were both involved lay sleeping, or laughing, perhaps, at my perplexity. He believed himself to be free, now he wore my clothes. They were his people who suffered here, and it meant nothing to him how lost they might become, how cruelly they might be hurt.

Once again the little plopping thud that had disturbed me in the dressing room sounded, close by, and I saw that it was the chestnuts falling from the trees onto the gravel path beyond the moat. No rising mist, no falling leaf, no pattering rain could have marked with such finality the end of summer. There was the whole of autumn in the sound. I looked up at the shuttered windows of the château, and wondered which was the round tower where the mother slept, and which the prayer cell of the daughter. Above me was the dressing room where I had stood so short a while before, and beside it the long windows of the bedroom.

The church clock struck the half hour, my signal for departure: I had lingered long enough amongst these people who were strangers to me. I dared not risk passing the dog again and perhaps disturbing the household, and I decided to pass through the gateway, cross the bridge, walk up the avenue of limes and so onto the road, and continue walking through the night to the nearest town.

The chestnuts continued to fall beside the moat, and this time, with no trees near, one hit me on the head and dropped beside me. I looked up, puzzled, and saw that a small window in a turret above the dressing room was a dark slit no longer, but held a peering figure, kneeling on the sill. As I watched another chestnut fell, striking me on the forehead, and then another, and another, thrown by the kneeling figure, who for some reason wished to attract my attention. Suddenly the figure rose to its feet and stood on the sill by the open slit, and I saw that it was a child, perhaps ten years old, wearing a white nightgown, and that one false move would send it headlong to the depths below. I could not distinguish sex or feature: all I could sense was danger.

"Go back," I called softly. "Go back into the room." The figure did not move. Another chestnut hit me on the head. "Go back," I called again. "Go back, or you will fall."

Then the child spoke, the voice coming clear and high and quite composed.

"I swear to you," it said, "that if you don't come to me by the time I count a hundred, I shall throw myself out of the window."

I did nothing, and the voice called down to me again.

"You know I never break my word. I'm beginning to count now. And unless you are with me by the time I reach a hundred, I swear by the Sainte Vierge that I will do it. One . . . two . . . three . . ."

A recollection of fever, saints and visions came crowding back into my mind. The conversation of the evening made sense to me at last. It had never occurred to me that the religious, saintly Marie-Noel might be a child. The voice continued counting, and I turned and went through the garden door to the terrace, and so to the front door, which had not been bolted. I groped my way up the stairs to the first corridor, blindly seeking for some second service stairway that might lead me direct to the turret above the dressing room. I found a swing door and kicked it open, for it no longer mattered that I might be heard and the household aroused: my only thought was to prevent disaster.

I came to a winding stair, lit by a dim blue bulb, and ran up it, two steps at a time. The steps led to a landing and another winding corridor, but directly in front of me was a door, and from behind the door I could hear the voice counting steadily, "Eighty-five, eighty-six, eighty-seven . . ." I burst through the door, and seized the figure from the window sill, and threw it down on its bed beside the wall. It stared up at me with enormous eyes and close-cropped hair, and I felt sick because it was a replica of Jean de Gué, and therefore in fantastic fashion of a self long buried in the past so forgotten.

"Why did you not come to say good night, Papa?" she said to me.

Chapter 6

She gave me no time to think what I should answer. She jumped from her bed and threw herself upon me, flinging her arms round my neck, covering me with kisses.

"Get off, stop it," I said, trying to disentangle myself.

She began to laugh, clinging the harder, like a monkey, then suddenly turned and somersaulted back onto the bed. When she had recovered balance she sat cross-legged at the end of it, tailor-fashion, watching me without a smile. I recovered my breath and smoothed my hair, and we stared at one another like two animals before battle.

"Well?" she said—the inevitable "*Alors?*" that is question and exclamation and retort all in one—and I repeated it, to gain time, to try and grasp the significance of this new and unexpected complication of a daughter, and then, endeavouring to hold my ground, I said, "I thought you were supposed to have a fever?"

"I did this morning," she said, "but when my aunt Blanche looked at the thermometer this evening I was only just above normal. Since I stood by the window it has probably shot up again. Sit down." She patted the bed beside her. "Why didn't you come to see me the instant you got back?" she asked.

Her manner was imperious, as if she was accustomed to giving orders. I did not answer.

"Joker," she said lightly. Then she put out her hand and seized my own and kissed it. "Have you had your nails manicured?" she asked.

"No."

58

"They are a different shape, and your hands are cleaner. I suppose that is what Paris does for men. Also you have a different smell."

"What sort of smell?"

She wrinkled her nose. "Like a doctor," she said, "or a priest, or a stranger who comes to tea."

"I'm sorry." I stared at her, nonplussed.

"It will pass off. It is evident you have been moving in exalted circles. Have you all been discussing me below?"

Some instinct told me children should be snubbed. "No," I said.

"That's not true. Germaine told me they talked of nothing else at lunch. Though there was also much fussation because you were late. What were you doing?"

I decided to speak the truth as far as possible. "I was sleeping in a hotel in Le Mans," I said to her.

"What a funny idea. Were you very tired?"

"I had drunk too much the night before, and hit my head on the floor. Also I believe I swallowed a sleeping draught by mistake."

"If you hadn't taken the sleeping draught, would you have gone away?"

"What do you mean?" I asked.

"Would you have gone off somewhere and not come back?"

"I don't understand you."

"The Sainte Vierge told me that you mightn't come back. That's why I got a fever." She was no longer imperious. She was watching me closely, her eyes not moving from my face. "Have you forgotten," she said, "what you told me before you went to Paris?"

"What did I tell you?"

"That one of these days, if life became too difficult, you would just disappear and never come home again."

"I'd forgotten I said that."

"I hadn't forgotten. When Uncle Paul and the rest of them began talking about the money troubles, and how you had gone to Paris to try and arrange things, and he had not much hope of your success, I thought to myself, Now is the moment for him to do this. I woke in the night and was sick, and the

59

Sainte Vierge came and stood at the end of my bed and looked sorrowful."

The direct gaze of the child was hard to meet. I shifted my eyes, and, taking up a well-worn rabbit lying beside her, played with the single ear.

"If I hadn't come back," I asked, "what would you have done?"

"Killed myself," she said.

I set the rabbit to dancing on the sheet. I had a hazy recollection that this had made me laugh years past, in the days when I had toys. The child did not laugh. She took the rabbit from me and put it behind the bolster.

"Children don't kill themselves," I told her.

"Then why did you run upstairs so fast just now?"

"You might have slipped."

"I couldn't have slipped. I was holding on. I often stand at the window. But if you hadn't come home, then it would have been another matter. I shouldn't have held on. I should have jumped out, and died. And then I should have burnt in hell. But I would rather burn in hell than live in this world without you."

I looked at her again: the small oval face, the close-cropped hair, the burning eyes. The passionate avowal was disturbing, shocking, something to be expected from a fanatic, not a child. I thought hard to find the right thing to say.

"How old are you?" I asked.

"You know quite well I shall be eleven next birthday," she said.

"Very well, then. You have the whole of life before you. You have your mother, aunts, grandmother, all the people here at home who love you, and yet you talk wild nonsense about throwing yourself from a window if I wasn't here."

"But I don't love them, Papa. I only love you."

So that was that. I wanted a cigarette. Unconsciously I fumbled in my pockets, and, seeing this, she jumped from the bed, ran to a small desk near the window, took out a box of matches from a pigeonhole, and in a flash was back by my side with a lighted match held ready.

"Tell me," she said, "is it true that measles can be bad for unborn babies?"

60

The switch of mood was beyond me. "I don't know," I said.

"Maman told me that if I catch it and pass it to her, and she passes it to the little brother, then he will be born blind."

"I can't tell you. I don't understand those things."

"If my little brother was blind, would you like him?"

She was not solemn any more. She began to pirouette about the room on her toes, first on one foot, then on the other. I did not know how to answer her. She kept looking at me as she danced.

"It would be very sad for a baby to be born blind," I said uselessly.

"Would he have to be put in an institution?" she said.

"No. He would be taken care of here at home. In any case it won't happen."

"It might. I may have measles, and if I have, I am sure to have passed it on to Maman."

I felt I had caught her out, and the slip was too good to miss.

"You told me just now that you had a fever because you were afraid I wouldn't come home," I said swiftly. "You didn't say anything about measles then."

"My fever came because I was visited by the Sainte Vierge. It is a sign of grace," she answered.

She stopped pirouetting, and got into bed, and covered her face with the sheet. I dropped my cigarette ash into a doll's saucer and glanced around the room. It was an odd mixture of nursery and cell. There was a second slit in the wall as well as the window where she had stood to throw chestnuts on my head, and immediately beneath this slit she had improvised a prie-dieu, made out of a packing case, with a piece of old brocade across the top. Above this was a crucifix, adorned with a rosary, and between two candles on the top of her prie-dieu was a statue of the Madonna. Close by, on the wall, were pictures of the Holy Family, the head of St. Thérèse of Lisieux, and incongruously, perched lopsided on a stool, a doll with paint splodges over its naked stuffed body, pierced through the heart with a penholder. Round its neck was a card with the words, "The Martyrdom of St. Sebastian." Toys, more suited to her age than the prie-dieu, lay about the floor; and by her bed was a photograph of Jean de Gué in uniform taken, judging by the youthful appearance, before she was born.

I stubbed out my cigarette and got up. The figure under the blanket did not move.

"Marie-Noel, promise something."

Still no movement. I supposed she was foxing sleep. It did not matter.

"Promise you won't climb on the window sill again," I said. Nothing happened, and then there was an odd scratching sound, which began faintly, stopped, and continued more loudly. I realised that she was scratching the wall beside her bed in imitation of a mouse or rat. This was followed by a squeak, then a kick under the blanket. Forgotten sayings of disapproving adults returned to me.

"You're being neither clever nor funny," I said. "If you don't answer me at once I shan't say good night." A louder rat squeak and more violent scratching on the wall was the reply. "Very well then," I said firmly, and opened the door. What I intended by this gesture heaven knew, for she held all the cards; she had only to go to the window again to prove it.

The threat, to my relief, succeeded. She threw down the sheet, sat up in bed and held out her arms. Reluctantly I went to her.

"I will promise, if you will too," she said.

Her reasoning was sound, but I sensed a trap. This was something for Jean de Gué to handle, not for me. I did not understand children.

"What must I promise?" I asked.

"Never to go away and leave me," she said, "or, if you must go, to take me with you."

Once again I avoided the direct question in her eyes. The situation was impossible. I had already placated the mother, pandered to the wife. Must I surrender to the daughter too?

"Listen," I said, "adults can't commit themselves to promises of that kind. No one can foretell the future. There might be another war."

"I'm not talking about war," she said.

There was a strange, age-old wisdom in her voice. I wished she were older, or much younger, or somehow different. She was the wrong sort of age. I might have dared to tell the truth to someone growing up, but not to a child of ten, still fast in her secret world.

"Well?" she said.

No adult awaiting a decision about the future could have been more calm or grave. I wondered why Jean de Gué had ever suggested to her that he might leave home and disappear. Had it been a threat to win obedience, like my trick of a moment ago? Or was the threat deliberate, so that when it did happen she would be prepared?

"It's no use," I said, "I can't make that promise."

"I didn't think you could," she said. "Life is hard, isn't it? We must both just hope for the best—that you will stay at home, and that I shan't have to die young."

The casual, somehow fateful tone of voice was worse than if she had shown emotion. She kissed my hand again. I took a chance.

"Listen," I said, "I promise you that if I do go away, I'll tell you first. I may tell nobody else, but I will tell you."

"That's fair," she nodded.

"And now will you go to sleep?"

"Yes, Papa. My blankets have come unstuck. Settle me, please."

The clothes were loose at the bottom. I thrust them in tight, so that she could not move. She watched me from the pillow. I supposed I was meant to kiss her.

"Good night," I said, "sleep well." And I kissed her on the cheek.

She was thin and bony, her face and neck small and the eyes much too big.

"You're not fat enough," I said, "you ought to eat more."

"Why do you look so awkward?" she asked.

"I'm not awkward."

"You've got the face on of someone who tells a lie."

"I continually lie."

"I know you do. But not as a rule to me."

"Well, that's enough for now. Good night."

I went out and shut the door. I listened a moment outside, but there was no sound of movement, so I went down the turret stair, through the baize door, and back along the corridor to the dressing room.

I felt suddenly very tired. The house was quite still. No one had been awakened by my rush upstairs, or by the barking of the dog outside. I crept into the bathroom and stood by the open bedroom door, listening. Françoise did not stir. I went close to the bed, and from the sound of breathing knew her to be fast asleep. I went back into the dressing room, took off my things and got into the bath. It had grown cold, but I didn't want to disturb her by running hot water. I dried, and put on the pyjamas I had worn at the hotel and the dressing gown that was lying across the chair. I brushed my hair with his brushes, as I had done in the morning, and then went over to the table and picked up the parcel that bore the initials M-N. It felt like a book. Carefully I undid the string and the wrapping, and it was a book, as I had thought. The title was *The Little Flower,* and with it was a large, highly coloured plate of St. Thérèse of Lisieux, bought separately and slipped inside. On the flyleaf Jean de Gué had written, "To my adorable Marie-Noel, with all my heart, Papa." I wrapped the book up again, and put it back on the table with the other packages. He must have chosen his presents with great care. I did not know what it was he had brought back for his mother, but it was something that she needed badly. The locket had dried his wife's tears and helped her to go to sleep believing in him. *The Little Flower,* when it lay open, as it would do, beside his picture in the turret room, would feed the imagination of his child, so that she might see visions, and dream dreams, and in doing so perhaps nag his conscience less—that is, if he had a conscience, which I doubted. I leant out of the window once again, and the chestnuts still fell from the trees onto the gravel path beyond the moat, and a mist was rising from the grass, spreading in wisps towards the murky trees.

One had no right to play about with people's lives. One should not interfere with their emotions. A word, a look, a smile, a frown, did something to another human being, waking response or aversion, and a web was woven which had no beginning and no end, spreading outward and inward too, merging, entangling, so that the struggle of one depended upon the struggle of the other.

Jean de Gué had acted wrongly. He had run away from life, he had escaped from the emotions that he had himself created. None of these people under his roof would be behaving as they had behaved tonight but for something he had done to them. The mother would not have turned to me with frightened eyes, the sister would not have left the room in silence, Paul would not have spoken with hostility, Renée would not have cursed me on the stairs, the wife would not have wept, the child would not have threatened to throw herself out of the window. Jean de Gué had failed. He was a greater failure than I. And that was why he had left me sleeping in the hotel in Le Mans and gone away. It was not a jest, but a confession of defeat. I knew now that he would not come back. He would not even bother to find out what had happened. I could do as I pleased, leave his home or stay. If I had never met him, if none of this had happened, I should have been tonight at the guesthouse in la Grande-Trappe, learning there what to do with failure. I should have heard the monks chanting their Office, said my first prayer. Now none of this was going to happen, and I was alone. Or rather I was not alone—I was part of the life of other people. Never before had I been concerned with the feelings of anybody but myself, except for the minds and motives of characters in history long since dead. Now I had a chance to do otherwise, through deception. I could not be sure if anything good ever came through a lie. I thought not—only trouble, war, disaster—but I did not know. If I had gone to la Grande-Trappe they would have told me, but instead I was in another man's home.

I turned away from the window in the dressing room, went into the bedroom and took off my dressing gown and slippers. Then I lay down beside his poor, pathetic wife, who was sleeping peacefully with the locket pinned on her shawl, and I said, "Oh, God, what am I to do? Ought I to leave this place, or should I stay?"

And there was no answer, only a question mark.

Chapter 7

I slept heavily, and when I awoke the shutters had been pushed back, daylight filled the room, and my partner had left my side. I could hear voices coming from the bathroom beyond, and I lay still, my hands behind my head, looking about me at the room, whose striped wallpaper seemed out of keeping with the dark woodwork and the massive furniture, which had probably never been moved in fifty years. An effort had been made to modernise the room with bright hangings and a frilly dressing table in the alcove. The cushions on the chairs were also striped, in an endeavour to match the wallpaper, but they were out of tone, a blend of pink and puce, distressing if the eye lingered upon them long.

The room served as boudoir also, for there was a small secrétaire near the fireplace, a tea table, a corner cabinet displaying porcelain, and a bookcase, yet oddly the effect was not to make the room more comfortable but the reverse. It gave a certain stiffness and formality to the whole, like furniture on show in a store window, or as though the arranger wished to surround herself with possessions that had once looked well in quite a different setting, but in this room were ill assorted.

The voices ceased, taps were turned on and off, footsteps went along the corridor. Somewhere there was a banging door, a distant telephone, the sound of a car starting up and driving away, and then, after silence, the brushing movement of someone sweeping the corridor. Sleep had had a strange effect on me. I had awoken in a different vein. The sudden anguish that had come over me the night before had vanished. The people in the château had reassumed their puppet quality, and the jest was with me once again. Last night I had sensed tragedy, and was so filled with compassion both for them and for myself that it had seemed to me I was destined to make amends for all that had gone wrong in their lives and my own. Now sleep had changed my values. The liability had become an escapade. It was nothing to do with me if Jean de Gué had been possessed by his family, and had then run out on duty. No doubt they were as much to blame as he. The self who had wakened this morning suggested that the whole unprecedented situation was but a prolongation of my holiday, and when it got out of control, as sooner or later it surely must, I could quit. The one embarrassment, discovery, would have happened last night if it was going to happen at all. The mother, the wife, the child, all three had been deceived. Whatever blunders I might make in the future would be put down to whim or freak of temper, for the simple reason that I was above suspicion. No spy in the service of his country had ever been given such a disguise, such an opportunity for probing the frailty of others . . . if that was what I wanted. What did I want? Last night, to heal. This morning, to be amused. There was no reason why the two should be incompatible.

I looked above my head at the old-fashioned bell rope, and pulled it. The brushing in the corridor ceased. Footsteps came to the door and someone tapped. I called out "*Entrez!*" and the blushing, rosy-cheeked *femme de chambre* who had served my dinner tray presented herself at the door.

"Monsieur le Comte slept well?" she asked.

I told her very well, and demanded coffee. I enquired after the rest of the family and was informed that Madame la Comtesse was *souffrante* and staying in bed; that Mademoiselle was in church; that Monsieur Paul had gone to the *verrerie;* that Marie-Noel was getting up; that Madame Jean and Madame Paul were in the salon. I thanked her and she went away. I had learnt three things from two minutes' conversation. My present to the mother had done her no good; Paul's business, the family business, was a glass foundry; and Renée, the dark woman, was his wife.

I got up, went to the bathroom and shaved.

Gaston brought my coffee to the dressing room, no longer in uniform and gaiters but wearing the striped coat of a *valet de chambre*. I greeted him as a friend.

"Things are better this morning, then?" he said, placing the tray on the table. "It is not so bad to be home again after all."

He asked me what I would wear, and I told him whatever he himself considered suitable to the morning. This amused him.

"It's not the coat that makes the morning gay," he said, "but the man inside it. Monsieur le Comte is all sunshine today."

I expressed concern for my mother's health. He pulled a face.

"You know how it is, Monsieur," he said. "When one grows old one becomes lonely and frightened, unless there is something very strong within." He tapped his heart. "Physically, Madame la Comtesse is stronger than anyone in St. Gilles, and in her mind as well, but morally it's a different matter." He went to the wardrobe, took out a brown tweed jacket and began to brush it.

I watched him as I drank my coffee. I thought how different it would be if I were back in a hotel bedroom in Tours or Blois, and he the *valet de chambre* who had come to wait on me. He would ask me, with a hotel servant's courtesy and indifference, whether the city pleased me, and whether I hoped to return next year, forgetting me as soon as the tip was paid, the luggage carried down by the porter and the anonymous key replaced in its pigeonhole. This man was my friend, but I felt like Judas as I watched him.

I put on the clothes he had laid out for me, and it was a curious feeling, like wearing the garments of someone dead who had been close to me. I had not felt like this in the travelling suit I had worn the day before. This jacket was personal. It had a rough, familiar smell about it, not unpleasant, and I could feel it had been in woods and under rain, had rubbed the ground, had lain on summer grass, been scorched by bonfires. Unaccountably, I thought of the priests of ancient days, who on ceremonial occasions wore the skins of the animals which had been sacrificed, to bestow upon their persons greater power through the strength of the slain beasts, and their warm spilt blood.

"Will Monsieur le Comte be going down to the *verrerie?*" asked Gaston.

"No," I said, "not this morning. Did Monsieur Paul suggest it?"

"Monsieur Paul will be back for lunch as usual. Possibly he is expecting you to go with him this afternoon."

"What's the time now?"

"Already after half past ten, Monsieur le Comte."

I left him seeing to my clothes, while in the bedroom the little *femme de chambre* was busy making the bed. I walked downstairs, the chill, impersonal smell of polish that greeted me at variance with the gigantic crucified Christ upon the wall. I could hear the murmur of women's voices from the salon, and I crept softly to the open door leading to the terrace, having no desire to join them, and so out and round to my previous hiding place under the cedar tree. It was a golden autumn day, no hard brilliance in the sky but soft translucence, the moisture from the ground drawn up into a spongy warmth, making the air gentle. The château, graceful and serene, protected from the outside world by the mellow walls guarding the sunken moat, might have been an island, separated as it was from village and church, lime avenue and sandy road; an island whose way of life went back to centuries long past, having no concern with the postman I saw wheeling his bicycle past the church above the bridge, or the high van bringing supplies to the *épicerie* at the corner.

Someone was singing near the archway leading to the outbuildings, and, walking left, so as to avoid the dog, I looked down and saw a woman kneeling beside a pool of water formed in the crevice of the moat wall and fed by the river. She was scrubbing sheets on a wooden board, splashing the soapy water over the rim of the crevice, and she looked up at me, brushing wispy hair from her forehead with a mottled hand, and smiled, and said, *"Bonjour, Monsieur le Comte."*

I found a door in the wall, and a narrow footbridge leading across the moat; and, turning left, avoiding the garage and stabling, I was at once amongst cow houses and straw and muddy earth, with a vegetable garden beyond covering three or four acres and enclosed by a rough stone wall, and beyond this cultivated fields surrounded by forest. Here by the cow house was a strawstack, tightly packed and golden brown, and beneath it, piled in heaps one upon the other, pumpkins smooth and round like the behinds of little boys, flesh pink, lemon, lime, and on top of them all a rake and fork, and a white cat blinking in the sun.

Inside the cow house the floors were newly washed, the water running in a groove, but the good cow smell, the manure, the milky tang, clung to the walls and the wooden partition. As I turned, an old woman emerged from some lair at the further end, smiling, toothless, her clogs clattering on the stone floor, bearing the yoke on her shoulders and the empty swinging pails. *"Benj̆ur, M'sieur le Camte,"* she seemed to say, and proceeded to talk rapidly, jerking her head and laughing, and I was lost for answer, her broad, toothless accent too unfamiliar to my ears.

I left her with a wave of my hand, passing a vast heap of cider apples ready for the press, and on through line upon line of vegetables—the sprouting purple-green of root crops, the dew upon them still, their pungent, earthy odour mingled with dried sunflower, tarragon and raspberry cane—and so out through another door, through another wall, and into the immediate château grounds beneath the chestnut trees, their falling leaves dappling the sandy path with patterns of green and gold. There was no formality about the grounds, and the dovecot was isolated amidst pasture for the cattle; but the pasture stretched to the woods, and the paths through the woods spread from a single centre, like the hours on a sundial, stretching out to all the points of the compass. The dell in the centre was dominated by a lichen-covered statue, the classic drapery chipped, the right hand of the huntress missing.

I walked up one of these long rides and looked at the château from the furthest point, seeing it now as a picture within a frame. The blue-black roof, the turrets, the tall chimneys and the sandstone walls had shrunk to fairy-tale proportions: it no longer held living, feeling people, but was a plate turned over in a book of illustrations, or something glimpsed on the walls of a gallery, noted momentarily for its beauty and then dismissed.

I retraced my steps past the seeking Artemis, down the ride to the dovecot, now filled with hay but still a nesting place for cooing fantail pigeons, who preened and postured, strutting in and out of their narrow entrances, bowing and spreading their tails. Then the long windows of the salon opened, folding against the shutters, and the figures of Françoise and Renée appeared on the terrace, waving to me, and from between them the child came running, calling, "Papa . . . Papa . . ." regardless of her mother, who scolded her to return. Crossing the footbridge spanning the moat, she sprang over the grass to join me, leaping high when almost on top of me so that I had to catch her in mid-air like a ballet dancer.

"Why didn't you go to the *verrerie?*" she asked, hanging round my neck, rumpling my hair. "Uncle Paul had to go without you and it made him in a bad temper."

"I was late to bed through your fault," I said, putting her down. "You'd better go back indoors—I can hear your mother calling you."

She laughed, pulling my hand, dragging me to the swing by the dovecot. "There is nothing the matter with me today. You are home," she said. "Now mend the swing for me. The rope has broken."

I fumbled with the contraption, clumsy-handed, while she watched me, chattering of nothing, asking questions that demanded no answer; and then when I fixed the seat for her she stood on it for a moment, working it with energy, her thin legs springy as a monkey's beneath the short frock, the bright checks draining from her face any colour she might otherwise have had.

"Come on," she said suddenly—I had gone to the back to push her, thinking she wanted to swing higher—and we walked off aimlessly together, hand in hand, she stooping to pick up chestnuts when we came to the path, filling a small pocket in her frock and then throwing the rest away.

"Do people always like boys better than girls?" she asked me inconsequently.

"No, I don't think so. Why should they?" I replied.

"My aunt Blanche says they do, but there are more women saints than men, for which there is great rejoicing in Paradise. Will you race me?"

"I don't want to race you."

She ran on ahead, skipping and leaping, passing through the garden door to the front terrace, through which I had gone the night before. Glancing up at the small window in her turret room, I saw how formidable was the height from that

71

sill to the ground below. I followed the child towards the stabling and outbuildings. She had sprung up onto the wall above the moat and was now picking her way along the top of it, amid tangled ivy. Then she jumped down again close to the archway, and the dog, which had been sleeping in the sun, stretched himself, wagging his tail, and she opened the gate of his run and let him out. He barked as he saw me approach, and when I called out, "Come here, then, what's the matter, old fellow?" he kept his distance and growled, standing beside Marie-Noel as though to guard her.

"Stop it, César," said the child, jerking at his collar. "Have you gone blind suddenly that you don't know your master?"

He wagged his tail again and licked her hand, but he did not come to me, and I stood where I was, with an intuition that if I advanced he would growl again, and my efforts to make friends would increase his suspicion rather than allay it.

"Leave him alone. Don't excite him," I said.

She let go his collar and he loped towards me, still muttering, sniffed, and then left me, without interest, and went off nosing at the ivy around the moat wall.

"He didn't give you any welcome," said Marie-Noel. "How extraordinary. Perhaps he isn't feeling well. César, come here. César, let me feel your nose."

"Don't bother him," I said. "He's all right."

I began to walk towards the house, but the dog did not follow me. He stood uncertainly, watching the child, who ran to him, and patted his great flanks and felt his nose.

I looked across the precincts of the château to the bridge and the village beyond, and I saw a woman turn down the hill from the church and come to the gateway between the entrance towers. She wore black, with a little old-fashioned toque on her head, and she was carrying a prayer book. I recognised her for Blanche. Looking neither to right nor to left, seeming to be unconscious of the day, she walked stiff and straight up the gravel driveway to the terrace steps. Even when Marie-Noel ran to meet her, her frozen face never relaxed an instant, the hard, set expression remaining unchanged.

"César growled at Papa," called the child, "and didn't seem

pleased to see him. It has never happened before. Do you think he is ill?"

Blanche glanced across at the dog, who now advanced towards her, wagging his tail. "If no one is taking him for a walk he had better be put back in his run," she said, and came up the steps, apparently unconcerned at the dog's behaviour. "As you are now well enough to be out of doors, you are well enough to come for your lessons with me after lunch."

"I don't have to do lessons today, do I, Papa?" the child protested.

"I don't see why not," I said, believing I might ingratiate myself with Blanche. "You had better ask your mother what she thinks."

Blanche made no comment. She walked straight past me into the house: I might not have been there. Marie-Noel took my hand and shook it crossly.

"Why are you in such a bad humour with me today?" she said.

"I'm not in a bad humour."

"You are. You don't want to play with me, and it isn't anything to do with Maman if I have lessons this afternoon or not. You know that very well."

"Am I supposed to give the orders?"

She stared at me, her eyes round. "You always do," she said.

"Very well then," I said firmly. "It won't hurt you to have lessons, if your aunt can spare the time. Now come upstairs —I have something for you."

It occurred to me suddenly that the giving of the presents would be much simpler if it were done at the table, while we were all assembled there having lunch, than if I gave them to each one individually. But the child might have hers now, as a sop, because I had taken an unpopular attitude over the lessons.

She followed me up to the dressing room, and I went to the table and gave her the book in its wrappings. She tore them off, and when she saw what the book was she exclaimed in delight and hugged it to her.

"It is just what I wanted," she said. "Oh, my darling sweet Papa, why do you always guess the right things?"

In her enthusiasm she flung herself upon me, and once

73

again I was forced to undergo the arms round the neck, the cheek thrust against mine, the random kisses falling anywhere. This time I was expecting it, and as I swung her round in my arms it was like playing with a lion cub, or a long-limbed puppy, or any young animal that attracts one because of its youth and grace. Instead of being awkward with her I found myself responding. I pulled her hair and tickled the back of her neck, both of us laughing, her very naturalness with me making me unafraid, confident of myself and of her. It was stimulating to realise that if this attractive clinging object knew I was a stranger she would be repelled and scared, withdrawing herself immediately, and we should have no point of contact, that she would be totally indifferent to me, just as the dog had been.

"Must I do lessons?" she said, sensing intuitively my sudden response, trying to turn it to advantage.

"I don't know," I said. "We can decide that later."

Putting her down, I stood beside the table again, looking at the other packages.

"I'll tell you something," I said. "I've brought presents from Paris for everyone. I gave your mother hers last night, and one to your grandmother too. We'll put these in the dining room, and they can open them at lunch."

"For Uncle Paul and my aunt Renée?" she said. "Why, it's not either of their birthdays."

"No, but it's a good thing to give presents. It shows appreciation. I have one for your aunt Blanche too."

"For my aunt Blanche?" She stared at me, amazed.

"Yes, why not?"

"But you never give her anything, not even for Christmas or the New Year!"

"Well, I'm giving her something now. It might make her better-tempered."

The child went on staring at me, and began biting her fingers. "I don't think it's a good idea, putting the presents on the table," she said, her voice worried. "It's too much like a fête or a celebration. Nothing is going to happen, is it, that you haven't told me?"

"What do you mean?"

"My little brother isn't going to be born today?"

74

"No, of course not. That's got nothing to do with it."

"The Wise Men from the east brought gifts . . . I know what you gave Maman, because she was wearing it. She told my aunt Renée that it cost a lot of money, and it was very naughty of you, but it showed how fond of her you were."

"What did I tell you? It's a good thing to give presents now and again."

"Yes, but not in front of everyone, when it's special. I am glad you did not put my *Little Flower* in the dining room. What have you brought for the others?"

"We'll see later."

She opened her book, crouching on her knees to do so, with the book laid out on the floor of the dressing room, and I remembered dimly how as a child one never adopted an adult position, but invariably read lying flat, drew standing up, and for preference ate walking about instead of sitting down. It struck me that I ought to go upstairs and enquire after my mother, and I said to Marie-Noel, "Come and see if your grandmother is better," but she went on reading, not taking her eyes from the book, and said without lifting her head, "She is not to be disturbed. Charlotte said so." Nevertheless I went upstairs, oddly confident now about everything I did.

I found my way without difficulty to the second floor, and the third corridor, and the room at the end. I tapped on the door, but there was no answer, not even the barking of the terriers. I opened the door cautiously and found the room in darkness, the shutters closed, the curtains drawn. I could distinguish the form under the covers on the bed, and I went close and looked down on her. The face had a dirty, greyish pallor to it, and she was breathing heavily, lying on her back, the sheet drawn to her chin. There was a close, stale smell about the room. I wondered how ill she was, and thought it remiss of Charlotte to leave her there without attention. I could not tell whether she really slept, or simply lay there with her eyes closed, and I whispered, "Do you want anything?" but she did not answer. The heavy breathing sounded harsh and painful. I went out of the room, softly closing the door, and at the end of the corridor came face to face with Charlotte.

"How is she?" I said. "I've just been in to her, but she didn't hear me."

I caught a flicker of surprise in the woman's small black eyes.

"She won't wake now before the afternoon, Monsieur le Comte," she whispered.

"Has the doctor been?" I asked.

"The doctor?" she repeated. "No, naturally not."

"But if she is ill," I said, "wouldn't it be wise to send for him?"

The woman stared. "Who told you she was ill? There is nothing wrong."

"I understood from Gaston . . ."

"I only gave the usual message in the kitchen that Madame la Comtesse was not to be disturbed."

She sounded on the defensive, as though I were unfairly attacking her for something she had not done, and I realised I must have made some sort of error in coming upstairs to enquire after her patient, who now appeared not to be a patient, but merely sleeping.

"I must have misheard him," I said shortly. "I thought he said she was ill," and I went downstairs and back to the dressing room to fetch the presents I was about to bestow upon my unsuspecting relatives. The child was still there, reading intently, and it was not until I stirred her with my foot that she became aware of my existence.

"You know, Papa," she said, "she was just an ordinary child like me. No one thought anything special about her when she was little. She could be troublesome sometimes, and cause grief to her parents. And then God chose her as a divine instrument to bring consolation to hundreds and thousands of people."

I picked up the packages from the table. "That sort of thing doesn't happen often," I said. "Saints are very rare."

"She was born at Alençon, Papa, and it's hardly any distance from here. I wonder if there is something in the air that is likely to turn a person into a saint, or whether there is something one must do?"

"You had better ask your aunt."

"I have. She told me prayer and fasting alone aren't any

76

good, but that God's grace can descend suddenly, without warning, if one is really humble enough, and pure in heart. Am I pure in heart?"

"I doubt it."

I heard the sound of a car driving up to the château, and Marie-Noel ran to the window and craned out.

"It's my uncle Paul," she said. "His present is the smallest of the lot. I shouldn't like to be him. But, being a man, I suppose he can hide his feelings."

We went down like conspirators and into the dining room, which I had not seen—a long, narrow room facing the terrace, immediately to the left of the entrance—and cunningly I told the child to lay the presents in their proper places, which she did with evident enjoyment, her earlier doubts allayed. I noticed, to my surprise, that Blanche sat at one end of the table, not Françoise, as I should have thought. The head of the table was presumably my own place since she laid no present there; and she put Renée's package next to it, and Paul's next to Blanche, and her own book of *The Little Flower* on my other side. Françoise, then, sat between Paul and the child. I puzzled on the jigsaw arrangement, until Gaston came into the room, changed from his valet's rig to a dark coat, followed by the rosy-cheeked Germaine and another whom I had not seen before but who, judging from her plumpness and frizzled hair, was daughter to the woman I had seen washing sheets in the pool beneath the moat wall.

"What do you think, Gaston," said Marie-Noel, "Papa is giving everybody presents, even my aunt Blanche. It is not in celebration of anything, it is just a sign of appreciation."

I saw Gaston dart me a quick look, and I wondered why it should be so unusual a thing to do, to present gifts on returning home. Did he assume I had been drinking again? A moment or two later he flung open double doors at the end of the room, leading to what appeared to be a library, and said, "Madame la Comtesse is served." The little group which his action revealed might have been a conversation piece executed rather stiffly by an eighteenth-century painter. Françoise and Renée were seated in hard chairs some distance apart, the one reading, the other sewing, Paul was leaning on his wife's chair, and the tall, thin figure of Blanche was

77

silhouetted against the further door. They looked up as the child and I advanced into the room.

"Papa has a surprise for you all," Marie-Noel said, "but I am not going to tell you what it is."

I wondered, had it been Jean de Gué himself who entered, whether he would have seen them as I did then, or whether, because they were his own family and he belonged to them, familiarity would have blunted perception, their pose seeming natural and without significance, merging into the background that he knew so well. As a stranger I was like a spectator at a play, but I was also in a sense producer too: circumstances were forcing them to follow my lead, and upon my actions would depend their own. I was Merlin, I was Prospero, and the child a sort of Ariel to do my bidding, an intermediary between two separate worlds. I saw, in that moment, apprehension on both Françoise's face and Renée's, but to a different degree, and surely from a different cause: the one expressed doubt, a fear of being hurt, and the other, more guarded, wary, seemed to imply misgiving. Paul, openly hostile, threw me a glance full of suspicion and dislike, and Blanche, by the door, betrayed no interest whatsoever. But I saw her figure stiffen, and she looked not at me but at the child.

"What is it, Jean?" said Françoise, rising to her feet.

"Nothing," I replied. "Marie-Noel likes to be mysterious. It's only that I have brought back a small present for everyone, and we put them on the table in the dining room."

The tension eased. Renée relaxed, Paul shrugged his shoulders, and Françoise smiled, fingering the locket which she wore pinned onto her jumper.

"I'm afraid you spent too much money in Paris," she said. "If you continue giving me presents like this one, there'll be nothing left at all."

She passed by into the dining room, and we followed her. I made a pretence of tying my shoe, allowing the others to sit, so as to make sure that I was right in assuming my place to be at the head of the table. This was correct, and I sat down. There was a momentary hush while Blanche said grace and we bowed our heads over our plates. I noticed Marie-Noel watch her aunt in fascination, and, looking to the end of the table,

I saw that Blanche's eyes were on the package beside her napkin. Her usual frozen immobility changed to incredulity. Had the package been a live snake she could not have expressed greater horror or disgust. Then her mouth tightened, she regained composure, and, ignoring the package, she took the napkin and placed it on her lap.

"Aren't you going to open it?" said the child.

Blanche did not answer. She broke the bread beside her plate, and I saw then that the others were all looking at me with curiosity, as if something quite without precedent had occurred. For one second I wondered if my action in sitting down, the way I held myself, some involuntary gesture, had at last betrayed me, and they knew me for an impostor.

"Well," I said, "what's wrong? Why are you all staring at me?"

The child, my familiar spirit, gave me the answer. "Everyone is surprised because you have given a present to my aunt Blanche," she said.

So that was it. I had acted out of character. But I was still undiscovered.

"I felt in a generous mood," I announced, and then, remembering the words of Jean de Gué in the bistro in Le Mans, and how his choice of gifts must have been deliberately chosen to suit the recipient, I added, "I hope I have given everybody what they needed most. It's part of my system."

"Look," said Marie-Noel, "Papa has given me a life of the Little Flower. It was certainly what I wanted most. He can't have given my aunt Blanche a life of St. Thérèse of Avila because it's the wrong shape. I could tell by the feel of it."

"Suppose you stop talking," I said, "and get on with your food. They can open their presents later."

"There's only one present I want," said Paul, "and that's the renewal of the Carvalet contract, and possibly a cheque for ten million francs. You haven't been able to oblige, by any chance?"

"I would say your present also is the wrong shape," I answered, "and I dislike talking business when I am eating. On the other hand, I am perfectly willing to come with you to the *verrerie* this afternoon."

My sense of power was unbounded. I knew nothing about

79

the contract or the business, but I felt my bluff to be superb, and it must have worked, for they were all attacking their plates. My self-confidence mounting every moment, I signalled to Gaston to pour me out a glass of wine. I recalled my success with the mother the night before and began to tell the same tale again, the visit to the theatre in Paris, the meeting with old friends, and just as she had fed me with information then, so now I picked up here and there a clue. As the meal went on I learned that during the war Jean de Gué must have fought for the Resistance, that Paul had been a prisoner, that Jean de Gué and Françoise had met and married soon after the Liberation. Little scraps of family history fell on my ear before the conversation drifted to something else totally unconnected. What I gleaned would have to be sorted and sifted at leisure, and still I could not be absolutely sure of the relationship between Jean de Gué and Paul and Renée, except that the last two were husband and wife, and Paul obviously directed, or helped to direct, the family business. The likeness that made the tie between Jean de Gué, his mother and his child showed no trace in the colouring or features of the sister Blanche; while Paul and Renée, both being dark in hair and complexion, could have been blood relations had I not known the contrary.

Blanche took little part in the conversation, and never once addressed herself to me; and Françoise, surprisingly, proved my greatest source of help and information. The note of complaint had gone from her voice, she seemed happy, even gay, and I guessed that the locket she so constantly fingered was the cause of this. Renée, whom I had expected to dominate the table, was silent, even sullen, and when Blanche enquired after her migraine she replied briefly that it was as bad as ever.

"Why don't you take something for it?" said Paul irritably. "Surely in these days somebody has invented a cure? I thought Dr. Lebrun had given you some tablets."

"You know perfectly well they don't touch it," she answered. "I shall lie down this afternoon and try to sleep. I had a wretched night."

"Perhaps Aunt Renée is getting measles," said Marie-Noel. "They say that begins with a headache. But it wouldn't hurt her if she was, because Aunt Renée isn't going to have a baby."

The remark was unfortunate. Renée flushed and darted a look of venom at her niece, while Françoise, turning the subject rather too adroitly, asked Paul about one of the workmen at the *verrerie* who had burnt his arm in a furnace, at the same time frowning at the child.

"If what we pay out in benefits and sickness could only go into the business, we should be in a better position to face the future," said Paul. "As it is, the men seize any excuse to be idle, knowing they will be kept at our expense. It was very different in my father's day."

"Our father happened to have brains and integrity," said Blanche, surprisingly. "His sons unfortunately have neither."

Good for Blanche, I thought, looking towards her in astonishment. But Paul, thrusting out his chin and flushing as darkly as his wife, said swiftly, "Are you suggesting that *I* am dishonest?"

"No," said Blanche, "misled."

"Oh, please," said Françoise wearily, "must we have this at the table? I thought for once we were going to keep off family affairs."

"My dear Françoise," said Paul, "if Jean cared to put into the business one quarter of what he spends on ridiculous trinkets like the brooch you are wearing, there wouldn't be any need to discuss family affairs. No one would complain. Least of all myself."

"You know perfectly well it's the first present he has given me for months," she said.

"Possibly. But perhaps other people have been more fortunate."

"Such as who?"

"Don't ask me. Jean is the traveller. I stay at home. That is the prerogative of the younger brother."

Unpleasant innuendo, but I had it. He was also a de Gué, the *cadet*. And, judging from his manner, he resented his position. The jigsaw fitted into place, but I was not certain that Renée made a comfortable sister-in-law.

"If you are trying to hint," said Françoise, "that Jean wastes money on other women . . ."

81

"But he does," chipped in the child. "Papa has given a present both to Aunt Renée and Aunt Blanche, and I, for one, want to know what he has brought."

"Will you be quiet," said Françoise, turning to her, "or do you want me to send you from the table?"

The leg of mutton had been eaten and taken away, the vegetables served, and we were now at cheese and fruit. I felt it was time to ease the tension.

"How about opening the presents?" I said cheerfully. "I agree with Françoise. Let's stop discussing family. Come on, Renée, a gift to chase the migraine."

Marie-Noel asked my permission to get down, and then ran round the table to stand beside her aunt. Reluctantly, I noticed, Renée untied the ribbon. The fancy paper was laid aside, and the layers of tissue. I caught a glimpse of lace, and Renée paused and said hurriedly, "I'll open it upstairs. I might spill something on it here."

"But what is it?" said Françoise. "A blouse?"

The child forestalled the covering hand of her aunt, and drew from the folded tissue the flimsiest of nightgowns, gossamer light, a frivolity for brides on midsummer eve.

"How pretty," said Françoise. But her tone lacked warmth.

Renée had taken the piece of nonsense away from Marie-Noel and was folding it back again between the concealing paper. She did not thank me. It was only then that I realised I had made a faux pas. The gift was not intended for public display. The child had been right when she told me that presents were personal things, and that people liked to open them in privacy. Too late to make amends. Paul was staring moodily at his wife, and Françoise wore the false, bright smile of someone who tries to pretend that all is well. On Blanche's face was nothing but contempt. Marie-Noel was the only one delighted.

"You will have to keep that for best, Aunt Renée," she said. "The pity of it is that only Uncle Paul will see you wearing it."

She darted round to his side of the table. "I wonder what Papa has given you?" she said.

He shrugged his shoulders. His wife's gift had taken the edge off expectation. "I've no idea. You had better open it," he said.

Excitedly she snipped the string with a knife, while I sought to make excuses for Jean de Gué. I thought back to the past evening, and my encounter downstairs, and I believed I knew now what had been expected of me. Tête-à-tête, with Paul absent, the frivolous gift might have come apropos. But it hardly belonged in the dining room with the cheese. At least, I decided, the blunder might be rectified by the fact that Jean de Gué had brought a present for his brother too. But I was wrong. Worse was to come. The child, with puzzled face, drew forth a small bottle from corrugated wrapping.

"It's medicine," she said. "It's called Elixir." And, looking at the printed folder enclosed with it, she read aloud, "To tone the organs. A hormone preparation to counteract impotence. . . . What does impotence mean, Papa?"

Paul snatched the bottle from her to prevent further reading from the folder. "Give that thing here and be quiet," he said, stuffing the bottle in his jacket and turning to me in fury. "If that's your idea of a joke, I don't see it."

He got up and went out of the room. The silence was appalling, and this time I could find no excuses for Jean for such a wanton piece of cruelty.

"What a shame," said Marie-Noel reproachfully. "Uncle Paul was disappointed, and I don't blame him."

I felt Gaston's gaze on me from the sideboard, and lowered my eyes to my plate. Hostility surrounded me on all sides. I dared not look at Renée, and Françoise's deprecating cough warned me that I could expect no sympathy from her. Jean de Gué, in all the glory of his cups, could not have made so fabulous a botch as I had done. Apology was useless. "For what we have received may the Lord make us truly thankful," said Blanche, and rose from her seat. Françoise and Renée followed her, and I was left sitting at the table.

"Aunt Blanche," called the child, "you haven't taken your present." She ran after the others, holding the third package in her hands.

Gaston came with a tray and brush to sweep the crumbs. "If Monsieur le Comte is going to the *verrerie* the car is outside," he said.

I met his eyes and saw reproach. And this upset me, because his devotion gave me confidence.

"What happened just then," I said, "was not intentional."

"No, Monsieur le Comte."

"It was, in fact, an error. I had forgotten the contents of the packages."

"Evidently, Monsieur le Comte."

There was no more to say. I went out of the dining room to the hall, and so to the terrace, and drawn up below the steps was the Renault, and Paul waiting by the open door.

Chapter 8

There was no escaping him. The situation was my responsibility. Whatever Jean de Gué may have intended to do, discreetly and in private, I had now wrecked with brash and false bonhomie.

"All right, get in. You drive," I said curtly, and as I climbed in beside Paul I realised that in assuming the personality and presence of the other I must also make amends for the faults I committed in his name. In a strange way it seemed a point of honour.

"I'm sorry for what happened just now," I said. "The whole thing was a mistake. Everything got mixed up in my valise."

He did not answer immediately, and glancing at him, as we turned left up the village hill and past the church, I saw in the narrow mouth, with the droop at the corners, for the first time a resemblance to Blanche. But the prominent nose and thick eyebrows were his own, and the muddy complexion was quite different from hers, which was smooth and pale and fine.

"I don't believe you," he said. "If any gesture was deliberate, yours was, to make me look a fool in front of everyone, even the servants. Can't you imagine them now, laughing their heads off in the kitchen? I should be, if I were them."

"Nonsense," I said. "Nobody even noticed. And I've told you already it was a mistake. Forget it."

He turned out of the village, past a cemetery, and along a straight road towards the line of forest.

"I've put up with practical jokes from you all my life," he said, "but there are certain limits. What might be amusing

84

at a club, or between ourselves, is a different thing from jeering openly before our wives, and hurting them into the bargain. Frankly, I didn't know that even you were capable of that amount of bad taste."

"All right," I said, "I've apologised. I can't do more. If you won't believe the thing was a mistake, there's no more to be said."

The forest closed in upon us, not a forbidding darkness but golden green, a tangle of oak, hornbeam, chestnut, beech—all the trees whose leaf gives light instead of shadow, whose branches spread with time, whose stems grow paler. Unlike the conifer, so deeply black in winter and in summer, they mellow with the changing season, and now, in the fall of the year, they spilled colour on the ground.

"Another thing," said Paul, "don't you think it's time you stopped treating Renée as if she were a second Marie-Noel? If you want to make a pet of your own daughter it's your affair, not mine, but I object to my wife being turned into a doll merely to gratify your desire for popularity."

The rôle of apologist was not an easy one, and I tried to think what Jean de Gué would have done if he had committed the blunder of producing the nightdress in public.

"All women like to be spoilt," I said. "Didn't you see what I gave Françoise? Naturally I brought back something pretty for Renée too. Did you expect me to give her the life of a saint, like the child?"

Paul turned the car to the right, and we were off the tarred surface onto a sandy byroad. The forest was thinning, and there was a clearing ahead.

"Your choice was vulgar and your timing crude," said Paul. "I happened to be watching Françoise as well as Renée. Anyway, next time you decide to give my wife a present, consult me first."

The road narrowed, and I saw that it was a cul-de-sac. Straight before us was a long line of workmen's cottages, and to our right a great shedlike building with a sloping roof and tall stovepipe chimneys, standing in a wide expanse of rough ground surrounded by other sheds, the whole fenced in and separated from the road and cottages. Workmen were passing in and out of the sheds with barrows, and there was a truck running along rails, backing against a tipped heap of waste. From the chimneys came a peculiar gasping, choking sound of smoke expelled by a furnace. Paul drove the car in through the open gates, stopping in front of the small lodge immediately beside them, and, getting out, without another word to me he walked away across the ground towards a second building, behind the shed with the high chimneys.

I followed him, and as I picked my way between the trolley rails I realised, from the crunching beneath my feet, that the ground was covered with minute particles of glass, fine as sand upon a beach. It was everywhere, part of the soil, part of the mud, and the waste heaps were glass as well, blue and green and amber. Workmen pushing barrows stopped to let us pass, and I noticed that, although they nodded to him, to me they smiled; not with any particular deference or respect, but with a certain camaraderie and warmth, as if they were genuinely glad to see my face. The welcome flattered me, boosted my morale, and I felt meanly gratified that the esteem, or whatever it was, had been shown to me, not Paul.

He made straight for a long, two-storied, eighteenth-century house, with an old, red-tiled, lichen-covered roof, and, opening the door, led the way into a square shabby room with panelled walls and a stone floor. There was a table in the middle covered with books and files and papers, and a big desk in one corner. A bald-headed man with spectacles and hollow cheeks, wearing a dark suit, rose from a seat at the table when he saw us.

"*Bonjour, Monsieur le Comte,*" he said to me. "You are feeling better, then?"

I realised that Paul must have told him some story of sickness or a hangover, or both, and I noticed that his smile was tremulous, nervous, not warm and friendly as that of the workmen had been, and behind the spectacles he had anxious eyes.

"There was nothing wrong with me," I said. "I was merely idle."

Paul laughed—not the laugh of humour, but the disparaging sound of one who is not amused. "It must be pleasant to lie in bed in the mornings," he said. "It's something I haven't been able to do for a long time, or Jacques either, for that matter."

The man made a deprecatory gesture, glancing from one to the other of us, wishing to offend neither, and then he said quickly, "Is there anything you wish to discuss in private? If so, I can leave you."

"No," said Paul, "the future of the *verrerie* is as much your concern as ours. Like you, I am waiting to hear what was achieved in Paris."

They looked at me, and I looked back at them. Then I went over to the chair by the desk, sat down, and took a cigarette from the packet lying there.

"What do you want to know exactly?" I asked, bending over to light the cigarette, the action enabling me to hide my face, which might otherwise have betrayed my uncertainty of the proper reply.

"Oh, *mon Dieu* . . ." said Paul in exasperation, as if my cautious, hedging question was the ultimate straw, the final insult to patience too long shown. "There's only one issue, isn't there? Do we, or do we not, close down?"

Somebody—was it the mother?—had said something about a contract. The visit to Paris hinged on a Carvalet contract. Jean de Gué was expected to bring it back with him. Very well, then, they should have it.

"If you mean did I succeed in getting Carvalet to renew the contract, the answer is yes," I said.

Both men stared at me, astounded. Jacques burst out with a "Bravo!" but Paul interrupted, "On what terms, what stipulations?"

"Our terms," I said, "and they made no stipulations."

"You don't mean to tell me they are willing to take our stuff on precisely the same conditions as before, in spite of the lower quotations they are getting from other firms?"

"I persuaded them to do so."

"How many discussions did you have?"

"Several."

"But what's the explanation? Why all those letters? Were they bluffing, trying to make us lower our figure, or what?"

"I couldn't tell you."

"Then you came away completely satisfied, and we carry on for a further period of six months?"

"That's about it."

"I can't understand it. You've achieved something I frankly believed to be impossible. My congratulations."

He took the cigarettes from the desk and handed them to Jacques, lighting one for himself. They began discussing something, without reference to me, and I swivelled round in my chair and looked out of the window, wondering what I had been talking about. In a moment, perhaps, they would begin again with the questions which meant nothing to me, and my wild ignorance would betray itself, but in the meantime . . . in the meantime, what? I looked out and saw a tangled orchard, golden in the sun, with apple trees, heavy laden, bowing their branches to the earth. An ancient horse with a flowing white mane browsed in a field beyond. A woman in a black apron, with a grey shawl round her shoulders and sabots on her feet, was hoeing between the vegetables, hens pecking in her path. The scene framed itself in the windowpane like a print, peaceful and soothing, and I wished it could continue with me as onlooker, not participating in any way, a traveller sitting in a train watching the world go by. Yet this was what I had complained of in life hitherto—the non-participation, the lack of contact with the ways of other people.

"Have you got the contract with you?" said Paul.

"No," I answered. "They're sending it."

The woman hoeing lifted her head and looked towards the window. She was large, elderly, broad-hipped, with a lined brown peasant's face, and her first glance at the house was watchful, suspicious; but when she caught sight of me she smiled, and, leaving the hoe, she plodded across the ground towards the house.

"I suppose it's all right to tell everybody there's no question now of a close-down, Monsieur Paul?" said the man Jacques. "I've said nothing, naturally, but you know how rumours get around. The whole of last week there was speculation here amongst the men."

"I know it only too well," said Paul. "The atmosphere's been impossible. Yes, spread the news as soon as you like."

The woman was now directly beneath the window, and Paul, noticing her for the first time, said, "There's Julie, all ears as usual. Wants to be the first to spill good news or bad."

He leant out of the window. "Monsieur Jean succeeded in Paris. Don't pretend you don't know what I mean."

The half-smile broadened on the woman's face. She reached out and plucked a bunch of grapes dangling from the vine on the wall beside her, and offered it to me with the gesture of a queen.

"There you are," she said. "Grown especially for you, Monsieur le Comte. Eat them at once before the bloom is off them. So all is well, then, after all?"

"All is well," said Paul, suddenly human, relaxed.

"It's what I thought," said the woman. "It needs someone with brains to kick these people where they feel it most. And who are they, I should like to know, thinking that because they have a big name up in Paris they can dictate to us? It's time they learnt their lesson. I hope you made them feel small, Monsieur Jean." She had the solidity of Gaston, and his strength, and the same flame of loyalty in her eyes, but she would not hesitate to criticise if those to whom she gave devotion failed. I looked away from her warm, brown, wrinkled face to the drooping apple trees, and the browsing horse, and the line of forest trees beyond the fields. "So the furnace will continue to roar, and the chimneys to smoke, and the glass to cover the floor of my lodge with filthy dust, and nobody will think about the future for another six months," she said. "You will remember to come and say a word to André presently, Monsieur le Comte? You heard about his accident, naturally."

I remembered there had been talk of an injured workman. "Yes," I said, "I'll be along later," avoiding those loyal yet curious eyes. She went off again to her vegetables, scattering the chickens who fluttered at her feet, and, turning my head, I saw that Paul was hanging up his coat and putting on overalls.

"There's not been much correspondence in since you were away," he said. "It's all there, on the desk. Jacques will show you."

He opened the door through which we had entered, facing the sheds, and went out, and I was left alone with Jacques and a little stack of letters and papers. I opened them one by one, and they were mostly invoices, curt demands for payment for goods supplied by other firms, a query from a

89

haulage contractor, a statement from the railway. As I looked through them I knew that I understood nothing, absolutely nothing, of what I was supposed to do or say or dictate or write: the jumble of figures was meaningless, and I was as helpless as a child dumped suddenly into an adult world.

Strangely, to speak the truth was the only way out. I swept the file aside and said, "What is all this? What do you want me to do about it?" Strangely, too, Jacques smiled—he seemed more at his ease now that we were alone together and Paul had gone—and replied, "It's not necessary to do anything, Monsieur le Comte, now that the contract has been extended. They are only routine matters, and I can deal with them."

I got up from the desk, went to the door and opened it, and stood on the threshold, looking out on the line of sheds, the workmen passing to and fro, a lorry being driven out of the gates, the pleasing, somewhat incongruous proximity of a farm and farm buildings some fifty yards from the foundry shed itself. Geese were strutting in the yard, a woman spreading linen on a hedge to dry, and mingling with the lowing of cattle from beyond the farm gate came the intermittent clanging of metal within the shed. The smoke billowed out from the stovepipe chimneys, the old bell on the patched corrugated roof was caught in a sudden gleam of sunshine, and at the entrance two plaster statues, one of the Madonna and Child and the other of St. Joseph, stood with raised hands to bless the small community and all who worked and dwelt there. I knew instinctively, because of the age of the buildings, and the atmosphere, that this had been happening in the same way for two or three hundred years, that wars and the Revolution had not altered it. It continued because the family and the workmen believed in it, because they wanted it that way. The small, unchanging glass foundry was part of the background of their bit of country, like the farmhouse and the fields and the ancient apple trees and the forest, and to destroy it would be like tearing the roots of a live thing from the soil.

I looked over my shoulder to Jacques, sitting at the table, and said, "How long can a foundry like this compete against big firms with modern machinery, paying high wages?"

He raised his head from the invoices and papers that I had not understood, his eyes blinking nervously behind his spectacles.

"That depends on you, Monsieur le Comte. We know very well it can't go on much longer. It's a rich man's hobby that has become a liability instead of a source of revenue. If you don't mind losing money it's your affair. Only . . ."

"Only what?"

"You would not be losing quite so much today if a little more trouble had been taken in the past to look after what belongs to you. Forgive me, I am being frank. I have no business to say this. How can I put it to you, Monsieur le Comte? A business is like a home: it must have a head, a core, a centre, and depending upon that centre, it either thrives or falls to pieces. As you know, I never worked for your father, it was before my time, but he was much respected, he was just and fair, and Monsieur Duval was another like him. Had he lived he would have made his home here in the house, and there would have been a sense of continuity. He understood the workmen, he would have known how to adapt himself to the changing conditions, but as things are . . ." He looked at me apologetically, unable to finish his sentence.

"Are you blaming me or my brother?" I asked.

"Monsieur le Comte, I blame neither. Force of circumstance has been against us all. Monsieur Paul has a great sense of duty, and he has devoted himself to this small business since the war, but after all he has been fighting a losing battle against costs and wages, and you know as well as I do that he is not at ease with the workmen, and sometimes that makes things very difficult."

I thought how unenviable was this man's position, the buffer, the go-between, cursed probably by employer and employed, yet bearing on his shoulders the real sweat and toil of the business—checking orders, pacifying creditors, working overtime, trying to keep some sort of balance, the last prop and support of a tottering system.

"What about me?" I asked. "Come on, be frank. Aren't you trying to tell me the failure's mine?"

He smiled, with a deprecating, indulgent shrug of the shoulder that explained a world of feeling without words.

"Monsieur le Comte," he said, "everybody likes you—no one ever says a word against you. But you are not interested, that's all. The *verrerie* could fall to pieces tomorrow for all you care. Or, at least, so I believed until you told us the news this afternoon. We all imagined you were going to Paris simply to amuse yourself, instead of which"—he gestured with his hands—"as Monsieur Paul said, you've achieved the impossible."

I looked away from him to the open door, and I saw Julie plod back across the waste ground outside the sheds to her little lodge at the entrance. Some of the workmen called to her, laughing, and she shouted back to them, chaffing them, her hoe over her shoulder.

"You are not offended, Monsieur le Comte, at what I said?" Jacques asked with a touching humility.

"No," I answered. "No, I'm grateful."

I went out, crossing the short distance to the main foundry shed. Inside, near the furnace, the men were working stripped because of the heat. All round me were vats and tubs, rods and connecting pipes, and there was a roar and a clanging and an odd pungent smell which was not unpleasant. When I advanced to watch what was going on, the men stood back smiling, the same welcoming smile that I had noticed before, half familiar, half tolerant, the smile that adults assume sometimes to a child, indulgent in the sense that if the child wishes to amuse himself he might as well, since whatever he chooses to do can never be anything but play.

Presently I went out again into the cool air, to the other sheds, where men in overalls were working with different tools, with moulds and mixtures, and I turned in my hands the blues and greens and ambers of rejected glass that seemed to me perfect, little flacons and bottles of every shape and size. And so to the sorting and the packing sheds, with consignments ready to be dispatched, and never for one moment was there an impersonal, automatic, factory feeling. What I saw was individual, intimate, a little industry possessed by and possessing the people who worked there, having an enduring quality which the passing of time could not change.

"Amusing yourself, Monsieur Jean?"

I looked up from the glass I held in my hands, and there

was the broad smiling face of Julie, the woman from the lodge.

"You can put it that way if you like," I said.

"Leave the solid work to M'sieur Paul," she said. "It has always been like that. Will you come and see André now?"

She led the way through the entrance and down the sandy road past the line of cottages. They were yellow-washed, like the house inside the *verrerie* ground, with the same mottled tiled roof and dormer windows, separated one from another by small plots of garden and broken fences. She took me into the third cottage, which was living room and kitchen and surely bedroom in one, for a man was lying there before the hearth on a tumbled wooden bed, while a bright-eyed boy about the age of Marie-Noel played with a broken truck in another corner.

"Now then," said Julie, "here is Monsieur le Comte come to see you. Sit up and show that you're alive at least."

The man smiled, hollow-eyed, pale, and I saw that he was bandaged from the neck down to the arm.

"How are you?" I said. "What happened?"

Julie turned from scolding the boy, who had not risen when I came into the kitchen.

"What happened?" she said. "He nearly burnt his right side off, that's all. So much for your modern furnaces and machinery. You can have the lot. Sit down, Monsieur Jean, sit down." She threw a cat off the single chair, and dusted it. "Haven't you anything to say?" she asked the man, who looked too ill and wan to speak. "Here is Monsieur le Comte back from the gay life in Paris, and you can't even raise a smile for him. It's enough to send him straight back there again. Wait, I'll make some coffee."

She bent over the stove, rattling the fire with a bent poker.

"How long will you be laid up?" I asked the man.

"They won't tell me, Monsieur le Comte," he answered, a wavering eye on the woman, "but I'm afraid it may be some time before I am fit to work again."

"That's all right," said Julie. "Monsieur Jean understands that perfectly. No need to fuss. He will see you get paid all right, and compensation too. And nobody is going to be out of work either, for a long time to come, isn't that so, Monsieur Jean? We can all breathe again. Those sharks in Paris know better than to say no to us. Now then, drink your coffee. You like a lot of sugar in it, I know. You always did." She fetched a small packet of sugar cubes from a cupboard, and the boy, seeing this, came to beg one from her, calling her grand-mère.

"Get off with you," she said. "Where are your manners? Ah, since your mother went there's no holding you," and aside, in a loud hiss that the child must obviously have heard, "The trouble is he misses her, poor little one, and with André laid up I'm obliged to spoil him. Go on, drink your coffee. It might bring some colour into your pale city face."

It was André on the bed who needed colour, not I, and coffee too, but she did not offer him any, and, looking above and about me, I saw that the plaster was coming off the walls, and there was a great patch of damp on the ceiling that would spread with the first rain. She noticed my glance, with her shrewd brown eyes.

"What can one do?" she said. "I must try and patch it up one of these days. It's a long time since any of these cottages were repaired, but what's the good of coming to you with our grumbling? We know you're short of money, like the rest of us, and you have enough on your hands already. In a year or two, perhaps . . . How is everybody at the château? Is Madame la Comtesse well?"

"Not very well," I said.

"Well, there it is. We are all getting older. I will go up to see her one of these days, when I can get away. And Madame Jean, when is she expecting?"

"I'm not sure. I don't think it's very long now."

"If you have a fine boy a lot of things will be different. If I were younger I would come up and nurse him—it would remind me of old days. They were good times, you know, Monsieur Jean. People are very different today, nobody wants to work any more. If I didn't work I should die. You know what is wrong with Madame la Comtesse? She hasn't enough to do. Drink your coffee. More sugar. Here, another lump."

I saw André watch me drink, his wan eyes fixed upon my cup, and the boy too, and I knew that they both wanted coffee and sugar and would not get any, not because Julie wished to keep it from them but because there was not enough to go round. And there was not enough to go round because they had no money to buy coffee or sugar in any quantity. André did not earn enough at the *verrerie*, and the *verrerie* belonged to Jean de Gué, who did not mind whether it closed tomorrow. I put the cup and saucer back on the stove.

"Thank you, Julie," I said. "It's done me good."

I got up, and without protesting, the ritual visit over in fitting fashion, she went with me to the door.

"He won't work again," she said to me outside. "You understood that, of course. It's no use telling him, he would only fret. Well, there it is, that's life. Luckily, I'm here to look after him. My respects to Madame la Comtesse. I'll cut her some grapes from the vine: she used to enjoy them in the old days. After you, Monsieur le Comte."

I let her go back alone, though, to the foundry, telling her I had to fetch something from the car, and watched her cross the rough ground, passing the dumps of waste glass, crunching the scattered powdery fragments with her sabots, her stolid, powerful figure in its dark shawl and apron part of the background, merging against the grey-washed sheds. When she had disappeared into the tangled garden behind the old house I got into the Renault and drove back along the highroad, the way we had come, with the forest on either side. About four kilometres west, before the road dipped, I drew up at the side of the road, lit a cigarette, got out and looked down to the country below.

The little community of the glass foundry was tucked away in its clearing in the forest behind me, and now below, out of the line of forest, stretched acres of fields and scattered farms and distant villages, each village crowned with a church spire, and beyond them again further fields and further forest. Immediately below me was the village of St. Gilles, and I could see the church spire, but the château was hidden by the mass of trees. Only the farm buildings showed, chrome-coloured, mellow under the autumn sun, and the enclosing walls of the domain, a line of grey against the dark alleyways and trees.

I wished I could feel detached: I wished I could look down on the village of St. Gilles and the walls of the château with dispassionate eyes. My morning mood had somehow gone awry. The amusement, the schoolboy sense of fun, was miss-

95

ing; playing at spies hit back, like a boomerang. The feeling of power, of triumph that I was outwitting this little group of unsuspecting people, had turned again to shame. It seemed to me now that I wanted Jean de Gué to have been a different sort of man. I did not want to discover at each step that he was worthless. It might have been an inspiration to take on the rôle of someone fine—the change of skin would have acted as a spur to endeavour. Instead, I had exchanged my own negligible self for a worthless personality. He had the supreme advantage over me in that he had not cared. Or had he, after all? Was this why he had disappeared?

I went on gazing at the quiet, secluded village. I could see a line of black and white cattle, prodded by a child, ambling past the church, and then from behind me I heard a voice. Turning, I saw the smiling, nodding face of the old curé, riding, of all things, a tricycle, his long cassock hitched above black buttoned boots. It was an oddly touching sight, moving because it was ridiculous.

"It's pleasant there in the sun?" he called.

I felt a sudden urge to confide in him, and I went up to the tricycle and put my hands on the handlebars and said to him, "Father, I'm in trouble. I've been living a lie for the past twenty-four hours."

His face puckered in sympathy, but the nodding head was so much like a mandarin figure in a china shop that I lost faith the instant I had spoken. What could he do, I asked myself, here on top of the hill, astride his tricycle, for someone like myself caught up in deceit and trickery?

"When did you last make your confession?" he said to me, and I was reminded of my schooldays, when the matron, having asked me a somewhat similar question, followed up her query with a purge.

"I don't know," I said. "I can't remember."

He went on nodding, in sympathy, and also because he could not help it, and said, "My son, you had better come and see me later on this evening."

He had given me the answer I deserved, but it was no use to me. Later on would be no good. I wanted to be told now, on the hillside, whether to drive away and leave the people at the château to get on with life as best they could.

"What would you think of me," I asked, "if I left St. Gilles, went off and disappeared, and did not come back?"

The smile returned to his old pink baby face, and he patted me on the shoulder. "You would never do it," he said. "Too many people depend on you. You think I would condemn you? No, it would not be my place. I should continue to pray for you, as I have always done. Come on, now, enough of your nonsense. Remember, if you are depressed and low in spirit, it's a good sign. It shows that the *bon Dieu* isn't far away. Go and finish your cigarette in the sun and think about Him."

He waved his hand and rode off, his cassock catching in the pedal, and I saw him free-wheel down the hill, enjoying his little spin. I watched him turn into the village, avoiding the cattle, and then he dismounted by the steps of the church, propped his tricycle against the wall and disappeared. I finished my cigarette, climbed into the car and drove after him, through the village and over the bridgeway to the château entrance. I saw Gaston by the archway to the out-buildings, and called to him to take the car back to the *verrerie* for Paul. Then I went indoors and up the stairs to the dressing room, and on the table I found the packet of letters that I remembered seeing in the pocket of the valise.

Among them was one with the name and address of the Carvalet people stamped on the back. I read it through, and it was as I feared. They said that they regretted their unfavourable decision, in view of so much business between us in the past, and especially after the last personal interview they had had with me, but on further consideration they found themselves unable to renew their contract.

Chapter 9

I did not, for the moment, mind about Jacques or any of the family here at the château, because presumably they had prepared themselves for the worst, and were merely surprised and relieved that they were able to believe the contrary. Here they could continue to live on the revenue from their

97

land, or on their inherited income, the château becoming shabbier, the grounds more ill kept, they themselves growing older and more discontented, blaming the outside world for everything that had happened. I minded, immediately, for the workmen I had seen at the *verrerie* this afternoon, stripped and sweating beside that furnace, and the others, working in the sheds at their separate skilled tasks, and above all for André, with his burnt, bandaged side, lying in bed in the cottage, and Julie, who had given me coffee and sugar from her small hoard. I minded that their eyes should change, that when I went back again to the foundry they would discover that the good news was not good news after all but bad, that I had lied to them, that the contract with Carvalet had not been renewed. Instead of that tolerant, indulgent smile of welcome they would look away, ignoring me, not even bothering to show contempt; and when Jacques explained to them that the whole thing had been a misunderstanding, and unfortunately, things being as they were, Monsieur le Comte could not afford to run his business at a loss, their faces would show—to a lesser degree, because they were not physically in pain—the same blank look of the burnt André. Something would have damaged them which they themselves were powerless to prevent, but which Monsieur le Comte could have foreseen and guarded against, had he only cared. They would watch Paul and myself drive back to the château, and then, the machinery suddenly idle, the furnace quiet, and the heap upon heap of little bottles waiting to be packed, they would return to the line of cottages in the sandy lane, with the plaster peeling and the damp on the ceilings, and say to one another, "It doesn't matter to him, but what about us? What happens to us now?"

The thing that puzzled me most was why I cared. The loyalty in Julie's eyes, the patient acceptance in André's, the swift change from hostility to something near admiration in Paul's, and still more in Jacques's, the welcome camaraderie in the workmen's, all this had not been given to me but to Jean de Gué. The scorn and disenchantment which must now follow would therefore go to him in the same way, and could not touch my inviolate self. This person who walked about wearing another's clothes, parading his features, colouring

98

and manners, was guiltless, he was merely a covering, a façade, as remote from its original as a violin case from the instrument it protects. Emotion should have no part in this. I had never for one moment been so blind as to imagine that any show of warmth coming from these people was due to qualities of my own, springing suddenly to the surface and finding a response: they came alight for him and for him only, however misplaced the glow. What was happening, then, was that I wanted to preserve Jean de Gué from degradation. I could not bear to see him shamed. This man, who was not worth the saving, must be spared. Why? Because he looked like me?

I sat in the dressing room, staring at the polite yet definite letter from Carvalet, and I wondered what had passed through the mind of Jean de Gué when he put it in the pocket of his valise. I knew I must come to a decision—either to tell Paul directly he returned to the château that I had lied about the contract, or to allow him to go on believing it had gone through. The first would bring recrimination, scorn, admission of the lie to all the workpeople, and the immediate closing down of the foundry—which, I assumed, was what would have happened anyway had Jean de Gué returned. The second would bring even greater chaos: the manufacture and dispatch to Paris of goods which had not been ordered, and, when the first consignment arrived at the Carvalet works, astounded telephone calls demanding an explanation.

The present contract might have a few days or a few weeks to run. I did not know. Even if facts and figures were put before me, presumably they would make little sense. I knew nothing of business. My sole financial dealings were with the academic establishments which paid my modest fees, and with those editors and publishers who printed my articles and lectures. What, I asked myself, would be the procedure of the owner of a glass foundry seeking to get in touch with the firm which bought his wares? No doubt, if the matter were urgent, the office telephone. I was not in an office. I was in the dressing room of a château in the depths of the French countryside, and I did not even know where the telephone was kept.

I put Carvalet's letter in the inside pocket of my coat and went downstairs. It was almost four o'clock. There was no one about, and a feeling of siesta brooded over the place. The aftermath of lunch still clung to the air, escaping from the kitchen quarters, where I had not yet penetrated, suggesting that the dishes had been washed and dried and yet something of their substance clung to dark walls and a low ceiling, and that vegetables, earthy from the kitchen garden, awaited rinsing and shaking before the evening meal. I ventured to the door of the salon, half ajar, and after listening a moment and hearing nothing I stepped across the threshold and saw that it was empty, except for Françoise, who was lying on the sofa asleep. I crept out again and went back to the hall. Renée was doubtless doing the same upstairs, whether to ease her migraine or to try on the gossamer gift I neither knew nor cared. Marie-Noel, forced into lessons through my abrupt departure to the *verrerie*, was perhaps in that bare, bleak bedroom with her aunt Blanche, while outside the sun shone on the dovecot and the swing. I found the telephone. It could not have been worse placed, jammed between macintoshes in the dark, and the machine itself was an old-fashioned one, the mouthpiece fastened to the wall and the receiver hanging at one side. Pinned above, so that the eye must inevitably rest upon them, was further proof of Blanche's care for souls: two martyred saints, decapitated, their splashing blood licked by ravenous hounds.

I unhooked the receiver and waited, and after a moment there was a buzz and a nasal voice intoned the fact, *"J'écoute."* I was not surprised when, fumbling with the local directory, I discovered that my number was St. Gilles 2. Nothing could have been changed since installation. I asked for Paris and the number printed on Carvalet's letter, and waited for what seemed eternity, crouched in my dark hole. When I was told at last that Carvalet were on the line I panicked, dropping both letter and receiver, thinking I heard footsteps on the stairs. The exchange repeated its information, the singsong patter echoing from the dangling receiver, and, seizing Carvalet's letter to decipher the sprawling signature at the bottom, I murmured into the mouthpiece my request for Monsieur Mercier. Who wanted him? came the question. The

Comte de Gué, I replied. And suddenly the enormity of my deception appeared greater than ever, now that I could not actually be seen. I was told to wait, and in a few moments the Monsieur Mercier of the letter announced that he was at my disposal.

"Monsieur," I said, "a thousand apologies for disturbing you without first warning you of my intention to do so; also for my discourtesy in not acknowledging your letter. I was obliged to return home very suddenly, owing to illness in my family, or I would have called upon you again to raise one or two points which were not quite clear. I have now seen my brother and gone over the points with him, and we are prepared to lower our figure and meet your demands."

There was silence at the other end of the line, and then the polite but exceedingly surprised voice answered, "But, Monsieur le Comte, the whole question was gone into very thoroughly between us last week. You made your position quite plain, which we appreciated. Do you mean to say you now want to reopen negotiations between your firm and ours?"

"Exactly," I said. "My brother and I are prepared to make any personal sacrifice in order to keep the foundry working and our men employed."

Another silence. Then, "Excuse me, Monsieur, but this is in complete contradiction to what you yourself gave us to understand."

"I know," I said, "but frankly I was acting without full consultation with my family. It is, you know, a family concern."

"Naturally, Monsieur, and because of this we have always given you every consideration. We greatly regretted that a revision of the contract should have become necessary, and above all that you would have to close down if we could not come to terms, which unfortunately turned out to be the case. I recollect your saying that your personal feelings were not involved, and that the *verrerie* had become a liability you could not afford."

The smooth, cool voice ran on, and I had a vision of the speaker and Jean de Gué sitting confronting one another on leather chairs, exchanging shrugs and cigarettes, the whole concern dismissed from their minds as soon as the interview was over. Here was I, a stranger, making myself ridiculous in a lost cause because I did not want a handful of workmen, and a peasant woman, and her maimed relative to despise their employer, who would not know if they did, and would not care.

"Everything you are saying is perfectly correct," I said. "What I am trying to tell you now is that I have changed my mind. I will agree to any proviso, if we can continue to keep the foundry working. Our production costs are my affair. I am asking you to renew your contract on your own terms, whatever they may be."

A more prolonged silence. Then, swiftly, "Of course, Monsieur, because of our long connection with you and your family, we were upset that it should be severed, but there seemed to be no other solution. However, if you are now prepared to meet us over figures—obviously this cannot be agreed off-hand over the telephone—I must again consult my fellow directors. Then I see no reason why the ultimate result should not be satisfactory to us both?"

The query in his voice brought instant affirmation to my own. Letters were to be written, and the present contract could be renewed under different terms. We exchanged compliments, and I heard him hang up. I reached for my handkerchief—or rather Jean de Gué's—and wiped the sweat off my forehead because it was not only hot in the small space amongst the macintoshes, but the effort I had made had been mentally exhausting. I had committed myself to something without having the slightest idea of how to carry it through. If the price Carvalet paid for the glass phials did not cover the cost of running the plant and paying the wages, which it assuredly could not—otherwise why the present crisis?—then the money would have to come from another source. It was at this moment that I heard someone breathing down the receiver, which I still held, unthinking, against my ear: the unmistakable sound of a person listening at an extension, waiting for further information. I did not do anything. I went on waiting, holding the receiver close. Presently the exchange cut in, asking if I had finished with Paris, and when I said yes, and the line went dead, I heard the breathing again, and then a gentle click, proving that whoever listened within the château had now hung up. I could not be sure, but I felt there was little doubt that my conversation with Paris had been overheard. By whom? Where was the extension? I hung up and went out into the hall. The footsteps I had fancied hearing on the stairs, when my call came through, may have been imagination and anxiety mixed. At any rate no one had come down, and all was still. The breathing into the telephone had not been imagination. I went out onto the terrace, for it hardly mattered now if I were seen or not, and looked up at the château, but I could see only the main telephone wire, entering the château roof at a point between tower and wall. The tall chimneys, the turrets, even the gargoyle heads hid any other signs there might be of electricity and telephone, nor was I sufficiently knowledgeable about these things to guess what lead went where.

Discovery of the extension, and of the eavesdropper, were things that must wait. I felt it more immediately important to find out something about Jean de Gué's personal finances. The half-finished cheque book in the dressing room upstairs, which I went to fetch, bore cryptic figures and initials but no balance, and its only worth-while information was the name of the bank and the branch address in a neighbouring town. There was no desk in the dressing room. Somewhere in the château there must be a room where the owner wrote his letters and kept personal possessions. I remembered the library where the family had assembled for lunch. I went down again to the hall, and through the dining room to the double doors of the library, now closed once more, and, entering, I found it in half-darkness, someone having folded the shutters of the long windows at the end as protection against the sun. I opened them, and then saw what I was looking for—a desk in the corner. It was locked. The bunch of keys—part of Jean de Gué's personal belongings, along with his change, and his wallet, and his cheque book, and his driving licence, none of which I had found occasion to use until this moment—had been with me ever since I had worn his clothes. I tried them now, and one of them fitted. My burglar's action did not worry me; I was playing spies again, and no one was being hurt.

The opened desk revealed the usual muddle and disorder of somebody else's things, unlike my own meticulously kept papers at home, with bulging pigeonholes, envelopes spilling their contents, letters, bills, receipts, all thrown in haphazard. The drawers, when I tried them, were no better. One half-inch open and they jammed, choked with books and documents, papers and photographs, surely the life history of the man himself and the entire family of de Gué for generations. Their persistent refusal to emerge from the dusty drawers drove me to recklessness. I wanted bank statements and I could not find them, only the stubs of cheque books long since used and put away. Balked in my search, like a thief who cannot find the string of pearls he is seeking, I was determined to snatch at something, anything, to appease frustrated curiosity. Finally, my eye caught the red leather cover of what might be a ledger. I tugged and squeezed it out of the reluctant drawer, only to reveal a game book, with list upon list of pheasants, partridges, hares, shot long before the war. The gap it left gave space for my wandering hands, and, roaming past a revolver, they found another bulky volume, smelling of mould, which showed itself to be an album full of photographs, most of them faded, stuck tightly into old-fashioned slots.

I let the bank statements go. A glimpse at the past was irresistible. The album bore a crest on the first page, a hound's head and a tree, and underneath was written "Marie de Gué" in a long sloping hand. When I turned the page there was the mother, unmistakably, a young woman in her mid-twenties, the present heavy jowl a rounded and determined chin, the shock of grey hair blonde, profuse, set in waves by tongs, a frilly blouse adorning the sloping shoulders that were now hunched and covered with a multitude of wraps; and the photograph might have been one of myself decked out in female dress, impersonating, with wig and props, some feminine character in charades. Beside it was the date, 1914. Then followed, one by one, the others: Jean de Gué, the father, suggesting Paul but with a bristling moustache, the eyes alert, taken against an impossible studio background of draped hangings and false flowers; the two of them together, gazing down with fond parental pride at what must have been a much cosseted and beribboned Blanche; and then friends and relatives of an older generation, an uncle this, an aunt that, an aged grand-père in a wheeled chair. The dates were not always given, and often I had to guess for myself what summer it was when a small boy and a girl straddled a pony, or what winter, the dovecot shrouded in snow, the same pair posed in mufflers, their arms round each other's necks. The couple were seldom apart. Wherever one stood, holding fishing rod or gun, the other would be lurking; and with a little shock of surprise—even, oddly, of distaste—I saw that this second hovering figure, Blanche, was as a child almost a replica of the Marie-Noel of today, with the same long legs, thin body and close-cropped hair. It was only later, when she must have been about fifteen, that she began to change, the oval face lengthening, the expression in the eyes becoming more watchful, more solemn; but even so I could not recognise in that grave and surely sympathetic face the tight-lipped spinster of today.

The young Jean was never solemn. Every snapshot showed laughter, or a comic attitude, or some mockery of the camera that seized him, and I thought how different they were, though our features were identical, from snapshots taken of myself as a boy, glassy-eyed and anxious. Paul did not figure much in the album. He was often out of focus, the dimmest figure in a group, or bending to tie a shoelace when the camera clicked. Even the clearest photograph of all three children in their 'teens, which was thrust loose in the album, showed him half obscured by Jean's robust shoulder and eclipsed by Jean's devastating smile.

I recognised odd figures here and there in groups: the curé, slimmer, younger, yet cherubic then, and, flicking back the pages to the baby days, there was surely Julie of the *verrerie*, nursing Paul. There was one man called Maurice who appeared often in the latter pages of the album. He was amongst groups at the glass foundry, and at the château, and there was one of him and Jean together, standing by the stone statue in the park. Then, abruptly, the snapshots ended. Three or four empty pages remained, waiting to be filled.

Whether the elder Jean de Gué had died, or the war had come, or the mother had grown suddenly tired of taking snapshots, it was impossible to say. An era was over, a cycle closed.

I shut up the album with a curious feeling of nostalgia. Long used to delving in the historical past, familiar with old letters, documents and records of centuries ago, this furtive glance at a family background of my own time, my own generation, was oddly moving. I minded, not that the handsome countess at the beginning of the album should grow old and the blonde hair turn to grey, but that she had aged in the way she had, those dominating, confident eyes turned searching, restless, the proud mouth voracious, the rounded neck and shoulders slumped to useless fat. I minded that Blanche, so lithe and winning as a child, so serious and watchful as a growing girl, could become warped out of recognition, crude as a caricature. Even Paul, smudged in his snapshots, hidden behind the laughing Jean, had been somehow touching as a child, standing on one foot at the end of groups, a lock of hair always falling in his eyes. Yet today he was unsympathetic, heavy, betraying emotion only when I had probed a hidden sore and mocked—heaven knows without intention—the failing that he felt was shameful.

These pictures of a past when all seemed well were disturbed by an intrusion from the present. I heard someone fumble with the double doors that led into the dining room, and, pushing the album back into the desk, I turned, and there was Renée, who had no part in the faded snapshots, any more than Françoise. These two belonged to the bleak aftermath, the drabness of St. Gilles without the charm. She closed the doors behind her and stood watching me.

"I heard the car," she said, "and I thought Paul might be with you. Then I met Charlotte in the passage, and she told me you were alone. Françoise is still resting in the salon, and I guessed you would be here. Well, aren't you going to apologise for your behaviour at lunch?"

The wretched mishandling of the gifts was to be thrown up at me again. No doubt, in her judgment, I deserved it. I sighed and shrugged my shoulders.

"I've already apologised to Paul," I said. "Won't that do?"

Pent-up emotion showed in the tense body, the nervous hands, and she looked at me with an expression half baffled, half distraught, that was disturbing and irritating all in one, so that I felt instant sympathy for Paul, who must surely bear the brunt of all her moods.

"Why did you do it?" she said. "Isn't it difficult enough without making them suspicious, and above all hurting Paul? Or were you deliberately setting out to make a fool of me as well?"

"Listen," I said. "I had so much to drink in Le Mans that I couldn't remember what I had put in those packages. For all I knew I had brought everybody books."

"You expect me to believe that?" she asked. "There was no mistake in what you gave Françoise, was there? However much did it cost, or haven't you paid?"

Here, surely, was the worst sort of feminine spite, the grudge of a gift from husband to wife. I was glad that Françoise had the locket with the miniature, and not Renée.

"I gave Françoise something I knew she would value," I said. "If you are disappointed in your own present, it's too bad. Give it to Germaine. I don't mind in the least what you do with it."

If I had hit her I could not have moved her more. She stared at me, colour flooding her face, and, leaving the door, she came slowly across the room to the desk, which I had now locked again, pocketing the key. Before I realised what she was about she had her arms round me, her face against mine, and I was standing stiff and wooden like a third-rate actor in a provincial play.

"What is it?" she said. "What's the matter with you? Why are you so changed? Are you afraid to make love to me?"

So that was it. Perhaps I should have guessed, but her words came as a shock and filled me with dismay. I did not want to kiss her. The clinging arms repelled, and the seeking mouth, too eager, froze response. Whatever Jean de Gué might have done in idleness was not to be practised now by his surrogate.

"Renée," I said, "someone may come in . . ."—weak, futile excuse of every cowardly lover not in immediate stress—and I backed ungallantly from this unexpected and embarrassing

107

proximity. But even now, half hunched as I was against the desk, she followed me, her hands striving to caress, to cling, and I thought how lacking in grace and dignity is the male under assault. A woman, if she is attacked by a bully, has at least feminine frailty to lend charm.

My show of appeasement was not convincing: the clumsy pat on the shoulder, the muffled kiss in the hair, must have seemed poor fare, and I sought to keep her off by a flow of words.

"We have to be careful," I said, "and not lose our heads about this. I think Paul understands about that piece of nonsense I gave you. I made very light of it, and I can do the same to Françoise. But we mustn't go on meeting in this way. The servants might see us, and once suspicion got into their minds there would be no end to every sort of complication."

As I listened to my own voice pouring out a torrent of excuses in her ear I realised, hopelessly, that I was actually committing myself more deeply. I was taking intrigue for granted, and letting slip in the most cowardly fashion the blessed opportunity now given me to say frankly and brutally, "I don't love you and I don't want you. That's final."

"You mean," said Renée, "that we must meet somewhere else? But how? Where are we to go?"

No tears from her. No touching demand for affection. One thing and one thing only in her mind. What Jean de Gué had doubtless started as a pastime had turned to a liability. I wondered to what extent he had been committed, and how deeply, after the first excitement, bored.

"I'll think of something," I said, "but remember what I say, we must be careful. We can't risk future happiness by stupidity now."

Jean de Gué himself could not have spoken with greater duplicity. How easy it was, after all, to be a cad. My words had calmed her, and the contact, brief as it had been, must have eased the tension and given her release. Then, to my relief, I heard the child's voice in the room beyond. Renée, with an exasperated shrug, moved from my side.

"Papa? Where are you?"

"In here. Do you want me?"

She burst into the room. Instinctively I opened my arms, wondering, as she sprang into them monkey-fashion, whether I could use her from now on as a buffer against the demands of an adult world.

"Gran'mie is awake," she said. "I have been in to see her. She wants us both to go to her room for tea. I have been telling her about the presents, and how disappointed Uncle Paul was in his. And do you know, Papa, you made a mistake with the one for my aunt Blanche? She would not open it, so Maman and I unwrapped it for her, and inside a note, 'For my beautiful Béla, from Jean,' not Blanche at all, and it was an enormous bottle of scent called 'Femme,' in a lovely box wrapped in cellophane, and the price upon it still, ten thousand francs."

Chapter 10

As we went upstairs together hand in hand, Marie-Noel said to me, "It's a funny thing, but everybody seems to be in a bad mood about those presents. Maman was so pleased with hers this morning, and then after lunch she took it off and put it with the rest of the things in her jewel case. As for Aunt Renée, she scarcely looked at hers, and just now, when I told you about the mistake with Aunt Blanche's present, I thought she was going to hit us both. Who is Béla, Papa?"

I was thankful I did not know. It saved further complications. Yet Jean de Gué might have had the foresight to scribble more than the initial B.

"Someone," I said, "who likes expensive scent."

"Does Maman know her?"

"I doubt it."

"I doubt it too. When I asked her she crumpled up the note and said it must have been some business friend in Paris who had asked you to dinner, and the scent was a return of politeness."

"Possibly," I said.

"The trouble is, you know, your memory's getting worse.

Fancy making such a muddle and giving it to Aunt Blanche instead. I knew there was something wrong. Why, you haven't given her anything as long as I can remember. I've never quite understood why—grown-up people behave in the strangest way. But even I can see there is not much point in giving Aunt Blanche a present when she hasn't spoken to you for fifteen years."

Fifteen years . . . This sudden piece of information, dropped in so casual a fashion, made me pause halfway up the stairs to stare at the child, forgetting my rôle, and she tugged at me impatiently. "Come on," she said. I followed silently, profoundly shaken. What I had taken to be temporary disapproval was so deep-rooted that it must affect the relationship of the entire family. The casual love affair with Renée, if it could be called that, was nothing in comparison. No wonder the giving of a present had been out of character. The revelation was disturbing, even sinister, especially when I remembered the snapshots of the two children with their arms about each other. Something personal and bitter had come between Blanche and Jean de Gué, yet it was accepted by all, even by the child.

"Here we are," said Marie-Noel, throwing open the door of the vast bedroom, and once again, as on the evening before, a wave of heat engulfed me from the stove. The small terriers, absent earlier in the day, were back again. They leapt from the bed, barking shrilly and refusing to be quietened by the scoldings and patting of the child.

"It's fantastic," said Marie-Noel. "The dogs in this place have all gone off their heads. César was the same this morning, barking at Papa."

"Charlotte," said the comtesse, "did you take Jou-Jou and Fifi for their walk or were you gossiping below all afternoon?"

"Naturally I took them, Madame la Comtesse," said Charlotte, at once pricked to self-defence. "They came with me up and down the park for nearly an hour. Am I likely to neglect them?"

She darted a look at me, as though I had been the one to accuse her, and I thought how unfavourably she compared with the honest, stalwart Julie of the *verrerie*, the small beady eyes, the narrow frame, even the niggardly way she poured out the tea suggesting something crabbed and sour.

"Go on, get out," commanded the comtesse angrily. "The child will look after us." Staring up at me from her bunch of bolster and pillow, the face still grey and flabby, deep shadows beneath her eyes, she put out her hand and pulled me down beside her. As I kissed the sagging cheek I thought how odd it was that this filial embrace, which should have been repellent, was somehow comforting, while the brush with the handsome Renée had been distasteful, crude.

"*Mon Dieu*," she whispered, "how the little one made me laugh!" Then, pushing me away, she said aloud, "Sit down and drink your tea. What have you been doing all day besides getting your parcels mixed up?"

Once again I was at ease with her; I could talk, I could laugh, she conjured a gaiety out of me I did not know was there. We made a trio perfectly at ease with one another, the comtesse, the child and I, the comtesse slopping her tea into a saucer and sipping it in gulps, the last drop lapped by the begging dogs, while the child, enthroned as pourer-out, picked fastidiously at toast, her eyes upon us.

I told of my visit to the *verrerie*, speaking with greater confidence now that my furtive call to Paris had produced, or might produce, a temporary solution, and the comtesse, without prompting, enlarged upon past glories as old people will, to my secret interest and the child's delight. She told us of the days when the glass was blown by hand, which she remembered well, and how long ago, before her time, the furnace was fed by wood from the nearby forest—that all glass foundries were established in forest country for this reason—and how in olden days, a century ago, there had been a hundred and sixty horses working, and women and children. The names of the workmen and their families were all written down somewhere in a book, in the library, perhaps, she did not remember.

"Oh well," she said, "that's all over. No more of that. The old days can never come back."

I was reminded of Julie, who had shown the same acceptance of change, the same dismissal of things that were finished, but when I told her about my visit to the cottage, and the poor burnt André lying in bed, she shrugged her shoulders, grown suddenly callous.

"Oh, those people," she said. "They'll squeeze the last franc out of us if they can. I wonder how much Julie has got out of me in her time. As for her son, he's always been a good-for-nothing. I don't blame the wife for running off with a mechanic in Le Mans."

"That cottage is in a shocking state of repair," I said.

"Don't do anything about it," she answered. "Once you begin, they'll ask for something else. We're beggared enough without bothering about them. And likely to remain so, unless Françoise produces a son, or . . ." She stopped, and although I did not understand her words, a certain tone in her voice, and the sidelong glance she gave me, were somehow acutely disconcerting. After a moment she went on, "These days people must fend for themselves. And what are they grumbling at? They have no rent to pay."

"Julie didn't grumble," I said. "She asked for nothing."

"I should hope not. She's got a nice sum, no doubt, tucked away under a floor board. I wish I had as much."

Her attitude troubled me. I felt disenchanted. Julie, who had seemed so honest and so loyal, was now shown as grasping, and the comtesse, a moment ago laughing and generous, was suddenly heartless, lacking perception. The wave of sympathy which I felt for both, instinctive, sincere, was somehow dulled, and puzzling this, while Marie-Noel poured me out another cup of tea, I realised that it was not the comtesse who lacked perception, but myself. I was a sentimentalist. I wanted people to be kinder, more generous, than they were.

"You know," said Marie-Noel, suddenly breaking into the conversation, "it was very curious when Maman and I opened that present in front of my aunt Blanche. Maman said, 'Don't be so obstinate, Blanche, it can't kill you, and if Jean has brought you something it must mean he has some feeling, surely, and wants to tell you so in this way.' And my aunt Blanche looked down, and after ages she said, 'You open it, then. I don't mind—it's nothing to me.' But I am sure she was curious too, because she put her lips in a way she has sometimes. So we opened the parcel, and when Maman saw the great big bursting bottle of scent she said, 'Good heavens, why ever this?' and my aunt Blanche had to look then, and do you know she went dead white, and she got straight up and went out of the room. I said to Maman, 'It's not medicine, like Uncle Paul's present. Why should she mind?' and Maman said, in a funny sort of way, 'I'm afraid it must have been a joke after all, and rather cruel.' Then of course we found the note to the other person, Béla, and Maman said, 'No, it isn't a joke, it's a mistake. This is for someone else.' But I still don't see why either of them should have thought it cruel."

Her words seemed to make a hole in silence. Waves of nothing hung about the air. In a curious way the child and I were together. My ignorance, and her innocence, made us one. The mother stared at me, and there was something in her eyes I could not read. It was neither condemnation nor reproach, yet there was speculation: a kind of wondering search that touched a chord, suggesting, though I knew it could not be, that some inner sense of hers had pricked my identity, uncovered my secret, knew me for a fraud. Yet when she spoke her words were for the child.

"You know, little one," she said, "the ways of women are very mysterious, especially one who is religious like your aunt. Remember that, and don't turn into a fanatic like her."

She looked suddenly tired and old. Hilarity was spent. The gesture with which she brushed away the terriers was pettish, weary.

"Come on," I said to Marie-Noel, "let's put the tea table out of the way."

We moved it back against the wall, beside the dressing table, on which I caught a glimpse of a large tinted photograph of Jean de Gué in uniform prominent amongst the silver brushes. Some intuition made me glance at the bed. The mother was gazing at it too, the same odd look of speculation on her face. When our eyes met we dropped them simultaneously. At that moment Charlotte came into the room, followed by the curé. The child went to him and curtseyed.

"Good evening, Monsieur le Curé," she said. "Papa has given me a life of the Little Flower. Shall I fetch it for you to see?"

The old man patted her head. "Later, my child, later," he

said. "When I come down you shall show it to me." He advanced to the foot of the bed and stood with hands clasped over his rounded belly, looking down at the grey, exhausted face of the comtesse.

"Well," he said, "so we are not so bright today? Too much excitement yesterday, perhaps, followed by a wakeful night and bad dreams. St. Augustine has something to say about that. He suffered too."

He drew a book from the folds of his cassock, and I saw the comtesse, with a supreme effort, force her wandering attention to his words. She motioned to the chair I had just left, and the curé, spreading his skirts, sat down. At the far end of the room Charlotte also composed herself to listen, hands folded, head bowed.

"May I stay?" whispered Marie-Noel, her eyes shining with excitement as though she was asking permission to watch some spectacle. When I nodded, uncertain what was expected of me, she fetched the stool from the dressing table and planted it close to the curé. Then, like a child actress living her rôle, she changed her expression of bustling preparation to one of rapture, eyes closed, hands clasped, lips moving silently in response to the old man's prayers. I glanced at the comtesse. Courtesy and training kept her propped against her pillows, but weariness caused the massive head to droop, ever so slightly, to the chest, and the flickering eyelids were symptoms, not so much of reverence as of intolerable fatigue.

I left the room and went downstairs and out into the park, wandering in those paths beyond the stone Artemis, now grey and solemn in the falling light. The château, which had seemed a jewel in sunlight, was more forbidding at the approach of dusk. The roof and turrets that had blended against blue took on a sharpened tone against the changing sky. I thought how like a bastion it must have been when water filled the moat, before the eighteenth-century façade of the central portion linked the early Renaissance towers. Were they any more lonely, the silken ladies peering through those slits, than the Renée and the Françoise of today, with the clammy water damping the mouldering walls, and the forest, thick and shaggy, shrouding the very doors? Did the

114

wild boar, fiery-eyed, come rooting where the cattle wandered now, and the thin horn of the huntsman sound in early morning when the mist still clung about the trees? What drinking, roistering nobles of Anjou must have clattered forth over the drawbridge to hunt and fight and kill; what love-making by night, what long uneasy births, what sudden deaths? And now, in another time, how much of this was repeated, oddly, in a different way, with stifled emotions and hungers more obscure. Cruelty was of a deeper kind today, wounding the spirit, hurting the secret self, but then it was more openly brutal: only the tough survived, and the lonely Françoise or the frustrated Renée of that age went like blown candles into disease and death, lamented or forgotten by their lord, who, prototype of Jean de Gué, feasted and fought, shrugging a velvet shoulder.

Someone was going round the château, closing the shutters and folding the long windows one by one, and the shutting out of night was like withdrawal into privacy. What happened within was dead, was finished, was no more; the château was a tomb, and only the cattle lived, grazing beside me, snuffling the wet grass, and the jackdaws, fluttering to roost, and a dog barking in the village beyond the church.

This second evening of my masquerade took shape and substance like a second night at school. I was familiar now with my surroundings. The blank astonishment had gone. My audacity, an intoxicating drug the night before, seemed natural, and when I opened a door, or went into a room, or came face to face with one of the family I no longer felt a shock of surprise. I recognised sounds, smells, voices; knew which chair was whose; heard bells without inwardly flinching; washed my hands and was not amazed at the action; changed my coat and shoes for dinner with the same herd instinct as a new boy aping his fellows at school, who does as the others do, letting his old home self and habits slip away until next holiday, and for the moment of his term assumes a hard bright shell, a glittering mask to win the approval of boys and masters, and is himself deceived and fascinated by the new personality walking in his stead. Eating, drinking, picking up a paper were suddenly actions interesting in themselves because they were not mine but

115

those of Jean de Gué. The strangeness of a dream is alway
natural to the dreamer, and I began to move with eas
amongst my phantoms, who talked to me, smiled at me c
ignored me. The ritual was already established; the whee
that had always turned continued turning, and I was merel
borne by it, unprotesting, part of the framework.

Dinner was a silent affair. We were only four. Marie-Noe.
I discovered, had soup and biscuits at seven and did no
join us, while Blanche, according to Gaston, wished to fas
She was in her room, he said, and would not be comin
down again this evening.

Conversation languished. Françoise, the prop at lunch
looked tired, and with flagging interest touched upon littl
topics to stir the silence: illness in the village, the curé
evening visit, a letter from a cousin in Orléans, troubles i
Algiers, a train crash north of Lyons. The dullness of it soothe
me. Her voice, when the complaint was out of it, was clea
and pleasant. Renée, wearing a high-necked blouse that be
came her well, with hair again brushed up to show her ear
had put a spot of rouge on either cheekbone, whether t
dazzle me with her charm, or wound me with her wit, c
make me jealous with sudden bright chat to Paul I did ne
know. The scheme, if scheme there was, failed. I was u
moved, and Paul did not notice what she was about. H
concentrated upon his food, which he ate noisily, gruntir
replies between mouthfuls, seldom raising his eyes from h
plate; and directly dinner was over he moved to a cha
under the best light in the salon, and, lighting a cigar, w.
hidden to view by the wide-open sheets of *Figaro* an
L'Ouest-France.

Marie-Noel came down in a dressing gown, and sh
Françoise and I—Renée was on the sofa with a book who
pages she never turned—played draughts and dominoes,
peaceful family trio who must have done the same befor
night after night, time without number, until nine o'clo
struck and Françoise, yawning with fatigue, said, "Well no
bedtime, *chérie.*" The child, without demur, got up, tidi
away the draughts and put them in a drawer, kissed h
uncle and her aunt and her mother, and, taking my han
said, "Come on, Papa."

This, I supposed, was the nightly routine, and we marched upstairs to the nursery-bedroom in the turret. The doll, no longer stabbed by a penholder, had been rescued from martyrdom and was now a penitent, forced to a kneeling position beside an inverted tin that served as a confessional, while a large lopsided Donald Duck, with one leg missing, had been cast in the rôle of priest, the sailor's hat draped in black cloth to suggest a biretta.

"Sit down," the child commanded, and then, taking off her dressing gown, hesitated a moment before, as I thought, going to her makeshift prie-dieu to say her prayers.

"Would you like to watch me mortify the flesh?" she said.

"What do you mean?" I asked.

"I sinned, you know, in saying I would kill myself last night," she said. "I told my aunt Blanche, who said it was very wrong. It's too soon to make my confession, so I've decided to give myself a penance to fit the crime." She slipped off her nightgown, and stood thin and bony before me. "The spirit is willing, but the flesh is weak," she said. She went to the untidy bookcase, and, rummaging a moment, fetched out a small leather dog whip with a knotted end. She shut her eyes and then, before I realised what she was about, lashed herself swiftly across her back and shoulders. There was no feint about it. She jumped involuntarily, drawing in her breath with pain.

"Stop it," I said, and, getting up, tore the whip out of her hand.

"You do it," she said, "you whip me instead."

She watched me, bright-eyed, and I picked up the nightgown she had thrown on the floor.

"Put it on," I said curtly, "and hurry up. And then say your prayers and get into bed."

She obeyed, and the prompt response, the eager willingness to do what I told her, was somehow worse than if she had shown defiance. She was excited, tense, beneath the dutiful façade, and although I knew nothing about children, knew nothing of their games, the excitement seemed to be wrong, unnatural.

The prayers at the packing-case prie-dieu were interminable. She did not say them aloud, so I could not tell if this was pretence or not, but presently she crossed herself, and rose, and with a subdued expression climbed into her narrow bed.

"Good night," I said, and bent to kiss her, but whether the cool, tight face upturned to me was intended as further punishment for herself or for me it was impossible to tell. I went out and shut the door, and, glancing down at the worn, knotted whip, turned left, after passing through the baize door at the bottom of the turret stairs, and went on sudden impulse to the room in the tower at the far end of the first corridor. I tried the handle. It was locked. I knocked on the door.

"Who is there?" said Blanche.

I did not answer. When I knocked again I heard footsteps and the sound of a key being turned in the lock, and then the door opened and Blanche stood there in a dressing gown, her hair released from the screwed knot and hanging straight about her face, giving her, in an instant, that same childish look of Marie-Noel upstairs. The expression in her eyes, incredulous, alarmed, defeated my purpose. The feud between her and her brother was not my affair. She could, at least, be warned about the child. I thrust the whip into her hands.

"Keep this," I said, "or throw it away. Marie-Noel was trying to use it on herself. I suggest you tell her that scourging drives the devil in, not out."

The expression in her eyes turned to hatred so intense that I stared fascinated, almost hypnotised, by the sudden savagery in that pale, impassive face. And then, before I could say anything more, she had flung herself against the door and locked it, leaving me in the corridor outside, having done no good, perhaps having antagonised her even further. I walked slowly back along the corridor, shocked, dismayed, haunted by the thought of those eyes, so venomous and unforgiving, that surely must once have been wide and full of trust.

As I came to the head of the stairs, wondering which way to turn and what was the procedure now, I met the three of them coming up the stairs to bed, one behind the other. Françoise heavy, leaden-eyed and pale; Renée, the spot of colour on her cheek still vivid, the high-necked blouse empha-

118

sising the high-dressed hair, and Paul, his hand on the light switch, yawning, another newspaper, a local one, underneath his arm. They looked up at me, the three faces caught in the feeble jet of light, and because I was not one of them as they believed, but was outside, a stranger, peering down into their world, it was as though all three of them were naked, without masks. I caught the anguish of Françoise, uplifted on a breath and instantly cast down again in disillusion, with only endurance to sustain her after the one magic moment; Renée triumphant because she believed her body to be beautiful, flaunting desire so that it might be given her again, forever returning, forever unfulfilled; while Paul, bewildered, tired and envious, wondered what miracle might be achieved, or what oblivion.

We bade each other good night, pairing off like couples at a set of lancers. As I followed Françoise along the corridor I wondered, dispassionately, how I should have felt had it been otherwise, had Renée been the wife of Jean de Gué. Were attraction and revulsion so near in kind that forced proximity could bridge the gulf between them and make them one? I was spared further speculation because I found that an alteration had taken place in the dressing room. There was now a bed in the room, a camp bed, with bolster, sheets and blankets. Oddly, my first instinct was not relief but guilt. What had happened? What was the matter? Then, going to the chest of drawers, I saw standing on it the huge bottle of scent, with the glaring motif "Femme." It was untouched.

I thought a moment, and then passed through the bathroom to the bedroom. Françoise was sitting by her dressing table, pinning her hair.

"Do you want me to sleep in the dressing room?" I asked.

"Wouldn't you prefer it?" she said.

"I don't mind one way or the other," I answered.

"That's what I thought."

She went on pinning her hair. This, I thought, is one of those issues in married life making for reconciliation or tears or interminable argument, and it would not have happened but for the bottle of "Femme" with the initial B so carelessly scribbled upon it. We had both of us bungled, her husband

and myself, and because I believed he would have responded with silence, that was the course I chose too.

"Very well," I said, "I'll sleep in the dressing room."

I went back into the bathroom and began to run the water, and as I cleaned my teeth, remembering which was my toothbrush and which my glass, it was once again like those scarce-remembered, queerly familiar second nights at school. The bathroom fittings were no longer strange, the running water came with a sound that was not the home sound yet was now part of a settled scheme; and when Françoise brushed past me to fetch a pot of cream, neither of us talking, she might have been some dormitory companion of a bygone era from whom I was temporarily estranged. I felt it neither incongruous nor strange to be in vest and pants while she was in a trailing wrapper. I had become part of the bathroom background, and so had she. Only the silence was out of key, and when, in pyjamas and dressing gown, I went to say good night and found her reading, and she turned to me a pale, indifferent cheek, with none of last night's anguish and none of last night's tears, I felt again not so much relief as guilt—guilt that the sins of Jean de Gué had been increased tenfold by his scapegoat.

I went back to the dressing room and opened the window. Tonight the chestnut trees were still, and there was no clarity, no stars, and no lone figure, either, in the turret room above. As I climbed into the camp bed and lit a cigarette, with the thought that this was my second night under the château roof and that twenty-four hours or more had passed since I came to St. Gilles, I knew that everything I had said or done had implicated me further, driven me deeper, bound me more closely still to that man whose body was not my body, whose mind was not my mind, whose thoughts and actions were a world apart, and yet whose inner substance was part of my nature, part of my secret self.

Chapter 11

When I awoke the next morning I knew there was something I had to do. Something urgent. Then I remembered the telephone conversation with Carvalet, and how I had committed myself, or rather the *verrerie* of St. Gilles, to continued production on their terms, without the remotest knowledge of the family resources. All I possessed was Jean de Gué's cheque book, and the name and address of his bank in Villars. Somehow I had to get to the bank and talk to the manager, inventing some excuse for my ignorance. He would surely be able to give me a rough idea of the financial situation.

I got up and bathed and dressed while Françoise was still breakfasting in her room, and while I drank my coffee in the dressing room I tried to visualise in my mind's eye the layout of the Michelin map and the road along which we had come from Le Mans. Somewhere along that road, surely not more than fifteen kilometres or so from St. Gilles, was Villars. I remembered noticing the name when I looked up my original course northwest from Le Mans to Mortagne and la Grande-Trappe. I no longer had my maps, but the town should be easy enough to find. When Gaston came into the dressing room to brush my clothes I told him I was going into Villars, to the bank, and I wanted the car.

"At what time," asked Gaston, "does Monsieur le Comte wish to go into Villars?"

"Any time," I said. "Ten, half past."

"Then I will have the Renault outside at ten o'clock," he said. "Monsieur Paul can take the Citroën to the *verrerie*."

I had forgotten there was a second car. This would simplify matters. There would be no questions from Paul, no suggestion of coming with me to the bank, which I had feared. I was reckoning, though, without the complications of family shopping. Gaston, naturally enough, must have passed round word of my intention, for I was putting change into my pockets, and was about to go downstairs, when the little *femme de chambre* knocked at the door.

"Excuse me, Monsieur le Comte," she said, "but Madame Paul asked if she may go with you into Villars. She has an appointment with the coiffeur."

I wished Madame Paul another attack of migraine. The last thing I wanted was another tête-à-tête with her, but there seemed no possibility of excuse.

"Does Madame Paul know I'm leaving at ten o'clock?" I said.

"Yes, Monsieur, she has fixed her appointment for half past."

I wondered if it was a deliberate scheme for my company. I told Germaine that of course I would take Madame Paul to the coiffeur, and then, with a sudden inspiration, passed through the bathroom to the bedroom, where I found Françoise sitting up in bed.

"I'm going into Villars," I said. "Do you want to come?"

Then I remembered that surely every husband kisses his wife good morning, even if he has been banished from her side the night before, and I went up to the bed, and kissed her, and asked her how she had slept.

"I was restless," she said. "It was as well for you that you had the camp bed next door. No, I can't come into Villars. I shall stay in bed. I'm expecting Dr. Lebrun sometime this morning. Why must you go? I had hoped you would see him."

"I have to go to the bank," I said.

"Gaston could go for you," she said, "if you want some money."

"It isn't that. I've got business to discuss."

"I believe Monsieur Péguy is still away ill," she said. "I don't know who is doing his work. The senior clerk, I suppose. He won't be much use."

"It doesn't matter."

"We ought to make up our minds finally, you know, whether I should go into Le Mans for the baby or have it here." The plaintive note had come back into her voice, the aggrieved tone of one who feels herself neglected.

"What do you want to do?" I asked.

122

She shrugged her shoulders, apathetic, resigned. "I want you to make the decisions," she said. "I'd like to feel the whole nightmare lifted from me, and that I don't have to worry any more."

I looked away from the accusing eyes. This was the moment, I supposed, for problems, intimacy, discussion of the many little troubles of daily life that must be shared by a husband and wife. But because it was not my problem, and the moment not of my choosing, I felt impatient with her that she must produce it now, when all I could see ahead of me was the necessity of getting to the bank.

"Surely Dr. Lebrun is the right person to take charge of all this?" I said. "We have to go on his advice. Ask his opinion when he comes this morning."

Even as I spoke I knew that I was wrong. It wasn't what she meant. She needed reassurance, and felt herself to be alone. I wanted, desperately, to say, "Look, I'm not your husband. I can't tell you what to do . . ." so that the burden of guilt would lift from me. Instead, as a sop, an attempt to ease my conscience, I added, "I won't be long. I'll probably be back before he's gone."

She did not answer. Germaine came in to take away the breakfast tray, and behind her Marie-Noel, who, having kissed us in turn, and bidden us both good morning, immediately demanded to be taken into Villars too.

Here was the perfect counterplot to Renée: I wondered I had not thought of it myself. When I said that she might come the child watched me with dancing eyes, wriggling impatiently while her mother brushed her hair.

"It's market day," said Françoise. "You are not to go pushing in those crowds or you'll catch something. Fleas, if nothing worse. Jean, don't let her go wandering in the market."

"I'll look after her," I said, "and anyway, Renée is coming too."

"Renée? Whatever for?"

"My aunt Renée has an appointment at the coiffeur," said Marie-Noel. "As soon as she heard Papa was going into Villars, she came along to Aunt Blanche's room to telephone."

"Ridiculous," said Françoise. "She washed her hair only four or five days ago."

I heard the child say something about Aunt Renée wanting to look nice for *la chasse*, but I did not listen. I fastened onto a single flash of information, which was that the telephone extension was in Blanche's room. Blanche, then, had lifted the receiver and listened when I spoke to Paris. If not Blanche, who else? And how much had been heard?

"I'll try and keep Dr. Lebrun until you come back," said Françoise, "but you know how he is, he never can stay long."

"What's he coming for?" asked Marie-Noel. "What's he going to do?"

"He's going to listen to baby brother," said Françoise.

"Suppose he doesn't hear anything—will it mean he's dead?"

"No, of course not. Don't be so silly. Run along now."

The child looked from one to the other of us, anxious, expectant, and then, for no apparent reason, suddenly turned a cartwheel.

"Gaston says I have very strong limbs," she said. "He says most girls can't stand on their hands at all."

"Look out . . ." warned Françoise, but it was too late. The flying feet overbalanced and crashed upon the little table near the fireplace, scattering a porcelain cat and dog onto the hearth, smashing them irrevocably. There was a moment's silence. The child picked herself up, scarlet in the face, and looked at her mother, who sat up in bed gazing at the disaster, stunned.

"My cat and dog," she said, "my favourite pieces. The two my mother gave me that I brought from home." I thought for a moment that the shock of this sudden accident would be too great for her to feel anger, but a tumult of feeling must have swept over her on that instant, breaking all control, and the bitterness of months, perhaps of years, surged to the surface.

"You little beast," she said to the child, "with your horrible clumsy feet, smashing the only things I possess and value in this house. Why doesn't your father teach you discipline and manners instead of filling your head with all this nonsense about saints and visions? You wait until you have a brother, then he'll get the petting and the spoiling and you'll take second place, and a good thing it will be for you and for everybody else. Now leave me, both of you. I don't want either of you, leave me alone, for God's sake . . ."

The child, her face drained of colour, ran from the room. I went over to the bed.

"Françoise . . ." I began, but she pushed me away, her eyes tormented.

"No," she said. "No . . . no . . . no . . ." She flung herself back on her pillows, burying herself against them, and in a futile endeavour to be useful, to do something constructive, however late, I picked up the fragments of the porcelain animals and carried them into the dressing room, so that her eye should not fall upon them when she looked again. Mechanically I wrapped them in the cellophane and paper that had served for the great bottle of scent still standing on the chest of drawers. There was no sign of Marie-Noel, and remembering the night before, and the whip, and—even worse —the threat of the open window, I went out of the dressing room and up the back stairs to the turret room, running three steps at a time in sudden fear. But when I came to the room I saw with relief that the window was closed, and that she was undressing, folding her clothes neatly on a chair.

"What are you doing?" I asked.

"I've been naughty," she said. "Don't I have to go to bed?"

Suddenly I saw the adult world through her eyes, the strength of it, the absence of logic and understanding, so that the calm undressing at a quarter to ten, when she had only been up perhaps an hour, and the sun was streaming into her room, became things accepted without question because this was how a grown-up person punished.

"I don't think so," I said. "I don't think it would do much good. And anyway you were not naughty. It was bad luck."

"But I can't come to Villars now, can I?" she asked.

"Why not?"

She looked bewildered. "It's a treat," she said. "A person can't have a treat when they've broken something valuable."

"You didn't intend to break the figures," I said. "That's the difference. The thing to do is to try and have them mended. Perhaps we could find a shop in Villars."

She shook her head in doubt. "I don't think there is one."

"We'll see," I said.

"I shouldn't have overbalanced but for my hands," she

said. "I had them too near the table, and my wrists went weak. I've done it heaps of times before out in the park."

"You chose the wrong place, that's all," I said.

"Yes."

Her eyes searched mine, as though in hungry confirmation of some unspoken thought, but I had nothing more to tell her and nothing more to say.

"Shall I put on my dress again?" she asked.

"Yes. Then come downstairs. It's nearly ten o'clock."

I went down to the dressing room, and picked up the broken pieces in their wrapping paper. Downstairs the car was ready waiting, and Renée was standing in the hall.

"I hope I haven't kept you waiting," she said.

There was a world of anticipation in her voice, and of confidence too, as she walked past me onto the terrace and down the steps; and the very way she moved, and then called good morning to Gaston standing by, with a glance above her at the warm bright sky, betrayed excitement and avidity. The scene was set, this was to be her day. Then the child came running across the terrace after us. She wore white cotton gloves and a white plastic handbag dangled from her wrist on a chain

"I'm coming with you, Aunt Renée," she said, "but it's not a treat. I have some rather serious shopping to do."

I had never seen expression alter so swiftly from assurance to dismay.

"But who said you could come?" exclaimed Renée. "Why aren't you doing your lessons?"

I caught Gaston's eye, and the understanding that I glimpsed, the appreciation of the situation, was so superb that I wanted to wring his hand.

"It suits Aunt Blanche better when we do lessons in the afternoon," said Marie-Noel, "and Papa is glad of my company, aren't you, Papa? May I get in front? I shall be sick if I sit in the back."

For a moment I thought Renée was going to return to the château, the frustration was so shattering, so complete. Then she pulled herself together, and without looking at me climbed in behind.

I need not have worried about the road to Villars. The truth, as usual, proved an easy way out of difficulty.

"We will pretend," I said to Marie-Noel, "that I'm a stranger and don't know the way, and that you have to direct me."

"Oh yes," she said, "what a good idea."

It was as simple as that.

As we drove out of St. Gilles, and along the side roads through the shimmering countryside, golden green under the October sky, I thought how easily and happily children lend themselves to fantasy, and that life for them is only bearable because of this facility for self-deception, for seeing things other than they are. If I could have told Marie-Noel the truth about myself without destroying her faith in Jean de Gué, with what passionate intensity she would have given herself to complicity, and what a wizard's aide she would have been, the genie to Aladdin's lamp.

Soon we were out of the magic of field and farm and forest, of sandy byways and falling poplar, and back on the hard, straight *route nationale* and so to Villars, the child announcing in a singsong chant each turn I had to take, while behind us our passenger kept silence—except once, when I braked swiftly before a suddenly slowing vehicle in front, and the smothered "Ach!" of shock and exasperation, as the jolt shot her forward, betrayed the mood within.

"We'll drop Aunt Renée at the coiffeur and put the car in the Place République afterwards," said Marie-Noel.

I stopped in front of the small establishment with the waxen lady's head in the window all crimped and curled like a sheep ready for shearing, and opened the door for Renée, who got out without a word.

"What time will you be ready?" I asked, but she did not answer. She went straight into the shop with never a backward glance.

"She seemed in a bad mood," said Marie-Noel. "I wonder why."

"Never mind about her," I said, "go on directing me. Don't forget I'm a stranger here."

The absence of Renée put an end to restraint, and my mood, like the child's, turned festive. We found parking

127

space beside a line of lorries, and heedless of the warnings about fleas, plunged into the market in the Place beside the church.

Nothing was on a grand scale, as it had been in Le Mans. Here were no beasts, no cattle, but trestle tables crammed together in a small space, spilling over with aprons, jackets, macintoshes, sabots; and the child and I moved leisurely between them, our eyes caught foolishly by the same objects —by spotted handkerchieves, scarves, a china jug shaped to a cock's head, pink rubber balls, chunky coloured pencils, red one end and blue the other. We bought some grey and white checked slippers for Germaine, and then, distracted by a rival firm which was offering the same thing in a lively green, shamelessly took our custom to them; and hardly were the slippers wrapped and paid for than desire seized us both for yellow boot laces, both for ourselves and for Gaston, and two sponges on a string, and finally a great hunk of milk-white soap, a mermaid riding a dolphin embossed upon its surface.

We turned in the crowded alley, laden with our wares, and I saw we were being watched with intense amusement by a blonde woman in a bright blue coat, her own arms full of dahlias, and she said over the child's head, and as though to the stallkeeper beside her, "It must be true, then, that they are closing down the glass foundry at St. Gilles and turning it into a *bon marché* store." And as she brushed past us, going in the opposite direction towards the church, she murmured for my ear alone, "*Père de famille* for a change?"

I looked back at the blue coat swinging down the alley, amused, intrigued, and then Marie-Noel, pulling at me, said, "Oh, Papa, there's a little lace cloth. Come quickly— it's just what I want for my prie-dieu." And we were involved in purchases once more as she darted from stall to stall, and I, indulgent, lazy in the warmth of the sun, forgot all about my purpose in coming to Villars, until the church clock boomed half past eleven and I thought, aghast, of the bank closing at twelve, and nothing achieved.

"Come on, hurry," I said, and we went and spilt our purchases in the car. While she was arranging them on the back seat I glanced once again at the cheque book to memorise the address of the bank.

"Papa," said the child, "we've never seen about mending the broken porcelain for Maman," and, looking at her, I saw anxiety in her face, the happiness gone.

"That's all right," I told her, "we'll do it later. The bank is more important."

"But the shops will be shut," she urged.

"That can't be helped," I said. "We'll have to risk it."

"I wonder if they mend porcelain in that place by the Porte de Ville," she said. "You know, where they have candlesticks."

"I don't know," I said, "I shouldn't think so. Look, will you sit and wait for me here in the car? It will be very dull in the bank."

"I don't mind. I'd rather come."

I was not sure I wanted her sharp ears overhearing all I said.

"Listen," I answered, "I may be some time. And there will be a lot of talk. It is much better for you to stay here, or go and wait with Aunt Renée."

"Oh no," she said, "that's much worse than the bank. Oh, Papa, couldn't I go to the shop by the Porte de Ville and see if they would mend the porcelain, and then come and meet you at the bank?"

She stared up at me expectantly, delighted with this solution. I hesitated.

"Where is it?" I said. "I've forgotten. What about traffic?"

"Just inside the Porte de Ville," she said impatiently. "There's never any traffic. You know, next to the umbrella shop. And then I'll come back past the church and straight to the bank. It's barely four minutes."

I looked up and down the avenue where we had parked the car. The flamboyant Gothic spire of the great church topped the trees. Wherever she meant to go could not be any distance.

"All right," I said, "here's the parcel. Be careful, now." I put the broken pieces wrapped in cellophane and paper into her hands.

"Do they know you in the shop?" I asked.

"Oh, surely," she said. "I've only got to say the name de Gué."

I watched her across the road and then turned left, back to the market place and to the obvious bank building standing at the corner. I pushed through the doors, and with a brilliant feat of memory asked for Monsieur Péguy.

"I'm sorry, Monsieur le Comte," said the clerk, "Monsieur Péguy is still away. Is there anything I can do for you?"

"Yes," I answered, "I want to know how my account stands."

"Which one, Monsieur?"

"All of them."

A woman typing at a desk behind the counter looked up and stared.

"Excuse me, Monsieur le Comte," said the clerk, "do you mean you require the bare balances, or do you want to see a full statement of figures?"

"I want to see everything," I repeated.

He disappeared and I lit a cigarette, leaning against the counter and listening to the click-click of the woman's typewriter beating against the slower tick of the clock on the wall. There was the close, airless smell familiar to all banks, and I thought of the many times I had cashed small traveller's cheques in similar branches throughout the country, and now, like a gangster, was preparing to probe the secrets of another. The clerk returned with a sheaf of papers in his hand.

"Perhaps you would like to take a seat in the office, Monsieur le Comte?" he said, and he led the way through to a small room with a glass-fronted door.

He left me alone with the file, and as I turned the papers I realised that I was as lost before these columns of figures as I had been before the bills and statements in the *verrerie*. I looked them over one by one, but could make nothing of them, and then the clerk returned to find out whether I wanted any more information.

"Is this all?" I asked. "You have no other papers of mine?"

He looked at me enquiringly, a little puzzled, and said, "No, Monsieur le Comte, unless, of course, there is anything you wish to look at in your safe in the vault."

I had a vision of clinking bags of gold in some massive

safe. "In my safe?" I asked. "What have I got in my safe?"

"I don't know, Monsieur le Comte," he said, looking offended, and murmured something about its being unfortunate that Monsieur Péguy was away.

"Is there time for me to look in it before you close?" I asked.

"Certainly," he replied, and he disappeared again and came back with a bunch of keys, and I followed him down a long flight of stairs to the basement. He opened a door with one of the keys, and we were in a vast, low room like a cellar, the walls lined with safes, all numbered. He stopped before number 17, took another of the keys on his bunch, put it in the lock, and turned it. I waited for the door to open, but instead he withdrew the key, stood back, and looked at me expectantly. Seeing that I made no move, he said with a puzzled air, "Monsieur le Comte has forgotten to bring his key with him?" Cursing myself for a fool at not knowing what he expected of me, I felt in my pocket and brought out Jean de Gué's bunch of keys. One of them—longer and bigger than the others—looked to me as if it might be right, and, stepping forward with an air of confidence which must surely seem as false to him as it did to me, I put it in the lock, and thank God it turned, and when I tried the handle of the safe the door swung open.

The clerk, murmuring that he would leave Monsieur le Comte to find the papers he wanted, went out of the vault, and I put my hand in the safe, to find no bags of gold but another mass of papers, all of them tied with tape. Oddly disappointed, I took them to the light. The title of a document caught my eye, "Marriage Settlement of Françoise Bruyère," and I was beginning to untie the tape when the clerk returned.

"Your little girl is outside," he said. "She asked me to tell you that everything is arranged about the porcelain, and can she go back in the lorry with Madame Yves?"

"What?" I asked impatiently, preoccupied with the papers in my hand.

He repeated the message stiffly, but it made no sense to me, and I did not want to enquire what lorry he was talking about or who Madame Yves might be, for clearly I should know.

131

"All right, all right," I said, "tell her I'll be along in a moment."

Now I had the tape undone and had opened the document, and I immediately forgot about being in the vaults of the bank, for this was familiar ground in spite of the legal jargon. I might have been browsing through archives back in Tours or Blois, or in the Reading Room at the British Museum. "*Régime dotal . . . majorat . . . usufruit . . .*"—here were all the perplexities of French matrimonial law, the sort of thing I found fascinating and incomprehensible in one; and, time of no account, I sat down and began to read.

The father of Françoise, a Monsieur Robert Bruyère, had evidently been a rich man with little faith in the stability of Jean de Gué, and no desire to bolster the tottering fortunes of the family of St. Gilles. Her dowry, which was considerable, was therefore in trust for the male heir, but the income from this trust could be used during the minority of the said heir, husband and wife having joint control over it. In default of a son, when Françoise reached the age of fifty the trust funds were to be divided between her and any surviving daughters of the marriage, or, if she predeceased her husband before she reached the age of fifty, between the husband and any daughters. The point was that the income from this vast trust could only be used by the parents on the birth of a male heir, and if no male child was born no one could touch a sou of the money until Françoise reached the age of fifty —unless, of course, she were to die before that age. On the date of the marriage itself a capital sum had been allotted to the husband for his own use, but this was less than a quarter of the total dowry.

I read the complicated document over a dozen times, and I understood at last the allusions dropped by Françoise and the others to the advantage of the next child being a boy. I wondered what whim had caused her father to tie up his fortune in this fashion, and whether Jean de Gué, on his marriage, had simply seized his share of it and gambled on a son. Poor Marie-Noel, no trust money for her if a brother came along. As to Jean de Gué himself, he would get control of half the capital itself only if there was no heir and Françoise died before the age of fifty. . . .

"Excuse me, Monsieur le Comte, but will you be much longer? I have to go to lunch. We close at twelve, as Monsieur le Comte is no doubt aware, and it is already twenty past."

The clerk stood beside me, wearing the injured expression of one who has lost valuable minutes of his time, and with an effort I brought myself back to reality. For a moment it had been as though I were sitting in that vast bedroom in the tower, hearing again the comtesse's voice—"Beggared . . . and likely to remain so, unless Françoise produces a son, or . . ." Now I understood the words, though the hidden meaning of her tone, her covert glance, were still a mystery. I only felt, dimly, that there was a bond between us unbreakable and strong, a secret world of mother and son which no outsider, neither wife nor child nor sister, could enter; and the masquerader that was my outward self hovered on the fringe of discovery, seeking, yet fearful of what it might find.

"I'm coming," I said. "I didn't realise it was so late."

I put the documents back in the safe. As I did so, a paper fell out which had not been tied up in tape with the others, but seemed to have been thrust hastily in. I glanced at it, and saw that it was a letter from a lawyer called Talbert, written two or three weeks earlier. Odd words caught my eye—"*verrerie*," "*rentes*," "*placements*," "*dividendes*"—and, sensing that here might be the clue to the whole financial tangle, I put it in my pocket. Once more we went through the ritual of the keys, and then I followed the clerk out of the vault, up the stairs and into the little office.

I looked about me, still absent in thought, my mind filled with the details of the marriage settlement, and then I remembered and said, "Where's the child?"

The clerk replied, "She's been gone some time."

"Gone? Gone where?"

"Monsieur le Comte, you said I was to tell her it would be all right for her to do as she asked and go with this person in a lorry."

"I said nothing of the sort!"

I spoke sharply, furious with myself and with him, and he repeated, more offended than ever, the words that I had used, giving them a sense I had never intended. I saw that my own impatience had been to blame—I had spoken quickly, thoughtlessly, wanting to read the document.

"Who was this person, did you say? Where did she go?" I asked, responsibility flooding me, with a sudden vision of gypsies, kidnappers, little girls murdered in woods.

"I rather think it was one of your own lorries from the *verrerie*, Monsieur le Comte," said the clerk. "Some of your workpeople had been to the station. The child seemed perfectly at ease. She climbed up in the front seat with the woman."

There was nothing to be done about it. Marie-Noel must take her chance. She would either be delivered safely at the château or butchered in the forest. If there was any mischance, I should be to blame.

The clerk led me past the counter, empty now and silent, and let me out, locking and bolting the door behind me. I turned left and went across the Place towards the church, for I must at least discover what had happened about the broken porcelain. Marie-Noel had said something about the Porte de Ville. Where was the Porte de Ville? I went back in the direction I had seen her take, beyond the car, and although irritated now, and anxious, I was at the same time struck by the beauty of the town, the curious charm of canals winding peacefully past the old houses, little footbridges leading across the water to back gardens, roofs yellow with age, overhanging eaves and twisted beams. At last I came to the Porte de Ville itself, an ancient gateway to the once fortified town, with a stone bridge where the drawbridge used to be. I passed under the archway to what was evidently the main shopping street of the town, and at once I saw, on the righthand side, the place that the child must have meant, an antique shop with china and silver in the window. But the door was fast shut, and there was a notice beside it saying they closed from midday until three.

I turned away, and then saw that a man was watching me from a shop on the opposite side of the street.

"*Bonjour, Monsieur le Comte,*" he said. "Are you looking for Madame?"

I was evidently known, but I did not want to become involved.

"It doesn't matter," I said. "It's not important."

A sort of half-smile appeared on his face. He seemed amused. "I don't wish to be indiscreet," he said, "but Madame can't hear the bell when the door is shut. It would be better to take the garden entrance."

He went on smiling, delighted to be of use to me, but I had no intention of walking into any back garden and disturbing the antique merchant during the sacred siesta hour. I thanked him and went back under the Porte de Ville, and, glancing leftwards, in vague curiosity, saw how the shops and houses of the narrow main street backed onto the canal, and that the rear of the antique shop itself was in reality a small eighteenth-century house, with a balcony and strip of garden fronting the canal like a miniature palazzo on a Venetian backwater. The windows were wide open to the sun, and a cage with budgerigars stood on the balcony. A narrow plank bridge led from the road to the garden. It was one of those corners that a tourist brochure describes as "picturesque," and I wondered how many coloured replicas on postcards were on sale within the town. As I stood there, pausing to light a cigarette, someone came out onto the balcony to feed the birds, and I recognised in an instant the blonde woman in the bright blue coat who had laughed at Marie-Noel and myself in the market place. Was she the keeper of the antique shop? If so, then I had no objection to asking what arrangements had been made to mend the broken porcelain.

I advanced towards the plank bridge, feeling a little over-bold. "Excuse me, Madame," I called, "I tried the shop just now, but the door was locked. Did my daughter visit you this morning?"

The woman turned round, surprised, and then to my intense astonishment burst into laughter.

"Idiot," she said. "I thought you'd gone home. What are you doing, hanging about at the street corner and playing the fool?"

The familiarity, the use of the intimate "tu," shook me off balance. I could only stare, wondering how to answer in character. She looked away to her right, past the Porte de

Ville to the Place St. Julien. It was truly the siesta hour. The streets were empty.

"There's no one about," she said. "Come on in."

The reputation of Jean de Gué in Villars was evidently a light one. I hesitated, and then, glancing across the square, saw the decisive factor in favour of acceptance. It was Renée, whom I had forgotten all about, long finished at the coiffeur, tramping the town in search of me. With a sudden flood of realisation I remembered that, now Marie-Noel had disappeared into the unknown in a lorry, I should have to drive Renée back to St. Gilles alone. I was trapped. The woman in the blue coat followed my eyes and saw my dilemma.

"Quick," she said, "she hasn't seen you—she's looking the other way."

I dashed across the little bridge and onto the balcony, and, laughing still, she pulled me into the room.

"There's luck," she said. "A moment later she'd have caught us."

She shut the long window and turned to me, smiling, the same look of intense amusement on her face that I had noticed and indeed shared in the market place. But now there was nothing guarded about it, or disguised: her whole expression was open and free.

"That child of yours is adorable," she said, "but it was very naughty of you to send her here. And why for heaven's sake did you wrap up those pieces of broken porcelain in cellophane and paper with a card addressed to me? She said something about a mistake, and a friend of yours in Paris, but one of these days, my angel, your jokes will go too far." She put her hand in the pocket of her blue coat and pulled out a piece of crumpled cellophane and some string. "I'll see to your broken porcelain, and anything else you care to send in from St. Gilles, but don't use your child or your wife or your sister as your deputy, because it's making fools of them and I have too much respect for your family."

She dived into the other pocket and produced a crumpled card. On it was written "For my beautiful Béla, from Jean." The porcelain dog and cat lay in pieces on a table. The only link that was missing was the outsize bottle of "Femme."

Chapter 12

Although she had closed the long window, the billowing casement curtains masking the view, the room was full of sun. I had an impression of blue-grey walls and cushions, but the effect, instead of being cold, was light as air. The dahlias that I had seen her carrying from the market place were red and gold, and now they spilt in profusion from a vase in the corner, the sun upon them still. There was a bowl of fruit upon a table, a bookcase, a Marie Laurencin drawing hanging above the fireplace. Deep chairs stood about the room, and a Persian cat cleaned its paws in one of them. Close to the window was a low flat table with artist's materials upon it, thin, small brushes and a special sort of paper. There was a smell of apricots.

"What are you doing in Villars in the middle of the day?" she asked.

"I went to the bank," I said, "and forgot the time. I was supposed to pick up one of the family from the coiffeur."

"You've left it rather late," she said. "Does she enjoy walking about the streets?" She went to a corner cupboard and brought out a bottle of Dubonnet and two glasses. "Where's the child?"

"I don't know. She disappeared in a lorry with some workmen."

"That shows good taste. You've brought her up well. Are you going to have lunch with me? It's all here—ham, salad, cheese, fruit and coffee." She opened a hatchway between this room and another, and there was a tray laid ready, with food upon it.

"How can I," I asked, "with my sister-in-law waiting for me outside?"

She went over to the window and opened it, and looked out across the balcony to the Place St. Julien.

"She's not there any more. If she has any sense she will

137

go and sit in the car, and then, when she becomes tired of waiting, drive back to St. Gilles."

I wondered if Renée could drive. I did not care. It was more interesting to speculate on why my companion called herself by the name of successive Hungarian kings. I sat down in one of the deep chairs and sipped Dubonnet. I felt suddenly devoid of responsibility, and content to let things take their course. Jean de Gué had too many women in his life.

"You can imagine how I felt," she said, "when Vincent came to me just this morning and told me that your small daughter was in the shop asking if we would mend something very precious belonging to her mother. I couldn't imagine what had happened—for one moment I thought your wife had found out that I had done the miniature. What about the miniature? Did you give it to her? Did she like it?"

I paused a moment, considering my words, trying to understand the proper sequence of events. "Yes," I said, "yes, it was a great success. She was very pleased."

"And you managed to get the setting I told you about? They kept the locket for you, after my telephone call?"

"I did. It was quite perfect."

"I'm so glad. It was a marvellous idea of yours, and must have come to you in one of your better moments. The child didn't mention it, so of course I did not either. She said her mother had been very much upset by the breakage this morning, so I gathered the dog and cat were precious. They won't mend, of course, but I can get duplicates from Paris. They're Copenhagen—I suppose you realised that? Come on, let's eat. I'm hungry, if you are not."

She laid the table, drawing it up to my chair, and I thought to myself that this was, so far, the most effortless moment of my masquerade. It could be termed a gift, even, on the part of Fate, which had been sparing of indulgence up to date. The only trouble was Renée, walking the streets of Villars getting angrier every moment.

Jean de Gué's Béla must have divined my thought, for she said, "Vincent will be back from lunch directly. When he comes I'll send him out to see if she's in the car. Did you leave it in the Place de la République?"

"Yes." Had I? I wasn't sure.

"Don't worry. She'll drive it home. It's what I should do in her place. And then Gaston can bring it back again. Were you joking when you said the child had gone off in a lorry?"

"No, it's true. They gave me the message in the bank."

"You take it very calmly."

"I think it was a lorry from the *verrerie*. And what could I do? She and the lorry had disappeared when I came up from the vaults."

"What were you doing in the vaults?"

"Looking in my safe."

"That must have been a shock to you."

"It was."

I was eating the ham and the salad and breaking bread, and it struck me how much more pleasant was lunch today, with this woman opposite me, than it had been yesterday in the dining room at the château. This train of thought led me to the one undelivered present.

"There's a bottle of scent for you," I said, "on the chest of drawers in the dressing room at St. Gilles."

"Thank you. Am I supposed to go and fetch it?" she asked.

I told her without lying, able to laugh at it now, about the mistake in the initial B.

She looked bewildered. "I don't see how it happened," she said, "since you never speak to your sister. Or had you really brought her something as a peace offering at long last?"

"No," I answered, "my mind wasn't functioning properly. Too much to drink in Le Mans the day before."

"You must have been insensible and dead drunk on the floor to have made a blunder of that magnitude," she said.

"I was both."

She raised her eyebrows. "The visit to Paris was not successful?"

"Very unsuccessful."

"Carvalet weren't co-operative?"

"They wouldn't extend the contract on our terms. I came back and told my brother Paul they had. My family and the workmen at the *verrerie* all believe it has gone through. Yester-

139

day I reopened negotiations on the telephone, and the result is an extension of the contract on their terms. Nobody knows but me. That's why I went to the bank this morning—to see if I can stand the loss. I still don't know the answer."

I looked up from eating and saw the wide blue eyes fixed upon me.

"What do you mean, you don't know the answer?" she said. "Surely you do? You told me before you went to Paris that the *verrerie* is working at a loss, and that if Carvalet wouldn't agree to your terms you were going to close down."

"I don't want to close down," I said. "It wouldn't be fair on the workpeople."

"Since when have you bothered about the workpeople?"

"Since I got drunk in Le Mans."

There was the sound of a door in the distance. She got up and went to the passage. "Is that you, Vincent?" she called.

"Yes, Madame."

"Go and see if the Comte de Gué's car is in the Place de la République, and if there is a lady waiting in it."

"Very good, Madame."

She came back and brought me the basket of fruit and the cheese, and poured me another glass of wine.

"You seem," she said, "to have made rather a mess of things since you returned. What are you going to do about it?"

"I haven't the slightest idea," I said. "I'm living from day to day."

"You've done that for a long time."

"I'm doing it more so now. From minute, in fact, to minute."

She cut a slice of Gruyère cheese and gave it to me. "You know," she said, "it's a good thing, now and again, to take stock of oneself in life. To see where one has gone wrong. I sometimes wonder why I go on living here in Villars. I barely make a living out of the shop, and I exist mainly on what Georges left me, which is precious little these days."

Was Georges perhaps a husband? Some kind of comment seemed necessary.

"Why do you go on living here?" I asked.

She shrugged her shoulders. "Habit, I suppose. It suits me.

140

I'm fond of this little house. If you think I exist for your occasional visits, you flatter yourself."

She smiled, and I wondered whether Jean de Gué did flatter himself. Either way, the result was beneficial.

"Do you think," she asked, "that your sudden feeling for the *verrerie* is because it is, after all, two hundred and fifty years old, and you may be going to have a son at last?"

"No," I said.

"Are you sure?"

"Perfectly. My feeling for it comes from having looked on it yesterday with new eyes. I watched the men working there for the first time. I realised they had a certain pride in it, and a feeling for its owner too. If the *verrerie* closes down they will be deceived in him, disillusioned, quite apart from being out of a job."

"It is pride, then?"

"I suppose it is. Pride of a sort."

She began to peel a pear and gave me the quarters from it. "You make a mistake leaving so much of the administrative part to your brother. If you weren't so infernally lazy you would do it yourself."

"That had occurred to me."

"Is it too late to start now?"

"Much too late. Anyway, I don't understand it."

"That's nonsense. You've watched it since you were a child. Even if you were never in the slightest bit interested, you must have picked up a working knowledge. I sometimes wonder . . ." She paused, and began to peel an apple for herself.

"What do you wonder?"

"No . . . it would be probing, and I never probe."

"Go on," I said, "I'm curious. I want to be probed."

"It's only," she said, "I sometimes wonder if your lack of feeling for the *verrerie* is because you don't want to think about it too deeply. You don't want to be reminded of what happened to Maurice Duval."

I was silent. This was the fringe of something. The man Jacques had spoken of, Maurice Duval: he was the man in the photograph album by the side of Jean de Gué.

"It could be," I said slowly, after a moment or two.

"You see," she said softly, "you don't want me to probe."

141

On the contrary it was essential to find out all I could about Jean de Gué. But not at the risk of committing another blunder.

"No," I said, "you're wrong. I want you to go on talking about it."

She took her eyes off mine for the first time, and looked above my head, into the distance.

"The Occupation was over fifteen years ago," she said, "his part of it. Yet people go on remembering him—what a fine man he was, and how he died. It can hardly make for peace of mind for those involved."

There was a tap at the door and a small thin man, wearing a beret, looked into the room. He smiled when he saw me.

"*Bonjour, Monsieur le Comte,*" he said. "It's nice to see you. How are you?"

"Very well, thank you."

"There was no lady in the car. But there was this note on the seat."

He handed it to me with a bow. It was short and to the point. "I have been looking for you and Marie-Noel for nearly an hour. I have hired a car to take me back to St. Gilles. R." I showed it to my hostess.

"Now you can relax," she said. "Vincent, be a dear, and put these things through to the kitchen, will you?"

"Yes, Madame."

"Peace, for how long? For me, till three o'clock. For you, as long as you care to stay. Do you want another cushion?"

"No. I'm perfect."

She cleared away the table and fetched cigarettes and coffee. "I'm rather glad you have this sudden sentiment for the *verrerie,*" she said. "It shows you have more feeling than you pretend. I still don't see, though, if it's losing money and you've arranged an even worse contract than before, how you can possibly afford to keep it running."

"Nor do I," I said.

"What about that friend who comes to shoot with you? He advises you, doesn't he? He'd be the one to ask."

She had thrown off the bright blue jacket, revealing a thin wool frock of indeterminate grey. It was restful to look upon her, and to know that in this room nothing was expected of

142

me. I wondered how often Jean de Gué came here from the château and sat with his head against a cushion, as I was doing now. Her casual friendliness was disarming, yet inviting, too. It held a quality of ease suggesting mutual understanding without emotional demand. I picked up the cat and stroked it. It would suit me, I thought, if this could be all my masquerade demanded of me: if, instead of being the owner of the château of St. Gilles, I might stop here indefinitely in the sunshine, sitting where I was sitting now, with the cat on my lap, being fed with slices of pear by Béla of Villars.

"Can't you sell some securities, or some land?" she asked. "What about your wife? The money's tied up, isn't it?"

"Yes."

"Unless you have a son. I remember now."

She poured me out another cup of coffee. "How is your wife? She's not very strong, is she? Who's looking after her?"

I thought a moment. "Dr. Lebrun," I said.

"He's getting rather old, isn't he? I should have insisted on a specialist. You've been oddly detached about it all along. I hope you show more sympathy at home."

I stubbed out my cigarette. She was the one person who wouldn't be hurt by the truth, yet oddly enough I should have hated her to know. I could imagine the raised eyebrows, the amused laughter and the practical approach, deciding what must be done, followed by quick, inevitable withdrawal and the courtesy one shows to a stranger.

"I'm not really detached," I said. "I try to show sympathy. The trouble is, I don't know enough about Françoise."

She gazed at me thoughtfully. The candid eyes were disconcerting.

"What's the matter?" she said. "It's not just finance, is it? It goes much deeper. What really happened to you in Le Mans?"

I thought of the old childhood game of hunt-the-thimble. I used to play it with a maiden aunt. It was a restful, easy game for the adult, who did not have to move but only to close her eyes while I, the child, tiptoed about a sitting room filled with furniture and, heart beating, hid the thimble behind a clock. Then, with opened eyes, the dreaded questions began. As her eyes travelled towards the clock, honesty would compel me to say, "You're getting warm," though reluctantly, fearfully, not wanting the small gold thimble to be revealed in its precious quiet seclusion. This time I closed my eyes and went on stroking the cat upon my knee. Safety lay in evasion, and in the truth as well.

"You said something a little while ago about taking stock of oneself," I said. "Perhaps that's just what I've been doing, over a period of time, and it came to a head that evening in Le Mans. The self I knew had failed. The only way to escape responsibility for failure was to become someone else. Let another personality take charge."

She did not say anything. I suppose she was considering. I could not see because my eyes were closed.

"The other Jean de Gué," she said, "the one who's been hidden for so long beneath the surface gaiety and charm, I've often wondered if he existed. If he's going to emerge, he'd better do so now. Time's getting on."

Intuitively, uncannily, she had understood something of my meaning, but not the real sense. The thimble behind the clock was safe, the guesser cold. It was peaceful lying in the deep chair and I did not want to move.

"You don't really understand what I'm trying to tell you," I said.

"Yes, I do," she answered. "You aren't the only one with a dual personality. We all have our multiple selves. But no one avoids responsibility that way. The problems remain to be tackled just the same."

Colder and colder. The seeker was looking at the other end of the room.

"No," I said, "you've missed the point. The problems and responsibilities are new, because the man in charge is somebody else."

"How does he seem to you, then, the man in charge?" she asked.

The great church in Villars sounded two o'clock. The sonorous bell of any church, any cathedral, always rings a summons, and this one, solemn, deep-toned, was far too near for peace of mind.

"Sometimes I see him without any feeling at all," I said, "and sometimes with far too much. One moment he's considering murdering those closest to him, and the next he's giving

144

up his life for a stranger. He says he believes that the only motive which moves the human race is greed, and by ministering to this greed he himself survives. I think he has twisted ideas, but he's terribly near to the truth."

I heard her get up, put my coffee cup on a tray, and carry the tray to the hatch. Then she came back and sat on the arm of my chair. It was strange that I resented, not the favour, which was casual and natural in itself, but that it was done to my other self, the Jean whom she believed me to be. I also resented the present on the chest of drawers at the château.

"The man in charge," I said, "why does he buy you 'Femme'?"

"Because he likes the smell, and so do I."

"Do you suppose that's ministering to greed?"

"It depends on the size of the bottle."

"It's a very big bottle."

"Then I call it foresight."

I was not sure if I knew the scent of "Femme." I had never given anyone a bottle, and most scented women I avoided and abhorred. This one was not scented: she smelt of apricots.

"The thing is, it isn't greed at all," I said. "It's hunger. That's where he's wrong. And if it's hunger, what about the conflicting claims? Mother, wife, child, brother, sister-in-law, even workpeople—I can't satisfy them all. Frankly, I don't know where to start or what to do."

She did not answer, but I felt a soothing hand on my head. Anonymity closed in upon me. I was on a border sea between two worlds. The narrow island that once confined me had slipped away, rock-bound and isolated; the crowded continent waiting to receive me, vociferous, demanding, was momentarily out of sight. Wearing another skin had spelt release, yet bondage too. Something had been resurrected but was also spent. If the claims could be forgotten and the oblivion kept, which man should I be, myself or Jean de Gué?

I put out my hands and felt her face. "I don't want to have to think," I said.

She laughed, and, hardly brushing them, kissed my closed eyes.

"That's why you come here, isn't it?" she said.

Chapter 13

When I came away from the house the sun of late afternoon had turned all the lichen-coloured roofs to gold. Boys and girls carrying satchels and schoolbooks ran out of the house next door and crossed the canal by another footbridge. A clip-clopping horse, drawing a covered cart, plodded past the Porte de Ville, the driver slumped on his seat, cracking a lazy whip. Shutters had been flung back and doors were open in the shopping street within. In the avenue of plane trees, close to the market place, beside which lorries and carts had parked during the bustle of morning, old men and women now sat about in groups, basking in the warmth before the air turned chill, while smaller children, chattering like birds, shuffled the falling leaves and kicked the dust. I wondered how it would look at nightfall, this town of Villars, turning early to sleep and silence like all provincial market towns, the inhabitants behind their shutters and in bed, the houses in shadow, the mellow roofs sloping to pitchy eaves, the flamboyant Gothic spire of the cathedral church stabbing an ink-blue sky; no sound, perhaps, but the passing footstep of a loiterer homeward bound and the hardly perceptible ripple of the canals still and dark beside the walls.

It was the sort of town that in the past had tempted me to pass a night en route. Having dined, no wayfarer but myself left in the street, I used to wander past the silent houses whose shuttered windows told me nothing, only now and again a glimmer of light through the chinks betraying the life within. Sometimes an open window on an upstairs floor revealed a gulf of darkness, or a candle threw a shadow on a ceiling, or a baby cried; but mostly all was still, and I would prowl alone in company with hungry cats who, sleek and stealthy, nosed the gutters of the cobbled street. How casually I would have passed that Porte de Ville, stared down into the canal, glimpsed the footbridge and the small house tucked in beyond, and so returned to my tourist's bed and been off by morning, none the wiser. Whereas now, in another mood, my whole life changed, some part of Villars was my possession.

The light of the late day gave warmth and colour; this was a friendly town where people smiled. The Renault, waiting in the Place de la République, was suddenly familiar as my own, and Marie-Noel's white plastic bag, left on the seat where she had thrown it with the market purchases, was not like any object in a stranger's car but full of meaning: I saw it dangling on the small wrist above the short white cotton glove. Even the bank at the corner had its own place and purpose in the background. Villars was a citadel, a refuge; and as I drove out of it I wondered why the gift of another man's mistress should prove such a curious antidote to strain. It seemed to me that nothing would move me now, neither tears from Françoise nor tantrums from Renée. The mother could be coaxed with affection, the child indulged to a limit set by reason, the brother pacified, the sister soothed: none of them seemed a problem, as they had done during those first forty-eight hours under the château roof.

The reason was hard to find. Physical ease alone was not enough: in the past I had proved it valueless. Could change of identity alter the body's pulse, release some matter in the mind hitherto held back by prejudice? The world was full of tragic misfit phantoms seeking escape by making love disguised. I was not one of them. The Béla of Villars completed a pattern, a pattern containing mother, wife and child. The warmth of one, the dependence of the second, the laughter of the third, shaped themselves to make a fourth of her, and, finding this, I lost myself in all. Here was a part of the solution, but not the whole.

I remembered the correct turnings to St. Gilles, and as I drove down the lime avenue, over the bridge, through the gateway to the drive and under the archway of the moat to the outbuildings that I had only seen from a distance, my confidence was supreme. Nothing could daunt me now. I found myself in a yard containing two garages with doors flung wide, a potting shed and an empty stable full of broken stalls. As I got out of the car and slammed the door, the old

147

woman I had spoken to in the cowshed the day before emerged from the entrance, and I heard her call over her shoulder to someone within. She said something about "Monsieur le Comte," and a man in blue overalls followed her from the stables. They smiled and came towards me, and the man asked whether I wanted him to wash the car. I told him yes, for this was probably routine, and once again the woman pattered a string of incomprehensibilities, and I smiled and nodded, catching a reference to *"beau temps"* and *"la chasse,"* the rest escaping me.

I went back under the archway, and the retriever ran forward in his enclosure, barking. I stood still, calling him softly by name, but, doubtful, he continued barking, his tail wagging uncertainly at the same time, and I went to the gate of his run and waited for him to smell my clothes. He sniffed, puzzled, not satisfied, and I saw the man in overalls watching from the stableyard.

"What's the matter with César?" he said.

"Nothing," I answered. "I must have startled him, that's all."

"It's funny," he said. "He generally goes nearly mad when he sees you. Let's hope he's not turning savage."

"He's all right," I said. "Aren't you, César?"

I reached through the gate and patted the dog's head; gradually reconciled to tone and touch, he was mute and continued sniffing. But when I moved away he began to growl again.

"If he behaves like that on Sunday he won't be much use to you," said the man. "Shall I give him a dose of oil after his food?"

"No," I said, "let him alone. He'll soon recover."

I wondered what was expected of the dog on Sunday. Perhaps if I took him myself for exercise he would come to know me, and the suspicious bark give way to whines of welcome? If not, attention would be drawn to him, his behaviour questioned, the poor animal accused of treachery towards his master, when in reality he had proved himself to be the only instinctive creature in St. Gilles.

I went up the steps to the terrace, and as I entered the hall Paul came out of the small cloakroom to the right of the stairs.

"Where the devil have you been all day?" he asked. "We've

148

been trying to get you since one o'clock. Renée lost all sight of you, had to come back in a hired car, and then, to our astonishment, Marie-Noel turned up alone as we were finishing lunch, announcing quite calmly that she'd had a lift in the lorry. Lebrun waited until two, and then had to go. He's just been through to me again."

"What's wrong?" I enquired.

"What's wrong?" he repeated. "Only that Françoise isn't at all well, and Lebrun has forbidden her to move from bed. If she isn't careful she'll have a premature baby and lose it, and more than likely be critically ill herself. That's all that's wrong."

The contempt in his voice was something I had to accept. The fault was not Jean de Gué's but mine. I had promised to be back in time to see the doctor. I had not kept the promise. I had not even remembered it.

"What's his number?" I asked. "I'll get on to him at once."

"No use," he said. "He's been called out again. I told him to try you later this evening."

He turned on his heel and disappeared through the dining room into the library. He was not going to question me further. For that I was grateful. I knew what I had to do. I went straight upstairs and along the corridor to the bedroom. The curtains were half drawn, the fire had been lit, and there was a screen at the foot of the bed to mask the light. Françoise was lying against her pillows with closed eyes. She opened them as I came into the room.

"Oh, it's you," she said, "at last. I'd given you up long ago. I told them you'd probably taken the train back to Paris."

The voice was flat, expressionless. I went up to the bed and took her hand.

"I should have telephoned," I said. "I was held up in Villars, and frankly I forgot. There's no more to it than that. I don't even ask you to forgive me. How are you feeling? Paul tells me Lebrun has ordered you to stay in bed."

The hand in mine felt limp and cold. She did not take it away.

"If I don't I shall lose the baby," she said. "It's what I've been afraid of all along. I've always known something would go wrong."

"It won't go wrong," I said, "not if you take care. The question is, how good is Lebrun? Wouldn't you like me to call in a specialist?"

"No," she said, "I don't want a stranger interfering at this point, upsetting me, upsetting Lebrun. I shall be all right as long as I stay quiet and nobody worries me. What with Marie-Noel coming back on the workmen's lorry, and Renée having to hire a car because you disappeared, I've been almost frantic with anxiety. And then, in the middle of the afternoon, I decided that I might as well give up and resign myself to the fact that you wouldn't be coming back—that you'd got rid of them both on purpose and had gone off to Paris."

The tired eyes searched my face, and I knew that the only answer was to keep as near to the truth as possible.

"I had a long session at the bank," I said. "I don't mind telling you, but I don't want the others to know. The fact is, I lied about the contract. I didn't succeed in getting an extension when I was in Paris, and only managed to arrange things by telephone, and through the bank, today. They've agreed to continue the contract, but on their terms. It means the *verrerie* working at an even greater loss than before, of course, but it can't be helped. Somehow I shall have to find the money."

She looked bewildered, and I went on standing there holding her hand.

"What was the point of lying?" she asked. "I don't understand."

"I suppose it was pride," I said. "I wanted everyone to believe I had succeeded. Well, perhaps I have succeeded, for a time. I haven't been into all the figures yet. But I want you to keep this to yourself. I don't intend telling Maman, or Paul, or anyone except you unless things turn out to make it absolutely necessary."

She smiled for the first time, and, as she half raised herself on her pillow, I saw that she meant me to kiss her. I did so, and let go her hand.

"I won't tell anybody," she said. "I'm only too glad that you've taken me into your confidence for once. It's funny, though, that you've bothered so much about the *verrerie*. The idea of closing down never seemed to worry you as it did Paul and Blanche."

"No," I said, "perhaps not. It began to worry me yesterday, when I went down there in the afternoon."

She asked me to give her a comb and looking glass from the dressing table, and, sitting upright against the bunched pillows, she combed the lank fair hair away from her face. It was a gesture similar to another I had seen scarcely two hours before, and because of the total difference of mood and personality, the one carefree and gay, the other so weary, lifeless, yet if possible more intimate still, I felt myself oddly moved: I wished the balance could be restored, and Françoise likewise vigorous and happy.

"Why didn't you tell me the night you came back?" she said.

"I hadn't decided," I replied. "I wasn't sure what I was going to do."

"Paul's bound to find out," she said. "You can't possibly keep it from him. Besides, what does it matter if he does know, since you've fixed the contract? Anyway, all these things will be solved when the boy is born." She put the mirror back on the table beside the bed. "Marie-Noel said you were down in the vaults at the bank. Everyone wondered what you were doing. I didn't know you kept anything there."

"Various securities," I said, "deeds, and so on."

"Is our Marriage Settlement there?"

"Yes."

"Did you look at it?"

"I did glance through it."

"If we have another daughter there's nothing to be done, is there?"

"No, apparently not."

"What happens if I die? You get everything, don't you?"

"You're not going to die. Now, shall I close the shutters and draw the curtains and put on your light? Have you anything to read?"

She was silent. She lay back on her pillows. Then she said, "You might get me the locket you brought me from Paris. I think I'll keep it here beside me, on the table."

I went to the dressing table in the alcove, took the small jewel case I saw there, and gave it to her. She lifted the lid and looked at the locket, snapping the miniature open as she had done before.

"Where was it you bought it?" she asked.

"A place I know in Paris," I said. "I can't remember the name."

"Renée tells me that the woman who keeps the antique shop in Villars does miniatures from time to time," she said.

"Oh? Perhaps. I don't know."

"If she does, we might get her to do Marie-Noel sometime, and the baby too. It would be cheaper than in Paris."

"Yes, probably."

She put the locket, with the miniature open, on the bedside table. "You'd better go down and make your peace with Renée," she said. "I was feeling too ill to cope with her when she arrived back—you know how impossible she can be when she loses her temper."

"She'll get over it."

I closed the shutters, and then I put a log on the fire.

"I suppose the child's with Blanche," she said, "or upstairs with Maman. I haven't felt well enough to see her. Tell her I didn't mean what I said this morning, that I was ill and wretched."

"I think she understood that."

"What did you do with the broken pieces?"

"Never mind. I've seen to them. Is there anything else you want?"

"No. No, I shall just go on lying here quietly."

I went through the bathroom to the dressing room and changed my shoes and coat, as I had done the evening before. The bottle of "Femme" was still standing on the chest. It was no longer impersonal, like something glimpsed in a shop-window, but had all the significance of my own intimate life. I put it away in a drawer, and because the drawer had a key something made me turn the key and slip it into my pocket afterwards. I went out into the corridor, and at the foot of the stairs I came face to face with Charlotte.

"Monsieur le Curé has just gone," she said. "Madame la Comtesse has been asking for you."

"I'll go to her now," I said.

Once again she preceded me up the stairs, as on my first evening. And that moment forty-eight hours ago seemed to me, following her a second time, like something in a distant past: the masquerader of that night was as different from the man who now climbed the stairs as he, in his turn, had been from the self waking in the hotel bedroom at Le Mans. It was as though the skin that covered me was like armour. Then my courage had been false; now it was invincible.

"Monsieur le Comte was detained a long time in Villars?" asked Charlotte.

I knew I was right to mistrust her and dislike her, and that every word she spoke was false.

"Yes," I said.

"Madame Paul had tea with Madame la Comtesse this afternoon," she continued. "She was very put out that she had been obliged to hire a car to bring her back, and she told Madame la Comtesse the whole story."

"There was no story," I said. "I was detained, that was all."

We were now on the upper corridor, and I walked past her and went on to the further passage and the room beyond. I entered, to be greeted with the usual yapping from the dogs, and, caring no longer, I kicked them out of the way and went at once to the chair by the fire, where the mother was sitting, her massive shoulders draped in a purple shawl. I bent and kissed her, relieved to see that Blanche was not with her and she was sitting there alone.

"Good morning and good evening," I said. "I'm sorry I never came to see you this morning. I left early. You've already heard all about it. I'm glad to see you up. Have you had a good day?"

The mocking, questing eyes met mine, and she grunted and pointed to a chair.

"Sit down," she said, "there, with the light on your face, so that I can see you. Get out, Charlotte. And no listening at the door. Go down to the kitchen and order two trays for dinner. Go on, hurry up. And take these things away first." She pushed the missal and prayer books on the table out of the way. The terriers climbed up and settled themselves on her

153

lap, and she remained silent until the servant went out of the room. I lighted a cigarette, feeling her eyes upon me still.

"Well," she said, "where were you?"

I guessed that everything Renée and Marie-Noel knew of my morning had already been told: the drive to Villars, the expedition to the market, the visit to the bank, and possibly, through a telephone call to the clerk, the actual moment of my leaving it. The fact that she asked where I had been showed ignorance of the house by the canal. This was something, then, which Jean de Gué withheld from his mother.

"I had business," I said.

"You left the bank before half past twelve," she said, "and it's now half past six."

"Perhaps I drove to Le Mans," I said.

"Not in the Renault. It was in the Place de la République all afternoon. The man who drove Renée home reported seeing it when he returned to the garage in Villars. I told Renée to telephone and ask him."

I smiled. The itching curiosity was blatant, like a child's.

"If you want the truth," I said, "I was trying to avoid Renée. And I succeeded. That's all I'm going to tell you. You can question me until midnight and you won't be any the wiser."

She chuckled, and I saw that once again my instinct not to lie had proved my salvation. "I don't blame you," she said. "Don't give in to her, or she'll prove insatiable."

"She hasn't enough to do," I said. "None of you women have enough to do."

"I had plenty to do once," she said, "when your father was alive, in the old days, before the war and before you married. There were no women sitting about idle then. Empty-headed fools like Françoise and Renée were children in their 'teens. I had something to live for. So had Blanche."

The sudden venom in her voice startled me. I looked up, and the mouth was narrow, hard, like her daughter's, and the eyes that had mocked me a moment ago were veiled under the hooded lids.

"What do you mean?" I asked.

"You know very well what I mean," she said, and then, as swiftly as it had come, her expression changed again, the mouth sagged, relaxed, and she shrugged her shoulders. "I'm

154

old and ill, that's my trouble," she said, "and it bores me, as it will bore you when your time comes. We're too much alike. We don't want to be bothered with our own ailments or anybody else's. How is Françoise this evening?"

I felt I had been near to some inner core of revelation that, could I perceive it for a moment, would bring understanding of what went on under the folds of flesh, but the new question came from another quarter, the quiet, elaborately casual tone was that of someone without heart or feeling.

"As you know, I missed Lebrun," I said. "He's going to telephone me later. She has to stay in bed. She isn't at all well."

I watched her fingers beating a tattoo on the arm of her chair. It went to a definite rhythm—three and two and three again. Glancing at her, I saw that she was not conscious of this; she did not even know that her fingers moved. The tattoo was keeping pace with a thought not clearly formed, to which she might, or might not, give expression.

"I saw Lebrun myself," she said. "He won't tell you any more than he told me. He's a bungler, and he won't admit it. She's going to have trouble with this baby, just as she did with the last—I've known it all along. The only difference is that this time she's succeeded in carrying it longer."

The tattooing on the chair arm continued. I watched it, oddly fascinated.

"Françoise doesn't want a specialist," I said. "I suggested it just now."

"You suggested it?" she asked. "Whatever for?"

"Why surely," I said, "if there's going to be difficulty, any sort of trouble . . ." Unaccountably, her eyes meeting mine, discomfort seized me. I remembered the terms of the Marriage Settlement, and that if Françoise died without giving birth to a son the whole vast dowry would be divided between Jean de Gué and Marie-Noel.

The room, already stifling, became suddenly unbearable. I got up, loosening my collar. I felt her eyes upon my back as I went over to the window, but she did not say anything as I stood there, wrestling with the shutters. I threw them back, lifting the sash of one of the windows, and leant out, drawing in a deep breath of air. Dusk had come, and with it mist. The

155

paths were shrouded, the huntress hidden, even the dovecot on the verge of grass below was black and humped into obscurity. Immediately beside me was a gargoyle's head, ears flattened, slits for eyes, the jutting lips forming a spout for rain. The leaded guttering was choked with leaves, and when rain came the whole would turn to mud and pour from the gargoyle's mouth in a turbid stream. How loud the sound of rain would be here, close to the roof, first pattering on the leads, then falling fast, seeping down the walls, swirling in the runways, choking and gurgling above the gargoyle head, driving sideways like arrows to the windows, stinging the panes; and to the owner of this room beneath the roof, lying alone in bed, there would be no other sound, perhaps, for hour after hour through the long winter's night but the falling rain, and the flood of leaves and rubble through the gargoyle's mouth.

I shut the window and looked back into the room. She was watching me still, but her hands no longer beat a tattoo on the chair.

"What's wrong with you?" she said. "You're nervous, aren't you?"

"No," I answered. "I couldn't breathe, that's all. You keep this room too warm."

"If so, it's partly for your sake," she said. "You always say the château is too cold. Come over here."

I went towards her slowly, against my will. Those eyes of hers, so like her son's, so like my own confronted in a mirror, surely had intuition of the masquerade. She reached for my hands and held them.

"Are you developing a conscience at long last?" she asked.

They say the touch of hands reveals the self. A child puts his into an adult's, and knows instinctively whether to trust or to dislike. Two nights ago these hands had clutched and pleaded, panic-stricken, lost, and now this evening they were stronger than mine, the grip was firm, the pressure ruthless. Her hands neither gave confidence nor sapped it: they turned the assurance I had to a different plane. The faith she had in her son was so intense that even if she did not know his secrets, or share more than a small part of his life, it was as

156

though he remained within her, bound and sightless as he had been before birth, and she would never loose him.

"Don't let's become sentimental," she said, "and trouble ourselves over what Fate sends us. It's too late, for you and for me. Life isn't a short affair, as everybody likes to make out; it's long, much too long. We are neither of us going to die for years. For God's sake let us both be comfortable, if we can."

A discreet tap at the door revealed Charlotte with the tray, followed by Germaine with a second, and once again there was the ritual of the meal, now familiar to me. The first evening the comtesse had barely tasted food, but tonight she sopped up her soup with soft pieces of bread, mushing it to a broth, her eyes intent, her chin nearly touching her plate. I thought of the ham and cheese and fruit in the house in Villars, and my companion there, and I wondered what Béla's life was in the evening; whether she went out and dined with friends, whether she sat alone, how it would seem there with the shutters closed. The mother turned to me, forking a piece of steak from her mouth to one of the dogs, and said, "Why are you so silent? What are you thinking about?"

"A woman," I said. "Nobody you know."

"Does she suit you?"

"Yes."

"That's all that matters. Your father kept a mistress for a time in Le Mans," she said. "I saw her once, red-haired, a perfect beauty. He used to go and see her every Friday. It made him better-tempered at weekends. Then she married a rich butcher and went off to live in Tours. I was sorry when she went; she did him good."

Charlotte brought us crème caramel in little pots. The dogs waited expectantly, paws lifted.

"So you let Marie-Noel drive back from Villars with Julie and her grandson," she continued, switching her train of thought. "She came to me full of it, said she preferred it to the Renault. 'Who drove?' I asked. One of the workmen, she said, the young one with curly hair. She said she liked his smell. 'Tell that to your aunt Blanche,' I said. 'See what she has to say.'"

So Madame Yves was Julie. I was relieved. In the return

157

to find Françoise ill in bed I had forgotten the child and the lorry.

"All children like driving in lorries," I said. "I probably did the same myself."

"You?" She laughed. "Better forget what you got up to at her age. Have you forgotten little Cécile who came to tea? You took her inside the dovecot and locked the door. Her mother never brought her again. Poor Cécile . . . Watch Marie-Noel, she's growing fast."

"It's not very amusing," I said, "being an only child."

"Nonsense, she loves it. She doesn't want other children. She likes them older. I know, I was the same at her age. I fell in love with all my grown-up cousins. Marie-Noel hasn't any cousins. She'll fall in love with the workmen at the *verrerie* instead."

There was a knock on the door. "Who is it?" she called. "Come in. I hate people who knock on doors."

Germaine stood in the doorway. "Dr. Lebrun on the telephone for Monsieur le Comte," she said.

"Thank you." I got up, laying down my napkin on the tray.

"Better say good night to me now. I shall be tired directly. Tell the old fool not to panic. All Françoise has to do is to keep her feet up, and she may produce a boy. Kiss me, then." The hands gripped me once again, the eyes held mine. "None of this nonsense about specialists. They cost too much," she said.

I went out of the room, down the stairs, and to the telephone in the cloakroom. Marie-Noel, in her dressing gown, was waiting by the instrument. She looked at me anxiously, her face pale.

"Can I listen in Aunt Blanche's room?" she asked.

"Certainly not," I said. "Dr. Lebrun wants to speak to me."

"Will you tell me what he says afterwards?"

"I don't know."

I pushed her out of the way, went into the cloakroom and shut the door. I said, "Hullo?" and the voice of the doctor answered, high-pitched, elderly, running on and on in a flurry of words.

"Good evening, Monsieur le Comte, it was so unfortunate that we missed one another this morning. I was in Villars this

158

afternoon and could have seen you there, even, had I known where to find you. Now I found Madame la Comtesse Jean in a highly nervous state, very apprehensive about herself, and certainly any agitation at this stage might easily bring things on before the natural term, and taking into consideration the difficulties she has had before, her anaemia and so on, she might have considerable trouble. In fact, it is essential that she should have complete rest during the next few days; this moment during the seventh month can be critical, you understand. I am not alarming you in any way?"

He paused two seconds to draw breath, and I asked him whether he would like a consultation with a specialist.

"Not at present," he said. "If your wife rests and has no further symptoms of malaise, above all no sign of haemorrhage, then all should be well. For the event itself I would suggest that she go to the clinic at Le Mans, but that can be discussed in a few weeks. At any rate, I shall be in touch with you constantly, and will give you another ring tomorrow. By the way, you are expecting me on Sunday, I suppose?"

Perhaps it was his custom to take lunch at the château on Sunday, or pay, not a visit of inspection to his patients, but a ceremonial call.

"Of course," I said. "We shall be delighted to see you."

"Luckily your bedroom faces the front. Your wife will not be disturbed. Very well then, we shall meet on Sunday."

"*Au revoir*, Doctor."

I hung up the receiver. "Your wife will not be disturbed. . . ." Was Sunday lunch so convivial that the sound of merriment echoed through the salon and rang to the rafters of the château? It was unlikely, and I wondered what he meant. I went out of the cloakroom, and Marie-Noel was still there.

"Well?" she asked quickly. "What did he say?"

"He said Maman was to stay in bed."

"Is the baby ready to come?"

"No."

"Then why was everybody saying that it was, and if it did come it would be born dead?"

"Who said so?"

159

"Germaine, Charlotte, everybody. I heard them talking in the kitchen."

"People who listen at doors always hear lies."

I could hear Paul talking to Renée in the dining room. They had not yet finished dinner. I went into the salon, the child following me.

"Papa," she said, and she was whispering now, "is Maman ill because I broke the porcelain and made her unhappy?"

"No," I said, "it's got nothing to do with it."

I sat down on the arm of the chair and pulled her to me. "What's the matter with you?" I asked. "Why are you so nervous?"

Her eyes flickered away from me, looked at everything in the room but me.

"I don't see why you want it," she said at last. "I don't see why you want to have this baby. Maman thinks it is a nuisance. She told Aunt Renée a long time ago that she wished she didn't have to have it."

Her question, so full of anxiety, was surely logical. Why was her mother obliged to have a child she did not want? I wished she could have asked the reason of Jean de Gué. I made a sorry substitute. In the circumstance it seemed easiest to tell the truth as I saw it myself.

"It's peculiar," I said, "and rather cold-blooded, really. Your grandfather Bruyère had a lot of money. He tied it up in such a way that your father and mother can't use any of it unless they have a son. So, even though they are perfectly content with their one daughter, it would make things much easier financially if they could have a son."

The instant look of relief upon her face was as though she had been given a blessed antidote to physical pain.

"Oh," she said, "is that all? Just for money?"

"Yes," I said. "Mercenary, isn't it?"

"Not at all," she said. "I think it's very sensible. Does it mean the more boys you have, the more money you and Maman get for yourselves?"

"Hardly," I said. "It just works for one."

In an excess of emotional release she slipped off my knee and turned a somersault from the sofa onto the floor, dressing gown and nightgown flying over her head, revealing her small

160

round behind. Shouting with laughter, her head hidden in the bunch of clothes, her quarters bare, she walked backwards to the screen as Blanche and Renée and Paul came into the room.

Blanche stood still, her eyes fastening onto the naked, capering animal into which the child had turned.

"What do you think you're doing?" she said swiftly. "Pull down your dressing gown at once."

Marie-Noel turned, shook herself free, the dressing gown falling about her, and, perceiving her adult audience, stood and smiled.

"It's all right, Aunt Blanche," she said. "Papa and Maman only do it for money, not because they want children. And that's why everyone in the world tries for boys—it's good for finance." She ran towards me and caught my hand, turning me round to face the relatives with a happy, proprietary air. "You know, Papa," she said, "Aunt Blanche told me that after you were born, when she was a little girl, everyone stopped loving her, nobody took any notice of her any more, and it was one of the lessons in humility that turned her to God. But when my little brother arrives everything will go on just the same. You will love me as much as ever, and perhaps the Sainte Vierge will teach me a different lesson in humility, not the one she taught Aunt Blanche."

It must have struck her that the frozen faces of her aunts and uncle did not reflect her own satisfaction. She glanced at me uncertainly, then back again to the sisters-in-law. Of the two women, Renée, if it were possible, looked the more outraged and shocked. The child sensed this, and smiled at her graciously.

"After all," she said, "there are other virtues besides humility. I could learn to have patience, like Aunt Renée. It's not everyone who can grow a baby. She has been married for three years to Uncle Paul, and nothing has happened to her yet."

Chapter 14

It seemed to me that I had reason to bless Françoise: her weakness gave me an excuse for absence upstairs. It was far simpler to sit with her in the bedroom than down below in the salon with Paul and Renée. I went upstairs and put the child to bed and when she was settled and tucked in for the night I returned to Françoise and did the same for her. I fetched hot water from the bathroom, and a sponge and soap and towel; then toothbrush and powder, pins for her hair, the pot of cream, the nightcap that tied with the ribbon under the chin. I waited on her like an orderly in hospital, or someone called urgently to minister first aid. I was reminded of those wartime days when, emerging from the tomb where I decoded documents, I took my turn at driving ambulances or whatever came my way during those feverish nights. The sudden intimacy with strangers then, most of them women and children, many of them frightened and in pain, had given me the same feeling of humility and compassion that came to me now as I helped Françoise prepare herself for the night. Her gratitude was intense, as theirs had been. She kept saying, in wonder and surprise, that I was kind.

"It's nothing," I answered. "What else would you expect?"

"I'm not used to it," she said. "You're not thoughtful as a rule. I've often come up early to bed, feeling tired, and you've stayed down talking to Paul and Renée. But perhaps you're avoiding them tonight in case they ask you what you were doing in Villars?"

She was as intuitive in her own way as the child was in hers, and I wondered, as I kissed her and turned out the light, whether she realised instinctively that I had disclosed only part of what had happened during the day.

As I went back to the dressing room, I remembered the letter from the lawyer Talbert which I had brought away from the bank. It was still in my pocket, and I took it out and read it. It was mercifully clear. The *verrerie*, he said, was running at a steady loss—that at least I already knew—and bankruptcy could only be avoided if it was subsidised from some other source, by the sale of land or securities, for instance, as Béla had suggested. The writer said that he would be glad to come to St. Gilles and discuss the matter with me at any time that suited me, and, as the matter was urgent, suggested that I might take the earliest opportunity to arrange an appointment. Presumably it was this letter which had made it so vital that Jean should see the Carvalet people in person and persuade them, if he could, to agree to more favourable terms.

The following day was Saturday, and I decided to go down to the foundry first thing in the morning, before Paul had dressed and had his coffee, to see if there was a letter from Carvalet. The directors could hardly have consulted before Friday, and a letter written afterwards would surely arrive today. I was up and round to the garage for the car before Gaston had come to brush my clothes and take away my tray. This time César let me pass without barking, and when I reached through his gate to pat him, and he wagged his tail, I felt that I had scored a triumph. Nobody was about. Sounds from the cow house beyond suggested that the old woman was with the cattle, and I could see the bent back of the man in overalls hoeing in a distant field. I turned left out of the village and up the hill to the straight forest road, and nothing of what I did seemed strange at all. It was all part of my life, more so than anything that had been in other days, this speeding along the smooth road between the oak trees and the chestnuts. And the feeling stayed with me when I drew the car to a standstill beside the gate of the foundry, and, getting out and slamming the door, called good day to the men already at work.

As I crossed the rough ground to the house behind the big foundry shed I met the postman walking away from it, and I knew my instinct to come early had been right. I went swiftly to the office door, and there was Jacques sorting the letters beside the desk. He turned round, looking at me in surprise.

"*Bonjour, Monsieur le Comte.* I didn't think you would be here this morning. Monsieur Paul said neither of you would be down."

I wondered why Paul should have told him so. Was it some sort of holiday?

"I thought Carvalet might have written," I said. "I'm expecting a personal letter from one of the directors."

He went on staring at me. Perhaps my brisk manner was unusual.

"I hope nothing is wrong?" he said.

"So do I," I replied. "Have you the mail there? Let's see if there is anything from them."

He looked down at the small pile of letters in his hand, and second from the top was a long envelope with the Carvalet stamped address.

"There it is," I said. "Thank you, Jacques."

I took it from him, and discreetly he moved away to the table in the middle of the room, while I read the letter with my back to the window. It was all right. It confirmed the telephone conversation and it enclosed the contract, extended for a further six months, drawn up on the new terms. The letter expressed satisfaction that the two firms had, after all, come to an agreement.

"Jacques," I said, "have you got our contract there? The old one?"

"You have it, Monsieur le Comte," he said, "in the file on your desk."

"Look for it, will you," I asked, "and I'll glance through the rest of the mail?"

He did not question me, but the expression on his face showed bewilderment. I watched him search through a file in a prominent position on the desk, while I flipped through the remaining letters, which were bills and receipts. He handed me the contract without a word, and I sat down at the desk and compared the two. The wording was identical, except for the crucial matter of the terms of sale. Knowing nothing of the business, nothing of the output of the *verrerie*, I could at least seize the salient fact that in the future Carvalet would pay less for the products sent them.

I felt in my pocket for the lawyer's letter and laid it before me, beside the contracts.

"I want to run through the figures," I said to Jacques. "Wages, production costs, the whole outfit."

He stared. "You saw them recently," he said. "You and Monsieur Paul and I checked everything before you went to Paris."

"I want to do it again," I said.

It took us about an hour and a half. It was tedious, incomprehensible and fascinating, and when we had done, and he went through to the kitchen to make some coffee, I was able to compare the final figures he had given me with what they would become under the new contract. The answer was that something in the nature of five million francs would have to be found from the personal account of Jean de Gué to balance costs. I saw his reason for closing down. There was nothing else he could do, if he did not want to sell land or securities. The glass foundry had been losing money under the old contract: under the new one it ceased to exist as a business at all. It became a luxurious toy, as ephemeral and brittle as the glass it made. My blundering sentiment had cost the owners dear.

I took the new contract, put it with both the letters in my coat pocket, and went through to the kitchen to find Jacques.

"There, Monsieur le Comte," he said, "a little refreshment after so much work." He handed me a cup of steaming coffee. "I am still marvelling at your success in Paris," he said. "You went really with no hope at all, more as a formality than anything else. But it proves the value of personal contact."

"No one," I said, "will be out of work. That's the important thing."

He raised his eyebrows. "Were you so concerned about the men?" he asked. "I hadn't realised that. Actually, after the first shock they would soon have found employment. They've been prepared for a close-down for a long time."

I drank my coffee, disillusioned. Perhaps I had meddled to no purpose after all. Someone knocked on the outer door and, excusing himself, Jacques went back to the office. I looked about me, and saw that I was standing in a fair-sized kitchen that must once have done duty for a family, the door beyond leading through to the rest of the house. Curious, I opened it, and saw a broad stone passage, with other rooms leading off it and a staircase rising to the floor above. I crossed the passage and looked into the rooms. They were empty, unfurnished, the walls discoloured, paint cracking, dust thick upon the floors. In the furthest one of all, a fine, square room with panelled walls, there were large pieces of furniture stacked against a wall, cases of crockery, chairs piled high one upon the other, the whole giving an appearance of neglect, as though the owner had put all his possessions to one side and forgotten about them. An old almanac was pinned to the wall, the date 1941, and beside it was a box of books. I bent down and opened one of the books. Inside was written "Maurice Duval."

A fluttering sound by the window made me turn my head. It was a butterfly, the last of the long summer, woken by sunshine, seeking escape from the cobwebs that imprisoned it. I tried to lift the window, but it was jammed. It could not have been opened for years. I released the butterfly from its prison, and it hovered a moment on the sill, then settled once more amongst the cobwebs.

I heard footsteps coming through from the direction of the kitchen. Jacques stood in the doorway, watching me. He hesitated, then advanced and waited uncertainly in the middle of the room.

"Were you looking for something, Monsieur le Comte?" he asked.

His manner was diffident, embarrassed. I wondered if he was in charge of these things, and whether I had broken some sort of family etiquette by exploring the house.

"Why do we go on keeping all this?" I said, pointing to the furniture.

He stared at me, then shifted his eyes. "It's for you to say, Monsieur le Comte," he replied.

I looked away from him, back to the stored furniture. There was something depressing about it, unused, forgotten, stacked there against the wall, and the room must have been lived in once, a salon or dining room.

"It seems such a waste," I said.

"Indeed, yes," he answered.

I considered whether I dared venture a question, a question that Jean de Gué would never have put because he would know the answer.

"Do you think we ought to make use of these rooms?" I

said. "Get someone to live in the house, instead of letting it stand empty?"

At first he did not answer. He went on standing there, ill at ease, looking about him at the room and the furniture but not at me. Then he said, "Who would you suggest should come here now?"

It was not an answer, merely another question, giving me no clue how to proceed. I strolled to the window and looked out. The sheds were away to the left, and to the right were farm buildings. Both were separated from the house and its immediate piece of garden by fences. There had been a paved path once, leading to the house from the road, and beside it stood a well, broken, no longer used.

"Why don't you live here yourself?" I asked.

His discomfort became even plainer, and I could tell from his expression that he thought I was attacking him in some way.

"My wife and I are very content where we are in Lauray," he said. "It is, after all, only a short distance away, no further than you are at St. Gilles. My wife likes to be where there is company. It would be too isolated for her here, besides which . . ." He broke off, distressed.

"Besides what?" I asked.

"Everybody would think it a little strange," he said. "No one has lived here for so long, and then . . . you must excuse me, Monsieur le Comte, but there are not very happy memories connected with the house when it was last inhabited. Few people would wish to live here now." Once more he hesitated, and then, seeming to gather courage, went quickly on, his words spilling out as if he were driven by something stronger than respect. "Monsieur le Comte," he said, "had there been fighting in the grounds of the *verrerie*, a battle between soldiers, that is something one accepts. But when the last man to live here, the master of the *verrerie*, Monsieur Duval, is woken from his bed in the middle of the night, and taken downstairs and shot by his own countrymen, and his body thrown into the well, cut to pieces with his own glass, even if it happened a long time ago and is something we all prefer to forget, yet it does not make anybody very anxious to come and live here, where it happened, bringing a wife and family."

I did not answer him. There was nothing I could say. The butterfly made another limp struggle to free itself from the cobweb, and, as I put my hand to it again to save it from the death it refused to avoid, my line of vision was caught by the rusted wrought iron of the ancient well, the stonework defaced, nettles at the base.

"No," I said slowly. "You are right, of course."

I turned and left the room and went along the stone passage to the kitchen, and thence to the office, which was impersonal because of the furniture, and the smell of stale cigarette smoke, and the files and papers. I stood by the desk for a moment, looking down at the bills and receipts and letters, but there was nothing further for me to do. I knew now about the figures—as much, probably, as I should ever know. The *verrerie* would continue to run until somebody, someday, discovered there was no more money to pay the wages or the bills.

"If you will give me an envelope addressed to Monsieur Mercier at Carvalet," I said to Jacques, who had followed me, "I can post their copy of the contract on my way back. I'll keep the duplicate."

But his camaraderie had vanished. We were both thinking of the empty part of the house, and a return to finance and business was out of the question.

"I only came down about the figures," I said. "There is no need to mention it to Monsieur Paul."

"No, Monsieur le Comte," he replied. He took an envelope out of the desk drawer and addressed and stamped it. As he gave it to me he said, the friendliness once more in his voice, "You are expecting me tomorrow? I think it's going to be fine. They gave a good forecast on the radio this morning. Half past ten, then, at the château."

He stepped forward to open the door for me, and I said, "Till tomorrow," and went out into the yard. Tomorrow was Sunday. Perhaps he and his wife came to Mass at St. Gilles and, with Dr. Lebrun, joined the family afterwards.

Something made me turn left outside the house and pass

through the small gate into the neglected orchard where Julie had been hoeing the vegetables the first afternoon. Viewed from this side, with none of the sheds visible, surrounded by creeper-covered walls, the house might have been any peaceful, late seventeenth-century manor farm set down in green fields and bounded by forest. Mellow beneath the sun, it surely belonged to another time; and what I had seen scarcely five minutes before, the broken well with the rusty chain standing in isolation amongst nettles, should belong to the same time too, remote and peaceful, giving life to the inmates of house and foundry from a pure spring deep in the earth, not serving as a charnel house for murder and destruction. The chain broken now that had drawn water from the well, and perhaps there was no more water either; perhaps the spring was dry or had turned its course elsewhere, leaving only dust and rubble and broken glass, and the links that had bound the *verrerie* and the master's house to the château of St. Gilles had also snapped, the unity had gone, the one no longer drew strength from the other. I wondered why I should mind, and why the thought of the murdered Maurice Duval, who had once been master here, should personify for me the virtues of permanence, a carrying over of the best of one generation to the next; and why the nature of his death, ugly, cruel, symbolic of all hatreds between people of the same race divided against each other, should suddenly seem my responsibility, something whose memory must not be allowed to suppurate unseen, but should be opened up and cleansed.

I left the orchard and went back past the sheds to the entrance of the *verrerie*, and there, standing by the small lodge, was Julie, her arms full of greenstuff. I called good day to her, and once again I was struck by the honesty of her face, the warmth and shrewdness of the brown eyes, the solidity and strength of her body. I knew that it was not sentiment on my part which made me trust her, but some intuition deep within myself that made me respond to her instinctively, as I had responded to Béla of Villars.

"You're an early one, Monsieur le Comte," she called.

"It's not often we see you at the *verrerie* on a Saturday morning, either. How are you? And how is the young comtesse? Not so well yesterday, they told me."

News must travel fast in a small neighbourhood. Then I remembered how she had taken Marie-Noel back to the château from Villars, and had talked no doubt to the servants afterwards.

"She has to take things quietly," I said. "She was better last night when I got home. I must apologise, Julie. The child went and bothered you yesterday in Villars. I didn't realise where she was or what she intended to do—they gave me a muddled message in the bank."

She laughed and gestured with her hands. "It's not for you to apologise, Monsieur Jean, but for me to thank you. We were just returning from the station, and there she was, running out of the Porte de Ville like a piece of quicksilver. Naturally I made young Gustave stop the lorry. I couldn't understand why the child was alone, and then she told me that her papa was in the bank, and nothing would content her but to come with us. We were only too pleased to have her, a sunbeam in the dark lorry. She never stopped talking from Villars to St. Gilles."

I had followed her to the patch of ground beside the lodge, where the few square yards were crammed with vegetables and flowers, and I watched her feed some rabbits in a hutch, talking to them all the while. I thought of the comtesse at the château feeding sugar to the terrier dogs. Suddenly it seemed to me that both women were strong, virile, tender, fundamentally the same; and yet one of them had grown awry, twisted, and in a strange way maimed, and it was because of something within herself that had never flourished.

"Julie," I said—and I knew that what I was asking would seem strange to her, coming at this moment, and was anyway something that Jean de Gué would have known and therefore never asked—"Julie, how was it, here at St. Gilles, during the Occupation?"

Oddly, she did not seem surprised at the question. Perhaps, then, de Gué might have asked it: perhaps he might have felt, as I did, that this peasant woman, so close to the

170

heart of things, might add a corner to the picture which no one else could.

"You understand, Monsieur Jean," she said after a moment or two, "that for a person like yourself, who was away fighting in the Resistance, war is something that is planned and carried out by the intellect. It is rather like a game that either succeeds or fails. But to those who are left behind it is very different. It is like being in a prison without bars, and nobody knows who is the criminal, who is the jailer, who is telling lies, which person has betrayed whom. People no longer have faith. If something you thought strong turns out to be weak, you are ashamed and wonder who is at fault. Is the weakness mine, is it yours, you ask, but nobody knows the answer and no one will take the blame."

"But you," I persisted, "what did you do, Julie? What did you think?"

"Me?" she asked. "What could I do but go on living here, as I had done for years, growing my vegetables, feeding my hens, looking after my poor husband, who was still alive, and saying to myself, This has happened before, it will happen again, it has to be endured?"

She turned away from the hutch, wiping her broad, strong hands on her apron. "You've seen them in the fields dying of myxomatosis?" she said. "Pretty, isn't it? We have come to this now, that for an animal to be free he has to be kept in a cage. I have no great opinion of the human race. It is just as well, now and again, that we have wars, so that men know what it is to suffer pain. One day they will exterminate themselves, as they have exterminated the rabbits. So much the better. The world will be peaceful again, with nothing left but the forest over there, and the soil."

She smiled at me and added, "Come in the lodge, Monsieur Jean, let me show you something."

I followed her into the small building, about the size of the dovecot on the château lawn There was a stove in one corner, with a pipe to the roof, a wooden table, a chair, and a cupboard the full length of the wall. A hen was sit-

171

ting fluffed before the stove. She shooed it with her foot and it ran squawking from the door.

"If she thinks she can lay in here she is mistaken," said Julie. "She is very cunning, that hen; just because she is old she tries to take advantage of me. Now wait, while I find you a snapshot."

She took a key from a pocket in her skirt beneath the apron, and reached up to the locked cupboard. It was full of papers, books and crockery, but neatly arranged, not huddled together in disorder. "Wait," she said, "I have it here somewhere." She searched among some papers and then brought out an exercise book, opened it, took an envelope from the middle, opened that, and from the envelope brought out a snapshot.

"There," she said, "you asked me about the Occupation. They accused me of being a collaborator because of this boy."

The snapshot was of a young soldier in German uniform. There was nothing very striking about him. He was not posing, or smiling, merely young.

"What did he do?" I asked.

"Do?" she said. "He did nothing. He was simply here for a few months, with many others. He was in trouble one day. There was to be an inspection, and he had stained his uniform messing with some dye. He came to me and asked, in his sign language with a few words mixed in, if I could clean it, so that he would not be punished. Monsieur Jean, I thought of my own two boys, André who was a prisoner and Albert who was killed, and there was this boy of the same age standing there, far from his home, asking me, who could have been his mother, to clean the stain on his jacket. Of course I cleaned it for him. And he came back afterwards and thanked me and gave me this snapshot. It made no difference to me whether he was German or Japanese or had fallen from the moon. He was no doubt killed later, like many others—they were all born to die, those boys, ours as well. But because I had cleaned his jacket the mayor of St. Gilles and many others did not speak to me, no, not for two years. So you see, when war comes to one's own village, one's own doorstep, it isn't tragic and impersonal any longer.

172

It is just an excuse to vomit private hatred. That is why I am not a great patriot, Monsieur Jean, and why I do not care to discuss the Occupation in St. Gilles."

I gave her back the snapshot and she replaced it with the rest of the letters and papers and books in the cupboard. Then she turned to me, her lined, weather-beaten face calm and impassive.

"So," she said, "everything is forgotten in time. That's life. But if I had shown you that snapshot some years ago, Monsieur le Comte, I wouldn't be here today, would I? A cord round the neck for old Julie, and the nearest tree in the forest out there."

I said nothing because I could not. War had never touched my country as it had hers. Hatred, cruelty, terror, these were emotions I had never known. I had only experienced failure and futility in my own person. I could understand the Jean de Gué who had run away from his responsibilities, leaving me to shoulder them: Jean de Gué, officer of the Resistance, eluded me. Did he believe, in those days, that if he was to survive he must minister to greed? What private conflict had driven the gay, laughing figure of the photograph album to cynicism and indifference? I felt within me a sudden absurd and impassioned desire to tell her, in the name of the Jean de Gué whom she believed me to be, of my sorrow for everything that had happened to her over the years, for bitterness and poverty and suffering and loss, for whatever might have come her way to cause her distress. But it would, I knew, have startled and embarrassed her if I had said anything of the sort, and instead I put my hand on her shoulder and gave it a pat. Then we went out together to the car, and she opened the door for me and stood smiling, her arms crossed under her shawl.

As I waved my hand to her and drove away, I thought that life would surely be delectable always and purged of pain, if it could be spent in the company of Julie of the *verrerie* and Béla of Villars, and perhaps Gaston thrown in for good measure. But as I pictured them all three in some house together, ministering to my needs, I realised that each one was too self-assertive and too individual to like the others, and in twenty-four hours their quarrels would have torn asunder the harmonious pattern my sentimentality had sketched. Which means, I thought, as I drove along the forest road once more, that relationships between people are largely valueless, because those to whom we are drawn never like one another, so that the chain dissolves, the message is lost. My compassion for Françoise, lying in bed in the château, cannot help the mother, likewise solitary, cut off, brooding on the past in her room in the tower. Nor can my instant appreciation of Marie-Noel, with her grace and youth and beauty, embrace the hard, embittered shadow that is Blanche. Why should Béla of Villars bestow her person as a gift, demanding nothing, and Renée of St. Gilles throw tentacles round her lover like an octopus? When is the first seed of destruction sown?

I had learnt three things from my morning. First, that through my telephone conversation to Carvalet I had committed the glass foundry to a course which could only bring about its ruin; secondly, that the last, well-loved master of the foundry had been butchered on his own doorstep and his body flung down the well; and thirdly, that the people of St. Gilles, like everyone else in the world, had seized defeat as an excuse to turn upon their friends.

Before I reached the village I stopped the car and felt in my pockets for the contract and Jean de Gué's wallet. In the latter was his driving licence, and I took it out and opened it. The signature, as I had expected, was a typically flowing French one: I had seen it, or its like, on hundreds of French documents in my travels and studies. A dozen attempts at copying it were enough to give me confidence. When I took up the contract again and, in a sudden change of mood, wrote his name with a flourish at the bottom of the page, de Gué himself would have hesitated to denounce it as a forgery. Then I drove down the hill to the village and through the gateway to the château, stopping only to post the contract.

The front door stood wide open and there was commotion in the hall. Gaston, with sleeves rolled up, was edging a heavy sideboard through to the dining room, assisted by the man in overalls from the garage, another man whom I had not seen before, Germaine, and the stalwart daughter of the woman who washed the linen. As soon as Gaston saw me, and while I was wondering how, without betraying my ignorance, I could find out what this furniture-moving signified, he gasped a message over his shoulder. "Monsieur Paul has been looking for you all the morning, Monsieur le Comte. He says you have given no orders yet to Robert. Germaine, go through to the kitchen and see if Robert is still there." Then, returning to his labours, he said to the man whom I did not recognise, and who looked as though he might be a gardener, "Now then, Joseph, up with the leg at your end. Heave, now."

Germaine disappeared to the back regions. I waited in the hall uncertainly. Who was Robert, and what orders was I supposed to give? In a moment the *femme de chambre* appeared again, followed by a small, thickset man with grizzled hair and a scar on his cheek, dressed in breeches and leggings. "Here is Robert, Monsieur le Comte," she said.

"Good morning, Robert." I held out my hand to him. He shook it, smiling. "Well?" I asked. "What is it you want to know?"

He looked up at me, puzzled, then burst into uncertain laughter, as though I had made a joke at his expense and he wasn't quite certain how to take it.

"It's for tomorrow, Monsieur le Comte," he said. "I thought you would have sent for me yesterday to discuss arrangements, but Gaston told me you were out all day, and then, Madame la Comtesse being unwell, I did not like to disturb you last night."

I stared down at him. We were alone. Germaine and the others had retired to the kitchen, their labours finished.

"Tomorrow," I repeated, "yes, of course. Quite a number of people seem to be coming. Were you by any chance wondering what we were going to eat?"

He flinched as though the joke had gone on too long. "Why, Monsieur le Comte," he said, "you know perfectly well it is nothing to do with me what you eat. What I must know is your programme for the day. Monsieur Paul says you have not discussed it with him at all."

I had a sudden wild vision of beating the bounds, of stripping the willow, of bobbing for apples, or whatever the custom might be on the second Sunday in October—some cere-

175

mony at which I, as seigneur of St. Gilles, must play a leading part. I would willingly resign the rôle to Paul instead.

"You don't think," I began cautiously, "that for once we might leave the arrangements to Monsieur Paul?"

The man stared at me, astounded. "Why, Monsieur le Comte," he exclaimed, "you have never done such a thing in your life. In all my years in St. Gilles you have never suggested it. Ever since Monsieur le Comte your father died, it is you who have organised the Sunday of the *grande chasse.*"

This time it must have been I who looked, and certainly felt, as if he had made a joke in poor taste. The *grande chasse* —idiot that I was. There had been constant allusions to it during the past two days, and none of them had made any impression on me. Tomorrow, Sunday, must be the big annual shoot in the district, centring in the domain of St. Gilles, planned and wholly organised by the seigneur, Jean de Gué.

Robert watched me anxiously. "Are you quite well, Monsieur le Comte?" he asked.

"Listen, Robert," I said, "I've had a lot on my mind since I came back from Paris, and, frankly, I've not yet worked out tomorrow's programme. I'll see you later."

He looked baffled, frustrated. "As you say, Monsieur le Comte," he answered, "but time is getting on and there is much to be done. Will you see me at two o'clock?"

"At two o'clock," I said, and to be rid of him I went through to the lobby as though to telephone, and waited until I heard him pass through the service door. Then I crossed the hall and went out to the terrace and down to the shelter of the cedar tree that had been my refuge the first night. Two o'clock or midnight could make no difference—I should have no programme and no plan. Lecturing on French history had not equipped me for *la chasse:* I did not shoot.

Chapter 15

I remember hearing the midday Angelus sound from the village church, and soon afterwards voices from the château, as the gardener Joseph, and I think Robert with him, emerged from a side door and made their way towards the outbuildings. I was concealed by the low branches of the cedar tree, and they did not see me. When they had gone I went through the gate in the wall to the grounds beyond, and walked swiftly across the moat to the path beneath the chestnuts, and so to one of the long rides and away into the woods. It did not matter to me where I went, or how far; all I knew was that I had to put myself out of the range of call and somehow decide upon a course of action. The most obvious one was to feign illness—a sudden dizziness, or mysterious pains in my limbs—yet to do so would demand the immediate attention of Dr. Lebrun, who would surely know at once that there was nothing wrong. The mere pretext of a chill, of some vague malaise, would never serve. The seigneur of St. Gilles would not take to his bed on the day of the big shoot because of stomach-ache. Besides, it was not only tomorrow that made the nightmare. It was today, at two o'clock, with Robert coming for orders once again.

I wondered if I could make Françoise the excuse, but it was too much out of character. However sick his wife might be, it would not matter to Jean de Gué. I could, of course, take the car and disappear, make this my exit from the masquerade. Nothing prevented me from doing so, at any hour of the day or night. Now, perhaps, was the moment. I had survived up to the present because nothing had really constituted a challenge. The relationships within the family had not defeated me, or the intimacy without, or the tricks of language, the hazards of unaccustomed routine, the impossibilities of business and finance. I had plunged into this unknown world like a reckless walker into a morass, each step

177

taking him deeper, each wild flounder committing him more inescapably. But, more fortunate than such a man, if I felt myself held fast and sucked into the depths, I had only to throw myself backwards to be free, to return to the past and take on the self discarded in Le Mans.

I crossed and recrossed the rides, now deep in the dark woods, then suddenly emerging from the shadows, each ride converging in its turn upon the statue in the centre, surrounding it with compass points of light. I could see no way out of my dilemma, no real answer to the ridiculous situation in which I found myself, except by admitting defeat.

I walked slowly down one of the rides to the statue and stood beside it, looking towards the château. The sky had clouded. There was not the radiant blue of yesterday, and an autumn pallor masked a watery sun. The château itself looked grey and frigid on its plot of ground encircled by the moat, and although the long windows of the salon were thrown open they were not inviting: only darkness came from within. The black and white cattle cropped the grass by the dovecot, and a few yards away a bonfire smouldered, a tongue of flame rising now and again through a column of blue-grey smoke, the rank and melancholy smell of charred wet wood and sodden leaves coming towards me on a wisp of air.

I was filled increasingly with self-disgust. The sense of power and confidence had seeped away, and my likeness to Jean de Gué was nothing but a clown's covering, a ludicrous mask of paint and powder, already melting, falling away in strips, showing me to myself unchanged, the useless nonentity I had always been. A lifelong inability to handle weapons, to aim with effect at anything, was now to prove my downfall. Anyone with rudimentary training might have bluffed his way to glory by blazing away at everything on sight: I hadn't even the knowledge to do that. I knew the butt end from the barrel, but beyond that all was mystery.

I thought of the laughter of Jean de Gué, the laughter of anyone told suddenly of my predicament. Humiliation is not easy to bear, especially when it follows upon complacency. I had been very sure of myself driving away yesterday from Villars, with a picture in my mind of Béla feeding her birds on the balcony. I had been confident again this morning, not an hour ago, coming from the foundry with the contract in my pocket. Now I was deflated, the bubble of conceit exploded, lost in the air.

As if it were a symbol mocking me, Jean de Gué's watch, which I wore on my left wrist, suddenly fell to the ground, smashing the glass. I bent and picked it up. The strap had given—I should have noticed it was worn. Irritated by this new mishap, I walked slowly on, the watch in my hand, and I saw that the naked hands now stood at half past twelve. It was almost time for the midday meal, for sitting at the head of the table in the dining room, for facing the family, for giving my orders for the shoot. I came to the dovecot, and was protected now by its rounded walls, unseen from the château windows. Marie-Noel must have been playing here earlier, for her cardigan lay forgotten on the swing. I stood by the bonfire, stirring it with my foot, till the bitter, pungent smoke rose up and stung my eyes, and suddenly I was reminded of the well in front of the master's house in the *verrerie*. There were nettles here, too, and tangled grass, and Marie-Noel's swing looked as old and neglected as the well had done before the house. The rope had broken again and lay thrown down, useless as the links of the chain; and as I looked at it I saw in my mind's eye the well chain wrapped about a man's limp body, binding it, and the body thrust down the deep black hole of the well to water. I saw the group of men holding to the ironwork, looking down, and then suddenly, in fear and horror, seizing handful after handful of broken glass from the reject dumps behind the sheds, hurling the jagged pieces down into the dark water with the body, covering it, sinking it, until finally there was nothing left to see but the patch of night sky reflected in the water.

Another gust of smoke came from the bonfire, blown by a gust of wind, and, as suddenly as the image of the dead man's body had come to me, I knew what I was going to do. I waited for the smoke to drift, then tossed the watch I was holding into the fire. I saw it fall against a heap of glowing embers. Then I knelt down and thrust my hand amongst them until I had the watch. I cried out with the searing agony of pain and collapsed sideways onto the grass, clutching my hand, seizing leaves, grass, anything to cover the scorched flesh, while the broken watch lay forgotten beside me.

I lay a moment, waiting for the faintness to pass, and the retching that I could not prevent, and then, because of the intensity of the pain, I got to my feet and began to run towards the château. I had only one thought—to stop the pain, to get away from light, from air, into the darkness of the open windows. I remember stumbling across the threshold and falling onto the sofa, and seeing the staring, frightened face of Renée, and hearing her cry out; and then the darkness that I had sought was with me and about me, but the pain continued. I heard Renée call for Paul, and Paul for Gaston, and I was surrounded by questioning, anxious faces, trying to uncover the hand that I still held against me, shielded by my coat. But I could only rock backwards and forwards, shaking my head, unable to tell them to go away, to leave me alone, because there was only one thing with me, which was pain.

Gaston said, "We must find Mademoiselle Blanche," and Renée ran out of the room screaming for Blanche. I heard Paul say he was telephoning for the doctor, and I thought dimly, through the pain, that if only I could faint the pain would stop. Gaston was kneeling beside me, and he asked, "Have you cut yourself, Monsieur le Comte?" and I said, "No, burnt myself, you idiot," turning away from him, and thinking to myself that if I could swear and blaspheme in English it might help to ease the pain.

Then the others came back, crowding around me once more, the same words passing stupidly from one to the other. "He's burnt himself . . . it's his hand . . . he's burnt it . . . but where . . . but how?" Then the peering faces backed away and Blanche was there, kneeling where Gaston had knelt. She put out her hand to take mine, but I exclaimed, "No, it hurts too much." She said, "Hold him down," to Paul and Gaston, and they seized me by the shoulders and pinned me against the cushions. Blanche reached for my hand and covered it with something cool and cleansing, spattering the contents of a tube that splayed all over the seared back of my burnt hand. Then she put a bandage over it and fastened it loosely, and told the others that in a moment or two the pain would ease. I shut my eyes and heard the low hum of voices discussing me, always asking the same question—how could it have happened?—and slowly, very slowly, the agony began to be something that could be borne and eventually explained by the sufferer, who was no longer a focus point of pain but someone who had other limbs as well, another hand, a body, legs, eyes that could open at last and stare up at the people gathered about him.

"Is that better?" asked Paul, and I waited a moment and then said, "Yes, I think so," still uncertain, because the release from immediate pain was still too new. I saw that Marie-Noel had now joined the circle and was staring down at me, her eyes enormous in her small white face.

"Whatever did you do? What happened?" asked Renée, and beyond her was Gaston, troubled, unhappy, standing with a glass of brandy that I did not want.

"My watch fell off my wrist into the bonfire," I said, "the bonfire out there by the dovecot. I didn't want to lose it, so I bent to pick it up and burnt myself instead. My own fault entirely. An idiotic, senseless thing to do."

"Didn't you think what you were doing?" asked Renée.

"No," I said. "I didn't realise the fire was so hot."

"You must be completely crazy," said Paul. "You could have fished the watch out with a stick, any piece of wood by the bonfire."

"It never occurred to me."

"You must have been very close to the bonfire for it to have fallen off your wrist into the middle of it," said Renée.

"I was. The smoke got in my eyes. I couldn't see properly—that was part of the trouble."

"I've telephoned for Lebrun," said Paul. "He's coming out right away. The first thing he said was did Françoise know? I said no. He warned me she shouldn't be told. Just the kind of thing to upset her."

"I shall be all right," I said. "It's not hurting now. Blanche has worked wonders." I looked round for Blanche, but she had disappeared. She had taken away the pain and gone.

"One thing's evident," said Paul. "You'll be in no shape to shoot tomorrow."

"That's the first thing I thought of," I said.

They stared at me in sympathy. Gaston made a little clicking sound of vexation. "It's what you most enjoy, Monsieur le Comte."

I shrugged my shoulders. "It can't be helped," I said. "The rest of you will enjoy yourselves. Anyway, I saved the watch. It's out there somewhere in the ashes."

"All that trouble for a watch," said Renée. "I've never heard of anything so stupid, so unnecessary."

"And it's not even his gold one, Madame," said Gaston. "The gold one is still in Le Mans, being repaired. Monsieur le Comte has been wearing his old steel watch, the one Monsieur Duval gave him on his twenty-first birthday."

"That's why I didn't want to lose it," I said. "Sentiment."

There was an odd silence. Nobody said anything. Gaston put the glass of brandy down on the table, and after a moment Paul offered me a cigarette.

"Anyway," he said, "it's a good job it wasn't worse. The back of your hand caught the damage—you haven't even singed your coat sleeve."

Marie-Noel hadn't said a word all the time. I was sorry if I had frightened her. "Don't look so solemn," I smiled. "I'm all right now. I'll get up in a minute."

"Here's your watch," she said.

She had been holding her hands behind her back. Now she advanced and held out the watch, blackened by the fire. I had not noticed her run to find it. She must have done it in a moment.

"Where did you find it?" asked Renée.

"In the ashes," she said.

I held out my left hand for the watch and put it in my pocket. "Now let's forget it," I said. "I've caused enough commotion for one morning. Why don't you start lunch? It must be after one." I thought a moment. "Françoise will wonder why I haven't been in to see her," I said. "Better say I'm out with Robert, and am not yet back. And somebody stop that woman Charlotte from blabbing everything to Maman upstairs. Now clear out and leave me. I don't want any lunch. I'll see Lebrun in here when he comes."

I was now tired, and sick inside. My hand hurt in a different way, not so much physically as in my mind, which was vividly aware of the raw tender flesh. I closed my eyes again and they all went away. Some time later there was a bell, and in a minute or two the elderly bearded face of Dr. Lebrun was looking at me, pince-nez on the bridge of a large nose, side by side with the impassive Blanche.

"What have you been doing to yourself?" he asked. "They tell me you've been playing the fool with a bonfire."

Resigned to it now, and bored, I went over the story again, and to justify myself I pulled the blackened watch out of my pocket.

"Well, well," he said, "we all do foolish things now and again. Let's have a look at the damage. Mademoiselle Blanche, just unwrap this for me."

Blanche, cool and calm, took my hand again between hers, and together they looked at the hand. The doctor anointed it with some ointment he had brought and did it up again in a kind of bandaged packet, and to my intense relief they had neither of them hurt me. The pain was with me, but no longer active.

"There," said the doctor, "now you'll be more comfortable. It's not too serious, I assure you, and in a few days you won't be able to see where you hurt it. These dressings to be renewed night and morning, Mademoiselle Blanche, and I think we shall have no trouble. What concerns me most is that you won't be able to shoot tomorrow."

"Don't worry," I said. "You'll do quite as well without me."

"I'm afraid not," he smiled. "You're like the mainspring of the watch there. If that's out of action the rest of the works collapse."

I saw Blanche looking at the watch, and from the watch to me. Our eyes met, and there was something questing, searching, in her expression that made me feel, during one instant of fear, that she knew the truth, and this was the reason why she had come to bandage my hand and relieve me of pain—because she did it to a stranger. Guilt made me drop my eyes, and then she turned to the doctor and asked him to come with her to the dining room and have something to eat. He thanked her, saying he would follow her in a moment.

She left us alone and he began to talk about Françoise,

183

repeating what he had told me on the telephone. I tried to absorb what he was saying, but while he talked, emphasising his points with his pince-nez, stabbing them in the air, I was still thinking about Blanche and the expression in her eyes, and wondering how and why she could have penetrated my disguise. Or was it after all imagination on my part?

Gaston appeared with a tray of food, but I waved him away.

"This evening you will feel like eating, not now," said the doctor, and he gave me some tablets from his bag with instructions about one every two hours, and two if my hand pained me, and then went off to join the others having lunch.

Gaston hovered about me still, a rug for my legs, another cushion, and I thought how his devotion and concern would turn to bewilderment and then to disbelief and finally to contempt if he should know the truth—that I was a shadow mimicking his master and then deliberately maiming myself for fear of discovery. It would be beyond his comprehension, and that of all of them at St. Gilles. People did not behave like that. What was the point of the deception if it brought so much trouble to the deceiver? What did he gain by it? Here was the point indeed. What did I gain? I lay back on the sofa, looking at my bandaged hand, and suddenly I laughed.

"You are feeling better, then?" said Gaston, his kind face broadening in sympathy, laughter a release for both of us.

"Better from what?"

"Why, better from your burn, Monsieur le Comte," he said. "It's no longer hurting you as it did?"

"It hurts in a different way," I told him, "as if it wasn't I who had burnt my hand, but somebody else."

"Pain can be like that," he said, "or else you feel the hurt in another spot. You remember my brother who lost his leg in the war? He always said he felt the pain in his arm. My grandmother was Breton. In the old days they wished pain or illness onto animals. If someone had smallpox they took a fowl and hung it up in the room alive. And at once the sickness left its human victim and went to the fowl, and in twenty-four hours it was rotted, dead, and the sick person

184

had recovered. It might be a good idea if I sent for a fowl and hung it up beside Monsieur le Comte."

"I'm not so sure," I said, "it might work the other way round. The fowl could be diseased and pass its sickness on to me—if not smallpox, something equally disagreeable."

The question was, which of us had escaped, Jean de Gué or myself?

When the family had finished lunch they came flocking back into the room to enquire after me, and I put the second part of my plan into action. "Paul," I said, "you can arrange everything for tomorrow with Robert. Now I'm out of it I prefer to be quit altogether. You can organise the whole thing between you."

"Oh, nonsense," exclaimed Paul. "You'll be feeling more like it in an hour or so. You know you've always done it. If Robert and I run it you'll only criticise us and say we've wrecked it."

"I won't," I said, "you go ahead. If I can't shoot I'm not interested."

I got up from the sofa, telling them that I wanted to rest alone in the library, and I could tell by their faces that they believed my decision came from bitter disappointment, and also because I was still in pain. I saw Renée draw the doctor aside and question him, and he shook his head. "No, no, I assure you, he's quite all right. It's just a question of shock. A burn like that is a very painful thing. . . ." You're right, I thought, especially when it's self-inflicted and totally unnecessary. For, my first panic at the prospect of the shoot over, I knew that all I need have done was to say that I did not want to take part. They would have swallowed it, they would swallow anything, because it never entered their heads for a moment that I was not the man they thought.

As I went into the library the heavy sloth of afternoon descended upon the château, and I realised then that my penance worked both ways. I was spared the preparations for the shoot, only to doom myself to inactivity, and after "resting" I should be at the mercy of the enquiries I wanted to avoid. To make the hours pass I pushed a chair over by the desk and, struggling one-handed with the drawer, pulled out the photograph album once again. This time I had no interruption. I could take my time, and after looking again through the earlier snapshots I passed on in leisurely fashion to the adult pictures. I noticed things that had escaped me in my previous hurried glimpse. Maurice Duval appeared quite early in the groups at the *verrerie*. He was standing in a back row, a youngish man, in a group that had the date 1925 beside it; and then, rather like house groups at school, he advanced year by year to a more prominent position, until, towards the end of the album, he was promoted to a chair beside the Comte de Gué himself, looking confident, at ease, the captain of the house beside the housemaster. I liked his face. It was strong, wise, trustworthy, a face that surely would command affection and respect.

I closed the album and pushed it back into the drawer. Perhaps there were others, but with one hand useless I could not rummage for them. I still had the new contract in my pocket—I wondered what Maurice Duval would have thought of it . . . I must have slept in the chair, because suddenly it was six o'clock, and it was not Paul or Renée or the child who had come to disturb me but the curé. He had switched on the light beside the desk and was peering down at me, his old head nodding in concern.

"There now, I've woken you. I didn't intend to do that," he said. "I just wanted to make sure you were not in pain."

I told him all was well and the sleep had done me good.

"Madame Jean has also slept," he said, "and your mother too. All the invalids at the château have been resting quietly. You have nothing to worry about. I took it upon myself to explain about your little accident, making light of it, as I thought best. You don't mind my having done that?"

"On the contrary," I said, "I'm very grateful to you."

"Good. They are neither of them anxious, only sorry that you won't be about to shoot tomorrow."

"That's nothing. I'm perfectly resigned to it."

"Now you are being brave. I know what it must mean to you."

"I'm not brave, Monsieur le Curé. Quite the opposite. A physical and moral coward, to be perfectly frank."

He smiled at me, still nodding. "Come now," he said, "it's not as bad as that. Sometimes it's a sort of indulgence to

186

think the worst of ourselves. We say, 'Now I have reached the bottom of the pit, now I can fall no further,' and it is almost a pleasure to wallow in the darkness. The trouble is, it's not true. There is no end to the evil in ourselves, just as there is no end to the good. It's a matter of choice. We struggle to climb, or we struggle to fall. The thing is to discover which way we're going."

"It's easier to fall," I said. "The laws of gravitation prove it."

"Perhaps," he said. "I don't know. The love of God doesn't always concern itself with the laws of gravitation, though both are miracles. Now I think we might both give thanks that you were not more seriously burnt by the fire."

He knelt down. He was a big, heavy man, and it was not easy for him. He folded his hands, bent his head and began to pray, his head nodding all the while, and thanked God for preserving me from harm, for sparing me pain, and added finally that, because I liked the shoot so much and to miss it was such a deprivation, would God in His goodness send His grace to me as consolation, so that I would not consider the accident as a bitter disappointment but as a blessing?

As he struggled to his knees I thought about his analogy of the pit, and I wondered how much further I had to fall, and if the sense of shame that overwhelmed me was merely wallowing in darkness, as he had suggested. I got up from my chair and accompanied him to the hall, and watched him disappear across the terrace and down the steps to the drive. It was beginning to spit with rain, and he went off under an immense umbrella, like a bent gnome under a mushroom.

I had played the coward long enough: I could at least show the others that I was not in pain. I found Françoise sitting up in bed, reading *The Little Flower* to Marie-Noel. The curé had done his mission well. She was sympathetic but not concerned. She seemed to think I had singed my fingers and no more, and kept lamenting over and over again how disappointed I must be that I could not shoot, and how glad she was that it was not her fault, that it was not her delicate health that had caused the trouble.

Marie-Noel was oddly quiet and subdued. She did not

187

join in the conversation, but when her mother began to talk she took the book and went and sat in a corner, reading it to herself. My mishap must have worried her, and she had not yet got over it. I went downstairs for dinner, Charlotte having sent word that Madame la Comtesse had gone to bed early and was not to be disturbed—for which I was thankful, since it would not have been easy to answer her questions.

Paul and Renée were both full of the arrangements for the shoot, the time the guests were to arrive, the names of some of them, the plans for lunch at a farmhouse if it was wet. It was as though, in some fortunate way, my ridiculous action had given them purpose and authority. Paul obviously enjoyed his part of organiser, and Renée, with Françoise out of the way, saw herself, through Paul's promotion, suddenly acting hostess. She said something about receiving the guests on the terrace, wet or fine; she kept asking Paul if he had remembered this or forgotten that, reminding him that last year such-and-such a thing had not been done, referring to me for approval; and there was something touching about their enthusiasm and their keenness, like understudies cast at a moment's notice into leading rôles.

Blanche, after her swift ministration at midday, had relapsed once more into silence. She showed little interest in the arrangements for the following day, merely reminding us, as she rose from the table, that whether or not the guests met on the terrace at half past ten Mass was at nine, as usual. I wondered whether she had forgotten that Dr. Lebrun had asked her to dress my hand, and the same thought must have struck Renée, for as we passed into the salon she said, "If you want to go up early, Blanche, I can do Jean's hand. Where are the dressings?"

"I'm going to do it now," Blanche replied briefly, and in a moment she was back again with the dressings that the doctor had given her, and she put out her hand to take mine, still without a word to me.

When she had finished, she said good night to the others but not to me, and Renée, settling herself on the sofa, remarked, "Isn't Marie-Noel coming down for her game of dominoes?"

"Not tonight," said Blanche. "I'm going to read to her upstairs."

She left the room, and after a moment Renée said, "How unusual for the child to miss her dominoes."

"She was upset about Jean," said Paul, picking up one newspaper and throwing me the other. "I noticed it at the time. You'd better watch out, or she'll start seeing visions again. I'm not sure that giving her a life of St. Thérèse de Lisieux was a very sensible thing to do."

The evening wore on, the newspapers our distraction, and now and again Renée glanced at me and smiled, the smile of sympathy, of collusion, framing her lips in the silent question, "Does it hurt? Is it any easier?"—to show me, I suppose, that because of my injury I was now pardoned for my neglect of yesterday. I was worried about the child. She might have taken upon herself some new trick of martyrdom, strangling herself with an iron collar or lying upon nails, and at half past nine I said good night to Paul and Renée and went upstairs. I made straight for the little room in the turret and opened the door. The room was in darkness, so I fumbled for the switch and turned it on. The child was kneeling at her prie-dieu, clutching a rosary, and I realised I had stumbled upon some meditation.

"I'm sorry," I said. "I'll come back when you've finished."

She turned blank eyes towards me, holding up her hand for silence, and I stood there waiting, uncertain what I was meant to do, whether to switch off the light or leave it on. But in a moment or two she crossed herself and laid her rosary at the feet of the Madonna, then stood up and climbed into bed.

"I was doing my Stations of the Cross," she said. "It puts me in the right state for Mass tomorrow. Aunt Blanche always says it helps to do the Stations if one is thinking about something else."

"What were you thinking about?" I asked.

"This morning I was thinking about the shoot and what fun it would be," she said, "which I'm sure was a sin in itself. The rest of the day I've been thinking about you."

Her eyes were more puzzled than concerned. I was relieved. I did not want her to have been frightened. "You needn't

189

worry about me," I said, tucking her up with one hand. "My hand is much better tonight, and Dr. Lebrun told me it would be quite all right in a few days. It was a silly thing to happen, the watch falling off—I ought to have remembered that the strap was loose."

"But it didn't fall off," she said.

"What do you mean?"

She stared up at me, turning red, and began picking at the bedclothes in embarrassment. "I was in the dovecot," she said. "I had climbed up to the top, and was looking through that little gap beside the hole where the pigeons go in and out. I saw you come down from the ride swinging the watch in your hand. I was going to call out to you, but you looked so serious I didn't like to. Then you stood a few minutes by the bonfire, and suddenly you threw the watch right in the middle of it. There was no smoke getting in your eyes or anything. You did it on purpose. Why?"

Chapter 16

I sat down on the chair beside the bed. It was easier than standing up. The gap between us lessened, and I was someone on her level, not just an adult talking to a child. I realised she must have interpreted my action as a deliberate deed to rid myself of the watch, and then, regretting it, had burnt myself retrieving it. Self-inflicted pain had not occurred to her, yet it was something she would readily understand.

"The watch was really an excuse," I said. "I didn't want to shoot tomorrow. I didn't know how to get out of it, and then, standing by the bonfire, the idea came to me to burn my hand. It was simple, but stupid. I did it rather too effectively, and it hurt more than I intended."

She listened calmly. She took up my bandaged hand and examined it.

"Why didn't you pretend to be ill?" she asked.

"It wouldn't have worked. People would have realised nothing was the matter. A burnt hand is genuine."

"Yes," she said, "it's never pleasant to be found out. Now you have mortification and have learnt your lesson. May I see the watch again?" I felt in my pocket and gave it to her. "Poor thing," she said, "he's black, and he has no glass. He's had his day. Everyone was wondering at lunch why you should take so much trouble to rescue him. I kept my secret to myself. I did not tell them that before you tried to rescue him you had thrown him into the fire. It was rather a shame to make the watch suffer. Didn't you think about that?"

"Not exactly," I said. "I was a bit muddled in my mind. I was thinking about someone who had been shot, murdered, a long time ago, and in a flash I'd thrown the watch in the fire and burnt my hand pulling it out again. It was as quick as that."

She nodded. "I suppose you were thinking about Monsieur Duval," she said.

I stared at her, surprised. "As a matter of fact I was."

"Very natural," she said, "since he gave you the watch and he was shot. The two things go together."

"What do you know about Monsieur Duval?" I asked.

"He was master at the *verrerie*," she said, "and according to Germaine some say he was a patriot and some say he was a traitor. But he had a horrid death and I'm forbidden to talk about it. Especially to you and to Aunt Blanche, so I never do." She handed me back the watch.

"Who told you not to talk about it?" I asked.

"Gran'mie," she said.

"When?"

"Oh, I don't know. Ages ago, when I first heard the story from Germaine. I was telling it to Gran'mie and she said, 'Shut up. Never repeat servants' gossip. It's a string of lies.' She was very angry, and she's never talked about it since. Tell me, Papa, why don't you want to shoot tomorrow?"

Here was the question, and I did not know how to answer it.

"I just don't," I said. "I have no reason."

"You must have a reason," she insisted. "It's the thing you like doing best."

"No," I said, "not any more. I don't want to shoot."

She considered me gravely, her large eyes suddenly and

191

rather terribly like the child Blanche in the family album.

"Is it because you don't want to kill?" she asked. "Is it suddenly a sin to you to take any life, even a bird's?"

I should have told her instantly no, that my reason for not wanting to shoot was because I was afraid of shooting badly, but instead I hesitated, seeking a loophole for escape, and my hesitation was taken as assent. I could see, by the glowing excitement in her eyes, that she was weaving some fantasy in her mind about her father being sickened suddenly of all blood, all slaughter, and that he had burnt his hand so that he should not be tempted to kill again.

"Perhaps," I said.

As soon as I had spoken I realised my mistake. I had not deliberately lied to her before. Now I was doing so. I was building for her a false image of Jean de Gué, giving her what she asked for so that I might be spared the truth myself.

She knelt up in bed, and, careful not to touch my bandaged hand, put her arms round my neck. "I think you've shown great courage," she said. "It's just like the verse in St. Matthew: 'Wherefore, if thy hand or thy foot offend thee, cut them off, and cast them from thee; it is better for thee to enter into life halt or maimed, rather than, having two hands, or two feet, to be cast into everlasting fire. And if thine eye offend thee, pluck it out . . .' I'm glad it wasn't your eye; that would have been much more difficult. As it is, your hand will heal, but still, it was the intention that matters, or so Aunt Blanche always says. It's a pity we can't tell her, though I'd rather we kept it as a secret between us both."

"Listen," I told her, "there's no need to make a great mystery of this business. I burnt my hand, I can't shoot, I don't want to shoot, and there's an end to it. Now forget it."

She smiled, and bent down and kissed my bandaged hand. "I promise I won't mention it," she said, "but you can't prevent me from thinking about it. If you see me looking at you tomorrow in a very particular way, it will mean I am thinking of your great act of humiliation."

"It wasn't a great act. It was a foolish one."

"Fools are wise in the eyes of God. Have you ever read about St. Rosa of Lima?"

"Did she put her hand in a bonfire too?"

"No, she wore a great iron belt and never took it off, and it bit so deeply into her that all the flesh went bad. She wore it for years, and gloried in it. Papa, Aunt Blanche would like me to be a nun. She says I shall never find happiness in this world, and I believe she is right. I think so more especially now I am reading about the Little Flower. What do you think?"

I looked at her. She was standing up now, small and serious in her white nightgown, her hands crossed.

"I don't know," I said. "I think you're a bit young to decide. Just because Aunt Blanche hasn't found happiness in the world, it doesn't mean you won't. It all depends what you mean by happiness. It's not a crock of gold at the foot of a tree. Ask Monsieur le Curé, don't ask me."

"I have. He says that if I pray hard enough, one of these days God will show me the answer. But Aunt Blanche never stops praying, and she's years older than I am and hasn't got the answer yet."

The church clock struck ten. I was tired. I did not want to discuss the spiritual state of Blanche, or Marie-Noel, or myself.

"Oh well," I said, "perhaps you'll be luckier than she is, and know the answer sooner."

She sighed and settled herself in bed. "Life is a great problem," she said.

"I agree."

"Do you think it would be easier to be somebody else?" she asked.

"That's what I'd like to find out."

"I wouldn't mind being another child if I could be sure of getting you as my father," she said.

"You're wrong," I told her. "The whole thing is an illusion. Good night."

Oddly, her devotion depressed me. I turned out her light and went downstairs to the dressing room and the camp bed. It was not my burnt hand that prevented me from sleeping—that didn't hurt any more—but my realisation that the façade was everything, the skin and semblance of Jean de Gué all that any of them wanted. César, who had known

193

me for a stranger, had been the only one to recognise the fact and yet be reconciled—he had permitted me to pat him this morning, and had wagged his tail.

I slept restlessly for a few hours, and was woken by Gaston throwing back the shutters to a grey damp morning with a thin drizzle. Instantly the whole day loomed before me—the shoot, the guests, the ritual of the hours to come, as foreign to me as a tribal feast—and it seemed to me desperately important that I should let none of the family down, that I should not disgrace the de Gué or the château of St. Gilles, not because I had any respect for the absent seigneur but because something within me acknowledged tradition. I was aware of footsteps in the corridor and voices on the stairs, and the church bell began to ring for Mass. I thanked heaven I had shaved and had only to struggle into the dark suit laid out for me—and there was a tap on the door and Marie-Noel came in and was able to help me.

"Why are you so late?" she asked. "Is your hand worse?"

"No," I said, "I'd forgotten the time." Together we went into the bedroom to wish Françoise good morning, and then downstairs and onto the terrace. We could see the little family party going on ahead—they had passed through the gateway and were already crossing the bridge, Paul and Renée and Blanche, and on Blanche's arm, huge, massive and bent, a black figure that I did not recognise. I was about to question the child when it suddenly dawned upon me that there was the comtesse herself, whom I had only seen seated or in bed. The two black figures, one so large and dominating, leaning upon the other, stiff and upright beside her, looked like silhouettes cut out against a paper background of hillside and ancient church, the whole framed in a wan grey sky.

We caught them up and I offered the mother my other arm so that she could lean upon both Blanche and myself. I saw that she was even taller than I had thought: we were of equal height but her massive frame made her seem taller still.

"What's all this about your burning yourself?" she asked. "Nobody ever tells me the truth." We had reached the timbered entrance of the church as I finished my story and the bell ceased ringing. "I don't believe it," she said. "No one but an imbecile would have done such a thing. Or have you suddenly become one?"

A little knot of village people standing in the porch drew back to let us pass, and as we went through and up to our places, the comtesse still leaning upon Blanche and myself, I thought how incongruous it was that the family of de Gué came here to pray and ask forgiveness of their sins, when two members of it had not spoken to each other for fifteen years. The little twelfth-century church, so worn and simple without, the lichened stonework plain and unadorned, was garish within, smelling of varnish like a Methodist chapel, the windows violet-blue, while near to the chancel steps a doll-faced Madonna, wearing a crown too large for her, stared down surprised at the infant Jesus in her arms.

I had thought that once inside the church, and taking part in Mass, I might forget the masquerade and become the seigneur of St. Gilles indeed. Instead, a latent sense of guilt rose to confuse me. I was more than ever conscious of deception, conscious that I was tricking not so much the family I knelt beside, who were already familiar to me and whose faults I knew and somehow shared, but the villagers in the church of whom I knew nothing. More important still, I was tricking the good old curé with his pink cherubic face, whose prayers encompassed me, but whose ample form, topped by the nodding head, reminded me suddenly and irreverently of a witch doctor in an African scene, so that I had to avert my eyes and cover them with my hand, as if overcome by fervour.

I was caught between two moods—the one of self-abasement for my deception, making me feel that every word of the Mass must surely be a solemn declaration of my fault; and the other of intense awareness of the discomforts suffered by those beside me—of the mother, groaning audibly as she shifted on her knees, of Paul, with a smoker's morning cough, of Renée, whose sallow face was pallid without powder, of Marie-Noel, slavishly imitating every action of her aunt Blanche, bowing lower and lower over her clasped hands. Never had the Mass seemed so long, so pregnant with inner meaning, yet heard with such lack of grace, and when it was

195

over and we shuffled down the aisle, the comtesse leaning heavily on my arm, the first words she muttered were, "I suppose that fool Renée is going to doll herself up like a parrot because Françoise is in bed. I've a good mind to stay downstairs and spoil her fun."

In the porch Blanche came to take her other arm, and the three of us went slowly down the hill back to the château. So we entered the domain, brother and sister mute on either side of the mother, who professed herself delighted to see the rain, for the day would be a failure, the guests soaked to the skin, Renée in popinjay feathers bedraggled if she put her head out of doors, while Paul, in charge of the *chasse*, would make a fool of himself from first to last. "And so," she said, squeezing my arm, "you'll have the laugh of them after all."

We were on the terrace by half past ten, standing in mizzling rain as the first cars drove through the gateway. Poor Renée, her innocent plan thwarted, was hidden from view by the massive figure of her mother-in-law, who, leaning on a stick, a great shawl covering her shoulders, stood in the place of honour at the entrance to the château, regally offering a word of welcome to each as he arrived. Because her appearance was so unexpected, even the burnt hand of the seigneur was passed off as a small mishap, and the absence of Françoise not even noticed. Madame la Comtesse was "receiving"; nothing else counted.

The transformation was complete. I could hardly believe that the woman who stood here holding court, surrounded by every sort of guest from the neighbouring estates, was the one I had seen crouching in her chair upstairs or lying grey and exhausted in the great double bed. Every remark she made held in its tail a sting about the day's proceedings. "Better pick chestnuts and leave your gun behind," to one, and to another, "If you want some exercise, take my terriers for a walk. They'll give you more sport in ten minutes than Paul will in five hours."

I stood apart, not wishing to be involved in her malice, but my silence was misconstrued and taken for irritation at my accident. My reiteration of "Don't ask me anything—ask Paul" was obviously thought to be mockery of his efforts, and

I could see the impression spreading that the day would be a hit-and-miss affair, with nobody in charge and the whole thing slightly ridiculous. Paul, nervy and harassed, was looking at his watch, anxious to be off, his schedule already behindhand, when I felt someone touch my elbow. It was the man in overalls who lived in the cottage by the garage, and he had César by his side.

"Here is César, Monsieur le Comte," he said. "You had forgotten him."

"I'm not shooting today," I said. "Take him to Monsieur Paul."

The dog, excited to be loose and sensing the sport in store for him, roamed round searching for his master, and took no notice when Paul called him to heel. In his bewilderment he charged a rival, a well-trained retriever squatting sedately upon its haunches, and immediately there was an uproar, a fury of growling and snarling, the retriever's elderly owner shouting at the top of his voice, and Paul, livid, calling to me, "Can't you control your dog?" The gardener Joseph and I hurled ourselves upon the unfortunate César, but I could do little with one hand. Somehow we controlled the dog at last and had him leashed, everyone laughing at the ridiculous affair—except the owner of the dog and Paul himself, who as he passed me said, "Another of your jokes, I suppose? It amuses you to start the whole day wrong by letting your half-trained dog run wild."

There was nothing I could do. César's total disregard of me did not look like disobedience on his part, but amused and cynical indifference on mine.

"So you won't bother to come with us?" someone said.

"Not immediately. I'll follow later," I replied, and they began to move off in scattered groups, laughing and shrugging their shoulders, one or two glancing up at the heavy rain clouds and grimacing as though to say, "The show's a failure. We might as well all go home."

As they disappeared I turned to the comtesse and said, "All right. You set out to ruin the day for Paul and Renée, and you've done it. I hope you're proud of yourself."

She stared at me without comprehension, her eyes ex-

pressionless. "What do you mean?" she asked. "I don't understand you."

"You understand me very well," I said. "Here was the
one chance for Paul and Renée to show some sort of authority,
and you deliberately stood in their way, making a mockery
of the whole thing. No one spoke to Renée, Paul was ignored,
the day is as good as finished for them both. What sort of
sport the rest will have, God only knows."

Her face turned suddenly grey, whether from shock or
anger I could not tell. I had thought we were alone, but
Charlotte was waiting for her just inside the hall, and she
came forward now and took her arm, and the pair of them
turned and began to climb the stairs without a word. There
was no sign of Renée, no sign of Blanche; only the child
remained as second witness to the scene, and she looked
away from me awkwardly, her face flushed, pretending she
had not heard.

I had lost my temper playing another man's part, and it
was something he would never have done. He would have
laughed with his mother, encouraging her, had he found
himself in my position. I knew that what had angered me in
truth was that the situation would never have arisen had
Jean de Gué been there. If some accident had prevented him
from taking an active part he would have directed the shoot
just the same. It was not the mother's fault that the day was
ruined, but mine.

Marie-Noel stood first on one foot and then on the other.
She was dressed in macintosh and hood for walking, and
she must have hoped that both of us were to follow the
others and watch.

"Is your hand hurting?" she asked.

"No."

"I thought it must be, and that was why you didn't bother
much with the guests. I suppose you're sorry now not to be
shooting?"

"I'm not sorry. Only sick of the whole mess-up."

"Gran'mie will be ill now. She'll have one of her bad turns.
Why were you so cross with her? She only did it for you."

It was no good. All our motives were false. I had tried to
do the right thing in the wrong way, or the wrong thing in

the right way—I did not know which. My plan had not worked, and neither had the mother's. Even the dog was in disgrace because he had been given no directions.

"Where's your aunt Renée?" I asked the child.

"She went upstairs. Her hair was getting spoilt. She also looked as if she was going to cry."

"Tell her Gaston shall take us all in the car to join the *chasseurs*."

Her face brightened and she ran off.

I asked Gaston to bring round the car, and saw, to my relief, that he was putting a case of wine into the back. The best solution for the day, so far as everybody was concerned, seemed to be refuge in drink. I looked across the drive, and Renée and the child were walking towards us, and with them César, wagging his great tail.

"We don't want the dog," I called.

They stopped, surprised. "You'll want César for the birds, Papa," cried Marie-Noel.

"No," I said. "Since I'm not shooting there's no need to bring him. I can't manage him with one hand."

"You don't have to," the child said. "He always obeys your command. He didn't this morning because you never made him. Come on, César."

"Hasn't he a lead?" said Renée. "Where's his lead?"

I gave in. I could not argue; the day was out of my control. I climbed into the back of the Renault, with the dog on one side of me and the child on the other, Renée in the front and Gaston driving. As we jolted over a rough cart track to the woods, and I swayed against César, a mutter rose in his throat, forerunner to a growl, and I wondered how long his natural dignity would keep him courteous, and how soon an affront to his comfort would make him turn.

"What's wrong with César?" asked Renée, looking over her shoulder. "What does he keep growling for?"

"Papa's teasing him," said the child, "aren't you, Papa?"

"No, by God, I'm not," I said.

"Half-trained dogs get so excited," said Renée. "Don't forget he's only three."

"Joseph remarked on his behaviour two days ago," said Gaston. "He has growled at Monsieur le Comte several times."

"What shall we do if he goes mad?" asked Marie-Noel.

"He won't go mad," I said, "but somebody's got to see that he's kept on his lead."

Suddenly the car stopped, and we found ourselves quite near to the *chasseurs*, who were spread out in a thin line along the ride. We climbed out of the car, and I knew instinctively that it was a mistake for me to have come at all, for I hadn't the faintest notion what I ought to do next. Worse still, I saw that my instructions about César had not been followed. He was loose, roaming around as he had done in the drive, in a vain search for his master.

"Come here, César," I called. The dog took no notice. He was running along the line, his progress accompanied by angry shouts of "Catch that dog!", bewildered not to be claimed, and Renée made a click of disapproval. "Really, Jean, you ought to control him better."

"I knew it was a mistake to bring him," I said. "Marie-Noel, run and fetch him."

She was about to do so when there came shouts from within the wood, a whirring sound of flight, and the birds were over our heads. Suddenly the air was filled with the banging of guns, and the bodies of birds came rocketing down. I ducked instinctively, closing my eyes, a townsman out of his milieu, untrained to death in the field.

"What's the matter—are you faint?" asked Renée, but even as I straightened myself César, forgetting all he had ever been taught, dashed forward unbidden to retrieve the nearest bird, which surely, so his dog mind must have told him, would be his absent master's prey. As he did so, he ran headlong into his enemy of the terrace, the well-trained retriever belonging to the man on my right, whose bird it presumably was, and before the strangled summons "César!" could rise in my throat the hideous battle between them started once again. The retriever's master, a little old fellow in an out-at-elbows jacket and battered tweed hat, screamed at me, purple in the face, "Call off your dog!" and the three of us, Renée, Marie-Noel and I, flung ourselves into the mêlée of infuriated animals, joined now by a third. The *chasseur*, hysterical with rage, whirled away from us to fire at a couple of latecomers who now winged their way above us, but in his wild emotion he missed them both so that they swerved and dipped to safety in some cover far behind.

He turned to us, pale as death and almost speechless with fury. "What are we invited here for?" he yelled. "To be made fun of? That's the second time you've set your dog on mine. I'm going home."

César, secured at last, was dragged from the scene of action by Renée and the child, and now the other *chasseurs*, drawn by the sound of the barking dogs and the violent shouting of their neighbour, came flocking round to see what had occurred. Paul himself, appearing suddenly from the far end of the ride, ruffled, anxious, arrived in time to see his guest, still purple in the face, his gun under his arm and his dog limping behind, stalk off determinedly along the ride towards the road.

"What's wrong with the marquis?" called Paul. "I placed him there on purpose. It's the position he likes best. Wasn't he pleased?"

Out of the sea of faces I saw one I recognised. It was the fellow I had seen driving a car near the station in Le Mans, the first to mistake my identity. He was grinning. The débâcle of the drive seemed to amuse him.

"It was Jean playing the fool," he said. "I saw him as the birds came over. He dodged and ducked to amuse your wife, and then set César on to retrieve the marquis's bird and to fight old Justin. I shouldn't think the marquis will ever speak to either of you again."

Paul turned to me, his face white. "What's the idea?" he asked. "Is it because you can't have any fun yourself that you want to ruin the day for everyone else?"

Renée, mistakenly, spoke in my defence. "Don't be so unfair," she stormed. "Of course Jean was not playing the fool. His hand was hurting him—he nearly fainted. As for the dog, he got completely out of control. There's something the matter with him—he's turning savage."

"Then he'd better be put down," said Paul. "And if Jean feels ill, why did he come out at all?"

The guests drifted away discreetly. Nobody wished to listen in to a family row. The man from Le Mans winked at me, and shrugged his shoulders. I could see Dr. Lebrun hurrying down the ride in our direction.

"What is it?" I heard him say, his voice concerned. "Is it true that the Marquis de Plessis-Braye has shot himself through the foot?"

Paul uttered an exclamation and went off in pursuit of his outraged guest, whose stumpy figure was plodding steadily towards the distant lane.

"I think we too had better go home," I said to Renée, but her face fell, and so did the child's. Must I spoil their day also?

"We've only watched one drive," said Renée. "Surely you're not going to take any notice of Paul?"

"You both stay," I said. "I've had enough. Here, give me the dog."

I seized poor César's leash, and the dog, aware of disgrace yet scenting heaven knows what wounded prey that had dragged itself into the woods to die, leapt forward in a sudden bound, nearly tearing my arm out of its socket, and we plunged on, the pair of us, into a copse as thick and black as a witch's lair. I thought I heard a warning shout from Paul, but there was nothing I could do about it: my fate was linked to César's and his to mine, and we went off together through the wood, until, breathless and exhausted, we collapsed together upon a heap of cones. He watched me with a canine grin, saliva dripping from his jaws, and then, seeing he was neither beaten nor sworn at, turned his back on me and began to lick the wounds sustained in battle.

I lit a cigarette with a sigh, and, leaning back against a tree, wondered how far we were from St. Gilles. There was no sound of man or gun or bird, nothing but the light and dismal patter of the rain. Presently, damp and stiff, my bandaged hand starting to throb, I dragged myself to my feet, and with my hellhound in tow started off once more through the fastness of the wood, feeling, as the poet did before me, that my companion would be with me through the nights and through the days and down the arches of the years, and I should never be rid of him.

There was no break in the weeping sky to give direction.

I could not tell whether we walked north or south, east or west, and César was no help to me. Still leashed, he trotted at my side as docile as a poodle, stopping when I stopped, suiting his pace to mine. Suddenly he stiffened, and almost under my feet a pheasant rose and flew in alarm into the undergrowth ahead. As we scrambled through a belt of narrowing trees another bird took off, and yet another, for we must have inadvertently stumbled upon some hiding place or lair. In the distance I could hear shouts and then a shot, but away to the left of me, and the startled birds were swerving to my right.

Then I saw, some little way ahead, that at last the trees were clearing. We were coming to another of those broad rides traversing the woods which I had hoped to find before. We stumbled onto it, wet, bedraggled, as covered with leaves and brushwood as a poacher and his cur. And I perceived, not twenty yards away, Paul and Robert staring at me, while posted down the ride, like sentinels on guard, the line of *chasseurs* waited in ignorance for the birds I had prematurely scattered.

Chapter 17

Gaston appeared from nowhere with the car. He also had the flask, last seen in the hotel bedroom at Le Mans and now refilled with cognac, which I swallowed humped on the back seat of the Renault. Through the misty windscreen I watched the disconsolate figures of the sportsmen, balked of their prey, turn and disappear once more through the belt of trees in hopeful quest of less elusive quarry. Gaston, devoted, anxious, peered into my face, suggesting that Dr. Lebrun should be summoned to attend me, but he read my symptoms wrongly. My hand was not hurting me, nor was I in a high fever: the cognac was the solace that I needed.

After a while, the flask emptied, we jolted once again over ruts and muddy ridges. I recollect a low farm building, the trackway beside it already filled with cars, and waiting to welcome me at the doorway the tenant of the farm, immense, red-faced, bucolic, and his chattering shrimp of a wife. They led me into a huge barn, and I barely had time to huddle in the far corner, screened from the open door, before the *chasseurs* entered, thirsty, tired and steamy wet, turning the barn to babel until the rafters rang. Servants from the château hastened round with the wine which Gaston had brought. I remember Renée on one side of me and the man from Le Mans upon the other, and Renée telling him in great detail the story of the bonfire, and explaining that ever since I had been in a state bordering upon delirium, and nobody understood it except herself. Scarcely had she finished when the man from Le Mans started chattering about high finance, coups on the Bourse, gambles successfully won. My head reeled. Here was the one man who might have helped me—surely he must be the one Béla had spoken of?—and I didn't even know his business or his name.

"I'm flying to London late tonight," he said. "The usual monthly trip. If there's anything I can do for you there, you know where to find me."

In my haze of alcohol, I thought for one crazy instant that he had plumbed my secret. I stared at him, shaken, then caught at his sleeve and said, "What are you getting at? What do you mean?"

"Exchange of pounds," he replied briefly. "If you have any English friends, I know how to work it. Easiest thing in the world."

"Friends?" I asked. "Indeed I have English friends," smiling foolishly, knowing myself secure. Of course he had not guessed, of course he did not realise what I meant. "I have a very good friend in London who lives near the British Museum," I said. "He'd exchange pounds for francs any day of the week, if he could get them." And because I was speaking of the self who sat beside him, and the joke seemed to me exquisitely funny, I added, "Give me a piece of paper and a pen."

He handed me his pocket diary and Biro, and laboriously I wrote my own name and address in block capitals, and gave the diary back to him in drunken solemnity, saying, "Any assistance you give this chap you'll be giving to me; we're closer than brothers." Then I burst out laughing, thinking him extremely stupid not to see the point. Next I was aware of someone touching my elbow. It was Marie-Noel, and she was saying, "Uncle Paul wants to know if you are going to say a few words, or shall he?" Before I could answer the financier was clapping vigorously, and suddenly the whole company was banging and stamping, and the financier was patting me on the shoulder, saying, "Go on, Jean, make a speech." In a haze of alcohol surrounded on all sides by a sea of faces, I thought, This is where I make my mark as seigneur of St. Gilles. I may have ruined the sport this morning, but now I am in form.

"*Mesdames et Messieurs,*" I began, "once again it is my pride and pleasure to welcome you upon this happy occasion, and although, alas, an accident has prevented me from taking an active part in the proceedings, at least I am consoled by the fact that my brother has deputised so well. It is not an easy thing to do, to take another's place, as I am perfectly aware. The truth of this was forced upon me only yesterday morning when I was down at the *verrerie* looking through the accounts." I pulled myself up. What the devil was I saying? The two identities were merging into one. "Be that as it may," I floundered, "I am not here to talk about the *verrerie* but about shooting . . ."

I felt someone jogging my elbow—it was the financier, scarlet in the face, making signs to me to finish, murmuring for my ear alone, "Have you gone crazy, you idiot?" In front of me were the other faces, puzzled, uneasy, and it dawned upon me that my speech was not entirely a success, and that it would be best to finish it speedily with some jocular remark.

"In conclusion," I said, lifting my glass, "I will only add this—that my damaged hand today surely prevented disaster. The marquis was wise to go home when he did. If I had carried a gun"—and here I paused for emphasis—"some of you present might never have survived." I stopped, oddly relieved to have uttered my own truth, but I could not understand why nobody clapped. However feeble my joke may have seemed to them, surely courtesy demanded at any rate a show of applause? Instead, there was a shuffling of feet, and everybody began to move away and outside as though the barn had suddenly become unbearably warm and they longed for the open air. My words had been lamentably few, but I could not see how they had in any way been offensive.

Renée was with me again, and Dr. Lebrun. "I think you must have a touch of fever," he said. "It would be wise to get back to the château as soon as possible."

"Nonsense," I said, "my hand isn't hurting at all."

"All the same," he said, "you'd be wiser to lie down."

I was in no condition to argue. I allowed myself to be led by Gaston to the car, and as we turned out of the farmyard I could see the straggling line of sportsmen moving off to their afternoon objective. It was still raining, and I did not envy them.

"My speech didn't seem to go down very well," I said to the silent Gaston at my side, half excusing myself, half trying to turn it into a matter for laughter between us.

He did not answer for a moment. Then the corner of his mouth twitched.

"Listen, Monsieur le Comte," he said, his voice an apology, "you had a little too much to drink, that was all."

"Was it so noticeable?" I said.

I felt rather than saw the shrug. "People are sensitive," he said, "especially about the past. It doesn't do to mix up war and peace and make a joke of it."

"But I didn't do anything of the sort," I said. "I was speaking of something quite different."

"Excuse me, Monsieur le Comte," he said, "I misunderstood you. So did they."

We drove the few miles back in silence. As I got out of the car, and he stood waiting for further orders, it struck me suddenly that possibly not all the guests would be returning for refreshment later. It might be that some of them would now make excuses and go home. I put the point to Gaston.

"It is one of those things, Monsieur le Comte," he said, "that are best left to the discretion of those concerned. In any case, if few turn up to drink in the dining room, I can promise you that the kitchen quarters of the château will be completely filled."

I went upstairs and crept softly into the dressing room

206

so as not to disturb Françoise. Throwing myself down onto the bed, I slept instantly. I was woken by someone whispering in my ear. The whisper was at first soft, part of a breaking dream. Then it came louder, and, opening my eyes, I saw that it was dark, raining still. A figure stood by the bed. It was Germaine, the little *femme de chambre*.

"Come quickly, Monsieur le Comte," she was saying. "Madame la Comtesse is unwell, she is asking for you."

I sat up instantly, switching on the light. Germaine looked frightened, and I did not understand why she should have come to me.

"Where's Charlotte?" I said. "Has she sent you for me?"

"Charlotte is downstairs, Monsieur le Comte," she whispered. "There is a great crowd in the kitchen eating and drinking, you understand, all those who were at the shoot today, and Charlotte told me to stay with Madame la Comtesse because she wanted to join the others below. It isn't often, she said, that there is company at the château, and surely for once I could stay upstairs and listen, for Madame la Comtesse was sleeping and would give no trouble."

I was up now, and struggling into my jacket. "What's the time?" I asked.

"It's after eight, Monsieur le Comte," she said. "There are still a few guests in the dining room with Monsieur and Madame Paul and Mademoiselle Blanche, but not so many came as were expected. Gaston told us that a number had gone home because they were wet through, and also because you, Monsieur, were unwell and things were not quite as usual."

I straightened my tie and smoothed my hair before the mirror. At least I was sober again.

"What's the matter with Madame la Comtesse?" I asked.

"I don't know, Monsieur le Comte," she answered, looking frightened once again. "She was sleeping, and then she started to groan and to ask for Charlotte, but Charlotte had told me not to go down for her, so I went to the bed and asked if there was anything I could do. I told a lie, I said I could not find Charlotte. Then she asked for you, not Mademoiselle Blanche or the doctor or anyone else, only

Charlotte or you, Monsieur le Comte, and she said to come at once, no matter where you were or what you were doing. I was frightened, she looked so ill."

She followed me out of the dressing room and up the stairs. Away below I could hear the sound of revelry from the kitchen quarters, curiously in contrast to the usual deep silence of St. Gilles. We passed through the swing door onto the third corridor, and at once the music and the laughter stopped. We were shut off from sound, enveloped in shadow, for this part of the château had no part in the merriment below.

When we came to the bedroom door I paused, something telling me I should go in alone, and asked Germaine to wait outside in the corridor. The room was dark. Only a feeble glow from the stove enabled me to distinguish the shape of the furniture, of the bed, and because I did not want to disturb the comtesse by turning on the light, I went to the window and eased the shutter so that a streak of pallor might at least fall upon the carpet and make the darkness grey. As I folded back the shutter I could hear the steady rain running in the lead guttering as I had imagined it would in winter, churning and tumbling the rubble of dust and leaves, sweeping them down to course out of the gargoyle mouth. Looking from the window, I saw that the mist had descended too. The château was isolated in its plot of ground above the empty moat, like a dead world lost in vapour.

Her voice came to me, faint and strangely guttural, from the depths of the vast bed. "Who is it?"

"It's I, Jean."

I moved away from the window and went to her. I could see nothing but her form under the covers, not her face.

"I'm ill," she said. "Why didn't you come before?"

Her words, *"Je souffre,"* do not lend themselves to another language. The distress is there, physical or mental, embraced in the single phrase.

"What do you want me to do?" I asked.

She moved restlessly, and I knelt down beside the bed and took her hand.

"You know perfectly what I want you to do," she said. There were medicines on the table beside the bed, and I glanced towards them, perplexed, but she shook her head, impatient, exasperated, and moaned, thrashing her head from side to side. "Charlotte keeps it next door," she said, "in the dressing room, in the drawer of the cupboard there. Surely you remember where it is?"

I got up, went into the dressing room, and switched on the light. There was only one cupboard in the small room, with a single drawer, and this I opened. Inside were two boxes, one of them still half wrapped in paper which I recognised. It was the same wrapping that had covered the gift in the valise, the gift which I had given into Charlotte's hands that first evening in the château. I took the wrapping off now, and opened the box. It was full of little ampoules packed one upon the other in layers of cotton wool. They contained liquid, and a label upon each, with the single word "morphine." I opened the other box. It held a hypodermic syringe. There was nothing else in the drawer. As I stood there, staring, I heard her calling me from the bedroom, "Jean, why don't you come?" Slowly I took the syringe out of its box, and one of the ampoules, and laid them on the table below. There was cotton wool on the table, and a bottle containing spirit, but in the days of the war, when these things had been familiar to me, kneeling beside a doctor on the floor of an air raid shelter, or in an ambulance, I had never had the feeling of revulsion that possessed me now. Then we acted in mercy, to deaden pain. This was different. I understood at last what it was that Jean de Gué had brought his mother from Paris. But his mother was not ill or dying, neither was she in pain.

I went back into the bedroom and turned on a light which I found concealed in the hangings of the bed. The woman lying there was not the one who had stood beside me on the terrace that morning, regal and commanding, but another, grey and old and frightened, her hands restless, her eyes staring, and she kept turning her head from side to side on the pillow in a movement that was horrible and inhuman, like something long imprisoned without food or light or water.

"What are you waiting for?" she said. "Why are you so long?"

I knelt beside her. My burn did not matter any more, and

I put both my hands behind her, and turned her head towards me so that she was forced to look at me and be still.

"I don't want to give it to you," I said.

"Why?"

The staring eyes searched mine, and the massive face, grey and sagging, seemed to crumple, becoming twisted and distorted like a paper mask fixed on the battered body of a Guy Fawkes dummy dragged by shrieking children in a foggy London street. It seemed to me, as I looked at her, that she had the same dead texture of skin, that her eyes were not eyes but sockets, her mouth a hoop, the tangled, unbrushed hair horse's hair, and the person I held a shell without life or feeling. But somewhere within the shell was a particle of light that flickered more faintly than the last glow of ash from a bonfire. It was concealed from me, but it was there, and I did not want it to die.

"Why?"

Once again she spoke, this time in anguish, and she pulled herself up in bed and held my shoulders. The mask became a face, and the face hers and mine and Marie-Noel's. The three of us were together, looking out at me from her eyes, and the voice was no longer deep and guttural but the voice of the child when she spoke to me the first evening and asked, "Papa, why did you not come and say good night to me?"

I got up and went into the bathroom. Breaking the neck of the ampoule, I filled the syringe, and came back and prepared her arm with the spirit as I remembered we had done in the war. Then I drove the needle into her arm, pressed the plunger and waited, and she leant back on her pillows and waited too. Her eyelids flickered, and for a moment, before closing them, she looked at me and smiled. I took the syringe back to the dressing room, washed it and replaced it in the box, and put the empty ampoule in my pocket. Then I shut the door and went and stood by the bedside once again. The anguish had gone from the face, and the likeness too. She was neither Marie-Noel, nor myself, nor the mother of Jean de Gué; she was something sleeping, unconscious, unaware of pain. I crossed the room to the window and opened the shutters. The pattering rain fell into the leads and the gutters and out of the gargoyle mouth down to the empty moat, and there was no sound anywhere at all but this sound of falling rain. I looked at my bandaged hand, burnt yesterday in the fire through cowardice and shame for what it could not accomplish, and it seemed to me that what it had now done was more cowardly and shameful still. However much I tried to tell myself that what had happened in this room was compassionate and merciful, it was not true. I knew that I had done what the son and the mother had done before me—I had taken the easiest way out.

I went into the corridor and found Germaine still standing there, waiting. I said to her, "It's all right now, Madame la Comtesse is sleeping. I've left the light on. She won't notice it. You had better sit by the stove until Charlotte comes up."

I went along the corridor, through the swing door and onto the other landing, and the sound of laughter and music came floating up towards me once again from the back regions of the château. I could hear voices too coming from the salon—evidently the guests had not yet gone—and as I walked onto the terrace the door of the salon opened, the confusion of voices sounded louder, then quietened again as the door closed, and Marie-Noel came out and stood beside me.

"Where are you going?" she said.

She had changed into a blue silk frock, white socks and pointed shoes. She wore a little gold cross round her neck, and round her cropped fair hair was a blue velvet band. Her face was flushed with excitement. This was her festal evening; she was helping to entertain the guests. I remembered the promise made to her on my first evening.

"I don't know," I said. "I might not come back."

She knew at once what I meant, because the colour went from her face and she made a movement as though to rush at me and seize my hands. Then she remembered my bandaged hand and stood still.

"Is it because of what happened at the shoot?" she asked.

I had forgotten the futility of the morning, the ridiculous spoiling of the sportsmen's fun, the cognac and the wine and the ill-timed bravado of my speech.

"No," I said, "it has nothing to do with the shoot."

She went on looking at me, her hands clasped, and then she said, "Take me with you."

"How can I?" I asked. "I don't know where I'm going."

It was raining hard, falling onto her thin shoulders in the blue silk party frock. "Will you walk?" she said. "You can't drive because of your hand."

The simplicity of her remark brought me to the full realisation that I was without thought or plan. How indeed did I intend to get away? I had walked blindly out of that upstairs room and down into the hall with only one idea in mind—that I must leave the château as soon as possible. Instead of which the idiocy of the burnt hand kept me a prisoner.

"You see," said the child, "it's not very easy, is it?"

Nothing was easy, neither being myself nor being Jean de Gué. I was not born to be the son of the woman upstairs, nor the father of the child before me. I had nothing to do with them. They were not my people: I had no people. Being the accomplice in an elaborate practical joke did not mean I must be its victim too. Surely it should be the other way round, and it was for them to pay the penalty, not me? I was not bound to them in any way.

The voices sounded loud again from within the salon. Marie-Noel looked over her shoulder. "They are beginning to say good-bye," she said. "You will have to make up your mind what you're going to do." She suddenly did not seem a child any more, but somebody old and wise whom I had known in a different age, a different time. I did not want it to be like that, because it hurt. I wanted her to be a stranger still. "The time hasn't come for you to leave me yet," she said. "Wait till I'm older. It won't be long."

A footstep sounded in the hall, and someone came and stood in the entrance. It was Blanche. The fanlight above the door shone on her hair, and I could see the mizzle of rain strike slantwise against the light, then fall to darkness on the step.

"You'll catch cold," she said. "Come in out of the rain." She did not see me standing there, she only saw the child, and I realised that, believing herself to be alone with Marie-Noel, she spoke in a voice I had never heard before. It was gentle and affectionate, the hard, abrupt quality gone. She might

212

have been a different person. "Everybody is going in a moment," she said. "You only have to be polite a few minutes longer. Then I'll come upstairs and read to you, if Papa is still sleeping." She turned and went indoors.

The child looked at me. "Go on in," I said, "do what she says. I won't leave you." She smiled. Oddly, the smile reminded me of something. Then I remembered—it was release from pain. I had seen the same smile not ten minutes ago in the room upstairs. Marie-Noel ran back into the château after Blanche.

I heard the sound of a car coming down from the village and passing through the gateway. As it turned to the archway the headlights must have picked me up, for it stopped and Gaston got out. It was the Renault, and he came across the drive towards me. He looked flushed, a little awkward.

"I had not realised Monsieur le Comte was below," he said. "Forgive me, but it was raining hard, and I took Madame Yves and one or two other older people back who had been celebrating with us to the *verrerie*. I did not ask permission. I did not want to disturb you."

"That's all right," I said, "I'm glad you took them home."

He came nearer, and peered up at my face. "You look upset, Monsieur le Comte. Is anything wrong? Are you still feeling ill?"

"No," I told him. "It's just . . . a combination of circumstances." I gestured with my hand towards the château. It did not matter to me what he thought. I was not sure what I thought myself.

"Excuse me," he said, his manner diffident, yet somehow reassuring, gentle, "I don't wish to be indiscreet, but would Monsieur le Comte perhaps like me to drive him to Villars?"

I kept silent, not understanding, hoping that his next words would make his meaning plain.

"You have had a hard day, Monsieur le Comte," he went on. "At the château here everyone believes you to be in bed. If I drove you now to Villars you could spend several hours there in comfort, without anxiety, and I could come back for you early in the morning. I only suggest it because at the present moment Monsieur le Comte cannot drive himself."

He glanced away from me, apologetic, tactful, and I knew

213

that what he suggested was so profoundly the answer to my
turmoil of mind and body and spirit that he expected no comment even, no word of affirmation. He went to the car, re-
versed it, and brought it back to the driveway below the terrace. He opened the door for me and I got in, and as he drove
along the pitch-dark lanes to Villars, the rain beating against
the windscreen, neither of us speaking, it seemed to me that
there was nothing left now of that former self who had
changed identity in the hotel bedroom at Le Mans. Every one
of my actions, instincts, weaknesses, all had merged with
those of Jean de Gué.

Chapter 18

I thought for a moment it was the rain pouring from the gargoyle mouth, bearing away the silt and débris of the years,
and the gargoyle himself, with flattened, evil ears, was cracking at the base, the stonework crumbling, so that he too would
moulder and soften with the flood. Then the horror of the
dream departed and it was day, and the sound was Béla's
bath water running. The darkness had gone and the rain with
it, and the early morning sun was turning the rooftops gold.

I leant back, my hand behind my head. Through the open
window I could see the shapes and angles of the roofs, the
lichened tiles, the twisted chimneys, the dormer windows, and
behind and above them all the fluted spire of the cathedral.
From the street below came the first movements of the day:
shutters thrown back, the sluicing of the pavement, footsteps
passing, somebody whistling, the waking to another week of
this small, unhurried market town. The running bath water
merged pleasantly with the bright street sounds and I was
filled with a lazy peace, aware of the presence nearby, so
close that I had only to raise my voice and she would turn off
the water and come to me, someone who asked no questions,
accepting me as part of a life shared at odd moments, depending upon mood and time—mine, not hers—just as the adult
puts aside work and occupation to attend to the child she
loves. My hand, untouched the day before, was now redressed,

rebandaged, cool in its oiled silk package; and the experience of being waited upon, ministered to, with nothing demanded of me and no show of possessiveness, was novel to both the old self and the new. It was something I was reluctant to surrender: I wished to savour its delicacy as long as possible.

I could hear her throwing open the shutters in the room across the passage, talking to the budgerigars, putting their cages out onto the balcony, their twittering chatter a variation of the running water. Presently I called to her and she came at once from the other room, dressed in wrapper and slippers, and bent over me and kissed me with the quiet unconcern of someone in charge, whose heart and mind are free of trouble.

"Did you sleep well?" she asked.

"Yes," I told her, and it was a delight to feel her arms and her shoulders bare under the loose flowing sleeves, and to be aware of skin smelling of apricots and to know that being with her was stepping into yet a third dimension which was no part of the first world, or the second, but somehow contained them both, like the case of a Chinese puzzle.

"I'll make you coffee directly," she said, "and as soon as Vincent comes I'll send him for croissants from the baker up the street. Your hand doesn't hurt you? Good. I'll dress it again before you leave."

Then she was gone, and I gave myself up once more to lassitude and peace.

She had a quality of being surprised by nothing. Last night, when Gaston had deposited me outside the Porte de Ville and driven away, and I crossed the canal by the footbridge and tapped at the shuttered window, she had opened it instantly, without any startled query. Noticing at once my bandaged hand and general appearance of weariness and strain, she gestured to the deep chair where I had sat before, and fetched me a drink. She did not ask one question, and it was I who broke the silence first by feeling in my pocket for the broken phial and tossing it into the wastepaper basket beyond the chair.

"Did I ever tell you my mother took morphine?" I asked her.

"No," she answered, "but I suspected it."

"How?"

She hesitated. "From little hints you dropped from time to time. It wasn't my business to interfere."

Her voice was practical and cool, warning me that she accepted without praise or condemnation whatever Jean de Gué should choose to tell her, reserving her opinion for herself.

"Would it disgust you," I asked, "if you learnt that I supplied her with morphine, bringing it with me from Paris as a gift, just as I brought you the bottle of 'Femme'?"

"Nothing disgusts me, Jean," she said. "I know you too well to be repelled now by anything you choose to do."

She looked at me steadily. I leant forward and took a cigarette from the box on the table beside me.

"This morning she came downstairs and went with us all to Mass," I said, "and then received about fifty guests on the terrace of the château, in the rain. She looked magnificent. She did it, of course, from spite, to spoil Renée's day, who wanted to play hostess, Françoise being unwell and in bed. This evening the little *femme de chambre,* Germaine, called me to her—her own personal maid, Charlotte, was below—and I went up and found her . . ." I broke off, because it was vividly with me once again, the dark close bedroom, the dressing room, the cupboard above the washbasin. "I found her wanting me to give her that." I looked at the wastepaper basket where I had thrown the empty phial.

"And you did so?"

"Yes."

She said nothing. She went on looking at me.

"That's why I've come to you," I said, "in self-pity and self-disgust."

"Those are things you must deal with in your own way," she said. "I can't act as a purge and rid you of them."

"You have before," I told her.

"Yes?"

Perhaps it was my imagination. Was her manner harder, more abrupt than it had been that afternoon two days ago? Or merely without interest, unmoved?

"I wonder how many times in the past," I said, "I've come here to this house, to you, knowing what was going on at

216

home in the château, wanting to forget, and succeeding in forgetting because of what I found here?"

I pictured him leaving the car outside the Porte de Ville, crossing the footbridge, and tapping at the window as I had done tonight, shedding all the guilt and all the care as soon as he passed the threshold, ridding himself of trouble as I wished to now.

"If you don't remember," she said, "let it alone. It doesn't help the present. Anyway, you told me on Friday that your difficulties and problems were likely to be easier in the future, that you were going to tackle them in a different way. Hasn't the new Jean de Gué been successful after all?"

Now she was smiling, and the faint mockery in her voice made me realise that she had no faith in him and never would have, and that what I had told her on Friday about wanting to save the *verrerie* and safeguard the people working there had been dismissed as a moment's idle whim born of a drunken mood.

"He's failed," I said, "in precisely the same way that he's failed before. He gives his family what they ask for, through cowardice, through evasion, not only his mother but his daughter too. The only difference is that once it was done with gaiety and possibly charm. Now it's done with reluctance and distaste."

"That could be an advance," she said. "It depends on the point of view." And then the smile faded with the mockery in her voice. She came over to me, and took my hand, and said, "So you didn't shoot today. Do you want me to do anything about this? I hear you burnt yourself."

"Who told you?" I asked.

"One of the *chasseurs*," she said, "whose sport was not as usual, and who, after lunching at the farm, decided to return to Villars." She was undoing the bandage as she spoke. "I don't suppose this hurts you any more," she added, "but it needs redressing. I can manage that for you, if I can't purge you of your sins."

She went out of the room, and I wondered how much more Jean de Gué knew of her than I did, whether their intimacy dated back through months or years, and whether the photograph of the man in uniform on the mantelpiece, with

"Georges" written across it, was a likeness of a dead husband. Above all, I wondered how much she enjoyed, despised, accepted or tolerated, for money or for love, the man who was not me.

She came back with new dressings, as efficient in her own way as Blanche had been in hers, and as she knelt beside me and dressed my hand I said, "I burnt myself on purpose. I did not want to shoot." This surely would bring surprise to those candid eyes, so that the Jean de Gué she knew so well, whose character and faults could not disgust her, might take on a new aspect, might at least have some idiosyncrasy hitherto unsuspected.

"Why?" she said. "Were you afraid of shooting badly?"

The truth, coming from her, was such a shock that I did not answer. I waited for her to finish tying the bandage and then withdrew my hand, discomfited.

"Once before," she said, "your eye was out and your hands were hopeless, after a drinking bout like this one in Le Mans. You made some excuse—I forget what—not to shoot. It was over beyond Montdoubleau, not at St. Gilles. Burning your hand instead is rather drastic. But perhaps it was intended as a penance on the part of the man in charge?" The irony in the voice was back again, and as she rose to her feet she tapped my shoulder in a gesture half mocking, half affectionate. "Go on," she said, "sit back in the chair and finish your cigarette. I understand you had more to drink than to eat at midday, so possibly you can manage an omelette now."

She must know, then, about the speech as well, the lack of applause, the melting away of the guests. Her informant could be anybody, from the financier to the outraged Marquis de Plessis-Braye. It did not matter much. Disgrace was well established, and the seigneur of St. Gilles had brought no lustre to the day.

I followed her through to the small kitchen and watched her prepare the omelette. "At any rate," I said to her, "I broke my rule, and did not minister to the greed of the guests—on this occasion the greed for flattery and the meaningless banalities one utters on these occasions. I was only trying to be honest. I had no idea it would upset them so much."

"The truth is always embarrassing," she said. "You of all

people might have learnt that by now. At a picnic lunch it happens to be misplaced."

"I can't help it," I went on, "if my truth happened to be theirs as well. I only told them that if I had had a gun some of them might not have been alive by the end of the day."

She was busy beating the eggs with a fork. "Coming from a one-time Resistance leader," she said, "to a group of well-known collaborators, it must have sounded curious, all the same."

I stared at her blankly. It was my secret I had come near to blurting out at the farm, not the jigsaw past of Jean de Gué.

"But that's not what I meant," I said, seeing, through the confusion of wine and smoke and haze that had been the atmosphere of the barn, the scattered uneasy faces amongst others that had kept their serenity. "That's not what I meant at all."

"That's what they understood," she said, and the laughter behind her eyes was the same as the twitch at the corner of Gaston's mouth. She neither applauded nor condemned; what had been said was said. "Don't ask me how far they deserved the dig, intentional or not. I don't know what was happening here then—I was still trying to get out of Hungary."

Hungary? That helped to explain the Béla, if nothing else, though why she should bear a man's name was more than I could guess.

She poured the eggs into the pan and stood looking at me, the empty bowl and the fork in her hand. "If your new-found sense of responsibility wants to get things straight," she said, "surely there's only one person who can do that for you—your sister Blanche?"

She stared at me a moment, and then turned to the omelette. And the years that were gone, that I had no business to intrude upon, seemed to merge into a single entity, like the eggs and the butter and the herbs. They could never be separated now, or examined one by one. I was responsible for the present, not the past.

"How long can you stay?" she asked.

"Until the morning."

"No questions asked? No indignant wife or curious mother?"

"No. Gaston will see to that."

219

She had the omelette on a plate, and the plate on a tray, and the tray in an instant on the table beside the chair in the small salon, the wine uncorked and poured.

"So this new Jean," she said, "is not possessed by his family any more?"

"He never was."

"That's where you're wrong," she said. "The bond isn't easily broken. Wait till tomorrow."

And tomorrow had already come, and the budgerigars sang in their cages on the balcony, the cathedral chimed the half hour, someone called good morning to a passer-by in the street below, and the idyll I had stolen from Jean de Gué was over.

As I drank my coffee, dressed and ready to depart, on the balcony overlooking the canal, I saw that Gaston, faithful to his word, was sitting in the car outside the Porte de Ville. And my moment in time was like a dream within a dream, for I belonged neither to her world nor to the one that waited for me. The lover Béla had held in the night was a shadow who did not exist, and the master for whom Gaston watched was a ghost, dwelling only in his fancy, loved for what he once had been.

The journey to St. Gilles was as silent as the outward one, except for his brief word of assurance that all in the château believed me to be in my room. "I let it be known," he said, his eyes straight on the road ahead of him, "that Monsieur le Comte did not wish to be disturbed. I even took the liberty of locking both doors into the dressing room." He handed me the keys.

"Thank you, Gaston," I said.

We were coming out of the line of trees and approaching the valley. Below us was the village, the river and the bridge, and the domain, silver-wet from last night's heavy rain, glistened in the early morning sun.

"How many times, Gaston," I asked, "have you pulled me out of a scrape of my own making?"

He swerved left to the lime avenue, disclosing at the further end of it the still shuttered façade of St. Gilles.

"I have never counted, Monsieur," he said. "It is just something I look upon as part of my duty to Monsieur le Comte, and to his family also."

He did not take the car through the gateway and onto the drive, but circled the enclosing walls of the moat and so through to the garage outbuildings by a side approach. As I walked under the arch and past César's run without disturbing him, and stood for a moment under the cedar tree, it seemed to me the château had never looked more peaceful or more still. The quality it had now, in fresh untempered sunlight, was neither faerie nor austere; the changing shadows of dusk and midnight had vanished with the darkness and the rain, and walls and roof and towers were bathed in the radiance that comes only in the first hours of the day, soft, new-washed, the delicate aftermath of dawn. The people who slept within must surely bear some imprint of this radiance in themselves, must turn instinctively to the light seeping through the shutters, while the ghostly dreams and sorrows of the night slipped away, finding sanctuary in the unawakened forest trees the sun had not yet touched. I wished that this spirit of early morning did not have to turn to day, to the restless clash of will, of movement, of divided heart and mood, but that all of them, inside the château, might stay suspended, as it were, in time, like the courtiers in "La Belle au bois dormant," shielded from the future by a cobweb barricade.

I crossed the terrace under the shuttered windows and went into the dark, cold hall. In some way my very act of intrusion into the still sleeping château seemed to break the spell of peace and silence brooding there. I was aware of a sense of disquiet, of foreboding, as if when the house woke it would not be to the clear bright day without, but to some inner trouble that already hovered, malign and watchful in the shadow of the stairs. I crept up to the first floor and along the corridor to the dressing room, and turned the key in the lock. As I opened the door I stepped onto a piece of paper that had been thrust underneath it. It was pink, with a sprig of flowers in one corner, the kind of paper, I remembered dimly, that was packed in boxes with envelopes to match and given to children on birthdays or at Christmas. It said, in round, unformed letters, "My Papa, you told me you would not go away, and I believed you. But you never came to say good night, and your

221

door is locked. The Sainte Vierge tells me you are unhappy, and are suffering now for wrong done in the past, so I am going to pray that all your sins may be visited upon me, who, being young and strong, can bear them better. Sleep well, and have faith in Marie-Noel, who loves you dearly."

I put the paper in my pocket and sat down in a chair by the open window. The sense of oppression deepened. Some force had been put in motion which was no longer within my control. I wished now that I had never left the château, never had those hours of release in Villars. There, the community astir soon after five, the casual sounds of morning had rung cheerfully on the ear; but here, as the village church struck seven the hush continued, and the only living things were the black and white cattle moving like wraiths from the enclosing walls of the farm buildings into the park.

I went on sitting by the window, waiting for the customary time when Gaston would bring my tray. It must have been a little before eight when I first heard the hurrying footsteps along the corridor, the knocking on the bedroom door—Françoise's, not mine—and the confused babble of voices, exclamations, cries. Then, on the bathroom door, which I had not yet unlocked, there came a sudden further knocking, a rattling at the handle, and the voice of Françoise herself, urgent, shrill, "Jean, Jean, are you awake?"

I leapt from my chair by the window, took the key out of my pocket and opened the door. She was standing there in her nightgown, wan and pale, and behind her Germaine, and beyond, in the bedroom, the gaunt, accusing figure of Blanche, watching me without a word.

I put out my hand to steady Françoise. "It's all right," I said. "You don't have to tell me. It's Maman, isn't it?"

Her eyes swept me, incredulous, and so over my shoulder to the dressing room. "Maman?" she said. "Of course not. Why should there be anything wrong with Maman? It's the child. She's disappeared. Germaine has just been to call her, and the bed hasn't been slept in. She never even undressed. If she hasn't been with you, then she's nowhere in the château—she's vanished, gone."

Chapter 19

Their faces were turned to mine. I could see Paul, half dressed, standing at the bedroom door with Renée beside him, both roused by the same summons. As head of the house I was responsible: decisions, plans, must come from me. Françoise, shivering without a wrapper, was my first concern.

"Get back into bed," I said, "we'll soon find her. You can't do anything about it."

Blanche led her, crying, protesting, back to bed.

"She's probably in the park, or in the woods," I said. "It's not so unusual for a child to get up early. Do we all have to become hysterical?"

"But her bed has not been slept in, I tell you!" cried Françoise. "Germaine went in to call her, and the nightdress was lying folded, the sheets turned down, and nothing had been touched."

Germaine also was in tears, her plump red face suffused, her eyes swollen. "The bed was as I left it yesterday evening, Monsieur le Comte," she whimpered. "The child has not undressed. She has gone off wearing her best frock and her thin shoes. She will catch her death of cold."

"Who was the last to see her?" I asked. "What time did she go to bed?"

"She was with Blanche," said Françoise. "Blanche was reading to her, weren't you, Blanche? She sent her to bed about half past nine. She was restless and excitable."

I glanced at Blanche. Her face was set and strained. She did not look at me. "It's always the same," she said to Françoise. "Her father upsets her, works on her feelings, and she is capable of any foolishness after that."

"But Marie-Noel didn't see Jean all evening!" interrupted Renée. "Jean was asleep in his room. The mistake everyone makes is allowing the child to appear on every occasion and mix with adults. Yesterday she tried to be the centre of the picture throughout the day. I noticed it in particular. Of course she became overexcited."

"I had the impression she was quieter than usual," said Paul, "more subdued, at any rate in the evening. It's not surprising, when you think what happened during the day. I should imagine we're the laughingstock of the country, from Villars to Le Mans. You missed nothing," he added to Françoise, "you were well out of it."

Françoise, with swimming eyes, turned from him to me. "Did you drink so much?" she said. "What in the world will people think?"

Germaine, goggle-eyed, watched us from her corner.

"Go and tell Gaston to start searching the grounds," I said to her. "Tell him to get hold of Joseph, too, and anyone else who's about. Monsieur Paul and I will be down directly."

"If you want to know what I think," said Paul, "it's this. The child has run away because Jean made an exhibition of himself in public. She was ashamed. So were we all."

"Marie-Noel was not ashamed," said Renée. "I heard her telling everyone that Jean was the most courageous man in the world and nobody but herself knew why. Heaven knows what they thought of her precocity. It made me most uncomfortable."

"Courageous? What did she mean by courageous?" asked Françoise.

"It did take courage of a sort," said Paul, "deliberately to wreck the day for those who had taken infinite trouble to try and make it a success. It was a curious thing that, out of about fifty people invited here after the shoot was over, only twenty or so turned up. It's not the personal slight I mind, but the slight on the family."

"It was the weather," said Renée. "Everyone was wet through."

The bickering was interrupted by a knock on the door, and we all turned, in hope and expectation, but it was only Charlotte, self-importance upon her thin mean face.

"Excuse me, Monsieur le Comte, and you too, Madame la Comtesse Jean," she said. "I have just heard about the child. I think I was the last to see her. When I went upstairs last night I happened to look along the corridor and she was kneeling outside the dressing-room door. She wanted to say good night to her papa. She could not make you hear, Monsieur le Comte."

"That's not surprising," said Paul.

"Why didn't she try my door, then?" asked Françoise. "I was not asleep. She must have known perfectly well that she had only to knock and I would have answered."

"That was my fault, Madame la Comtesse Jean," said Charlotte. "I told the child on no account to disturb her Papa, who must have so much on his mind at the present time, or to disturb you, Madame, who need sleep so badly with the little one soon to be born. A little playmate, I told her, sent from paradise, whom she must learn to love and cherish."

The small button eyes flickered towards me and fell, and she looked from one to the other of us with a half-smile, servile, obsequious, upon her pinched mauve lips. I thought of the dressing room adjoining that other bedroom in the tower, and I knew that because of the rearranging of the boxes in the cupboard above the washbasin she must be aware of my visit there last night. She would not betray me, any more than she would betray herself. I was an accomplice, and I hated the fact, but there was nothing I could do to alter it.

"Well," I asked, "what happened next?"

"She seemed a little upset, Monsieur le Comte. I was quite shocked. She said, 'My papa needs me, and nobody else. He only wants a boy to bring money into the family.' Those were her words. I told her it was not the way to speak, and that Monsieur le Curé would not approve, or anyone in St. Gilles. When the baby comes we shall all love him, I said, from her papa down to César, we had all waited for him so long. Then she came with me as far as the service door, and on to her own staircase, and I went above to Madame la Comtesse, who was sleeping peacefully, like an angel."

Who was, in fact, lying unconscious, because of what I had done to her. Perhaps it was the same thing. It did not greatly matter now. The only thing that mattered was that Marie-Noel was missing, and she was missing because I had gone to Villars instead of staying at the château.

"Is it possible, Mademoiselle," suggested Charlotte, turning to Blanche, "that the little one has run down to the church? After all"—she hesitated, watching me an instant, the expression of servility on her face deepening—"if she has anything on her mind of which she is ashamed, she would surely go to Monsieur le Curé and ask to make her confession?"

"No," said Blanche, "she would come first to me."

Paul shrugged his shoulders. "It would be more to the point if we all got dressed, wouldn't it?" he asked. "Blanche can go down to the curé, while Jean and I search the grounds with Gaston. That is," he added, throwing me a glance, "if you're sufficiently recovered from yesterday."

Without answering, I turned and went back into the dressing room and, crossing to the window, looked down into the moat. There was nothing in it but the tangled grass, the ivy and the weeds. It was only in imagination that I saw the small body in the blue dress lying in the ditch, broken and useless.

It was Gaston who came to tell me that the dog was missing. Joseph had gone to feed him, and had found the kennel empty. This news brought an odd sense of relief. If Marie-Noel had taken César with her he would act as protector, at least from this world's dangers. Nor would a child bent on self-destruction take a dog with her.

Once outside the château, Paul and the men and I divided between us the ground to be searched, and my territory took me towards the scene of yesterday's shoot. The woods were soggy with the rain of the day and the night, the fallen leaves like paper under my feet, the brushwood soft and rotten. But the bright day, penetrating the cover, gave sharpness to the outline of the trees, which yesterday had been blurred and obscure. This morning there was no mist, no patter in listless branches sweeping dull and humid to the ground, only a clear intensity of sunlight turning the undergrowth silver where the raindrops, glistening like pools, shimmered a moment in the hollow of a leaf before the leaf melted and became one with the soil.

I knew, tramping the long rides, climbing the ditches in the black woods, that she would not be there, in front of me, a small Artemis with her hound at the end of the ride, or a babe in the woods asleep at the foot of a tree. It was only an

226

exercise I set myself because there was nowhere else to search, and the shouts and halloos of the rest of them, closer to the château grounds, could not reach me here, with their irritating, useless frequency. It was as idle to call as to prod a haystack with a fork, which I had seen Joseph do in all seriousness. If the child wanted to be found she would be found, not there, not here, but waiting, hidden, before her own symbolic shrine.

When I broke finally from the forest and emerged into fields once more, I saw that my walk had brought me in a half-circle, this morning's brightness showing what yesterday's mist had hidden, and there, a couple of fields away, were the foundry sheds, half obscured by a fence enclosing their plot of ground, and the chimney itself, a pencil against the sky. I climbed under the wire surrounding the wood, crossed the fields past the white horse browsing beside the hedge, and, opening a small gate embedded in briar and nettles, came once more to the apple orchard behind the master's house. The windows, facing west, were blank and dim, but the tangled garden glistened like the raindrops in the wood, a cobweb veil of dew encompassing the crops, a cover for tumbled, crimson apples, while the earth was steamy with the warmth drawn from it by the sun. The house slept, yet was not desolate. The creeping vine protected the windows and the walls, and the teeming garden and orchard, spilling vegetables and fruit that were never gathered, seemed an echo and a promise from a past still unfulfilled—a past that became suddenly blended with the present because of a half-open window beside the blistered door, a window that on my visit only three days before had been fast shut and crusted with the years.

As I watched, I saw someone come to the window and stand there, looking out at me, and I walked over the wet earth and the fallen apples. When I stood beside the window I saw the figure was Julie, and she had her finger to her lips for silence.

"You came quickly," she whispered. "I only sent word to the château ten minutes ago. I could get no reply by telephone."

Her words had no meaning for me. Yet I was afraid. The brown eyes, usually so warm and full of life, were troubled.

The intuition that I had learnt never to mistrust turned to apprehension.

"I had no message," I said. "I came by chance."

I climbed through the window into the room. It was the same that I had entered before, where the furniture was stored, the onetime salon of the master's house. The windows faced two ways: the one where Julie stood looked out upon the orchard and the garden, the other to the well. A shaft of sunlight fell upon the child, white and still under a heap of blankets, and upon the dog, his muzzle between his paws, stretched at her feet. It was what my fancy had conjured, yet, strangely, more poignant still. Not dripping from a pool, not torn or mangled, merely alone, a speck in isolation.

"One of the workmen found her because of César," said Julie. "The dog was standing guard beside the well. She must have climbed down the ladder to the bottom and lain there, amongst the glass and rubble, all the night. She was asleep when he brought her up, and she was sleeping still when he carried her into the house and called to me."

Asleep. I had thought her dead. I turned to Julie, but the wrinkled face was puzzled and awed, not stricken. Still whispering, taking me by the arm, she said, "It was Madame la Comtesse who walked in her sleep in the old days. It is perhaps part of the little one's inheritance, Monsieur Jean. No doubt she had something on her mind."

I felt in my pocket for the scrap of paper. It belonged to Jean de Gué, yet it was also mine. Mine too the image of the drugged woman on her pillow. Jean de Gué's mother had smiled when I took away her pain, but I had not carried it far: I had left it with his child instead.

The small face against the dark blanket looked like something carved from stone, an angel's head, remote, intangible, lost in a cold cloister.

"Poor little one," said Julie, "it is always at this age they take fancies into their heads. For myself, it was a boy in the village. I followed him everywhere. My sister had a passion for her teacher. This one is religious, like Mademoiselle Blanche. It will pass."

She patted the blanket, her hand brown and strong and wrinkled like her face, her thumbnail black with soil. The letter in my pocket, which had seemed precious, a key to unlock a door, became suddenly a scrap without meaning. I had a vision of it found in a forgotten drawer, years later, by a woman looking like Blanche, who, before throwing it into the wastepaper basket with a frown, wondered when she had written it, and why, remembering nothing of the suffering and pain she had taken with her to the well.

"You know what it is," said Julie. "In a house full of women like yours, it is time someone prepared her for what is to come. She is growing fast. They are like young plants at this stage, they shoot quickly. Ernest, who lives next door to me and who found her and carried her up, is father of three daughters. The first thing he asked me was her age. Not eleven yet, I told him. That's nothing, he said. His youngest was ten when she matured. It can be frightening, you understand, Monsieur Jean, when a child becomes a young girl and still knows nothing. It would not surprise me if it happened soon."

I wished I possessed Julie's common sense, her tenderness, her perception. I wished I had the knowledge of Ernest, who lived next door and had three daughters. Lecturing on Joan of Arc was no preparation for a *père de famille*, and I was not even a *père de famille*, I was someone acting a part in a masquerade.

"I don't know what to tell her," I said. "I don't know what to do."

Julie stared at me in pity. "These things are never difficult for us," she said, "but for you people at the château life is full of complications. Sometimes I wonder how you live at all. Nothing is natural."

The child stirred in her sleep but did not wake. The blankets, rough and hairy, brushed her chin. It would be simpler after all if she could stay there, poised in time, without the turmoil of the years to come. To Julie she was a seedling requiring sun; to me, something of my own self lost. In the dark the two combined together in a single point of pain.

"It's odd," I said to Julie. "When they told me at the château she had disappeared, I kept thinking of her drowned."

"Drowned?" she said, puzzled. "There is nowhere here to drown." She paused and looked over my shoulder to the window. "You know there has been no water in the well for fifteen years."

She turned and met my eyes, and I said, feeling suddenly that I could keep the truth to myself no longer, "I didn't know. I don't know anything. I'm a stranger here."

Surely she must understand? Her honesty would not be fooled: she must recognise me for what I was, an intruder and a fraud.

"Monsieur le Comte was always a stranger at the *verrerie*," she said. "That was the trouble, wasn't it? You neglected your inheritance and your family, and allowed another man to take your place and bear your responsibilities."

She patted my shoulder, and I knew that she was speaking of the past and I the present. We were two people in two different worlds.

"Tell me how to live," I said. "You're practical and wise."

Her eyes crinkled in a smile. "You wouldn't listen to me, Monsieur Jean. You never have, not even when I put you across my knees and smacked your little bottom as a child. You made your own decisions always. If life is no good to you now, it's because you went for what was exciting, what was amusing, what was new—never for what was lasting, what endured. It's true, isn't it? Since you were so high. And now you're nearly forty, and it's too late to change. You can't bring back your young days any more than you can bring back poor Monsieur Duval, whose only crime was trying to preserve the *verrerie* while you were absent, for which you and your little group of patriots called him a collaborator, and shot him and let him die there in the well."

She looked at me with pity, as she had done before, and I realised that her words were neither accusation nor condemnation. She knew, his family knew, the whole countryside knew that Jean de Gué had killed Maurice Duval. Only I, the substitute, had not been sure.

"Julie," I said, "where were you the night he was shot?"

"In my lodge by the gates," she answered. "I saw nothing. I heard everything. It was not my business then, or now. It's finished, done with, a matter for your conscience, not for mine."

Her hand was still on my shoulder as we heard a lorry turn into the gates.

"Julie," I repeated, "did you like Maurice Duval?"

"We all liked him," she said. "No one could help it. He had all the qualities you lacked. That was why Monsieur le Comte your father made him master of the *verrerie*. I'm sorry, Monsieur Jean, but it's true."

I could hear footsteps coming now across the waste ground towards the house, and voices too, but the jutting wall of the sheds obscured the view. Julie turned her head.

"They got my message," she said. "Someone has come from the château. Perhaps you can carry the child to the car and back to her bed, and she will never know that she walked here to the *verrerie* in her sleep."

"She didn't walk in her sleep," I said. "She came deliberately. She wanted to climb down into the well. Everything you've just said goes to prove it."

My lie to Marie-Noel about my burnt hand, my behaviour at the shoot, my evasion of the preceding night, had all combined to make her think her father penitent. She had atoned for his deed in her own way, by acting the part of the victim. Only by doing this could she bring him absolution. I felt for the letter in my pocket and read it once again. It wasn't a scrap of paper after all: it was a testament of faith.

Someone was entering the house by the office. Footsteps were crossing the kitchen and the little hall, and passing to the nearer room. Julie went to the door, her fingers raised to her lips for silence.

"Quietly," she whispered. "The child is still asleep."

I thought it would be Gaston or Paul. It was neither. It was Blanche.

"Mademoiselle?" exclaimed Julie, and the wonder in her voice, the astonishment, the swift glance back to me and to the furniture stored against the walls betrayed some sudden emotion that she had not shown hitherto.

"You need not have come, Mademoiselle," she said. "I told Ernest to give a message that the little one was safe. I have been watching her, and Monsieur le Comte arrived only ten minutes or so ago."

Blanche said nothing. She went straight to Marie-Noel and

knelt beside her, gently turning the blanket, and I saw that the child had on a coat over her blue frock, and thick stockings and shoes that she had not worn the night before. The clothes were marked with lime and dust, and torn in several places, and I saw clearly each movement of the preceding night: the freeing of the dog, her walk through the rain, the dark buildings of the glass foundry outlined against the sky, the black hollow of the empty well, and then step by step, clutching the ladder, the slow descent, her coat brushing the green lime walls, and at the bottom, amongst the glass and rubble, the small round patch of night high above her.

Blanche, still kneeling at her side, turned to Julie. "Where did you find her?" she asked, her voice so low I could hardly hear the words.

Julie, for the first time strained, nonplussed, threw me a questioning glance as though in doubt for an answer.

"It was Ernest who discovered her, Mademoiselle," she said, "here, inside the house. Didn't he tell you?"

"He told me inside a shed," she answered, "but the sheds are always locked at night. She has been lying amongst broken glass and lime."

Inside the house or inside the shed, both were lies. Why did Ernest and Julie lie to Blanche? Julie had not lied to me. Blanche stared steadily at Julie, and Julie, who had been direct and frank, became another woman, lost, confused, with a sudden running babble of words about misunderstanding Ernest, she had not listened properly, she had been at the back of her lodge letting out the chickens when he had come to tell her that he had found the little one asleep in the master's house.

"Her pockets are full of glass," said Blanche. "Did you know that?"

Julie did not answer. Once again she looked at me as if for help, and Blanche, feeling in the child's coat pocket, drew out a handful of minuscule objects, a jug no larger than a thumbnail, a vase, a flacon, all miniature yet perfectly formed, and amongst them a replica of the château of St. Gilles, diminutive yet unmistakable, two towers smashed.

"These have not been made since before the war," said Blanche. "I ought to know, since I helped design them."

For the first time she looked about the room and away from the child—at the tables and the chairs and the bookshelves and the trunks, all of them stored there, untouched and unused. And suddenly, in a flash of comprehension, I realised that what she was looking at had once been part of her life. This empty room was as familiar to her as the chill, stark bedroom at the château, but animated, joyful, not dead as it was now. This dusty salon in the master's house was to have been a place possessed by two people who loved each other well, both faithful to the past and to tradition, both looking to a future that might, when war was finished, prove stable and secure. But something had gone amiss, sorrow had turned inward, creation ceased, the Cross she knelt before in her bedroom was not a Saviour but her own hope crucified.

On impulse, I took the letter out of my pocket and gave it to her. As she read it, lips moving, following the words, I knew that what had happened on a dark night nearly fifteen years ago had not come about by chance, but was something planned and done deliberately by a man without heart or feeling, who saw perhaps, in the other, someone finer than himself, possessing, as Julie had told me only a few moments before, all the qualities he himself lacked.

"The little one has blood on her hands," said Julie suddenly. "I did not notice it when I covered her with the blankets."

Blanche gave me back the letter without a word, and together we knelt beside the child. Taking the small clenched fists, Blanche opened one hand and I the other. In the hollow of each palm was the red weal of a recent cut, but the cut now dry, not bleeding. The hands were clean—there was no dust, no glass. I said nothing; nor did Blanche. Then slowly she raised her eyes.

"Julie," she said, "I want you to tell Jacques to telephone to Monsieur le Curé and ask him to come here at once. Then look in the directory for the number of the convent of the Sacré-Coeur at Lauray, and find out if it would be possible for the Mother Superior to speak to Mademoiselle de Gué."

Julie, bewildered, looked from Blanche to me.

"No," I said. "No . . ."

The urgency in my voice roused César. He stood on guard, ready to defend the child.

"Are you mad?" I said to Blanche. "Don't you realise she did it on purpose, that she did it for me, because I burnt my hand in the fire?"

"Julie," said Blanche, "do what I tell you."

I went and stood by the door, my back against it. Julie, distressed, looked from Blanche to me.

"There is no need for Monsieur le Curé," she said. "The child has not come to any harm. She has only cut herself with glass. It is full of glass at the bottom of the well."

"The well?" said Blanche. "She climbed into the well?"

Julie realised her mistake too late. The words were spoken. "Why, yes, Mademoiselle," she said. "What if she did climb into the well and lie there in the depths of it all night? It has been dry for fifteen years. What if she walked here to the *verrerie* asleep or awake, for both your sakes, or for her own, poor little one, because she has too much imagination? Does it make any difference to what is past and gone? Why doesn't someone in the château look after her properly, and love her for herself? It isn't the stigmata on her hands you want to look for, but what will be happening to her soon, in her own body."

Blanche turned white. Emotion, long controlled, fought for release. "How dare you blaspheme, how dare you?" she said, her voice outraged, passionate. "I've watched over the child since she was born. I've loved her, trained her, brought her up as if she were my own, because her mother is a fool and her father a devil. I won't let her suffer in this world as I have suffered. She was made for another world, another life. These marks on her hands are proof of it. God Himself is speaking to us, through her."

The tenderness had gone, the pathos too. The Blanche who had come into the master's house so full of memories, looking for the lost child, was another woman, fanatical, bitter, seeking a victim in the one she wished to save.

"The Seigneur does not act in that way, Mademoiselle," said Julie. "If He wants to call the child to Himself, He will do so in His own good time, and not because Monsieur le Comte killed the man you loved. The little one will suffer in this world only because of what you do to her; yes, you, and her father, and her grandmother, and everybody up at the château. You are used up, spent, good for nothing, the whole lot of you. They are right, the people who say it is time we had another revolution in this country, if only to rid ourselves of the jealousy and hate you have helped to spread. Now, look . . . you have woken her, the damage is done."

Yet it was Julie herself whose voice, loud and indignant, had caused César to bark and the bark to startle the child. Marie-Noel, her eyes suddenly open and alive with curiosity, stared at us from the heap of blankets. She sat up, instantly alert, staring at each one of us in turn.

"I've had the most atrocious dream," she said.

Blanche bent over her at once, her arms round her in protection.

"It's all right, my *chérie*," she said. "You're safe, you're with me. I'm going to take you where they will understand you and look after you. It will never happen again, the horror and the fear in the well."

Marie-Noel looked at her calmly.

"It was not horrible, nor was I frightened," she replied. "Germaine said it was haunted, but I never saw a ghost. The *verrerie* is a happy place. It's the château that is full of ghosts."

César, reassured by the sound of her voice, settled himself at her feet. Marie-Noel patted his head. "He's hungry, and so am I. Can we go across to the cottage with Madame Yves and get some bread?"

The telephone started ringing from the office at the end of the house. The sudden peal of it jerked us to reality. Julie moved automatically to the door. I opened it, and Blanche rose slowly to her feet. Faced with the living present, the three of us acted instinctively. Only the child looked troubled.

"I hope that's not the beginning of it," she said.

"The beginning of what?" I asked.

"The beginning of my ferocious dream." Pushing aside the blankets, she stood up, dusted her coat and put her hand in mine. "The Sainte Vierge is anxious about all of us," she said. "She told me Gran'mie wanted Maman to die. In the dream I wanted her to die too. So did you. We were all guilty. It was very wicked. Isn't there something you can do to prevent it coming true?"

Jacques must have arrived at the office, for the ringing ceased, and through the open door and the empty rooms beyond I heard his low voice speaking. Julie passed me without a word and went to the kitchen, and after a moment Jacques's voice ceased, there came the murmur of them both in discussion, and then Julie reappeared through the kitchen door. She stood motionless, then beckoned. I left Marie-Noel and went to her.

"It was Charlotte asking for Monsieur Paul," she said. "I told her you were here with Mademoiselle Blanche. She said would you both go back at once to the château. There has been an accident. She said not to take the child . . ."

This time intuition had not lied. Julie lowered her eyes. I looked over my shoulder to the inner room. Marie-Noel was kneeling, turning the small glass flacons out of her pocket, and arranging them, line upon line, upon the dusty floor. As she placed the château at the head, with its broken tower, she caught sight of her hands, and turning them, palms outward, called to Blanche.

"I must have cut myself," she said. "I don't remember how. Will the cuts fade and leave no mark, or will you have to bandage me as you did Papa?"

Chapter 20

The summons which should have united brother and sister divided us still further. Blanche said never a word to me, nor I to her, as the workman called Ernest drove us back in the lorry; the evil that encompassed us both was like a cloud impossible to penetrate.

The château was deserted. Everyone was out, still searching for the child. Only Charlotte was left, blabbing and hysterical, the woman who milked the cows, screaming in my ear, and the cook, whom I had not seen before but whom I knew to be Gaston's wife. As we entered the château she came from the kitchen premises, eyes startled, hair unpinned and falling loose, and said, "They brought the ambulance from Villars. I did not know where else to telephone." Only now did

236

it become clear to me that Ernest, whom Julie had sent to St. Gilles in the lorry because she could get no reply by telephone, had met Blanche coming from the church, and she had straightway driven back with him to the foundry without returning to the château.

All sense of time was lost. I did not know how long I had walked in the woods. The day, disjointed from that first moment when Françoise had hammered on the dressing-room door to tell me the child was missing, had been one without minutes, without hours; and now, looking up at that gaping bedroom window and down to the trampled grass of the moat below, it might have been midday or afternoon. Marie-Noel asleep beneath the blankets belonged to an era past and gone. Nothing was certain but that disaster, swift and sudden, had come upon the château when it was empty.

The crooked finger of the woman who milked the cows stabbed at the patch of grass as she turned first to me and then to Blanche, and her voice, unintelligible and shrill, repeated again and again the only words I understood, "I saw her fall . . . I saw her fall . . ." The jabbing finger, the up-turned eyes, the sudden sweeping gesture of her hand as she mimed the falling body, was terrible and vivid, the drama of a witch, and Charlotte, plucking at Blanche's sleeve and babbling, "She was still breathing, Mademoiselle, I put a mirror to her lips," became her partner in the dreadful play.

The nightmare ride began again. Out of the drive, through the gateway, up the avenue and onto the road to Villars, in the wake of the ambulance that could only have preceded us by some twenty-five minutes. And still, despite the premonition that had now turned to certainty, Ernest, driving us in the lorry, was the only link between us.

"I was in church," said Blanche, "I was in church, praying, when it happened."

"I saw no ambulance, Mademoiselle," said Ernest. "You must have come out of the church and met me with the lorry before the ambulance came."

"I should have gone back to the château," said Blanche. "I should have gone back and told them that the child was safe. I might have been in time."

And a few minutes later, as always after disaster, the hopeless recapitulation of events to find how tragedy could have been avoided. "There was no need for everyone to join in the search. Some of us should have stayed. If one of us had stayed it would not have happened."

And lastly, "The hospital in Villars may not be prepared for emergencies. They should have taken her to Le Mans."

To the right, to the left, to the right, then straight ahead— the road that led to Villars was now so much part of my life that I felt I knew every twist and every turn. Here was the corner where yesterday evening Gaston had skidded. There was the puddle that early this morning had shone like gold. Villars, new-washed and radiant at six, was full of dust and noise now. Men were drilling a side road, cars were parked one behind the other, and the hospital building, which I had not noticed when Marie-Noel and I had walked the market place, now seemed prominent and large and ugly because of my own fears. It was Blanche who entered first, Blanche who spoke rapidly to someone white-coated, young, standing in the passage, and Blanche who pushed me into the bare impersonal waiting room while she disappeared after him through a further door beyond. The sister who returned with her was calm, impassive, trained like all her colleagues the world over to meet emotion, and her language was a universal language; it might have been taken from a phrase book of any country.

"I can't tell you the extent of the injuries. The doctor is examining her now," she said to me as she led us from the waiting room to a smaller private one.

Blanche did not sit down, although the sister drew forward a chair. She went and stood by the window, with her back to me. I think she was praying. Her head was bent, her hands clasped in front of her. I stared at a map of the region that was framed on the wall, and I saw that Villars was twenty kilometres from Mortagne, and from Mortagne a byroad led direct to the Abbey of la Grande-Trappe. On the desk was a calendar. A week ago tomorrow I had been driving to Le Mans . . . A week ago . . . Everything I had said, everything I had done, had brought this family closer to disaster and to pain. Mine was the responsibility, mine the guilt. Jean de Gué, laughing before the mirror in that hotel bedroom, had left me

238

to solve his problems as I chose. Each step I had taken during the past few days seemed now, in retrospect, to have caused suffering and harm. Folly, ignorance, bluff and blind conceit had brought about the moment that was passing now.

"Monsieur le Comte?" The man who entered, big, burly, would surely have given confidence to a waiting relative, but I had seen too many doctors' expressions in the war not to recognise finality. "I am Dr. Moutier. I want to tell you that everything we can possibly do is being done. The injuries are extensive, and it would be wrong of me to express any great hope. The comtesse is, of course, unconscious. I understand neither of you was present when the accident occurred."

Once again Blanche was the spokesman and the useless story repeated.

"The windows are large," said Blanche. "She had been unwell. She must have gone to the window feeling faint and opened it too wide, and leaning out . . ." She did not finish the sentence.

The doctor's brief "Naturally, naturally" was mechanical, and he added, "The comtesse was dressed. She was not in nightclothes. Presumably she was going to join you in the search for the child."

I glanced at Blanche, but her eyes were fixed on the doctor. "She was not dressed when the rest of us left the château. She was in bed. None of us dreamt for a moment that she would get up."

"Mademoiselle, it is always the unforeseen that produces accidents. Excuse me." He turned from us to speak to the sister outside the door. The low, rapid conversation was inaudible to us inside the room, but I thought I caught the words "transfusion" and "Le Mans," and I could see from Blanche's face that she had heard them too.

"They are going to give a transfusion," she said. "I heard him say they were sending the blood from Le Mans."

She was watching the door, and I wondered if she realised that these were the first words she had spoken to her brother for fifteen years. They came too late. They were no use. He was not there to hear them.

The doctor turned to us again. "You will excuse me, Monsieur, and you, Mademoiselle. Please wait here—it is more private than the other room. I will let you know as soon as there is anything definite to tell you."

Blanche caught at his sleeve. "Forgive me, Doctor. I could not help overhearing something of what you were saying to the sister. You have sent to Le Mans for blood?"

"Yes, Mademoiselle."

"Are you sure it wouldn't save time if my brother gave his blood? Both he and my brother Paul belong to blood group O, which I understand can be given to anyone without danger?"

For a moment the doctor hesitated, glancing at me. Appalled at what might happen, at the inevitable worsening of disaster, I said swiftly, "I'm not group O. I only wish to God I were."

Blanche looked at me, dumbfounded. "That's not true. You are both universal donors, you and Paul. I remember Paul telling me only a few months ago."

I shook my head. "No," I said, "you're mistaken. Paul, perhaps, not me. I belong to group A. It wouldn't be any use."

The doctor gestured. "Please don't distress yourselves," he said. "It is preferable to use the blood straight from the laboratory. There will be very little delay. Everything necessary is on its way now to Villars from Le Mans."

He paused, looking curiously from me to Blanche, and went out of the room.

For a few moments Blanche said nothing. Then oddly, terribly, it seemed to me, her expression of concern and anguish changed. She knows, I thought, she knows at last. I've given myself away. But I was wrong. Slowly, as though she could not believe her own words, she said, "You don't want to save her. You're hoping she will die."

I stared at her, aghast. Then she turned her back on me. She went and stood by the window once again. There was nothing I could say, nothing I could do.

We went on waiting. Sometimes there were voices in the passage and sometimes footsteps passed. No one came in. The midday Angelus sounded from the cathedral church. I looked at the map once more and saw that it was forty-four kilometres from Le Mans to Villars. The distance could be covered in forty minutes. Could forty minutes make all the difference between life and death? I did not know; I hadn't the medical knowledge. All I knew was that Jean de Gué and I had different blood, that we were dissimilar in the only thing that mattered now. He might have saved his wife, but I could not. Height, breadth, colouring, features, voice, we had everything in common but that. The discovery seemed to me symbolic of all that had gone wrong. He was the human reality, I the shadow. I could not replace the living man.

As I stood there, eyes on the map, following the course of the *route nationale,* it appeared so small a stretch between two points; yet each curve meant a slackening of speed. There might be a diversion, men working on the road, a traffic block, a sudden smash. I should not even know when the car or ambulance arrived. It would go very probably to another entrance. I went out into the passage, hoping that if I stood there somebody might come. But it was empty, save for a woman with a mop cleaning the floor.

At one o'clock Paul and Renée appeared at the hospital entrance. I pointed to the room where Blanche was waiting. I did not want to talk to them; she could tell them everything we knew. Renée went straight in, but Paul, after a second's hesitation, came to me.

"Ernest is still outside with the lorry. Shall I tell him to go?" he asked.

"I will," I replied.

He paused. "How is she?" he asked.

I shook my head, and went out of the hospital into the street, and told Ernest that he had better return to the *verrerie.* When he had climbed into the lorry and driven away, it was as though my contact with solidity and safety had gone. As with Gaston, with Julie, I sensed compassion in his eyes and in his voice, and I remembered what Julie had said about him, that he had young daughters. I wished I had not sent him away, but had climbed into the lorry and asked him about his wife, about his children. He might perhaps have given me strength and courage, but in the silent hospital room I should find misunderstanding, silence, even accusation.

I went out across the Place and began walking without thought, without intention; yet half consciously, I suppose,

I knew where I must go. I found myself before the closed door of "L'Antiquaire du Pont." The glass was shuttered and there was a notice in the window saying, *"Fermé le lundi."* I turned and went through the Porte de Ville, and stood by the footbridge looking up at the balcony and the windows of the house. They were closed too, the cage with the budgerigars was not on the balcony, and suddenly the house had no connection with anything that had happened. The self who had crossed the bridge and stayed there through the night was someone else. The room within, with the grey wallpaper, the blue cushions, and the dahlias, was a figment of my imagination, as was the other room beyond, looking over the rooftops. I had never passed the threshold, I had never seen the owner. Béla, with her warmth and her understanding, did not exist.

I retraced my steps through the Porte de Ville, glanced once more at the closed door, and went back to the hospital.

Paul was standing by the entrance. He said, "We've been looking for you."

I knew then it had happened. He took my arm, an odd, half-protective gesture, and we walked together along the passage to the small room. Dr. Moutier was there, with Blanche and Renée and the sister who had received us. He came to me at once and his voice was already changed. It was no longer brisk and professional, with the authority of one who must be about his business, but that of someone who was perhaps a husband and a father.

He said, "It's all over. I'm so very sorry."

They were all looking at me except Blanche, who turned away, and when I did not answer immediately Dr. Moutier added, "She never recovered consciousness. She was in no pain. I can assure you of that."

I said, "The blood transfusion—it was no good, then?"

"No," he said. "There was just a faint chance but . . . she had sustained too great a shock . . ." He gestured with his hands.

"It came too late?" I asked.

"Too late?" He repeated the words after me, puzzled.

"The blood," I said, "the blood from Le Mans."

"Ah no," he said, "it was here in half an hour. We gave

242

the transfusion at once. Everything that it was possible to do was done. Your wife did not die from any sort of neglect, Monsieur, please believe me. We did what was necessary to the very last moment. But alas, our efforts were in vain. We could not save her."

The sister said, "You would like to see her," her words a plain statement of fact, not an interrogation, and she led me down the passage and into a small room. We stood together beside the bed, looking down on Françoise de Gué. There was no sign of injury. She might have been sleeping. She did not look like a person dead.

The sister said, "I always think the real personality appears on the face during the first hour after death. Sometimes it is a consolation to believe this."

I was not sure. The Françoise lying dead looked peaceful, younger, happier, than the Françoise who had hammered on the dressing-room door that morning. The Françoise of the morning had been haggard, anxious, querulous. If this, the dead one, was true and the other false, then living had accomplished nothing: it had been a waste of time.

"It is very hard for you to have lost them both," said the sister.

Both? I thought for one moment that she meant Marie-Noel, that she had heard the story of the missing child. Then I remembered.

"There's a daughter," I said, "ten years old."

"Dr. Moutier told me you would have had a son," she went on.

She withdrew to the door and stood there, her eyes lowered, believing, I supposed, that I wanted to be alone, to pray. I did not pray, but I tried to think if I had said anything to Françoise in the week that had been deliberately unkind. I could not remember. So much seemed to have happened. I was glad I had given her the miniature my first evening. She had been happy then, and pleased. There was nothing else, unless it was waiting on her on Friday night. The record was unimpressive. I wished I had done more. I turned, and went back to the others.

Paul said to me, "You had better get home to St. Gilles. I've telephoned to Gaston to bring the Citroën. Blanche and

I will stay here to make arrangements, and Gaston can drive you and Renée in the Renault."

I could tell, by their faces, that they had been discussing what must be done. There was a certain quiet formality of tone and gesture that went with the aftermath of death. Nothing was referred to me direct. Mistakenly, the bereaved are left alone to indulge grief. It would have been better to give me something to discuss, to sign, to arrange. Instead I watched them, silent, ineffectual.

When Gaston came I sensed relief. They wanted me out of the way. Renée silently pushed me into the front seat, herself got into the back, and we drove away.

Gaston's face was shocked and drawn. He had not said anything to me when I had climbed into the car, but silently, gently, he had put a rug over my knees, a strange, touching gesture of sympathy for sorrow. I wondered, as he took the familiar road again, whether he thought, as I did, of the morning's drive and that of the preceding night, hours so remote that they seemed never to have been.

The closed shutters of the château were the first sign of mourning, and I supposed that Gaston, after Paul had telephoned from the hospital, had given orders for this to be done. Yet life would not be denied. Long rays of daylight stole through the chinks and patterned the floor in the salon, and the tribute of mourning to Françoise, lying still and peaceful in the small hospital room, seemed somehow useless and false. The sun and the warmth of day had never harmed her; it was we who had lacked forethought and care and had thrust perception out of doors.

Gaston had also given orders for a meal to be laid in the dining room, for none of us had touched any food. More to satisfy him, I think, than ourselves, we sat down and ate mechanically. Renée, subdued and gentle, revealing another facet of herself, told me how she and Paul had driven to every farm during the morning within a radius of ten kilometres, enquiring for the child, and had only returned to St. Gilles at half past twelve. It was strange, I thought, how sudden death, like war, brings instant sympathy. The challenging, sensual Renée of the past week was now natural, kindly, anxious to help us all, suggesting that she should make up a bed for Marie-Noel in Blanche's room so that the child would not be alone, or that Paul should move from their room and the child go to her, offering to fetch her from the *verrerie*—ready to do anything to make the sudden loss less frightening, less appalling for Marie-Noel.

"I don't think she will be frightened," I said. "I think—I can't explain why—she was prepared."

Renée, who a few hours before would have said immediately that everything Marie-Noel had done was outrageous, exhibitionist, and she should be severely punished, answered nothing, except that children who walked in their sleep should never sleep alone.

Presently she went upstairs and I continued sitting in the dining room, thinking. After a while I called Gaston and asked him to go to the *verrerie* with a message for Julie. Would he, I said, tell her that Françoise was dead, and that I wanted Julie to break the news to Marie-Noel?

"Monsieur le Curé is upstairs with Madame la Comtesse," he said to me, after a moment's hesitation. "Does Monsieur le Comte wish to see him now, or presently?"

"How long has he been here?" I asked.

"Madame la Comtesse sent for him as soon as Charlotte told her of the accident."

"When was that?"

"I don't know, Monsieur le Comte. Monsieur Paul and I could get no sense out of any of the women here when we returned and heard what had happened. They were too upset to explain anything clearly."

"I'll see Monsieur le Curé directly," I said. "Meanwhile ask Germaine to come to me."

"Very good, Monsieur le Comte."

Germaine was already in tears as she entered the room, and at sight of me her face crumpled afresh. It was a moment or two before she could control herself.

"That's enough," I said. "You only make it harder for all of us if you give way. There is something I want to ask you. Did you know Madame Jean had got up and dressed this morning before the accident?"

"No, Monsieur le Comte. I took her breakfast at nine, and she was still in bed. She said nothing to me about getting up.

Mademoiselle Blanche sent me to make enquiries in the village about the child, and when I came back I went straight to the kitchen. I never saw Madame Jean again."

The tears were welling into her eyes once more, and I had nothing else to ask her. I told her to send Charlotte to me.

It was a moment or two before Charlotte appeared, and when she did I saw at once that the hysteria of the morning was now over. She was watchful, self-possessed, and the small, beady eyes looked up at me almost with defiance. I did not waste any time. I said to her immediately, "When we all went out this morning to look for the child, did you go back again to talk to Madame Jean?"

There was a momentary hesitation in her eye, and then she said, "Yes, Monsieur le Comte. I just slipped in to say a word or two of comfort while she was having breakfast."

"What did you say to her?"

"There was nothing much I could say, Monsieur le Comte. I begged her not to worry. The child would soon be found."

"Did she seem very anxious?"

"She was more concerned about the little one's state of mind, Monsieur le Comte, than about her actual disappearance. She was worried that the child might have turned against her. 'She is too fond of her papa,' she said, 'and of Mademoiselle Blanche; she does not come to her mother as she should.' Those were her exact words."

"How did you answer that?"

"I told her the truth, Monsieur le Comte. I said that when a father idolises his daughter as Monsieur le Comte idolises Marie-Noel, it is always difficult for the mother. I had an aunt who experienced the same trouble. It was even worse when the daughter grew older; she and the father were inseparable, and my aunt had a nervous breakdown in consequence."

"Did you tell her that by way of comfort?"

"I told her because I was sympathetic, Monsieur le Comte. I knew that Madame Jean was often lonely here."

I wondered just how much damage Charlotte had done, now and in the past, in the château of St. Gilles. "Did you know Madame Jean meant to get up?" I asked.

Again the flicker of hesitation. "She said nothing definite,"

246

Charlotte answered. "She told me she did not like staying there all alone not knowing what was happening. She asked me if Madame la Comtesse was awake upstairs. I said not yet, that she was sleeping late. She said she might have some ideas about the child. Then I took her tray and went downstairs to do my washing and ironing. That was the last time I saw Madame Jean."

She shook her head slowly as she said this, and sighed, and clasped her hands, but there was nothing genuine about the gesture, like the flowing tears of Germaine.

"At what time did Madame la Comtesse wake?" I said.

Charlotte thought for a moment. "I'm not sure, Monsieur le Comte. I think it was a little before ten. She rang for me, but she did not want anything to eat. I told her about the child. She shrugged her shoulders; she wasn't interested. She sat in her chair, and I made her bed, and presently, seeing she did not need me, I went below again. I was still below in the sewing room, ironing, when the accident happened. Both Gaston's wife and I heard Berthe the cow woman scream, and we ran out . . . but you already know that, Monsieur le Comte."

She lowered her eyes and her voice and bent her head. I told her curtly she could go, and as she was leaving the room I said to her, "When you broke the news of the accident to Madame la Comtesse, what did she say?"

Charlotte paused, her hand on the door, then turned and looked at me. "She was horrified, Monsieur le Comte, stunned. Because of that I sent at once for Monsieur le Curé. I could not give her anything; it would not have been wise. You understand me?"

"I understand you."

When she had gone, I went upstairs to the dressing room and through the bathroom to the bedroom. Someone had closed the shutters here as elsewhere, and the window too. The bed had not been made, only the sheet and blankets pulled back. I went to the window and opened it, and the shutters too. The base of the window came to my hip. It was possible to sit on the sill, lean out, and lean too far. Possible, but not probable. Yet it had happened . . . I closed the window and the shutters once again. I looked around

247

the bedroom that gave no clue to what had passed, no hint of tragedy, and then went out and shut the door behind me. I walked along the corridor, up the stairs, through the door to the other corridor, and so to the room in the tower at the far end.

Chapter 21

I did not knock. I opened the door and went straight in. The room was shuttered like the others, the window closed, but here even the curtains were drawn too. No daylight penetrated; it might have been winter. A lamp was turned on by the bedside, and another on the table by the stove, and the fact that the sun shone brightly at four o'clock on the late, lingering, autumn afternoon made no difference to the changeless room in the tower, which was always dark, always barricaded against the day.

The dogs had been banished elsewhere, and the only sound was the low murmur of the curé, praying, and the echoing response from the opposite chair. Both had their rosaries in their hands; the curé was kneeling, head bowed, the mother sat huddled in her chair, shoulders hunched, chin touching her chest. Neither stirred when I entered, but I saw the mother's hand holding the rosary tighten an instant, then relax, and the Amen that followed the Pater and the Ave became louder, more fervent, as though the voice was conscious of a more earthly audience.

I did not kneel—I listened and waited. The murmur of the curé ran on, monotonous, soothing, stifling thought, and it seemed to me that this must surely be his purpose, whether he was praying for the living or the dead. The spirit of Françoise, lying in the hospital room, did not wish to be reminded of what had happened to her in the world she had deserted, and the mind of the mother here, who echoed the prayers, must not waken suddenly with a question. The cadence, smooth and toneless, the humming of a bee inside the petals of a flower, dulled interrogation, and my senses and my nerves, which had been strained, ready to snap, became gradually numbed, tuning themselves to the atmosphere and tempo of this room without life.

When the last Gloria was said, and the last Amen, there was a pause before the world took charge once more, the speaker became corporeal, the voice became the curé with his gentle old baby face and his nodding head. Rising to his feet, he came to me at once and took my hand.

"My son," he said, "we have been praying so hard for you, your mother and I, and we have asked that you may be given courage and support in this terrible moment of affliction."

I thanked him, and he continued standing, holding my hand and patting it, his face troubled for my sake, yet serene. I envied him his singleness of purpose, his belief that we were all of us erring children or lost lambs whom the Good Shepherd would gather in His arms or into the fold, whatever our omissions and our sins.

"The child," he said, "would you like me to tell her?"—going straight to what he felt must matter most to me. I replied no, I had asked Julie to tell her, but that presently both Paul and Blanche would be home, and perhaps he would arrange with them the many things that must be done.

"You know," he said, "that now, tomorrow and always I am at your disposal, ready to do all in my power for you, and Madame la Comtesse, and the child, and everyone at the château."

He blessed us both, took his books and left the room. We were alone. I said nothing. Nor did she. I did not look at her. Then suddenly, on impulse, I crossed to the window and pulled back the heavy curtains. I opened the windows wide and the shutters too, flinging them back against the wall, and air came into the room, and light. I went and turned out the lamps, and it was day. Then I stood beside her chair, and the sun of late afternoon shone down on her so that nothing was hidden; neither the grey pallor of her face, nor the hooded eyes, nor the raddled cheeks, nor the massive jowl, and as she raised her hand to shield her eyes from the sun the sleeve of her black wool coat fell back, showing the puncture marks between wrist and forearm.

"What are you doing? Are you trying to blind me?" she said, and she moved forward in her chair, trying to escape

249

the light. Her rosary fell to the floor, and her missal too, and I picked them up and gave them back to her, and then stood between her and the sun.

"What happened?" I asked.

"Happened?" She repeated the question after me, raising her head and staring, but she could not see my eyes because I was in shadow. "How do I know what happened, imprisoned here as I am, useless, nobody even answering a bell? I thought you had come to tell me what happened, not I you." She paused a moment, then she added, "Close the shutters and draw the curtains. You know I hate the light."

"No," I said.

She grimaced, and shrugged her shoulders. "As you wish. It's a strange moment to open them, that's all. I gave orders for Gaston to close the château. I presume he has done what he was told."

She settled herself back in her chair, and, taking up her rosary, put it between the pages of her missal, as though to mark the place, and then laid both on the table by her side. She eased the cushions at her back and moved the footstool under her feet.

"Now the curé has gone," she said, "I could tell Charlotte to bring back the dogs. They always make a nuisance of themselves when he is here. Why do you keep standing? Why don't you draw up the chair and sit down?"

I did not sit down. I knelt on one knee beside her chair, my hand on the arm of it. She watched me, her face a mask.

"What did you say to her?" I asked.

"What did I say to whom? To Charlotte?"

"To Françoise," I said.

Nothing happened, except that she sat more still. Her left hand ceased to play with the fringe of her shawl.

"When?" she asked. "I did not see her after she became unwell and went to bed. I had not seen her for several days."

"You're lying," I said. "You saw her this morning."

My reply was sudden. She did not expect it. I saw her whole body stiffen in her chair.

"Who says so?" she demanded. "Who's been talking?"

"I say so," I answered, "and nobody's been talking."

Purposely I kept my voice low. There was no accusation in it, or in my words.

"Did she recover consciousness? Did she say anything to you in the hospital before she died?" The question was sharp, abrupt.

"No," I said. "She said nothing to me, or to anyone."

"Then what does it matter? Why do you want to know? Suppose she did come here this morning, how can it help you now?"

"I want to know how and why she died," I answered.

She gestured. "What's the use? None of us can know. She became giddy and fell. Berthe saw her, didn't she, as she was crossing into the park with the cows? That was what Charlotte told me. Weren't you told the same story?"

"Yes," I said, "I was told the same story. So was Blanche. So were Paul and Renée, I imagine. So were the people at the hospital. I don't believe it, that's all."

"What do you believe?"

I stared at the face that told me nothing. "I believe she killed herself," I said, "and so do you."

I expected a denial, or an outburst, or an accusation—or possibly a crumpling of defence and a plea for sympathy. Instead, unbelievably, she shrugged her shoulders, and then she smiled and said without emotion, "And if she did . . ."

This answer, cold, inhuman, dismissing sudden death so casually, was yet a confirmation of all I had most feared. Indifference towards Françoise I had sensed from the beginning, but with something else as well, never uttered: a wish on the part of the mother that her daughter-in-law might die. Whatever the reason—possessiveness, malice, greed—the countess had wanted Françoise out of the way, and had believed, in her inmost heart, that her son wanted it too. Illness in pregnancy might have achieved this end: today's disaster made a swifter finish. It roused no pity in her that Françoise, unhappy, neglected, had perhaps surrendered on impulse without the will to live. Death, or the birth of an heir—either meant release from poverty; and Jean's mother felt only relief that matters were now resolved.

"Whatever happened," she said, "there can be no blame on you. You were not here. Therefore forget it. Play your part and mourn." She leant forward in her chair and took my face between her hands. "It's too late to develop a conscience," she went on. "I told you that the other evening. And if you thought that Françoise would survive the birth of the child, what made you gamble on her death?"

"What do you mean?" I asked.

"The day after you returned from Paris you telephoned Carvalet," she said. "Charlotte told me—she listened on the extension in Blanche's room, as she always does if there's anything being said below worth listening to, and then reports to me—and when I heard what you had said to the firm, the nonsensical agreement to their demands, I knew at once that it was a gamble. You were counting on the fortune that might come. Without an increase in capital you'd ruin yourself. No wonder you had qualms the next morning, and went off to Villars to the bank, and down to the safe to look through the Marriage Settlement. You could have spared yourself the trouble. There are duplicates of everything in the library, if you had taken the trouble to search for them. It was more amusing to go to Villars, wasn't it? You have a woman there. You told me so that evening when you returned."

The pattern of events was plain and could not be denied. My motives, misconstrued and twisted, were unimportant now.

"Françoise knew about the contract," I said. "I didn't keep it from her. I told her the truth."

"The truth?" The eyes that looked into mine were cynical and hard. The pain and anguish of the night before had gone. She might never have asked for my help, might never have suffered. "We all of us tell the truth when it happens to suit us," she said. "Françoise told me the truth this morning, when she came in here. Oh yes, you're right. I did see her. I was probably the last to do so. She came up dressed, ready to search for the child. 'What's upset Marie-Noel?' she asked. 'Why has she run away?' 'What's upset her?' I answered. 'She's afraid of being supplanted, that's all. None of us like to be deposed. She wants you out of the way, and the baby too.' That started it. She told me she'd never been happy here, she'd always been homesick, lonely, lost, and it was my fault, because I'd been against her from the start. 'Jean was never in love with me,' she said. I agreed. 'Even now he only wants the money,' she went on. 'Naturally,' I replied. 'Does he want me to die so that he can marry someone else?' she asked at last. I told her I did not know. 'Jean makes love to everyone. He has made love to Renée, even, here in the château, and he has a mistress in Villars,' I said. She told me she had suspected both these things, and that your kindness to her, the last few days, had been a blind, to make her believe otherwise. 'So the child isn't the only one to want me out of the way,' she said. 'Jean does too, and so do you, and Renée, and the woman in Villars.' I didn't answer her. I told her to stop being hysterical, and to take herself downstairs. That was all. Nothing more was said. She asked for the truth and got it. If she was not brave enough to face up to it, that was her affair, not mine. Whether she threw herself out of the window or fell because she was giddy is beside the point, and something we can't ever prove. The result is the same. You've got what you wanted, haven't you?"

"No," I shouted, "no . . ."

I pushed her back in the chair, and her expression changed. She looked bewildered, frightened, and the sudden switch from cynicism to apprehension at the sound of my voice, roused in anger against her, as she believed, and not against myself, made me realise the hopelessness of explanation, the useless wasted effort of trying to make her understand. Whatever she had said to Françoise, however truthful, however harsh, had been said for her son's sake. I could not accuse her.

I got up and went to the window, and stood there staring out across the park to the trees. Dear God, I thought, there must be an answer to this, there must be a way out—not for me, the impostor, but for them, for the mother, for the child, for Blanche and Paul and Renée. If Jean de Gué had fostered jealousy, dissension, animosity, he had the excuse of the past. I had no such pretext. I had followed him because I wished to remain hidden, to lose identity.

The night's rain had cleared the débris from the leaded guttering. A pool of water glistened on the gargoyle's tongue.

Something else in the gutter shone like glass. It was a morphine phial, empty, thrown out by Charlotte and now revealing itself because the leaves had gone. Seeing the phial lying there in the gutter, I wondered, had I not used the syringe the night before but had stayed here in the room, what might have been achieved, what hope, what understanding. I should not have gone to Villars, nor the child to the well. The tragedy would have been averted. Françoise would have lived. I turned away from the window, and looked back at the woman sitting in the chair, and I said to her, "You've got to help me."

"Help you? How?" she asked. "How can I help you?"

I knelt beside her chair and took her hand. Whatever wrongs there had been in the years that were gone, they could not be righted by a stranger. I could only build the present. But not alone.

"You told me just now that I had got what I wanted," I said. "Did you mean the money? For the glass foundry, for all of us, for St. Gilles?"

"What else?" she asked. "You'll be a rich man, you can do what you like, and you'll be free. That's all that matters to you, isn't it?"

"No," I said, "you matter to me. I want you to be the head of my house, as you used to be. And you can't as long as you take morphine."

Something fell apart, the layer upon layer of defence protecting every individual from assault so that no challenge can be heard, no signal seen; the core, left untouched in isolation, crumbled for one brief moment as I spoke, and I felt, in the hand that tightened on mine, the loneliness of years, the numbed senses, the mocking mind, the empty heart. It was as though, touching her then, these things became part of me and were now mine, and the burden was intolerable beyond belief. Then she withdrew her hand from mine, the armour folded about her once again, the face formed into features, and she became a person who had chosen a way of life because there was no alternative, and the man who knelt by her side, whom she believed to be her son, was trying to take away from her the only solace, the one method of oblivion.

"I'm tired and old and useless," she said. "Why should you grudge me something that makes me forget?"

"You're not tired or old or useless," I said. "To yourself, perhaps, but not to me. Yesterday you came downstairs and stood on the terrace, receiving the guests. You wanted to stand beside me, as you stood beside my father, you wanted to be the person you were once, long ago. But it wasn't just clinging to the past, or pride; it was also an attempt to prove to yourself that it could be done, that you were not dependent on the box of ampoules in there, and the syringe, and Charlotte. You could defeat them, and you did. You would have gone on defeating them but for me."

She looked up at me, watchful, guarded. "What do you mean?" she said.

"What did you think about," I asked, "yesterday morning, after the guests had gone?"

"I thought about you," she said, "about the past. I went back over the years. What does it matter what I thought? I began to suffer, that's all. When I suffer I have to have morphine."

"I made you suffer," I said. "I was the cause."

"What if you were?" she said. "All mothers suffer for their sons. It's part of our life. We don't blame you for it."

"It's not part of a son's life," I said. "They can't stand pain. I'm a coward and always have been. That's why I want your help, now and in the future, much more so than in the past."

I rose from my knees and went into the dressing room next door. The box of ampoules was still in the cupboard above the basin, and the syringe, and I took them out and brought them into the bedroom and showed them to her.

"I'm going to take them away," I said. "Perhaps it's dangerous to do so—I don't know. You told me I gambled on winning a fortune when I made that new contract with Carvalet. This is another gamble, a different kind."

I saw her hands tighten on the chair, and for a moment a look of terror, of despair, came into her eyes.

"I can't do it, Jean," she said. "You don't understand. I can't deprive myself suddenly, like this. I'm too old, too tired. Once, perhaps, but not now. If you wanted me to stop, why didn't you tell me so before? It's too late."

"It's not too late." I put the box down on the table. "Give me your hands," I said.

She put her hands in mine and I pulled her up from the chair. As she stood beside me she steadied herself, tightly clutching my bandaged hand, and I felt the pain shoot from my fingers to my elbow. She went on holding me, not realising, and I knew that if I took my hand away something would be lost to her, some confidence, some strength, which for the moment was part of her and gave her courage.

"Now come downstairs," I said.

She stood between me and the window, massive, huge, blocking the light, trembling a moment as she gained her balance, the ebony crucifix which she wore round her neck swinging against her breast like a pendulum.

"Downstairs?" she repeated. "What for?"

"Because I need you," I said, "and in future you'll come down every day."

For a long time she held onto me, never once relaxing her grip upon my hand. Then she released me and moved slowly to the door, majestic, dignified. She did not take my arm in the corridor but went forward, ahead of me, and opened the door of another room. At once the terriers rushed at her, barking, jumping, leaping to lick her hands.

She turned to me, exultant. "Just as I thought," she said. "These dogs are not taken out. Charlotte lies to me. Charlotte is supposed to take them in the park every afternoon. The trouble is there is no supervision in the château, no sort of order."

The dogs, released, ran to the stairs, and as we followed them she said to me, "Did I hear you tell the curé that Blanche and Paul were to make the arrangements for the funeral?"

"Yes," I said.

"They don't understand these things," she said. "There hasn't been a funeral in the château since your father died. It must be done properly. Françoise was a person of importance—she should have every respect paid to her. After all, she was your wife. She was the Comtesse de Gué."

She waited at the head of the stairs while I put the boxes in the dressing room. As we entered the salon we heard voices. The others had returned. Paul was standing by the fireplace, the curé beside him. Renée was in her usual place on the sofa, Blanche on another chair. They stared at us, disconcerted, and even the curé, startled, took a moment to recover before he came forward, solicitous, anxious to assist. But she waved him aside and went straight to the chair beside the fire, the chair where Françoise always sat. Blanche rose at once and went to her.

"You ought to be in bed," she said. "Charlotte told me you were very shaken, very exhausted."

"Charlotte's a liar," was the answer, "and you can mind your own business." She fumbled on her dress for the pair of spectacles that were hanging from a chain round her neck beside the crucifix, and put them on and looked at each one of us in turn. "This is a house of mourning," she said, "not a nursing home. My daughter-in-law has died. I intend to see that everything is done to honour her that should be done. Paul, get me a pencil and some sheets of paper. Blanche, in the desk in my room, in the top drawer, you will find a dossier containing all the names of the people who came to your father's funeral. Most of them are dead, but they have relatives. Renée, fetch me the telephone directory from the cloakroom. Monsieur le Curé, I should be obliged if you will come and sit beside me; I may have to refer to you for matters concerning the actual burial itself. Jean"—she looked up at me, and paused—"I don't expect any help from you for the moment. You had better take a walk, the air will do you good. You can exercise the dogs, as Charlotte failed to do so. But before you go," she added, "change into a dark suit. The Comte de Gué does not stroll about in a sports jacket when he has lost his wife."

Chapter 22

I left them in the salon, and went upstairs and changed. Then I called for Gaston and asked him to bring the car round to the drive.

"I want you to take me to the *verrerie*," I said. "I'm going to fetch the child."

"Very good, Monsieur le Comte."

As we drove out of the village and up the hill towards the forest he said, "My wife and I, Monsieur le Comte, and indeed everyone in the château, wish to express our deepest sympathy to you in this moment of stress."

"Thank you, Gaston," I said.

"If there is anything any of us can do, you have only to say so, Monsieur le Comte."

I thanked him again. There was nothing anybody could do to ease things, except myself; and I had started off by depriving an addict of morphine, which might lead to a tragedy worse than the first. I did not know. All I knew was that I had become a gambler, like Jean de Gué.

Gaston stopped the car outside the foundry gates. It was still early, yet no one was about. The men must have stopped work for the day out of respect for Françoise.

I got out of the car and went into the deserted grounds. Julie was not in her lodge. She must be in her son's cottage, and Marie-Noel with her. I told Gaston to wait, and walked towards the master's house, but the door was locked. I crossed the worn paving in front of the windows, and went and looked down into the well. I suppose it was about twenty feet in depth. The rickety ladder, with gaps here and there where the rungs were missing, was rotting away. The sides of the well were slimy, green with mould. Far below, at the base, I could see broken glass, and sand, and mud. That a child of ten could climb down into it, at night, without fear, coming to no harm, was unbelievable. Yet it was true.

I turned away from the well and looked through the dusty windows of the master's house. The blankets were still heaped on the floor where Marie-Noel had lain. I went round to the orchard at the back, and the window through which I had climbed that morning was now closed. But the hasp was not fastened—Julie must have shut the window hurriedly, after Blanche and I had left, and then taken Marie-Noel with her to her lodge, or to her son's cottage.

I threw open the window once again and climbed inside.

Then I went and stood beside the heap of blankets, as I had done that morning, and out of the emptiness I conjured the small, still face of the child as she lay sleeping, impervious, so it had seemed, to horror or to pain, but enduring behind the little mask the troubled burden of her ferocious dream. I bent and touched the blanket, and as I did so I was reminded of other moments, at Chinon, perhaps, or Orléans, when a line of tourist pilgrims, eyes agape, put grubby hands on a step where the Maid once knelt, so as to draw virtue from the stone. I had thought it foolish. It was foolish still. The blanket I touched had been flung round a child with too much imagination, after she had spent a night in a well. I felt in my pocket for the scrap of paper and read the last lines again. "The Sainte Vierge tells me you are unhappy, and are suffering now for wrong done in the past, so I am going to pray that all your sins may be visited upon me, who, being young and strong, can bear them better. Sleep well, and have faith in Marie-Noel, who loves you dearly." I replaced the scrap of paper. I was the only pilgrim . . .

I went out through the window and back by the way I had come, looking for a moment at the gnarled old trees laden with apples, the fallen sunflowers, and the vine climbing the house, heavy with grapes that nobody picked. Then I passed through to the front once more, by the sheds. Gaston must have told them at the cottage that I was here, for Marie-Noel was coming across the ground towards me.

Suddenly I did not know what to say to her. I had thought I should see Julie first. Julie would have told me how she had taken the news.

"Don't laugh," she called to me.

Laugh? I had never felt less like laughing in my life. I stood still, baffled, not knowing what she meant.

"I'm wearing Pierre's clothes," she said. "This is his jersey, and his black overall. Madame Yves made me change out of my blue frock because it was damp. Besides, it wasn't suitable."

I realised then that she was indeed wearing things that didn't fit. They were too short, making her legs longer and thinner than ever, and she had borrowed a pair of sabots too,

259

which were much too large, so that when she walked she had to shuffle her feet to keep them on.

"Look," she said, "I'm taller than Pierre, and he's twelve."

She showed how the sleeves of the overall did not reach her wrists, and stretched herself to make it seem smaller still.

"Yes," I said, "I see."

I stood awkwardly, looking down at her. Surely, I thought, there must be something that a father does or says at a time of tragedy like this? He would not just stand as I was doing, talking about clothes.

"I couldn't fetch you before . . ." I began, but she did not wait for me to finish. She took my hand and said, "I'm glad you didn't. Come and see what we've been making, Pierre and I," and she led me over to a mound of rubble beside a heap of waste glass. "There is the château," she said, pointing to the small glass model which had been in her pocket that morning, "and these other pieces are the houses in St. Gilles. That big block is the church. Look, Pierre has scooped up gravel to make roads. This line of pebbles is the river, and the bent twig is the bridge. We've been playing this all afternoon."

Julie couldn't have told her, then. She didn't know. I looked over my shoulder for Julie or Gaston, but I couldn't see either of them.

"Where's Madame Yves?" I asked.

"In the cottage," she said, "talking to Gaston and André. Pierre has gone to the farm for milk. I drank all theirs this morning; they only had a little in a jug. Guess what we had for lunch—chicken! Madame Yves went and caught a poor old limping cock who used to fight the others. She said it was time he went to his rest, and he went bravely, in honour of my visit."

She looked up at me, to watch my astonishment. I did not say anything. I was trying to think out how to tell her what had happened.

"Do you know," she said, and she lowered her voice, "it's very sad, but Pierre's mother doesn't live with them any more. She ran away to Le Mans some weeks ago, and that's why Madame Yves goes in and cooks for André and Pierre. It's such a shocking thing, for a boy to be without his mother and a husband without his wife."

I hadn't given Julie enough time. That had been it. Gaston had brought the message less than an hour ago. She had not yet found the right moment to break the news. But I was wrong.

"Our situation is very similar," she said. "You have even burnt yourself as André did, but his burn will last for a lifetime, and yours only for a few days. Also, we shall have the consolation of knowing that Maman is well cared for. After all, as Madame Yves explained, it is better to be with Jesus Christ in Paradise than with a mechanic in Le Mans." She stood up, brushing the sand from her knees. "When Ernest came back with the lorry and said that Maman had been taken to hospital, I knew what would happen," she went on. "My dreams have a habit of coming true. But at least this was an accident. In my dream we were trying to kill her on purpose. How did Maman come to fall from the window?"

"I don't know," I said. "Nobody knows."

"I shall find out," she said. "It will console Maman in Paradise if we know."

Then she picked up the glass château and put it in her pocket, and hand in hand we walked over to the lodge. Julie was coming in at the gate with Gaston. She carried the child's clothes over her arm.

"The things are dry now," she called. "You had better change. You can't go back to the château dressed like that. Quickly, then."

She bustled Marie-Noel into the lodge with the clothes, and then she turned to me. "She has been very courageous," she said softly. "You can be proud of her."

"It's happened too suddenly," I said. "She hasn't felt it yet."

Julie looked at me with pity, as she had done that morning when we stood together beside the sleeping child. "Do you know so little about children, Monsieur Jean," she asked, "that you imagine, because they don't cry, therefore they feel nothing? If so, you're much mistaken." She spoke quickly, as though she were trying to defend the child against some accusation. Then she recovered herself. "You must excuse me for speaking frankly. The truth is that the child won all our

261

hearts today. My condolences, Monsieur le Comte, in your great loss."

The proprieties were restored between us. The concierge of the glass foundry was speaking to the seigneur of St. Gilles. I bowed my head and thanked her. Then I turned to her again as a friend.

"You have done a lot for us today, Julie," I said. "I believed it better for you to break the news than anyone else. And I was right."

"She needed no telling," Julie answered. "It was she who told us. The dream had warned her, she said. For my part, I have never believed in dreams, Monsieur Jean. Only that children, like animals, are close to God." She looked over the waste ground towards the master's house and the well. "I suppose," she said, "there will be a police enquiry? You will not be bringing Madame Jean back to the château until it is over?"

"A police enquiry?" I repeated.

"No doubt it is for the doctors to arrange," she said, nodding. "It is to be hoped it will be quickly over. These things are unpleasant."

I had been too dazed at the hospital, and too distressed, to consider such a thing as an enquiry. But Julie was right, of course. This must have been one of the things discussed by Paul and Blanche at the hospital after I went.

"I'm not sure what the arrangements are, Julie," I said. "I left it all to Monsieur Paul and Mademoiselle Blanche."

Marie-Noel came out of the lodge, changed back into her frock and coat. She kissed Julie and we said good-bye, and Gaston drove us back to St. Gilles. As we passed through the gateway I saw there were four other cars in the drive below the terrace.

"There's Dr. Lebrun's car," said Marie-Noel, "and Monsieur Talbert's too. I don't know about the others."

Talbert—he was the lawyer who had written the letter which I had found in the safe. No doubt he looked after the family affairs. Then, as we drew up behind the cars and got out, we saw a man in uniform seated behind the wheel of the front one.

"That's the *commissaire de police*'s car," Gaston murmured.

"He must have come out from Villars with Maître Talbert and the doctors."

"Why do they all have to come?" asked Marie-Noel. "They aren't going to arrest anyone, surely?"

"They always come," I said, "if there's been an accident. I shall have to see them. Will you go and find Germaine and ask her to read to you?"

"Germaine reads badly," she said. "Don't worry about me. I promise you, now and forever more, I won't do anything to make trouble."

She went up the terrace and in through the door, and I turned to Gaston.

"The *commissaire* will probably have to question your wife," I said to him. "She was here at the time of the accident."

"Yes, Monsieur le Comte."

He looked anxious. I was anxious too. The nightmare of the day was not yet over. I entered the château and heard voices coming from the salon. They ceased as I opened the door, and everyone turned and looked at me. I recognised Dr. Lebrun, and Dr. Moutier from the hospital. The third was small, thickset, with greying hair. This was presumably the lawyer, Talbert. The fourth, who had a more official air, must be the *commissaire de police*.

My first thought was for the comtesse. I looked across the room at her, and saw that she was still sitting in the chair beside the fireplace, commanding, indomitable. She showed no sign of fatigue, and her presence filled the room, dwarfing the others.

"Here is my son, Monsieur," she said to the *commissaire*. And then turning to me, "Monsieur Lemotte has been so good as to come himself from Villars to ask the necessary questions."

The three men approached me, anxious to show their sympathy. "It is with regret that I intrude upon you in this moment, Monsieur," from the *commissaire de police*, and "So immeasurably shocked, Monsieur, permit me to share this time of trial," from the lawyer, and "I find myself so overwhelmed, de Gué, that I cannot find words to express my sorrow," from Dr. Lebrun. The murmuring of thanks, the shaking of hands, lent ease and dignity to the proceedings, helping to bridge the awkward gap before the questioning must begin. Then, the courtesies over, the *commissaire* turned to me.

"Both Dr. Lebrun and Dr. Moutier have informed me, Monsieur, that your wife was expecting a child within a few weeks, and I understand there was some increase in nervousness lately," he said. "Would you agree?"

"Yes," I replied. "That's quite correct."

"She was, perhaps, unduly apprehensive about the birth?"

"I think she was."

"Excuse me, Monsieur," interrupted Talbert, the lawyer, "Monsieur le Comte will forgive the explanation, but the birth was eagerly awaited both by him and by Madame la Comtesse Jean. They hoped for a son."

"Naturally," said the *commissaire*, "all parents are the same."

"But especially in this case," said the lawyer, "because under the terms of her Marriage Settlement the birth of a son meant an immediate increase of income, above all to Monsieur le Comte. I know, from what she said to me, that Madame la Comtesse Jean dreaded disappointing her husband, and indeed the whole family. This would, I think, account for more nervousness than usual in her case."

"Dread is surely a strong word, Maître Talbert." They turned to the speaker in her armchair by the fireplace. "My daughter-in-law had no need to dread any one of us. We are not so dependent on the terms of a Marriage Settlement that we cannot exist without its help. My late husband's family has been in possession here for three hundred years."

The lawyer flushed. "I was not suggesting, Madame, that Madame la Comtesse Jean was in any way intimidated by her situation. It was just that the position was delicate, and a responsibility to her. The birth of a son would have eased the financial difficulties considerably. She was aware of that."

The *commissaire* looked at Dr. Lebrun, who hesitated, glancing at the countess and then at me. "Madame Jean was certainly anxious for a son," he said. "In fact, she stressed the point when I attended her last week. No doubt this anxiety added to her nervous state."

"In short," said the *commissaire*, "Madame la Comtesse Jean was inclined to hysteria. Forgive me, Monsieur, I only wish to establish that your wife was particularly agitated at the time of the accident, and therefore, in her condition, more liable to attacks of giddiness. You would agree, Doctor?"

"Of course, of course."

"And you, Monsieur?"

"I suppose so," I replied. "She was also anxious about her little girl. You have been told what happened?"

"Monsieur Paul de Gué and Mademoiselle Blanche have given me their account of it. Also a *femme de chambre*. I am glad the little one was found eventually. So the last time you saw your wife was this morning, before you went to look for the child?"

"That is so, yes."

"Was she very disturbed?"

"Not more so, I think, than the rest of us."

"She did not suggest getting up and joining the search party?"

"No."

"You left her in bed, presumably to await your return with news of the child's safety?"

"Yes."

"Everybody, then, seems to have left the house, with the exception of the two *femmes de chambre*—Germaine, who took up Madame la Comtesse Jean's breakfast and was then sent to the village by Mademoiselle Blanche, and Charlotte; the cook, who was below; and of course Madame la Comtesse, who was in her room upstairs. I have examined the spot where your wife fell," he added to me. "I propose going to the bedroom directly, with your approval."

"Of course," I said.

"I have already questioned Berthe, the woman who tends the cows. She saw your wife leaning from the window, as though reaching out—so she described it—and then she grasped at the air, as it seemed, and fell. Berthe screamed for help, and was heard by the cook and Charlotte, who went instantly to the moat. The cook telephoned for the ambulance from Villars, and Dr. Moutier has told me the rest. I should like to establish that nobody else went to the bedroom after Germaine, the *femme de chambre* whom I saw just now, took up her breakfast."

"Charlotte might have done," said Renée.

"Perhaps you would ring for her, Monsieur?" suggested the *commissaire*.

"Charlotte is my personal maid: I will ring for her," said the comtesse. A hand went out from the armchair to the bell rope. "It was Charlotte who broke the news of the accident to me. She was hysterical. So, I imagine, were the others. You won't learn much from her. Servants always lose their heads in a disaster."

When Gaston answered the bell she told him the *commissaire* wished to speak to Charlotte.

"I don't quite follow," said Paul, "why it matters what Charlotte or Germaine said to my sister-in-law. It has no bearing on the fact that she became giddy and fell from the window."

"I am sorry, Monsieur," said the *commissaire*. "I quite understand the distress all this must cause to the family. It is just that, in order to conform with the requirements of the law, I must establish beyond any shadow of doubt that the cause of the fall was accidental. Unhappily, when someone falls from a height this is not always the case."

Renée, startled, turned suddenly white. "What do you mean?" she asked.

"Madame," explained the *commissaire* gently, "when a person is in a highly nervous condition it leads them, sometimes, to do dangerous things. I am not suggesting that is what happened in this case. As I have already said, in my view the cause is more likely to have been a sudden attack of giddiness. But I have to make quite sure."

"Do you mean," asked Blanche, "that my sister-in-law may have fallen from the window purposely?"

"It is possible, Madame. Not probable."

There was a sudden silence in the room, a silence filled, it seemed to me, as I looked from one to another of their troubled faces, with swift, unspoken denial, born of their inner guilt that each one of them might have contributed to Françoise's death. Blanche, who had so successfully taken from Marie-Noel the affection which otherwise would have

266

been given to the child's mother; Paul, with his endless complaints about the terms of the Marriage Settlement, which made it impossible for Françoise to finance the family business; Renée, who had cared nothing that her intrigue with Jean would cause Françoise unhappiness if it came to her knowledge; and the countess, whose fierce maternal possessiveness had deprived Françoise not only of her husband's tenderness, but also of her rightful place in the household—none of them was free from a measure of responsibility for the state of mind which had perhaps sent Françoise to her death.

The tension was broken as Charlotte came into the room, looking aggrieved and suspicious.

"You sent for me, Madame la Comtesse?"

"The *commissaire de police* has some questions to ask you, Charlotte," replied the countess.

"I want to know," said the *commissaire*, "whether you had any conversation this morning with Madame la Comtesse Jean before the accident?"

Charlotte flashed an angry look at me, and I realised, from her expression, that she believed he was asking her this question because of some remark or complaint of mine. She thought I had already told him about her visit to the bedroom, and that she was now to be reprimanded.

"I only saw Madame Jean for a few minutes," she said. "I spread no gossip, made no mischief. If Monsieur le Comte thinks I have been causing trouble he is wrong. I said nothing to Madame Jean about the telephone conversation."

"Telephone conversation?" said the *commissaire*. "What telephone conversation?"

Charlotte must have realised that she had made a mistake. She looked resentfully at her mistress, and then at me. Anxiety to cover her past actions had led to her own betrayal. "I beg your pardon," she said, "I thought Monsieur le Comte wanted to find fault with me. I happened to overhear a long-distance call of his to Paris, but I never mentioned this to Madame Jean. I knew my place. It wasn't for me to add to her worries."

Everyone turned in my direction, their expressions—from Renée's look of suspicion to Dr. Lebrun's evident embarrass-

267

ment—betraying the obvious conclusions which they drew from Charlotte's barbed sentences. It was the comtesse who broke silence first.

"My son's telephone call was a business one," she said. "It can have no possible bearing on the present situation."

The *commissaire* coughed apologetically. "I have no desire to probe into Monsieur le Comte's financial affairs, Madame," he said, "but anything that might have increased his wife's anxiety is of interest." He turned to me. "Did she know about this telephone conversation?" he asked.

"She did," I said.

"There was nothing about it to cause distress?"

"Nothing whatsoever. It referred to a contract I had negotiated in Paris."

The *commissaire* turned to Charlotte. "Why did you think the telephone call to Paris might have added to Madame la Comtesse Jean's worries?" he asked. His tone was not unkindly, merely abrupt.

Charlotte, already hostile, took it as further reproof. Once again she looked at me spitefully. "That is for Monsieur le Comte to say, not me," she replied.

Paul intervened. "This is quite ridiculous," he said. "My brother had renewed a contract with the firm of Carvalet in Paris, who take a large proportion of our glass. We were delighted he had done so. Failure would have necessitated closing down the *verrerie*. As it is, we have renewed on terms which will enable us to carry on, at any rate for a further six months. My sister-in-law was as pleased as the rest of us."

Talbert stepped forward, looking puzzled. "I don't want to contradict you, Monsieur," he said to Paul, "but your facts are surely wrong? Carvalet sent me a copy of the new contract only this morning. It is substantially different from the last: the terms are most decidedly to your disadvantage. I was amazed when I read it. Naturally, today's tragedy put it out of my mind, but since it is now mentioned . . ." He glanced at me. "Possibly Madame la Comtesse Jean was a trifle upset. She must have realised that the birth of an heir was more important than ever."

Paul stared at him, stupefied. "What do you mean?" he

said. "How can the contract be to our disadvantage? The terms are most favourable."

"No," I said.

I saw the *commissaire* glance surreptitiously at his watch. The tangled finances of the de Gué were not his concern.

"I can explain to my brother later about the contract," I said to him quickly. "I can assure you now that my wife was not in the least concerned about it. I took her into my confidence, and she appreciated it. There is nothing more I can say. Now, are you ready to go upstairs and inspect her room?"

"Thank you, Monsieur." He turned to Charlotte for his last question. "Apart from natural anxiety over the little girl, you found Madame la Comtesse Jean her usual self?" he asked.

Charlotte shrugged her shoulders. "I suppose so," she said sullenly. "I don't know. Madame Jean was easily discouraged and depressed. She told me this last upset of hers had come about because some favourite pieces of porcelain had been broken. She set great store by her possessions. She even dusted them herself, and would let no one touch them. 'At least they're mine,' she used to say. 'They're not part of St. Gilles.'"

The venomous parting stroke embraced us all. The château stood condemned. I wondered if the *commissaire* saw Françoise as I saw her, an isolated figure clinging to the treasures of the home she had left, lonely, neglected, sought after solely for her fortune.

He asked me whether he might now see the bedroom, and I took him upstairs, the others remaining below in the salon. As we went along the corridor he said to me, "I must again express regret, Monsieur, for all this inconvenience, and for adding to your distress at such a time."

"Please don't apologise," I said. "You have been very considerate."

"It is a curious thing," he said, "but generally, after a tragedy such as this, those most concerned with the deceased feel themselves, as it were, on trial. They wonder whether it was their fault, and what they could have done to prevent it. In this case, the answer is nothing. Everyone who mattered was out of the château. It was unfortunate, but nobody's fault. The only one to blame, perhaps, was your little girl, and she will never know."

I opened the door of the bedroom, and as we entered I saw that the shutters were no longer closed, as I had left them, but were flung wide, and the windows too thrust back against the wall. The child's body was across the sill, one hand grasping the window frame, the other, with her head and shoulders, out of sight. I heard the *commissaire* catch his breath. I put my hand on his arm. To dash forward was the impulse of us both, yet to do so might have startled her, causing her to lose the hold she already had. For the eternity of perhaps ten seconds we waited, immobile. Then the child's hand shifted its grip, the body wriggled back across the sill, and the whole of her emerged from the wide space between the windows. She slipped back into the room to face us, her eyes shining, her hair dishevelled.

"I've got it," she said. "It was caught on the ledge."

The *commissaire* found his voice before I did. I could not speak. I could only stare at Marie-Noel, who was safe and unaware of danger. She seemed to be holding what looked like a duster in her hand.

"What have you got, my child?" he asked gently.

"Maman's locket," she said, "the locket Papa brought her last week from Paris. She must have been shaking her duster out of the window, as she always did, and the locket was caught in it. They were lying together on the ledge below. I leant out and saw them." She came towards us. "Look," she said, "the pin of the locket is sticking into the duster. Unless I had climbed out as far as I did I couldn't have reached them. If Maman had only rung her bell, Gaston or someone would have rescued them for her. But she was impatient. She thought she could reach them herself." She looked at the *commissaire*. "Are you religious?" she asked.

"I hope so, Mademoiselle," he said, taken aback.

"Papa is not. He is a sceptic. But finding the locket and the duster was an answer to prayer. I said to the Sainte Vierge, 'I did little for Maman when she was alive. Let me do something for her now she is dead.' The Sainte Vierge told me to lean out of the window. I did not want to do it. It was unpleasant. But I found the locket. I still don't know

270

why that should help Maman, unless it is that to her, in Paradise, it seems better for her daughter to wear the locket than to let it lie sadly rusted and forgotten on a ledge."

Chapter 23

Before the *commissaire* left he assured me that he was perfectly satisfied my wife had fallen accidentally from the window, and asked me to call on him the next day at eleven o'clock. He understood that my brother had arranged for the body to be brought home to the château afterwards. Once again he expressed his condolences, once again I thanked him. A moment or two later he left in his car, closely followed by the two doctors. Only the lawyer now remained, and he had the grace to apologise for his presence.

"I only stayed, Monsieur," he said, "because I understand, from the conversation I have had with your brother, that he knew nothing whatsoever of the terms of the new Carvalet contract. I thought perhaps a few words now might clarify the position."

"Nothing will clarify the position," I said, "except for my brother to read it, which he is at liberty to do whenever he pleases. I have it upstairs in my dressing room now."

Paul hesitated. "I'm sorry to be persistent, especially at this moment," he said, "but you can hardly blame me. From what Maître Talbert has been telling me, the new contract differs from the old on the only vital points. Does that mean everything you told Jacques and me on your return from Paris was a lie?"

"Yes," I said.

"What's that to do with you?" interrupted his mother. "Jean owns the *verrerie*, not you. He had a perfect right to make what arrangements he pleased."

"I try to direct it, don't I?" said Paul. "God knows it's always been a thankless task. I never wanted to do it. There was nobody else. But why should Jean lie, that's what I want to know? What was the point of making fools of us all?"

"I didn't want to make fools of you," I said. "I thought

271

it was the only way to save the *verrerie*. I changed my mind after I came back from Paris. Don't ask me why. You wouldn't understand."

"How did you think you were going to raise the capital?" asked Paul. "Talbert says that under the new terms it would mean running the *verrerie* at a complete loss."

"I don't know. I hadn't thought."

"Monsieur was hoping for an heir?" suggested the lawyer. "No doubt that is why he confided the matter to Madame la Comtesse Jean? Of course, as things have turned out . . ."

He stopped. Discretion overwhelmed him. The comtesse stared at him from her chair beside the fire.

"Well?" she said. "Finish your sentence, Maître. As things have turned out—what?"

The lawyer spoke apologetically to me. "I am sure it is no secret to any one of the family, Monsieur, that under the terms of the Marriage Settlement you come into a considerable fortune on the death of your wife."

"No secret at all," I said.

"So that in point of fact," the lawyer continued, "whether the terms of the Carvalet contract are favourable or unfavourable, it doesn't matter so very much. Increase of capital will cover the loss."

Nobody seemed to have noticed, or even cared, that Marie-Noel was seated on a stool beside her grandmother, and was listening intently to the conversation.

"Does Monsieur Talbert mean that Papa gets some money after all?" she said. "I thought he only got money if I had a brother?"

"Be quiet," said her grandmother.

"Yes," said Paul slowly, "I suppose we did know that. But it's not one of the things people discuss in a family. Naturally, every one of us was hoping my sister-in-law would have a son."

The lawyer said nothing. There was nothing he could say. Paul turned to me. "I'm sorry," he said, "but if you don't mind, I still think it's only fair to me if I see the contract."

I threw the bunch of keys on the table. "It's in the valise in the wardrobe," I said. "Go and find it, if you like."

Marie-Noel jumped to her feet. "I'll find it," she said,

272

seizing the keys. She was out of the room before anyone thought of stopping her. Not that it mattered; the contract would have to be read.

"Really, Paul," said Renée, "you're being very inconsiderate. As Maître Talbert says, the position is changed now, because of poor Françoise's death, and I hardly think this is the moment to start talking business. It makes me feel extremely uncomfortable, and it must be very painful for Jean."

"It's painful for the whole family," said Paul. "I don't want the *verrerie* to benefit because of Françoise. I hate being made a fool of, that's all."

Maître Talbert was ill at ease. "I apologise," he said. "I would not have mentioned the matter had I known there was this unfortunate misunderstanding between you as to the terms. Naturally, I am at your disposal, Monsieur," he said to me, "for a full discussion on this and other matters at any time convenient to you after the funeral."

"The funeral will be on Friday," said the comtesse. "I have already arranged it with Monsieur le Curé. My daughter-in-law will be brought home the day after tomorrow and will lie here so that our friends and everyone in the district will have time to pay their respects. I shall of course receive them." The lawyer bowed. "You will have the kindness, Maître, to see that notification of the death goes to the newspapers this evening, so that it can be read in tomorrow's editions. I have written the notices myself." She took some sheets of paper from her lap, and handed them to him. "Monsieur le Curé is arranging with the Mother Superior of the convent at Lauray to send sisters to the château to watch during the nights of Wednesday and Thursday." She paused for reflection, tapping the arm of her chair with her fingers. "The bearers, of course, will be our own people on the estate. Let us hope the weather holds. My husband died in winter when the snow was on the ground, and the men found it very slippery as they carried him over the bridge."

The sound of Marie-Noel running down the stairs and across the hall could be heard through the open door.

"Not so much noise, child," said the comtesse as she burst

into the room. "One should tread softly in a house of mourning."

Marie-Noel went straight to Paul and gave him the document.

"Have I your permission?" he asked, glancing at me.

"Naturally," I said.

For a while there was no sound except the rustling of paper as Paul turned the crisp pages of the contract. Then he turned to me.

"You realise," he said, his voice expressionless, betraying nothing of what he must have felt, "that this contract goes against all we agreed to before you went to Paris?"

"Yes," I said.

"You've signed the duplicate and returned it to them?"

"I signed it in the office on Saturday, and posted it on the way home."

"Then there's nothing more to be done. As Maman says, you own the business, you can make what terms you please. It just means that, as far as I am concerned, trying to run it for you becomes impossible."

He stood up and handed me back the contract. His frustrated, harassed face looked suddenly old and tired. "Heaven knows I don't pretend to have brains," he said, "but if I had gone to Paris I could have done better than that. Only someone with immense capital behind him could afford to put his name to such terms. All I can conclude is that you were in an extraordinarily reckless frame of mind the whole time you were in Paris."

For a moment no one spoke. Then the comtesse reached for the bell beside the fire. "I think," she said, "that we needn't detain Maître Talbert any longer. A prolonged discussion on the future of the *verrerie* is quite out of place at the present time, and I am sure that he must have plenty to do in Villars, as we have here in the château."

The lawyer shook hands with all of us and followed Gaston from the room.

The comtesse turned to me. "You look tired, Jean," she said. "You've had a long, emotional day. Why not have a rest? You have just an hour before we go to church for the special service of prayers for the dead for Françoise

274

which Monsieur le Curé has arranged. After that we shall all drive into Villars to the hospital chapel."

She fumbled for the spectacles hanging beside the crucifix on her bosom, and began to scribble names and addresses on sheets of paper.

I went outside and stood in the grounds beyond the moat. The cattle had come to pasture, and the sun had dipped behind the trees. Beside the dovecot were the ashes of the bonfire, smoky white. Soon the mist would rise, encompassing the château, and already, with shutters drawn and windows closed, it stood remote from the evening world, from the jackdaws massing in the woods and the black and white cattle cropping the grass.

Paul came and joined me on the terrace under the windows. For a moment or two he smoked a cigarette in silence, then nervously he threw it away, saying abruptly, "I meant what I said just now."

"What did you say?" I asked.

"That it was impossible to run the *verrerie* for you any more."

"You said that? I'm sorry. I'd forgotten."

I turned and looked at him, and his face, perplexed, weary, seemed to merge into that of his sister Blanche, when, tense and watchful, she had stared at me only a little while before as we waited in the hospital. I knew that his sudden doubt of me, and his aversion, too, sprang not merely from feelings going back to boyhood days, to childish slights and jealousies and quarrels, turning later to suspicion and envy: they were due also to my own blunders in his brother's name, my own failings and weaknesses that could not be explained. I might, if I had tried, have drawn him to me as a comrade and a friend; instead I had antagonised him, sown still more discord and dislike, and his present mood was part of the damage I had done, like the still face of Françoise in the hospital bed.

"What's your reason?" I asked.

"My reason?" He stared down into the moat. "We've never got on, you know that. You had all the favours and I the kicks. I've been used to that my whole life. You asked me to run the *verrerie* for you because nobody else would take it on after Maurice was shot, and you were too idle yourself. I did it for the sake of the family, not for you. At least, up to date, I've respected your business judgment, if nothing else. Now I can't even do that."

His voice, resentful, bitter, sounded as though he had lost all faith not only in his work but in himself; as if what he had striven to do, through the years, had come to no account, the purpose gone. The foolish contract he had read, which had been set in motion by a stranger during five minutes over the telephone, might have been drawn up deliberately to mock him, tearing asunder everything he had with patience helped to build.

"Supposing," I said slowly, "that in future I rely upon your business judgment, not you on mine?"

"What do you mean?" His eyes, wretched, doubting, reminded me of those snapshots in the album, where he stood always on the fringe of a group, because the central figure claimed attention, and he, uncertain, somehow did not fit into the picture but was out of place.

"You said in the salon that you had no brains," I said, "but that nevertheless, if you had gone to Paris, you could have done better than I did. You're right; you could have done. Suppose, in the future, you take on that part of the business—travel, get the orders, go to Paris, London, any city you please, get fresh contacts, meet people, go all over the world if you like—while I stay here?"

He straightened himself and looked at me, puzzled, unbelieving.

"Are you serious?" he asked.

"Yes," I answered. Then, because he looked doubtful still, "Don't you want to travel? Don't you want to get away?"

"Not want to get away?" His laugh was short, mirthless. "Naturally I want to get away. I always have done. But there was never the money, nor the opportunity. Nor did you ever make it possible for me."

"I can make it possible for you now," I said.

Constraint, that had for the moment vanished, came near to us again. He looked away from me. "Because you've come into a fortune you're going to play benefactor, is that it?" he asked.

276

"I hadn't thought of it that way," I said. "It just struck me, suddenly, that your life hasn't been an easy one. I'm sorry."

"It's rather late for regrets after all these years."

"Perhaps. I don't know. You still haven't answered my question."

"You mean," he said, "that you'd give me a free hand to travel in Europe, or even America, visiting other factories, other small plants like ours, seeing how it is possible to keep going under similar conditions by using more up-to-date methods, so that at the end of six months or so, when I got back, we might incorporate them here at St. Gilles?"

The voice, which had been bitter and resentful, was suddenly interested, alert; and I, who had thought out none of the things he suggested, but was only profoundly sorry for having interfered in his life, realised that unwittingly I had stumbled upon an idea that would give his life new meaning. Instead of seeing himself as the younger brother, put upon, overburdened, never thanked, he would be transformed into the one who made decisions, bringing fresh blood to what had been decayed and dying, thereby saving both tradition and himself.

"I believe you could do all that and more," I said. "Talk to Renée, see what she says. I don't want to force you to it."

"Renée . . ." For a moment he frowned, thinking hard, then awkwardly, a little diffident, he said, "It might be the answer for us both. We haven't been very happy—you've known that. If I once got her away from here, everything might be different. She's felt herself wasted at St. Gilles, whereas if we were travelling, meeting people, and she had something to think about, she'd stop being bored and dissatisfied, and I'd be a better companion. I wouldn't seem the country boor that I do to her now."

He stood staring in front of him, the new image of himself taking shape and substance, and oddly, with a sort of poignancy, I saw the image too—the Paul he wanted to become, wearing flashier clothes, a gaudier tie, playing deck quoits on a transatlantic liner, drinking martinis with Renée in a bar. And through his eyes I saw Renée smiling upon him, elegant and sleek, the pair of them enveloped in a little cloud of their own success which would make them kinder to one another.

"Can I discuss this with Renée, now, tonight?" he asked abruptly. "Before there's any chance of your changing your mind?"

"I shan't change my mind," I said. "Good luck to you, Paul." And foolishly, like an old-fashioned figure in a drawing-room comedy, I put out my hand to him, and he shook it, stiffly, as though sealing a pact. I wondered if this was forgiveness of my own immediate blunders or whether it also included the past that was not mine.

He turned and disappeared into the château, and I went on standing there, watching the black and white cattle outlined against the dark trees, feeling the first chill of evening touch me from the long grass. Because no one came to join me, and I was undisturbed, I tried to make my own prayer for Françoise, who was dead through folly and neglect, a prayer which I should not be able to offer later at her special prayer service or in the hospital chapel, where acting her husband's part would make me a deceiver.

When the church bell tolled solemnly, breaking the stillness, and I went and joined the others in the hall, I saw that we were not to walk across to the village as we had done on Sunday, but were to go formally in the cars. Both were drawn up below the terrace, with Gaston in uniform at the wheel of the first and Paul at the second; and the three women, already in deep black, followed by Marie-Noel in a dark winter coat, entered the cars in some order of precedence which had already been decided upon—the comtesse, myself and the child in the Renault, and Paul driving his sister and his wife.

Slowly we proceeded through the gateway and over the bridge, foreshadowing the cortège of the Friday to come, and slowly, at the same sober pace, descended from the cars after two minutes' drive, entered the church, and took our places at the front as we had done on Sunday.

I wondered, kneeling there, listening to the prayers, what petitions went up in fervour or humility from those beside me, whether they asked for the repose of the absent Françoise or pardon for themselves; and it seemed to me that both

278

requests must by their very likeness fuse, the ultimate purpose of all such prayers being surely the abolition of anxiety and pain. The veils in which the mother and daughter and daughter-in-law were hidden lent similarity to their figures, so that the three of them together might have been the facets of one personality, the triptych of a single countenance. Whether they were sorrowful or secretive I could not tell; only the child, her close-cropped hair unveiled, was a symbol of what had been, the lost innocence, lost youth, for which the shrouded figures mourned.

The service over, we drove to Villars to stand for a few moments in the chapel. Strangely, it was not, as I had expected, distressing and macabre. The now waxen and infinitely remote figure of Françoise was not the person we had all betrayed but something mummified and distant, discovered after centuries in an Egyptian tomb. I watched the child, fearing perhaps tears or apprehension, but she gave no sign of either. She looked with interest at the two nuns, at the candles, at the flowers, and I realised that to her, as perhaps to the rest of us, sorrow and regret had no place here, but only curiosity and a vague surprise. Outside, Renée was the only one who wept. I saw her fumble for her handkerchief, and Marie-Noel, reddening, turned away her head, embarrassed to see an adult cry.

It was nearly half past eight by the time we returned to the château, the curé joining us for dinner. The comtesse, whom I had never before seen in the dining room, took her place opposite me at the end of the table, and her presence there, despite the solemnity of the occasion, gave sudden warmth and distinction to the room. Instead of being a mourning party, we might have been sitting down to a New Year dinner. Grotesquely, I expected to see Gaston bear in a turkey or a goose. There should have been chocolates in coloured paper, and a bunch of mistletoe hanging from the ceiling. The voices, which had started by being low, subdued, rose as the meal progressed, and after the dessert had been served and the tray of coffee cups taken to the salon, the comtesse leading the procession, it was almost as if, once the servants had departed, we were going to put on paper caps, play forfeits or roast chestnuts in the fire. Only when the curé had taken his departure did the comtesse, for the first time, flag; and, glancing at her, I saw that she had turned suddenly grey. The beads of perspiration stood out on her forehead and ran down her cheeks, and her eyes, flickering restlessly about the room, lost instantly all life and concentration. Paul had left the salon with the curé, and Blanche, Renée and the child, turning the pages of some book, had noticed nothing.

Quietly I said, "I'm going to take you upstairs."

She stared at me as if she did not understand, and then, when I put out my arm to her, she leant upon it, trembling. I said, loudly, so that the others heard, "I think it would be much better if we went over the lists together in your room."

She straightened herself, gripping my arm more firmly, and as we moved towards the door she said clearly, without difficulty, "Good night, good night, everybody. Don't disturb yourselves. Jean and I have matters we prefer to discuss upstairs."

They all rose instantly, and Blanche, coming forward, said, "You should never have come down, Maman. It has been too much for you."

Her words had just the necessary sting to waken response, and in a second her mother turned, loosening her hold upon my arm, retorting, "When I want advice from you I'll ask for it. There are four hundred envelopes to address before tomorrow evening. I suggest you make a start tonight, and the child can help."

We went out of the room and climbed the stairs together to the first corridor. As she paused there for a moment to regain breath she said, "Why did I say that? What are the invitations for?"

"The funeral," I said, "the funeral on Friday."

"Whose funeral?"

"Françoise's," I replied. "Françoise died today."

"Of course," she said. "For a moment I had forgotten. I was thinking of that time when we made lists for Blanche's wedding. We had the invitations printed, and then none of them were used."

She took my arm again and we mounted the second flight, and as we turned along the corridor to her room in the tower the shadows seemed to close in upon us, the silence deepen, and it was as though we were retreating to a past that was always there.

Charlotte opened the door for us, and I could see at once from her face that she was frightened. She darted a look at me, suspicious, anxious, and when the comtesse had passed through into the room she whispered to me, "The boxes have gone from the dressing room."

"I know," I said. "I took them away."

"What for?" she said. "I shall need them tonight."

"No," I said.

I pushed by her, following the comtesse, and I said, "Undress and get into bed, Maman. You may sleep, you may not. Either way, it doesn't matter. I shall stay here in the room with you tonight."

Her shadow, reflected on the ceiling, monstrous and over-powering like a witch, seemed part of the heavy curtains and the hangings to the bed; but when she turned and looked at me the movement dwarfed the shadow, the shadow shrank to the ground, and the smile belonged to the woman who downstairs in the dining room had held court and made a fiesta out of mourning, opposing tragedy with her own wit and pride.

"The tables are turned," she said. "It's a long time since one of us lay in bed and the other watched. You had a high temperature once when you were twelve years old. I sat in your room beside you and bathed your face. Is that what you're prepared to do for me tonight?"

She laughed and waved me from the room, calling to Charlotte. I went out into the corridor and down to the salon, and found the others turning out the lights, preparing to go to their rooms. Marie-Noel went towards the stairs hand in hand with Blanche, her small face white with fatigue now that the day had ended.

"You'll come and say good night, Papa?" she asked.

"Yes," I promised, and went back into the dining room for a cigarette. When I returned again into the hall I found that Renée had not followed the others, but was waiting for me on the stairs. Seeing her thus reminded me of that first evening, when, with my hand on the door leading to the terrace, I had suddenly heard her footsteps behind me, and she had stood there in her wrapper with her hair falling to her shoulders. Now she was no longer passionate or angry or disconsolate, but somehow wiser and a little shamed, as though recognising that the tragedy of the day was now a final barrier between us.

"So you want to get rid of us, Paul and me?" she said. "Have you been planning this ever since you returned from Paris?"

I shook my head. "There's no question of its being planned," I told her. "This evening out on the terrace the idea came to me, that's all. If you dislike the thought, put it out of your head."

She did not say anything for a moment. She seemed to be considering something, and then she said slowly, "You've altered, Jean. I don't mean because of today and the terrible shock to all of us; I mean for some little while. You're not the same."

"In what way have I changed?" I asked.

She shrugged her shoulders. "I don't just mean you've changed to me. I realise now that you were amusing yourself these past months. You were bored, there was nothing else for you to do, and I happened to be here. You've changed somehow in yourself, become harder, more withdrawn."

"Harder?" I said. "I should have thought the reverse. Softer, weaker in every way."

"Oh no." She considered me thoughtfully. "I'm not the only one to notice it. Paul said the same thing only a day or two ago, when you burnt your hand. You've been more detached, not only to me but to everyone. That's why it surprised us both that you made this suggestion that we should travel, and not you. From your behaviour the past week, you gave the impression that the one thing in the world you wanted was to get away."

I stared at her, disconcerted. "I gave that impression?" I said.

"Frankly, yes."

"It isn't true," I said. "I've never stopped thinking about all of you, day and night. The château, the foundry, Maman, the child, the whole family—you've been continually in my mind. The last thing I want to do is to go away."

She looked incredulous. "I don't understand you," she said. "I suppose the truth is that I never have. I was a fool to imagine I once did. You were never in love with me for one minute, were you?"

"I'm not in love with you now, Renée," I said. "I don't know about the past, but I rather doubt it."

"You see?" she said. "You are harder. You have changed. You can't even be bothered to pretend any more." She paused, and then slowly, reluctantly, she added, "Paul hasn't said so, but I'm sure he believes it, and I'm beginning to believe it too. Did you make that contract cold-bloodedly, deliberately, on the chance that . . . that what happened today might happen anyway?"

Her voice was low, yet I sensed a kind of urgency behind it, a mixture of wonder and horror that the man with whom she had been infatuated might have acted thus, and in doing so have somehow implicated her in his plans.

"If you think I made that contract believing Françoise would die, no, Renée," I said to her.

She drew in her breath. "I'm glad," she said. "In the chapel this evening I was suddenly . . . overwhelmed by everything that had happened. A week ago I couldn't have left St. Gilles, but now"—she turned and began to climb the stairs—"now I know I can't go on living here. I must get away—it's the only hope we have for the future, Paul and I."

I watched her disappear along the corridor, and I wondered whether it was in truth Françoise's death that had caused her shame, or whether it was my reserve, my indifference to her as a woman, that had killed her own desire.

As I switched off the light and climbed the stairs in darkness, it seemed to me that what I had done to these two, Paul and Renée, was not my own doing, the action of the solitary self of my former life, nor yet that of Jean de Gué, whose shadow I had become, but the work of a third—someone who was neither he nor I but a fusion of the two of us, who had no corporeal existence, who was born not of thought but of intuition, and brought release to us both.

Marie-Noel had asked me to say good night, and presently I went through the swing door to her own turret stair and turned the handle of her door, expecting to find her still dressed, or at her prie-dieu. But the long day had closed upon her at the last. She was in bed, asleep. The image of the chapel had not left her untouched, as I had thought. Two lighted candles stood at the foot of the bed, and the duck now knelt in prayer between them. A celluloid baby doll with a battered skull reposed in her arms, upon her breast, and on a piece of paper, pinned to the head of the bed, these words were written: "Here lie the mortal remains of Marie-Noel de Gué, who departed this life in the year of our Lord 1956, and whose faith in the Blessed Virgin brought peace and repentance to the humble village of St. Gilles."

I blew out the candles, and, leaving the window open, closed the shutters. Then I went down the turret stairs and through to the other side of the château, to that other room in the tower. Here there were no candles burning, only a light beside the bed, and the woman on the pillows was not asleep like the child, but awake and watchful. Her eyes, sunk in her grey, exhausted face, stared up to mine.

"I thought you weren't coming," she said.

I dragged the chair from beside the stove, and pushed it close to the bed. I sat down in it and put out my hand to her. She held it fast.

"I sent Charlotte to her room," she said. "I told her, 'Monsieur le Comte is looking after me tonight. I don't need you.' That's what you meant me to say, didn't you?"

"Yes, Maman," I answered.

Her grip tightened, and I knew she would hold it thus, through the night, as her defence against darkness, and I must not move, nor withdraw it, for if I did the bond would be loosened and the meaning lost.

"I've been thinking," she said. "In a few days' time, when everything's over, I shall leave this room and go downstairs to my old one. It's more practical. I can keep my eye on things."

"Just as you like," I answered.

"Lying here," she said, "I find my memory goes. I don't

know if I am in the present or the past. And I have bad dreams."

The gilt clock beside her bed ticked loudly, and the pendulum, showing through a glass case, moved backwards, forwards, the two combining to make the minutes slow. "Last night," she said, "I dreamt you were not in the château. You were fighting with the Resistance once again, and I was reading the note you smuggled to me the evening Maurice Duval was shot. I kept reading it over and over again until I thought my head would burst. Then, when you gave me the morphine, I didn't dream any more."

In Villars, Béla had a luminous clock in a small leather case, the hands showing white against the dark face, and the tick, rapid and so quiet that one barely heard it, was like the quick, live pulse of a human heart.

"If you dream tonight," I said, "I shall be here. It won't matter."

I leant forward and turned out the light with my burnt hand, and at once the darkness seemed to press upon me, enveloping me. The despair that was in the shadows invaded me, and she began to talk and mutter in a half-sleep that I could not share but could only listen to, with the ticking clock. Sometimes she called out, cursing, sometimes she fell into a prayer, once she broke into uncontrollable laughter; but never, as the fragmentary thoughts pursued her, did she clamour for relief, nor yet release my hand. When, just after five o'clock, she fell asleep and I leant forward and looked down at her, her face seemed to me no longer a mask, haggard, fearful, hiding the torment of months and years; but peaceful, relaxed and oddly beautiful, not even old.

Chapter 24

I knew now she would continue sleeping and I could leave her. I rose from the chair and went out of the room, down through the silent house to the salon, and, opening the shutters, let myself out onto the terrace. I crossed the moat and walked up the pathway under the chestnut trees, and so to the rides and the stone huntress standing in the midst of them. The air had the cold clarity that comes just before dawn, and the sky, no longer black with the intensity of the night hours, had grown dim, receding, as it were, before the challenge of the day, the stars more pallid, more with-drawn, the little cluster of the Pleiades already setting in the west, poised above the dark trees. Here on the high ground by the statue I could look down upon the château and the village beyond, the spire of the small church stabbing the sky, the group of houses beside the church, giving the appearance of one homestead, the rising ground to the east and the encircling forest, all of them making St. Gilles a single entity of château, church and village.

I sat by the base of the huntress and waited for the day, and as the sky paled, and the light came, and the village and the château took on shape and substance, the earth itself seemed to solidify, the warm wet tang of it rising with the sun, the moisture of the night and the dew of morning blend-ing together to fructify the soil. A white mist, warm and spongy, cloaked the trees, soon to evaporate, leaving them golden red, and miraculously, as soon as the sun topped the plateau beyond the village, the village itself awoke. In a mo-ment, so it seemed, there was smoke coming from a chimney, a dog barking, the lowing of cattle. I was no longer isolated, watching apart, numb with exhaustion, but one among many, part of St. Gilles. I thought of the curé waking to the day, his untroubled face clouding as he remembered the disaster at the château, and how at once he would surely pray for all bereaved, his faith, like a talisman, protecting them from harm, the same faith reaching out and embracing those about him. And I thought also of the people in the village, unknown to me, who had come to the special service last night from respect for Françoise, standing with bent heads and eyes averted. Ernest, the driver of the lorry, had been there, and Julie too, and her small grandson Pierre. I knew suddenly, with conviction, that it was not a stranger's curiosity that drew me to them, a sentimental attraction to the picturesque, but something deeper, more intimate, a desire so intense for their well-being and their future that although akin to love it resembled pain. This longing, strongly felt, was yet somehow impersonal: it did not spring from a wish to stand well with them, and it embraced, in some curious fashion, not only the village people and those who now seemed part of me, sleeping within the château, but inanimate things beyond—the contour of a hill, a sloping sandy road, the vine clinging to the master's house, the forest trees.

The feeling deepened, seeming to pervade my whole being, just as the physical burn of my hand three days before had touched each part of me; and the two things now mingled, what had been the searing, senseless hurt of Saturday merging to the enfolding fire within. As I sat there by the base of the statue, the sun rose and the morning mist dissolved. The château itself stood out clear-cut yet sleeping still, until the shutters of a room in the western tower opened suddenly, the sound coming to me sharp and distinct across the park, and I saw a figure stand for a moment by the long window, looking, not in my direction, to the statue and the alleyways, but upwards to the sky, the figure somehow remote, strangely forlorn, believing itself alone to watch the dawn. It was Blanche; and her sudden action, flinging wide the shutters of her room, made me wonder whether she too had held vigil all the night, and now at last, hungry for the sleep that would not come, had put the hope behind her for twelve more hours, and, flooding her cold room with light and air, was giving a grudging welcome to the day.

I got up and walked across the park towards the château, and it was not until I had crossed the moat and stood beneath her window that she noticed me. I saw her reach to the windows to close them again, but before she could do so I called up to her, "My hand is troubling me. Would you dress it for me?"

She did not answer but withdrew into her room, leaving the windows open, from which I concluded that, as always, her silence meant indifference to my presence, but she did not refuse to help me. Going to her room, I knocked, but, hearing no answer, turned the handle and entered. She was standing by a table unrolling a fresh dressing. Her face was set, expressionless. She was wearing a dark brown dressing gown, and her hair, swept back from her face and pinned in a bun behind, was as she wore it during the day. The bed was already made, the covers over it. Here was no disarrangement, nothing out of place; no tumbled disorder of a sleepless night showed in this chill bleak room. Only the flowers on her prie-dieu gave life, and colour too. They were dahlias, the same vivid flame that Béla had bought in the market place in Villars, which had filled the little salon of her house with life and warmth.

Blanche did not look at me, but, putting out her hand, took mine in hers and removed the dressing Béla had placed upon it on Sunday night. She must have seen that it differed from the one which she had put upon it herself on Saturday, but she showed no surprise; her action was that of an automaton, silent, unconcerned.

"If you made a vow of silence," I said to her, "you broke it yesterday, in the hospital. It isn't valid any more." She did not answer. She went on dressing my hand. "Fifteen years ago," I said, "the death of one person came between us. It took the death of another, yesterday, to loosen your tongue. Wouldn't it be simpler for both of us, and for the family too, if we made an end to silence?"

My hand seemed suddenly defenceless now it was bare. I could move it, clench the fist, and it no longer hurt. She took the new dressing and covered the burn. It felt fresh and cool and clean.

"It would be simpler for you," she said, without raising her eyes, "just as it was simpler for you to let Françoise die. It has made life easier for you. She's no longer in your way."

"I did not let her die," I said.

"You lied about your blood," she said. "You lied about that contract. You've lied about everything, always, through the years. I don't want to speak to you, now or in the future. We have nothing to say to one another."

She had finished the dressing. She let go my hand. The gesture was final, a dismissal.

"You're wrong," I said. "I have much to say to you. If you accept me as head of the family you are bound to listen to me, even if you don't agree."

She glanced up at me briefly, and then moved away, replacing the stock of dressings in a chest of drawers. "Coming into a fortune may give you a sense of power," she said, "but it doesn't entitle you to respect. I don't think of you as head of the family, nor does anyone. You've never done anything to justify the name."

I looked about me, at the severity, the coldness, the tortured pictures of the scourged Christ, the crucified Christ, that must face her upon the blank impersonal walls as she lay there in her high narrow bed, and I said to her, "Is that why you hang those pictures there? To remind yourself that you can't forgive?"

She turned and looked at me, the eyes bitter, the mouth hard and set.

"Don't mock my God," she said. "You've destroyed everything else in my life. Leave Him to me."

"Would you have hung them in the master's house?" I asked. "Would they have gone as part of your dowry to Maurice Duval?"

Now at last I had broken down reserve. The agony of years came to the surface, showing in her mouth and eyes like a sudden flame.

"How dare you speak of him?" she said. "How dare you even utter his name? Do you think I ever forget one moment, day or night, what you did to him?"

"No," I said, "you haven't forgotten. Nor have I. You can't forgive me—perhaps I can't forgive myself. In that case, why were we both so moved yesterday morning, when we discovered that Marie-Noel had gone to the well?"

What I had hoped for, and what I had also feared, then happened. Tears rose in her eyes, ran down her cheeks: not the grief of sudden loss or pain, but the anguish of years set free through innocence. She went over to the window and stood beside it looking out, her back defenceless, betraying the emotion that I could not see. I wondered how much of her life had been wasted here, confined, the bitter thoughts rising in her like a tide as she sat or lay or read or prayed. Presently she turned, dry-eyed now, composed, and yet more vulnerable because of the grief she had shown before me.

"That exhibition must have pleased you," she said. "It amused you, even as a boy, to see me cry."

"Then perhaps," I said, "not any more."

"In that case, what are you waiting for?" she asked. "Why are you still here?"

I could not ask forgiveness for something I had not done. As scapegoat, I could only bear the fault.

"I was looking in the album last week," I said. "I found the old snapshots of ourselves as children. And later ones as well. Groups at the *verrerie*, with Maurice there amongst them."

"Well?" she asked. "What of it?"

"Nothing," I answered. "Only that I wished what came about fifteen years ago had never happened."

Perhaps because what I said was out of character, unexpected, she looked up at me, startled momentarily out of her composure, and then, seeing that I spoke sincerely, without cynicism or any sort of mockery, she said quietly, "Why?"

My own truth was all that I could give her. If she did not believe it there was no more to say. "I liked his face," I said. "I had never looked at those photographs before. I realised, turning the pages, that he was good, and that the workmen must have loved and respected him. It came to me that when he was killed it was through jealousy; the man who shot him, or ordered him to be shot, did it not from mistaken patriotism but because he envied him, because Maurice Duval was finer than he was himself."

She stared at me, incredulous, and I supposed that what I was telling her was so alien to anything her brother might have said that she could not accept it.

"You think I'm lying," I said. "I'm not. It's true. I mean every word."

"If you want to make your confession," she said, "don't make it to me. It's fifteen years too late." She moved about the room, straightening things already orderly, using preoccupation to disguise emotion. "What use is it to either of us now," she asked, "to come here and accuse yourself? You can't restore the past. You can't bring Maurice back. You hadn't even the courage to shoot him yourself, but went that night to the *verrerie* pretending to be alone, asking him to hide you; and he came down and opened the door to let you in, and there you stood with your little band of murderers. God may forgive you, Jean, I can't."

She went and stood by the window once again, the air coming fresh and cool into the room. But when I followed her and stood beside her she did not move away, which seemed to me forgiveness in itself.

"From the first you were against Maurice, you and Maman," she said. "Even in the early days, when he first came to work at the *verrerie* and you and I were growing up, you were envious because Papa thought so much of him, even though you took no interest in the *verrerie* yourself and hardly ever went near it. Then later, when Papa gave him control and made him master, you began to hate him. I can see you now, you and Maman, in the salon, laughing, and Maman saying, 'Can it be that Blanche, the fastidious Mademoiselle de Gué, is amorous at last?' "

She did not look at me but stared out across the park, and her profile now was the profile of the girl in the album, already sombre, already reserved, possessor of a secret she did not wish revealed.

"Ridicule was your weapon always, yours and Maman's," she said. "Because Maurice came from the people you pretended to despise him. Papa was never like that, he understood. He wouldn't have tried to prevent us marrying, as you did. When the Armistice came, and the Occupation, you had your chance. So easy, wasn't it, to make murder seem heroic? It happened in other families. Ours wasn't the only one."

She gestured with her hands. It was suddenly over. The past was the past. She turned and looked about her at the alcove set in the tower, bare and simple like a convent cell, the prie-dieu in the corner, the crucifix above.

"Now I have this," she said, "instead of the master's house. If I was emotional yesterday morning, you know why."

I think that what endeared her to me most was that she tutoyered me still. The custom of a lifetime could not be broken by the silence of fifteen years. There was hope for the future in this if nothing else.

"I want you to go to the master's house and make it yours," I said. "I want you to make it come alive again, as it was when Maurice had it, to be the master now in place of him." Dumbfounded, she did not answer, only stared at me in disbelief, and swiftly, so that she could not reject me utterly, I went on talking. "I've told Paul he can go," I said. "He's only been directing the *verrerie* since the war through a sense of duty—

you know that. His heart's not in it. They ought to get away, to travel, he and Renée. It's the one likelihood they have, at the moment, of pulling their marriage together, apart from anything else. Paul has never had a chance of showing what he can do in business, in meeting people, outside St. Gilles. It's time he did."

Perhaps it was the note of urgency in my voice, belying cynicism, that most astounded her. She sat down, not realising, I believe, that she did so, and stared at me, clasping the arms of her chair.

"Some one of the family has to take over," I said. "I can't. I don't know the first thing about it, and have no desire to learn. As you said yourself, I've never had the slightest interest in it. If you had married Maurice you would have shared the *verrerie* between you, made something of it, instead of letting it decay and become out of date, which it is today. When Marie-Noel grows up it will be hers. If she marries it can be her dowry. Either way, the only person who understands and loves it is yourself. I want it to be your trust, your responsibility, because of Maurice, because of Marie-Noel."

Still she said nothing. I think if I had struck her across the face she could not have been more stunned. "The house is waiting there for you," I said. "It's been waiting for fifteen years. Pictures, china, tables, chairs, even his books, all the things you would have used together. You're wasted here— don't you realise it? Ordering meals, directing Gaston and the rest, who know what to do anyway, giving lessons to the child, which could be done by any capable governess . . . You belong to the *verrerie*, to that house; you could design and engrave again, as you did once, and create something delicate and fragile like the château the child found in the well. And then, instead of sending scent bottles and medicine phials to a firm like Carvalet, who would do better to buy them mass-produced, you could choose your own market, the market Paul will find for you, demanding fine workmanship, artistry, skill, which was what St. Gilles gave once, long ago, and can give again."

I paused, exhausted, drained suddenly of energy, of thought. And just as holding the mother's hand through the night had seemed to invest me with her own past phantoms of regret, so the eyes of Blanche upon me now, losing their bitterness, becoming reflective, considerate, even kind, gave light somehow to herself, healing her own sorrow, while the loneliness that had been hers was now my loneliness, my pain, engulfing me in a darkness that must be carried and endured.

I said to her, "I'm tired. I haven't slept."

"Nor I," she said. "I found I couldn't pray."

"We're quits then," I answered. "We've both been to the depths. But the child went first and wasn't afraid. When you go to the *verrerie*, Blanche, there's something you might do. Get your workmen to clear the rubble and find the spring once more. There ought to be water in the well."

I left her sitting there, and went out of her room and down the corridor to the dressing room. I flung myself on the camp bed, closed my eyes and slept dreamlessly until past ten, when I awoke to find Gaston shaking me by the shoulder, telling me that I had to be at Villars to see the *commissaire* at eleven o'clock.

I got up, shaved and bathed and dressed again, and went with him into the town. Gaston's wife and Berthe had asked whether they might come with me, as they wanted to visit the chapel. They stayed in the car during my brief conversation with the *commissaire*, who wished me to read and verify the notes he had taken the previous day. When I came out one of the officials told me that someone was waiting by the car to speak to me. It was Vincent, who helped Béla at "L'Antiquaire du Pont," and he had a small package in his hands.

"Forgive me, Monsieur le Comte," he said. "Madame could not get in touch with you in any other way. This package came from Paris yesterday. She knows now it arrived too late. She is so sorry for this. But she wanted me to give it to you, for the little girl."

I took the package from him. "What is it?" I asked.

"Some porcelain was broken," he said. "The little girl, your daughter, asked Madame if it could be mended. It was impossible, as I believe Madame told you. Instead, she sent to Paris for duplicates. She asked me to beg you not to tell the little girl that they are substitutes. She believes the child would be happier not to know, but to keep them now in

293

memory of her mother, believing they are the broken ones made whole."

I thanked him, and then, hesitating, asked, "Did Madame send any other message to me?"

"No, Monsieur le Comte. Just that, and her deep sympathy."

I got into the car. The others, Gaston and his wife and Berthe, were still patiently waiting for me, and we went, the four of us, to the hospital chapel, from where Françoise would be brought home the following day. Even in the few hours since the evening before she seemed to have become more remote, unapproachable, a part of time. Gaston's wife, who wept upon the instant, said to me, "Death is beautiful. Madame Jean might be an angel in the sky." I did not agree. Death was an executioner, lopping a flower before it bloomed. The sky had glories enough, but not the soil.

When we got back to St. Gilles I saw Marie-Noel waiting for me on the terrace. She ran forward and flung herself upon me, then, pausing until the others had gone with the car round to the garage, she turned to me and said, "Gran'mie was down early, before eleven. She's in the salon preparing it for Maman. Maman is going to lie there all tomorrow, so that visitors can come and pay their last respects." She looked excited, impressed. I noticed she was wearing the locket pinned onto her dark frock. "Madame Yves is helping Gran'mie," she went on. "Gran'mie sent for her. She said she was the only person who remembered how things were arranged when my grandfather died. They are arguing now about the position of the table."

She took my hand and led me to the salon. I could hear the sound of voices raised in dispute. I entered the room with the child, and saw that although the shutters were still closed the lights were switched on and the sofa and chairs had been turned to face the centre of the room. A long table, covered with a lace cloth, stood between the windows and the door. The comtesse was sitting on a chair beside the table, and Julie, with another white drapery over her arm, confronted her.

"But I assure you, Madame la Comtesse, the table was more in the centre and we did not use the lace cloth but the damask, this one that I have here, which I found myself just now at the back of the linen room, pushed anyhow, not touched, by the looks of it, since we had it for Monsieur le Comte himself."

"Nonsense," answered the comtesse. "We used the lace. The lace belonged to my mother. It was in my mother's family for a hundred years."

"Very possibly, Madame la Comtesse," said Julie. "I don't dispute it. I remember the lace cloth perfectly; you produced it when the children were christened and it made a fine background for the cake. But for mourning, that's another matter. The white damask is more suitable to pay tribute to Madame Jean, just as it did in 1938 for Monsieur le Comte."

"The lace hangs better," said the comtesse. "No one would know it wasn't an altar cloth. It would deceive Monsieur le Curé himself."

"Monsieur le Curé perhaps," said Julie. "He is shortsighted. It won't deceive the bishop. He has eyes like a hawk."

"I don't care," said the comtesse. "I prefer the lace. It may be more ostentatious than the damask, but what of it? I intend my daughter-in-law to have the best."

"In that case," said Julie, "there's no more to be said. The lace it will have to be. And I suppose the damask must go back to the linen room to be forgotten for another twenty years. Who looks after things nowadays at the château? I ask myself. It wasn't like this in the old days."

She sighed, folding the damask cloth on the end of the table.

"What else do you expect," said the comtesse, "with servants as they are today? They none of them have any pride in their work."

"Then it's the fault of the mistress," said Julie. "A good mistress makes a good servant. I remember when you used to come down into the kitchen we none of us spoke afterwards for half an hour, we were so frightened. Often we couldn't eat. That is how it should be. But today"—she shook her head —"it's another matter. When I came this morning little Germaine was listening to the T.S.F. True, it was a Mass, relayed from a cathedral, nevertheless . . ." She gestured, her sentence unfinished.

"I've been ill," said the comtesse. "Things have got out of hand. It will be different in future."

"I hope so," said Julie. "It was time."

"You say that because you're jealous," said the comtesse. "You always liked coming up here poking your nose into what didn't concern you."

"It does concern me," said Julie. "Anything that happens here to you, Madame la Comtesse, or to any of the family, concerns me. I was born in St. Gilles. The château, the *verrerie*, the village, that's my life."

"You're a tyrant," said the comtesse. "I hear your daughter-in-law ran off with a mechanic because you made life impossible for her. Now you have André and your grandson to yourself, I suppose you're satisfied?"

"I a tyrant?" said Julie. "I'm the most tolerant woman in the world, Madame la Comtesse. It was my daughter-in-law who nagged from morning till night. It's a good thing for my André she has gone. Now we shall have peace at last."

"You haven't enough to do," said the comtesse, "that's your trouble. Poking about in the *verrerie* grounds with a few chickens. In future you can come up to the château twice a week and help me set things in order once again. I was right, though, about the lace cloth."

"You are free to form your own opinion, Madame la Comtesse," said Julie. "I won't argue with you. But if it's the last word I ever utter, I shall insist that it was the damask cloth we used at the funeral of Monsieur le Comte."

They stared across the table at one another in perfect understanding. Then the comtesse, aware of my presence for the first time, wished me good day. "Everything went well?" she asked.

"Yes, Maman."

"The *commissaire* had nothing fresh to say?"

"No."

"Then we can proceed with the arrangements as planned. You had better help Renée with the addressing of the envelopes. Blanche has disappeared. I haven't set eyes on her all morning. I suppose, as usual, she's in church. Now go along, both of you, Julie and I have work to do."

We met Gaston in the hall. He was carrying the packet I

had left in the car. "Your parcel, Monsieur le Comte," he said.

I took it and went upstairs to the bedroom, the child following me.

"What is it?" she said. "Have you bought something?"

I did not answer. I undid the string and opened the paper. The Copenhagen cat and dog, perfect replicas of the ones that had been broken, lay revealed. I put them on the table where they belonged and then glanced at Marie-Noel. She stood with her hands clasped, smiling.

"You would never know," she said. "You could never tell that anything had happened. They are perfect. Just as if they hadn't been broken. Now I feel myself forgiven."

"How do you mean, forgiven?" I asked.

"I was showing off," she said. "I was careless, and so they got broken, and because they were broken Maman became ill. I wish we could stand them in the salon tomorrow, beside the candles, as a symbol."

"I don't think we can," I said. "It might look odd. I think if we leave them here, with all her things, it will mean the same."

We went down to the library, and the lists were waiting for us on the desk. But nobody was there addressing the envelopes, neither Paul nor Renée nor Blanche.

"Where are they?" I said to the child. "Where's everyone gone?"

She had already seized an envelope and was addressing it to the first name on the list in a careful sloping hand.

"I'm not supposed to say," she said, "because Gran'mie doesn't know. Aunt Renée is in her bedroom, looking through all her winter clothes. She told me, as a great secret, that after the funeral she and Uncle Paul are going away. They're going to travel, and later on, she said, they might even have a small apartment in Paris. She said she would ask me to stay if you and Gran'mie agreed."

"Is Uncle Paul also upstairs looking through his clothes?" I asked.

"Oh no," she answered, "he's gone down to the *verrerie*. Aunt Blanche isn't in church at all; she went with him, and that's a secret too. They were afraid that if Gran'mie knew she would interfere. Aunt Blanche wants to look through the furniture that's stored at the master's house. She told me that yesterday was the first time she had been inside the house for fifteen years. She said it was a waste nobody lived there, and it ought to be made habitable once again."

"Aunt Blanche said that?" I asked.

"Yes, she told me so this morning. She's going to do something about it. That's why she went down there with Uncle Paul." For a few moments she addressed the envelopes in silence. Then she raised her head, and, biting the end of her pen, said, "Rather a dreadful thought came to me just now. I don't know whether to tell it to you or not."

"Go ahead," I said.

"It's just that suddenly," she said, "since Maman died, everyone is getting what they want. Gran'mie, who loves everyone to notice her, has come downstairs. Uncle Paul and Aunt Renée are going to travel, which has made them pleased. Aunt Blanche has gone to look at the master's house, where, long ago, before I was born, she meant to live, so she told me once in private. Even Madame Yves is bustling with the linen, which makes her feel important. You have got the money you wanted, and can go spending now as much as you please. As for me"—she hesitated, her eyes troubled, a little sad—"as for me, I haven't been saddled with a baby brother after all, but have you to myself for the rest of my days."

I looked at her, a phrase forgotten or repressed forcing itself to my consciousness. Something about hunger, something about greed. Through the half-open double doors leading to the dining room I could hear the telephone. The sudden ring was an irritation, interrupting thought, for what she was saying to me seemed suddenly important, needing the right answer.

"The thing is," she said, "would any of these things have happened if Maman hadn't died?"

Her question, devastating, terrible, seemed to shake the foundation of all belief. "Yes," I said swiftly, "they had to happen, they were bound to happen. It's nothing to do with Maman dying. If she had lived they would have come about just the same."

Still she looked doubtful, not entirely satisfied. "When the *bon Dieu* arranges things, everything is for the best," she said, "but sometimes the devil tempts us in disguise. You remember what it says in St. Matthew—'All these things will I give thee, if thou wilt fall down and worship me'?"

The telephone ceased ringing. Gaston was answering it in the lobby. In a moment or two his footsteps sounded in the dining room, coming towards us.

"The point is to discover which is which," said Marie-Noel, "who gives us the things we want, God or the devil. It must be one or the other, but how do you tell?"

Gaston came to the double doors and said, "Monsieur le Comte is wanted on the telephone."

I got up and went through to the lobby in the hall. I lifted the old-fashioned receiver and listened.

"Who's there?" I asked.

Someone said, "*Ne quittez pas,*" the line blurred and indistinct, as though it came from a distance. Then, after a minute, another voice, a man's, said, "Am I speaking to the Comte de Gué?"

"Yes," I answered.

There was a pause. The speaker at the other end seemed to be thinking, deciding what to say.

"Who is it?" I repeated. "What do you want?"

Then softly, almost in a whisper, the voice replied, "It's me. Jean de Gué. I've just seen today's newspaper. I'm coming back."

Chapter 25

Instinct denied him. Mind, body, spirit united in revolt against him. He no longer existed. He was not real. The whisper at the other end of the telephone was imaginary, conjured up by fatigue. I waited, not answering. And then in a moment he spoke again.

"You are there?" he said. "The *remplaçant?*"

I suppose, because I heard a footstep in the hall—Gaston's, perhaps, it did not matter whose—caution seized me, and the conventional being who gives orders, takes them, makes arrangements and plans, spoke into the mouthpiece for me.

"Yes," I said, "I'm here."

"I'm speaking from Deauville," he said. "I have your car. I intend driving to St. Gilles later in the day. It's no use arriving before dusk—I might be seen. I suggest we meet at seven."

The cool assurance, the certainty with which he spoke, believing I would fall in with his plans, made me hate him the more.

"Where?" I asked.

There was silence for a moment while he thought. Then, softly, he said, "You know the master's house at the *verrerie?*"

I had thought he would suggest the hotel in Le Mans where he had played his first—and only—joke upon me. That would have been neutral ground. To substitute the master's house constituted a challenge.

"Yes," I said.

"I'll leave the car on a sidetrack in the woods," he said, "and come across the orchard. Wait for me inside the house and let me in. I'll be with you there as soon after seven as I can."

He did not say good-bye. The telephone clicked as he hung up, and that was all. I turned from the lobby and went into the hall. Gaston and Germaine were passing in and out of the kitchen quarters to the dining room with trays for lunch. Outside on the driveway I could hear a car, the Citroën. It would be Blanche and Paul returning from the foundry. Soon we should all assemble and eat together.

Although the emotion that filled me now was violent, overwhelming, yet at the same time I felt deliberate and calm. I was the possessor now, he the intruder. The château was my château, the people were my people, the family who in a few minutes would sit with me round the table were my family, my flesh and blood; they belonged to me and I to them. He could not return and make them his again.

I went into the salon, and the comtesse was still sitting there, surveying the room, the furniture of which had been altered yet again. Julie had gone, bearing the damask cloth with her. The comtesse was alone.

"Who was that on the telephone?" she asked.

"No one of any importance," I replied. "Someone who had seen the morning newspaper."

"In old days," she said, "no one would have telephoned at such a time. It shows want of tact. The courteous thing would be a letter of condolence, and flowers for me. However, good manners are a thing of the past."

I went over to her and took her hand. "I want to know how you feel," I said. "I couldn't ask you just now, in front of Julie."

She looked up at me and smiled. "We had a vigil, didn't we?" she said. "You slept in your chair. As for me, I never closed my eyes. If you think this business is going to be easy, you're mistaken."

"I never said it would be easy," I answered. "It's going to be the hardest thing you've ever done."

"I have to deny myself peace and pleasant dreams for your sake," she said. "That's what it amounts to, doesn't it? Just because you want me about the place. How do I know you won't change your mind again and banish me upstairs?"

"No," I said. "No . . . no . . ."

My sudden violence amused her. She reached up and patted my cheek. "You're spoilt," she said, "that's your trouble. Julie and I agreed upon it this morning. We all of us martyr ourselves because of you. If I become ill, which I very probably shall do, it will be your fault." She paused, and then, looking about her with satisfaction, said, "You know, I was agreeably impressed by Françoise in the chapel. She had breeding, for the first time. I shall be proud for everyone to come and pay their respects to her tomorrow. It's a great solace not to be ashamed of one's daughter-in-law when she is dead."

Gaston came into the salon and announced lunch, in his new hushed voice suited to mourning, and as we went out into the hall she said, "It will make all the difference when the salon is filled with flowers. Lilies above all, no matter what they cost. After all, Françoise will be paying. We owe it all to her."

The others were already in the dining room, and, glancing at Paul and Blanche, I saw they had the faces of conspirators —not furtive or withdrawn, but in the childish sense, sharing a secret that had turned out well for both. When Blanche, saying grace as she always did, looked at me afterwards, not smiling but somehow confident, assured, I knew that something at least had been achieved that morning, if not an end to silence at least a purge to pain.

As the mother took her seat opposite me I said, "Now you are back again, where you belong, I intend making other changes too. I've already discussed them with Blanche and Paul and Renée. Paul isn't going to direct the *verrerie* any more. He's going to travel, taking Renée with him."

My statement left her unmoved. Forking a piece of kidney from her plate to the terriers who crouched on either side of her, she said, "An excellent idea. They ought to have gone before. Unfortunately, none of us could afford it. Who will take his place? Not Jacques, surely? He hasn't the authority."

"Blanche," I replied. "She knows more about the *verrerie* than any of us. In future she will live at the master's house."

Even this failed to excite her. I don't know what I had expected. Abuse of Blanche perhaps, mockery, certainly a torrent of words. Instead she said almost placidly, "I always said Blanche had a head for business. I don't know where she gets it from—certainly not from me. Nor was your father brilliant. He looked upon the *verrerie* as a family tradition, not as a commercial proposition. But Blanche"—she raised her head and glanced across the table at her daughter—"she'll have the tourists here in no time at all. A shop inside the gates, selling replicas of the château and the church, ice creams from Julie at the lodge. It would have happened long ago, only that the war intervened."

She went on eating. Paul, throwing a look at me, said quickly, "You don't disapprove, then? Either of this plan or the other?"

"Disapprove?" she echoed. "Why should I disapprove? Both suggestions suit me well. What in the world would Blanche do with herself should I decide to come downstairs every day?" She crumbled a piece of bread. "Or Renée either, for that matter." She glanced at her daughter-in-law. "It's only when women have nothing to do that they get into mischief. They turn religious or take lovers."

So there was to be no argument. The child was right. Everyone had what they wanted. Relief showed itself on all their faces, and sitting there, watching them, I suddenly had a picture of what would be. Paul and Renée setting forth with luggage heaped at the back of the new car which I would buy for them, arriving in Paris feeling provincial and a little strange, but the feeling wearing off because of freedom; while Blanche, down in the master's house, sorting the furniture, turning over the books, coming perhaps upon a forgotten drawing or design, would find another freedom, escape from bitterness.

As I saw these things I was aware of Marie-Noel watching me from across the table. "Well?" I said. "What now?"

"Just this," she said. "You've made plans for everyone but yourself. What are you going to do when everybody's gone?"

Her question caught attention from the rest. They all looked at me, curious. Even Blanche, raising her head for one brief moment, stared, then dropped her eyes.

"I shall stay here," I said, "at the château, at St. Gilles. I've no intention of going away. I shall stay here always."

As I spoke I knew what I was going to do. I had remembered the service revolver in the drawer of the library desk. On Saturday I had burnt my hand to spare myself humiliation and discovery because I could not use a gun. Today was different. There would be no observers. The greatest fool on earth could hardly miss at point-blank range. I should have no remorse and no regret. He would receive the welcome he deserved. Even the rendezvous he had chosen, the master's house, was added justice. The only thing I minded was burning my car. Not that it seemed mine any longer, since he had taken it. It belonged to a past I had forgotten anyway. The project, born in an instant, took shape, becoming clear. I too would walk to the master's house through the woods, and, crossing the orchard at the back, climb through the window as I had done twice before. There would be no witnesses to this encounter. I stared in front of me, seeing nothing but the dark forest trees and the wet earth, and then, glancing up, I saw that they were still looking at me, puzzled, oddly strained. My last remark had sounded perhaps too vehement, too tense, and Marie-Noel, the only one without embarrassment, exclaimed, "When there's a sudden silence, and nobody speaks, it means there's an angel in the room, so Germaine told me. I'm not altogether sure. It could be a demon."

Gaston came with vegetables. The moment passed. Everyone began to talk at once, except myself. The mother, holding me with her eyes, framed with her lips the question, "What's the matter?" I shook my head, gesturing, "Nothing." I could see him climbing into the car at Deauville, driving off, confident, careless, assured of the little world that waited for him, the world which had become suddenly easier, his problems solved, the fortune he had always wanted now within his grasp; and I wondered whether it was his intention to dismiss me with a handshake and a smile, and then resume the life it had amused him to throw away. If so, his scheme would come to nothing. I was the substance now and he the shadow. The shadow was not wanted and could die.

After lunch my opportunity came. Blanche and the child went upstairs for lessons. The mother called the others to see the rearrangement of the salon. I went to the library, crossed over to the desk and pulled open the drawer. I saw the butt of the revolver beside the photograph album. I took it out and opened it, and it was loaded. I wondered why he kept it there, for what emergency, what strange purpose. Now it would be used against him. He had kept it loaded through the years for this. I slipped the revolver into my coat pocket, went upstairs to the dressing room and put it away in the drawer beside the boxes containing the morphine and the syringe.

When I came downstairs I realised I had been only just in time. They were moving into the library. The salon was now a place apart, waiting for tomorrow's ritual. Paul sat down at the desk, Renée at the table, and both of them began addressing envelopes. The mother, settling herself in a chair where she could watch them, put out her hand to me.

"You're restless," she said. "What's on your mind?"

As I looked at her I reminded myself that it was not her son I was going to kill but someone apart, without emotions, without heart, who had no feeling for her or anyone else. She recognised me as her son. In future I should do everything for her that he had failed to do.

"I want to bury the past," I said. "That's the only thing on my mind."

"You've been doing your best to resurrect it," she answered, "with your plan for Blanche."

"No," I said, "that's what you don't understand."

She shrugged her shoulders. "Just as you like," she said. "I ask for nothing better, if it works. The whole thing is a conspiracy, of course, to make life more pleasant for yourself. Come and sit down."

She gestured to the chair beside her and I sat down, still holding her hand. Presently, I saw she slept. Paul, turning his head, said quietly, "She's doing much too much. Charlotte said so just now. She'll suffer for it later. You ought to stop her."

"No," I said, "it's better this way."

Renée glanced at me from the table. "She ought to be resting upstairs," she said, "as she always does. Paul is perfectly right. She'll have a complete breakdown after the funeral."

"That's my risk," I said, "and my responsibility."

The long afternoon wore on. There was no sound but the scratching of the pens. I looked at the mother's face, asleep, and knew suddenly I must go before she woke, before the child came downstairs. Paul had his back to me, and Renée also. They must none of them know where I was going. Some impulse, like touching wood to ward off danger, made me kiss the mother's hand. Then I rose and went out of the room. No one looked up or called me back.

I fetched the revolver from the dressing room and went out of the front door onto the terrace and round the side of the château to the garden door. As I stood a moment under my first hiding place, the cedar tree, I saw César come out of his kennel. He lifted his head, sniffing the air, and looked towards me. He saw me, but he did not bark. Neither did he wag his tail. He accepted me as belonging to St. Gilles, but I was not yet his master. That would be one of my tasks. I went through to the park, under the chestnuts, and so out of the domain. Never had the forest seemed more beautiful or more benign, the hot sun gilding the falling leaves.

When I came to the field bordering the foundry grounds I lay down and waited. It was no use entering the master's house until Jacques had gone and the men had stopped work for the day. I remembered I had seen cans of petrol standing in the shed where they kept the lorry. Petrol was necessary for my purpose. Lying there in the woods, I could see the wisp of smoke coming from the foundry chimney, and I began to get impatient, restless. I wanted the men to go.

Two hours must have passed. I had no means of telling, without a watch, but of a sudden the air became more chill, the sun had dipped behind the trees, and I was aware of silence. All sounds from the foundry had ceased. I got up, and, crouching behind the hedge, looked at the orchard. No one was there. The windows of the office in the master's house were shut; the place seemed deserted. I crossed the orchard, keeping close to the hedge, and stood against the wall of the master's house. I waited a moment, then, sheltered by the vine, looked in at the office window. The room was empty, Jacques had gone home, and I had the place to myself. I moved along the house to the further end and climbed through the window once again. The room was full of traces of Blanche and Paul. Some of the furniture had already been shifted, tables and chairs pulled forward, pictures moved. She had not wasted time, then. She knew what she wanted to do. The room was no longer a shell, housing the past, but waited, expectant, for her to bring life to it once more.

I sat waiting, too, for the man I meant to kill. Sunlight went from the room, the shadows grew. In half an hour or less it would be dusk, and when he came, knocking on the window or the door, he would find that what happened to him was his own crime in reverse. He, and not I, would go back fifteen years.

I saw the handle of the door turn first, and because of disuse the knob fell to the floor. The door did not open, for I had bolted it. I crossed the room, picked up the knob and fitted it back. Slowly I withdrew the bolt, holding the revolver ready. I opened the door, the bottom of it jarring the stone flag, and it was thus, I thought, that Maurice Duval must have opened the door that night, and found him standing there in the darkness. Then I heard an exclamation from without and a voice—not his—said, "Hullo, is there somebody in the house?" It was not Jean de Gué, it was the curé. We confronted one another, I shaken and nonplussed, he smiling, nodding, until his eye, falling upon the revolver, oddly changed.

"Will you allow me?" he said, and he put out his hand and took the revolver from me before I knew what he was about. Then he emptied it, putting the cartridges in the pocket beneath his cassock, and the revolver also.

"I don't like those things," he said. "We had enough of them during the war, and during the Occupation too. They caused a lot of damage, and they could do so again."

He looked up at me, his head nodding agreement, and because I was without words, unable to speak, he patted my arm and said, "Don't be angry. You'll be glad that I took it away from you one of these days. You had planned destruction, hadn't you?"

I didn't answer him at once. Then I said, "Yes, Father."

"Very well," he said, "we won't discuss it. It's a matter for your own conscience and for God. It's not my business to ask you what is wrong. But it is my business to save life if I can. If that is what I have just done I find myself very thankful, and very humble too." He looked about him at the darkening room. "I've been visiting André Yves," he said. "Happily, in time, he may recover the use of his arm. He has great endurance. He said to me a week or so ago, 'It might be better if I put an end to myself.' 'Not so, André,' I told him. 'The future begins today. It's a gift, to which we wake each morning. Make use of it, don't throw it away.'" He paused, and then, pointing to the furniture, said, "So it's true then, what Mademoiselle Blanche told me this afternoon at the château when I called? She may come here to live, and it was your suggestion?"

"If she told you so, it's true," I answered.

"Then you certainly would not want to do anything to make her change her mind," he said. "There's an old saying— two wrongs don't make a right. Perhaps, if I had not happened to pass by, something would have happened to cause grief to all of us. There has been tragedy enough in your family without your adding to it."

"I wasn't going to add to tragedy, Father," I said. "I hoped to remove the cause."

"By destroying yourself?" he asked. "What good would that

do, to you or to them? By living, you can create their world afresh. Already I see signs of it, here in the master's house. That's what's needed, not only here in the *verrerie* but in the château too. Life, not death."

He waited for me to answer. I said nothing. "Well, now"— he hesitated, turning again to the door—"I can't offer you a ride—I came on my tricycle. I don't see the car outside. How will you go home?"

"I walked," I said, "and I shall return that way."

"Why not walk beside me?" he suggested. "I go very slowly, you know." He drew out his watch. "It's after seven already," he said. "They may be looking for you at the château. I know one who will be waiting anyway, the child. I'm dull company on the road, but I'd like you to join me."

"Not tonight, Father," I said. "I'd rather be alone."

Still he hesitated, his eyes anxious. "I'm not sure that I'm happy to leave you," he said, "after what I discovered just now. You might still do something rash that you'd regret."

"I can't," I said. "You've made it impossible."

He smiled. "I'm glad," he said. "I shall never regret it. As for your gun"—he patted his cassock—"perhaps I'll let you have it back again, one of these days. It will depend upon yourself. *Bonsoir.*"

He went out of the doorway into the dusk. I watched him pass the well without a glance, and so across the ground towards the sheds. I closed the door and bolted it again. The room was now filled with shadows, the day was done. As I went to the window facing the orchard a figure rose from beneath it, gun in hand, and, throwing his legs across the sill, climbed in. Laughing softly, pointing the gun at my chest, he said, "That's how I worked it once before, but this was far easier. No sentries on the road, no huts, no blocks, no wire. And instead of a bunch of lads who might give me away under threat, good Monsieur le Curé himself, who happened to pass by. You must admit that luck is always on my side. I was right, wasn't I, to come armed? It was the only thing I didn't leave you in my valise in Le Mans."

He pulled forward two of the chairs that Blanche had moved that morning.

"Sit down," he said. "You don't have to keep your hands up.

This isn't a threat, merely a precaution. I've always carried a gun since '41." He sat down in the other chair and straddled it, facing me. The back of it made a resting place for the gun. "So you planned to get rid of me, did you, and stay in St. Gilles? The sudden prospect of a fortune was too much for you? I sympathise. I felt that way myself."

Chapter 26

I couldn't see his eyes but only his features, dimly, which were mine. The absence of light made his presence, although more sinister, somehow easier to bear.

"What happened?" he asked. "How did she die? The notice I read this morning said by accident."

"She fell," I answered, "from the window of her bedroom. She had dropped the locket brooch you brought her back from Paris, and was reaching for it."

"Was she alone at the time?"

"Yes," I said. "There was a police enquiry. The *commissaire* was quite satisfied, and the death certificate was signed. To-morrow they bring her back to St. Gilles, and the funeral is on Friday."

"I read that in the papers," he said. "That's why I returned."

I made no comment. It was not the funeral of his wife which had brought him home, but what her death would mean to him hereafter.

"You know," he said, "I never thought you'd face it. When I left you in that hotel bedroom a week ago today, I imagined you going to the police, telling them your story, and, after many muddled explanations, persuading them to believe it. Instead"—he laughed, "you've succeeded in living a lie for seven whole days. My congratulations. What a boon you could have been to me twelve or fifteen years ago. Tell me, has no one had any suspicion?"

"No one," I said.

"What about my mother, and the child?"

"They least of all."

To say this gave me a strange sort of satisfaction that was

almost savage. He had not been missed; no one had regretted him.

"I wonder how much you learnt," he said. "It amuses me immensely to think of how you dealt with Renée, for instance, who already, before I left, was becoming a bore. And how you kept Françoise pacified. And whether, with misplaced courtesy, you tried to talk to Blanche. As for my mother, her demands can only be dealt with in the future by a doctor. Not our own, needless to say, but an expert. She'll have to go to a clinic. I'm already in touch with one, in Paris."

I watched the muzzle of the revolver on the back of his chair. I should never reach it. Expert in trickery as in all things, he would be too quick for me.

"There's no need to send her to Paris," I said. "Though I expect she will need medical care at home. She wants to stop the drug. I was with her all last night. She's made the first attempt."

I could feel his eyes upon me in the darkness. "What do you mean?" he asked. "You were with her all last night? What did you do?"

I thought back to the chair beside her bed, to the half-dreams, to the silence, to the threatening shadows that seemed to dissolve and pass. To tell him about the night now sounded trite, absurd. Nothing had been accomplished, only sleep.

"I sat beside her and she slept," I said. "I held her hand."

His laughter, infectious yet intolerable, rang through the dark room. "My poor friend," he said, "do you imagine that is the way to cure a morphine addict? Tonight she'll be a raving maniac. Charlotte will have to give her a double dose."

"No," I said. "No." But doubt assailed me. Already, when I left her sleeping in her chair, she had looked ill and exhausted.

"What else?" he said. "Tell me what else you've done."

What else? I searched my mind. "Paul," I said, "Paul and Renée. They're leaving the château, leaving St. Gilles. They're going to travel, at any rate for six months or a year."

I saw him nod. "That will break up the marriage even sooner," he said. "Renée will find the lover she's been searching for, and Paul feel himself more inferior than ever. Put him in the world and he'll look what he knows he is—a provincial boor. What want of tact, if I may say so, how lacking in finesse. Tell me more."

I remembered, as a boy, playing skittles. One bowled a ball along an alley, and the ninepin at the other end toppled and fell flat. This was what he was doing now to the plans I had conceived through love. It was not love, then, after all, but muddled sentiment.

"You turned down the Carvalet contract, didn't you?" I said. "I signed a new one. The *verrerie* won't close. No one will be out of a job. You'll have to back the loss with capital."

This time he didn't laugh. He whistled. The expression of dismay delighted me. "I suppose I can get out of it," he said. "It may take time. Your other moves were minor blunders, but this is serious. Even with Françoise's money behind me, propping up a dying business is no fun. Whom did you intend to look after things, with Paul away?"

"Blanche," I said.

He leant forward in his chair, tilting it, and thrust his face close to mine. Now I could see every feature, and his eyes as well. It was as it had been before, in the hotel in Le Mans. The likeness to myself was vile.

"You actually spoke to Blanche?" he asked. "And she replied?"

"I did," I said. "She came down here this morning. I told her the *verrerie* was hers from now on. She can do what she likes with it, she can build it up as a dowry for Marie-Noel."

He said nothing for a moment. The upsetting of all his preconceived ideas may have shaken him. I hoped it had. More than anything else, I wanted him to lose assurance. He did not do so.

"Do you know," he said slowly, "it might, in the long run, work. If Blanche took up designing again, and we could turn out cheap gimcrack stuff to attract the tourist, not bothering with Carvalet or any of the other good firms, we might attract a market in this part of the country that would undercut everyone else. Instead of every tourist driving through Villars to Le Mans down the *route nationale,* they would make a détour to St. Gilles. I believe, without knowing it, you've hit upon a plan." He paused. "Yes," he said, "the more I think of it, the more I like the idea. What an idiot I was never to

311

have thought of it. Blanche's intolerable attitude to me made it out of the question. How clever of you to flatter her ego, which I suppose you did. She used to think a lot of herself as a designer in old days, she and that pompous prig between them. If she comes down here to live she'll probably wear widow's weeds and pretend she married him secretly after all." He reached in his pocket for a packet of cigarettes, and handed me one, lighting his own. "You haven't done too badly, on the whole," he said. "What about Marie-Noel—where's she in the picture? Has she seen any visions this week, or dreamt any dreams?"

I did not answer. To tarnish the child was surely the ultimate evil. He might desecrate the mother, mock the sister and the brother, but to give him Marie-Noel as a butt for humour, that I would not do.

"She's all right," I said. "She stood yesterday's tragedy well."

"That doesn't surprise me," he said. "The two of them never got on. Françoise was jealous of the child, and the child knew it. Now, at last, you understand what it means to have a possessive family. And you were prepared to endure it, for the sake of the money. You came down here to the master's house determined to kill me, so that you could keep yourself in comfort for the rest of your days."

He tilted his chair back again, blowing smoke into the air, and his face was in shadow once more. Only his outline remained.

"You won't believe me," I said, "but I didn't think about the money. I happen to love your family, that's all."

My statement made him laugh once more.

"You have the audacity to tell me," he said, "that you love my mother, who is without exception the most egotistical, the most rapacious, the most monstrous woman I have, in all my experience, ever known; you love Paul, who is an oaf, a weakling, and a thoroughly disagreeable personality; you love Renée—presumably for her body, which I grant you is enchanting, but she has a mind like an empty box; you love Blanche, who is so twisted with repressed sex and frustrated passion that the only stimulation she gets out of life is to kneel before a bleeding crucifix. And I suppose you'll tell me that

312

you love my child for her sweetness and her innocence, which, let me tell you, can be put on for effect. What she really likes is being petted and admired."

I did not argue. What he said was true, according to his light, and perhaps mine too. The point was, it did not matter.

"I agree with you," I said, "your family are all those things. It doesn't prevent me from loving them, that's all. Don't ask me why. I couldn't answer you."

"I have affection for them," he said. "That's understandable. They happen to belong to me. But you have no reason. You've only known them a week. You're an incurable sentimentalist, of course."

"Perhaps."

"Did you see yourself as a saviour?"

"No. As a fool."

"That's honest, anyway. And what do you suppose is going to happen now?"

"I don't know. It's up to you."

He scratched his head with the butt of his revolver. I might have sprung at him then, but it wouldn't have worked.

"Exactly," he said. "What happens at St. Gilles is up to me. I can carry through your programme if I choose. Or tear it up, depending on my mood. What about you? Shall we walk into the forest and dig a grave? I can easily burn your car. No one would look for you. You'd simply disappear. It's happened to other people before now."

"If that's what you decide," I said, "then go ahead. I'm in your hands. Unless you prefer to throw me down the well."

I couldn't see him, but I could feel his smile. "Have you raked up that one too?" he said. "What a ferret you are. I thought the mud had settled years ago. I suppose you were shocked?"

"I wasn't shocked," I told him. "Your motive puzzled me."

"My motive?" he echoed. "Of course it puzzled you. You haven't been invaded since 1066. Complacency makes all your countrymen smug. We may be ruthless sometimes, but thank God we're none of us hypocrites. Do you also love your image of Maurice Duval?"

I considered a moment. Was love too strong a word? "I

313

regretted him," I said. "What I heard of him seemed to be good."

"Don't you believe it," he said. "He was a climber, like all his kind. Edged his way in with my father, with an eye to the future. Blanche was his greatest card, and I stopped him playing it. It's not very chic, you know, to sit back in comfort and make terms with your country's invaders to save your skin."

I had no answer. The quarrel was not my quarrel, nor the war my war. I only knew that people had suffered and died.

"It's not much use," I said, "discussing Duval or your family. I have my own picture of them. Nothing you can say will break it down. If you intend to kill me, as I intended to kill you, let's get it over. I'm ready."

"I'm not sure I want to kill you," he said. "It seems rather a waste. After all, we've deceived them once, we could do so again. I could let you know, we could arrange a rendezvous, I could disappear for a week or a month and you take my place. What do you think? Of course, I might have undone, in the meantime, all that you'd tried to do. But that wouldn't bother you. It might even add zest to your stay."

I hated him so much I could not answer. And, taking my silence for consideration, he went on, "You'd hardly have met my Béla," he said. "There wouldn't have been time. Nor, I dare say, the opportunity. She keeps a shop in Villars, and I call her Béla because she pretends she's descended from the kings of Hungary. Cooks like an angel, and that's not her only attraction. I visit her now and again to keep boredom at bay. Naturally, if we come to an agreement, she'll be part of the bargain. You wouldn't regret a visit, I can promise you that." Still I did not answer. "It would even," he said, "add a certain piquancy when I returned, if I thought you'd been deceiving Béla with the rest."

I got up from my chair. Instantly he rose too, covering me with the gun.

"Let's get it over," I said. "I've nothing more to say."

"I have, though," he answered. "Do you realise you haven't asked me any questions? Don't you want to know what I've been doing the past week?"

I was not interested. He had telephoned from Deauville. I

314

assumed, if I assumed anything, that he had been staying there. It was as good a place as any for escape.

"No," I said. "Frankly, I don't care. It doesn't concern me."

"But it does concern you," he insisted. "It concerns you very much."

"How?"

"Sit down again," he said, "and I'll enlighten you." He snapped a lighter, which I realised, in the light of the flame, was mine. And then I saw that his coat was also mine. But not the one I had been wearing in Le Mans.

"You see?" he said. "I played the game fair, just as you did. If you were taking my place—and I couldn't be sure, it was a gamble—then it was only sporting to take yours. I went to London. I went to your flat. I only flew back today."

I stared at him, or rather not at him but at his shadow. When I had thought of him, during the past week, it had been as a phantom, someone who existed no longer, a shadow, a wraith. And had I given the wraith substance I should have placed him perhaps in Paris, or in the south, in Italy, in Spain, anywhere but in my own life, deceiving my own world.

"You went to my flat?" I said. "You used my things?"

The duplicity, the outrage, seemed to me overwhelming. I could not believe it. Someone would surely have prevented it.

"Why not?" he said. "That's what you did at St. Gilles. I left you my family. You used them in the way you've described. Not my way, I admit, but that was the chance I took. You can hardly blame me for playing the game in reverse."

I tried to think. I tried to picture the scene. The hall porters would merely nod and say good morning or good night. The woman who cleaned my flat never came until after half past ten, when I had already left. In the evening, unless I dined with friends, I did for myself. Most people believed me away on the last week of holiday. There was no reason for anyone to telephone, to write. Bewildered, I still sought for proof that he was lying. "How did you know where to go?" I said. "How did you manage?"

"My poor idiot," he replied, "your card was in your valise, your notebook, your cheques, your keys, your passport—all

315

the things I was likely to need. I was even able to transfer the date for the car—the ferry service had a vacancy. To take over your very retiring personality proved the easiest thing in the world. I enjoyed myself. Your flat was a haven of rest. After the turmoil of St. Gilles I felt I was in paradise. I rifled your drawers, read all your letters, deciphered your lecture notes, cashed your cheques—fortunately your somewhat cramped signature was easy enough to imitate. I spent five days in complete and utter idleness, which was just what I needed."

The humour, and the justice, struck me at last. I had played about with human life; he had not. I had done my best to change his household; he had merely yawned and taken his ease. I had meddled; he had only spied. Then I remembered that he had, after all, returned. The news of Françoise's death, so promptly inserted in the papers by the lawyer, had found him at Deauville.

"If you enjoyed my London solitude so much," I asked, "what made you come back again to France?"

I felt him watch me in the darkness. He did not answer immediately, and when he did it was almost with embarrassment.

"That's where I have to apologise," he said, "but not more so, I think, than you, who by altering that contract may have let me in for very heavy loss. The fact is"—he paused, choosing his words—"the fact is, five days in London were enough. I couldn't have continued your dull, virtuous existence. In time someone would have arrived, friends would have written, the people at the university got in touch; and though I have never before questioned either my ability to take another's part or my command of English—I had plenty of practice in both during the war—I appear to have lacked your supreme confidence. The easiest thing to do, as I intended using your name and personality, was to change your mode of living. This was, to tell you the truth, just what I did."

I did not understand. I could not follow what he was trying to tell me.

"What do you mean?" I said. "How could you change my life?"

I heard him sigh in the darkness. "It may come as a shock," he said, "just as what you have been doing at St.

Gilles has come as a shock to me. First I wrote to the university, resigning your job. Then I told your landlord that I was going abroad immediately and wanted to give up the lease of your flat, and, flats being as few and far between in London as they are in Paris, he was only too glad for me—or rather you—to get out at once. I instructed a firm of auctioneers to sell your furniture. And finally, having found out from your bank statement how much money you had in the bank, I cashed a cheque for just that amount. It was, if you remember, a couple of hundred pounds. Not a fortune, but enough to tide me over comfortably for a month or two, until something else turned up."

I tried to grasp what he was telling me, to make myself realise that he was speaking of something which had actually happened, to think myself back into the person I had been. But all I could see was this shadow, wearing my clothes, who within a number of hours had destroyed that person's life.

"The French currency," I said. "You couldn't do it. How could you have changed two hundred pounds into francs? They wouldn't have given you more than the tourist allowance, and I had already spent three quarters of that."

He put his cigarette stub on the floor and squashed it with his foot. "That," he said, "was the cream of the joke. I have a friend who arranges these things, and he did it for me in a few hours. I should never have known he was in London but for the fact that you gave him your address—I couldn't imagine why, but in the circumstances it was a heaven-sent opportunity. When he telephoned on Monday morning I was never more surprised in my life, and it was then, of course, that I realised you were at St. Gilles. The point is that if I don't kill you, and if you won't agree to my little plan of deception that we share each other's lives from time to time, what are you going to do? There *is* no future for you."

The full meaning of his words was forced upon me. Unless I liked to make a fool of myself by writing to the university and saying it was all a mistake—that I had decided not to resign after all—I had no work. I had no money, save for one or two modest investments. I had no flat, and if I didn't get back to London soon I should have no furniture.

I did not exist. The self who had lived in London had gone forever.

"Of course," he said, "I didn't intend to come home. I was going to amuse myself spending your money over here. My friend is a wizard with currency, and he would have banked it anywhere—in this country or wherever I told him. Personally, I had in mind, to start off with, some little niche in Sicily or Greece. I would have taken Béla with me as a companion. She might have palled in time, but not at first. Hungarian women have the strangest charm. They get, as the Americans have it, 'under the skin.' But now"—he broke off, and I could dimly see the shrug of the shoulders—"poor Françoise dying has rather changed my plans. Instead of being an impoverished provincial count I might, with any luck, be a millionaire. Fate, or whoever arranges these things, has done what I wanted."

He stood up, the gun still pointing at me.

"It's a curious thing," he said, "and shows weakness of character. But apart from the money, and the sudden upheaval of plans, while I was driving from Deauville this afternoon I felt myself moved. The country was looking beautiful, the colours were exquisite. It is, after all, my country, and where I belong. The château, heaven knows, is falling to pieces and the grounds are unkempt and ragged, but I don't really mind. If you've been born in a place it does something to you. I neglect it, and curse it, and fight against all that it does to me, just as I curse my mother, for the self-same reason. And yet"—he laughed, and I saw him gesture with his hand—"and yet, driving south from Deauville, I felt I wanted her. In a strange sort of way I missed her, while I was gone. She's a devil and a brute, but I understand her and she understands me, and that's more than you can say, after your seven days."

Suddenly, with geniality, almost with affection, he shook my shoulder.

"Come on," he said, "I don't want to kill you. In many ways I'm grateful for what you've done." He pulled out a wallet—mine. "This will keep you for some considerable time," he said. "Naturally, there's no reason to cheat you now. At any time you decide upon deception, for a few

318

days even, I'll be delighted to oblige. What about it? Shall we play charades again now, and start to strip?"

I thought of the curé. I tried to remember what the curé had said. Something about the future, and every day a gift. He was now back in St. Gilles, putting away his tricycle. At the château they were waiting for dinner. They would be wondering where I had gone. Marie-Noel, anxious, perhaps, at my absence, was waiting for me on the terrace. I began to take off my coat.

The exchange of clothes in the darkness was macabre, even terrible. It meant, with every garment shed, a loss of the self I had found. When I stood in front of him at last, naked, and he had his revolver pointing at me still, I said, "Finish me off, I don't want to live."

"Nonsense," he answered. "No one refuses life. Besides, I don't want to kill you. The point has gone."

He began throwing off his clothes as he spoke, and, seeing that I fumbled with them as I put them on, he said, "What have you done to your hand?"

"I burnt it," I said. "I burnt it in a fire."

"What fire?" he asked. "Has there been a fire at the château?"

"No," I replied, "a bonfire in the grounds."

"How careless," he said. "You might have damaged your hand for good. Does it mean you're not able to drive the car?"

"No," I said. "It's better now."

"You'd better hand over the dressing. I can't appear without it."

The clothes, that had once been mine, seemed shrunken, small. The texture was too smooth. They didn't fit. The suit he had picked from my wardrobe in the flat was one I seldom wore. As I stood before him, dressed and ready, it was like wearing some sort of garment long outgrown, almost as if a man struggled once again into his schoolboy clothes.

He sighed in satisfaction. "That's better," he said. "I feel like myself again." He moved towards the window. "We'd better go out this way," he said. "It's safer. That gossip Julie may be in her lodge. There's another wicked old rascal for you. I suppose you loved her too."

He climbed from the window and I followed him. The

scent of the tumbled orchard filled the air. I brushed the vine with my shoulder as I passed.

"I'm sorry," he said, "I shall have to ask you to walk in front of me. I'll direct you to the place where I've left your car."

I stumbled across the orchard and the field. I saw the dim outline of the old white horse against the hedge. He snorted at sight of us, and made off.

"Poor Jacob," said my pursuer, "he's very old. Every tooth in his head is rotten—he can't even eat properly. I'll put a bullet through him one day to ease his troubles. You see, I can be sentimental too, at times."

The dark woods closed upon us, and even now I could not be sure, even now it might suit his plan to kill me and have done with me forever. I walked on, through darkness, undergrowth and moss, and now I had no present and no past, the self who stumbled had no heart or mind.

"There's the car," he said suddenly.

The Ford, familiar, spattered with mud, was drawn up beside the forest track. It seemed to me, like my clothes, a phase outgrown. I patted the bonnet with my hand.

"Get in," he said.

I settled myself in the well-known seat and switched on the lights and the ignition.

"Back her out into the track," he said.

He got in beside me and we drove along the path. We turned into the forest road and followed it to the top of the hill. Below us were the lights of the village, and the clock struck eight.

"It may not be easy," I said slowly. "They have become different. Your mother, I mean, and Blanche, and Paul, and Renée. Only the child is the same. The child hasn't changed."

He laughed. "Even if she had," he said, "she'd soon be mine again. I'm the only one who matters in her world."

We drove down the lime avenue and across the bridge. When I came to the gateway I stopped the car. "I won't go any further," I said. "It wouldn't be safe."

He got out and stood for a moment, an animal, sniffing the air. "It's good," he said. "It's part of the place. It's St. Gilles."

Now at last, when all decisions had been taken, he emptied his gun. He put it, with the cartridges, into his pocket.

"Good luck," he said, and then, with a smile, "Listen." He put his two fingers in his mouth and whistled. The sound was shrill and long. It was answered almost instantly by César. He began to bark. Not savagely, not as he would do to a stranger, but excitedly, high-pitched, the bark changing to a howl, to a whine. The sound went on and on, filling the air. "You didn't learn that trick?" he asked. "Of course not, how could you know?"

He smiled, and waved his hand, and passed through the gateway onto the drive. Looking towards the terrace steps, I saw a figure waiting there, the glow from the fanlight above the door shining upon her. It was Marie-Noel. When she saw the figure striding up the drive she gave a cry and ran down the steps towards him. I saw him swing her up in his arms and climb the steps. They went inside the château. The dog was whining still. I got into the car and drove away.

Chapter 27

What I did was automatic. I don't remember thinking anything. I turned the car up the lime avenue and then to the right, on the road to Villars. The way was so familiar now, even in darkness, that the action was mechanical. I drove cautiously because my injured hand was awkward still, and the part of my brain that was working told me I couldn't afford to make a mistake and risk landing the Ford and myself in a ditch. I concentrated on holding the wheel and watching the road, and the effort of doing so shut out thoughts of anything else. I made no image of the life I had left. It was as though, when he entered the château, something like an iron clamp had come down, shutting me from it and them, and I had to hide, I had to seek the cover of darkness.

Coming into Villars was a strange relief. The country roads held menace: they were nerve cells leading back to St. Gilles. Villars was lighted and had solidity, and people strolling in the streets. I turned down past the market place and stopped the car just short of the Porte de Ville. I looked across the canal and saw that the long window of Béla's room was opened wide onto the balcony, and was lighted too. She was at home. When I saw the light, and the open window, something stirred within me that had been frozen since Jean de Gué and I had changed clothes in the darkness. The iron clamp was between me and the château, not between me and her. She was outside the taboo. The light in her window was consoling, kindly. It stood for reality, too, for the things that were true. It seemed to me that this was important, to know the false from the true, and I could no longer distinguish between either. Béla could tell me, Béla would know.

I left the car and went over the footbridge to the balcony. I walked in through the open window. The room was empty, but she was there. I could hear her moving about in the kitchen across the passage. I stood there, waiting, and in a moment she was with me. She stood in the doorway, looking at me, and then she shut the door and came towards me.

"I didn't expect you," she said, "but it doesn't matter. If I'd known you were coming I would have waited dinner for you."

"I'm not hungry," I said. "I don't want anything."

"You look ill," she said. "Sit down, I'll get you a drink."

I sat in the deep chair. I did not know what I was going to say to her. She gave me cognac, and watched me while I drank. The cognac brought some sort of warmth to me, but the numbness remained. I felt the solidity of the arm of the chair under my hand, and it was safety.

"Have you been in the hospital chapel?" she said.

I stared at her. It took me a moment to realise what she meant.

"No," I said, "no, I was there this morning." I paused. "Thank you for the porcelain. The child was pleased. She believed they were the old ones, mended. It was right of you to suggest that."

"Yes," she said, "I thought it better that way."

She looked at me with compassion. No doubt I seemed to her strained and queer. She must believe I was still shaken by the shock of Françoise's death. It might be better to let her think that. Yet I could not be sure. I wanted something for myself alone.

"I came," I said, "because I was not sure when I should see you again."

"I understand," she answered. "Naturally the next few days, the next weeks, are going to be very hard for you."

The next days . . . the next weeks. They did not exist. It was not easy to tell her that.

"The child," she asked, "is she all right?"

"She's been wonderful," I said. "Yes, she's quite all right."

"And your mother?"

"My mother too."

She was still watching me. I saw her eye fall on my clothes. She did not recognise the suit. It was not dark, like the one I had been wearing since Françoise's death, but a tweed mixture. The shirt, the tie, the socks, the shoes—she had never seen any of them before. An odd silence seemed to come between us. I felt I must justify myself, give her some explanation.

"I want to thank you," I said. "You've shown me great understanding all this past week. I'm very grateful to you."

She did not answer. And suddenly I saw comprehension come into her eyes, the flash of intuition that sweeps an adult hearing the confession of a child. In a moment she was kneeling by my side.

"He has come back then?" she said. "The other one?" I looked at her. She put her hands on my shoulders. "I might have known it," she said. "He saw the notice in the paper. That brought him back."

Her words gave me such a sense of overpowering relief that all feeling of strain and tension went from me. It was like the stanching of a wound, the cessation of pain, the blotting out of fear. I put down the cognac and did something infantile and absurd. I laid my head on her shoulder and closed my eyes.

"Why you?" I asked. "Why you and nobody else? Why not the mother, why not the child?"

I felt her hands on my head, soothing, gentle. It was surrender, it was peace.

"I suppose I was not easy to deceive," she said. "I did not realise at first—I could not have told from looking at you, from conversation, any more than they could. It was not till later that I knew."

"What did I do?" I said.

She laughed, and the laugh was not mocking, as it might have been, or easy, or gay, but had a strange quality of warmth, of understanding.

"It was not what you did," she said, "but what you were. A woman would have to be a great fool not to distinguish between one man and another, making love." I felt rebuffed. Yet still I did not mind, because she was with me. "You have something," she said, "that he doesn't possess. That's how I knew."

"What do I have?" I asked.

"You may call it *tendresse*," she said. "I don't know another word for it." Then abruptly she asked my name.

"John," I said. "We share even that. Shall I tell you what happened?"

"If you want to," she said. "I can guess a great deal. The past is done with, for both of you. The future is what matters now."

"Yes," I said, "but not mine, theirs."

As I said this I knew with urgency, with conviction, that what I was saying was right and true. The old self of Le Mans was dead. The shadow of Jean de Gué had also vanished. In their place was something else that as yet had no substance, no flesh, no blood, but was born of feeling, that could not die, and it was like a flame, contained in the body's shell.

"I love them," I said. "I'm part of them now, forever. That's what I want you to understand. I shall never see them again, but because of them I live."

"I understand," she said, "and it could be the same for them. Because of you they also live."

"If I could believe that," I said, "then nothing matters. Then everything is all right. But he's gone back to them. It's going to be as it was before. It will start all over again—the carelessness, the unhappiness, the suffering, the pain. If that were to happen, I should want to go out now and hang myself on the nearest tree. Even now . . ." I stared over her shoulder at the darkness outside the window, and the iron barrier thinned, and it was as though I stood beside him inside the château, and I saw him smile, and I saw the mother look at him, and the child, and Blanche, and Paul, and Renée, and Julie too, and her son André.

"I want them to be happy," I said. "Not his sort of happiness, but the kind that is buried inside them, locked up, that I know is there. Béla, it exists, I've seen it, like a light or a hunger, waiting to be released."

I stopped, because what I said was perhaps nonsense. I couldn't explain myself. "He's a devil," I said, "and they belong to him again."

"No," she said, "that's where you're wrong. He's not a devil. He's a human, ordinary man, just like yourself."

She rose and drew the curtains, and then came back to me again. "Remember, I know him," she said, "his weakness and his strength, his good points and his bad. If he were a devil I shouldn't waste my time here in Villars. I should have left him long ago."

I wanted to believe her, but I could not be sure, when a woman loves a man, how true is her judgment. To see no evil could be the one blindness. Little by little I told her what I knew, the bits and pieces of the past I had put together during the week that had gone. Some of it she knew already; some of it she guessed. Yet as I talked, wishing to condemn him, it was as if it was the shadow I condemned, the man who had moved and spoken and acted in his place, and not Jean de Gué at all.

"It's no use," I said at last. "I'm not describing the man you know."

"You are," she answered, "but you're describing yourself as well."

There was the fear. Which one of us was real? Who lived, and who had died? It struck me suddenly that if I should now look at myself in a mirror I should see no reflection.

"Béla," I said, "hold me. Tell me my name."

"You are John," she said, "you are John, who changed places with Jean de Gué. You lived his life for a week. You came here twice to my house and you loved me as John, not as Jean de Gué. Is that reality for you? Does that help you to become yourself?"

I touched her hair and her face and her hands, and there was no falsity about her, no pretence.

"You've given something to all of us," she said, "to me, to his mother, to his sister, to his child. Just now I called it *tendresse*. Whatever it is, it can't be destroyed. It's taken root. It will go on growing. In future we shall look for you in Jean, not for Jean in you." She smiled, and put her hands on my shoulders. "Do you realise I know nothing about you?" she said. "I don't know where you come from, or where you are going, or anything at all except that your name is John."

"There is no more to know," I said. "Let's leave it at that."

"If he hadn't come back," she asked, "what was he going to do?"

"He was going to travel," I told her. "He was going to take you with him. Or so he said. Would you have gone?"

She did not answer at once. For the first time she seemed nonplussed.

"He's been my lover for three years," she said. "He's familiar, part of my daily existence. I believe he's fond of me. But he would soon find someone else."

"No," I said, "he would never find anyone else."

"What makes you so sure of that?"

"You forget," I said. "I've lived his life for a week."

I looked at the window and the curtains she had drawn across it.

"Why did you draw the curtains?" I asked.

"It's a signal," she said. "He doesn't come in when they're drawn. It means I'm not alone."

The same thought, then, had come to both of us. Once he had dined, and said good night to the child, and left his mother in the tower room alone, he might go down to the car once again, and drive from St. Gilles to Villars, and cross the footbridge as I had done. He belonged here, just as he did there. He was the man in possession, I the intruder.

"Béla," I said, "he doesn't know I've been here. He need never know, unless it comes out through Gaston, which is unlikely. Keep it from him, if you can."

I got up from the chair.

She said, "What are you going to do?"

"Leave the house," I answered, "before he comes. If I know anything of him, he'll need you tonight."

She looked at me thoughtfully. "I could leave the curtain drawn," she said.

When she said this I remembered what he had done to me. I remembered how he had not only taken up his own life once again but had destroyed the one that had been mine. I no longer had a job, or a roof in London, or anything that belonged to me but a suit of clothes, and the Ford, and a wallet containing some French money.

"I asked you a question a moment ago," I said to her, "but you never answered it. I asked you if you would have gone with him, travelling, had he suggested it."

"I suppose so," she said, "if I felt he wanted me."

"It would have been a sudden plan," I said, "without much warning. Remember, he couldn't have shown himself in Villars, in case he was recognised."

"He wouldn't have come to Villars," she said. "He would have written to me, or telegraphed, or even telephoned, asking me to join him."

"And you would have gone?"

She hesitated for one brief moment. "Yes," she said, "yes, I should have gone."

I glanced at the window. "Pull the curtains back when I've left the house," I said. "I'll go down the stairs and through the door to the street."

She followed me out of the room to the passage beyond. "What about your hand?"

"My hand?"

"It has no dressing."

She went to the bathroom and fetched an oilskin packet, similar to the one she had used on Sunday. As she held my hand, and dressed it, I thought of Blanche, who had done the same for me in the morning, and I thought of the mother, whose hand had lain in mine throughout the night. I remembered, too, the firm, warm clasp of the child.

"Look after them," I said. "You can do it, but nobody else. Perhaps he'll listen to you. Help him to love them."

327

"He loves them already," she said. "I want you to believe it. It wasn't just the money that brought him back."

"I wonder," I said. "I wonder . . ."

When she had dressed my hand and I was ready to leave, she said to me, "Where are you going? What are you going to do?"

"I have a car outside," I answered, "the one he took from me a week ago. The one he would have driven you in, to Sicily or Greece."

She came with me down the stairs, and, standing there, at the dark entrance to the shop, she paused a moment before opening the barred door and letting me out into the night, and in a troubled voice she said, "You're not going to harm yourself in any way? You haven't said to yourself, 'This is the end'?"

"No," I said, "it isn't the end. It may be the beginning."

She drew back the bolts from the door. "A week ago," I told her, "I was a man named John, who didn't know what to do with failure. I thought of a place I might go to, to find out. Then I met Jean de Gué, and went to St. Gilles instead."

"And now you are John again," she answered, "but you don't have to worry about failure. It doesn't exist for you any more. You learnt what to do with failure at St. Gilles."

"I didn't learn what to do with it," I said, "it merely became transformed. It turned into love for St. Gilles. So the problem remains the same. What do I do with love?"

She opened the door. The shops and houses opposite were shuttered and closed. There was nobody in the street.

"You give it away," she said, "but the trouble is, it stays with you just the same. Like water in a well. The spring remains, under the dried depths." She put her arms round me and kissed me. "Will you write to me?" she asked.

"I expect so."

"And you know where you're going?"

"I know where I'm going."

"Will you be there long?"

"I've no idea."

"This place, is it far away?"

"Oddly enough, no. Only about fifty kilometres."

"If they could have shown you there what to do with failure, can they also show you what to do with love?"

"I believe so. I believe they'll give me the answer you've given me now."

I kissed her, and then I went out into the street. I heard her shut the door and bolt it behind me. I went under the Porte de Ville, and climbed into the car, and reached for my maps. They were where I had left them, in the pocket beside the driver's seat. I found the route I had marked with a blue cross a week ago. The last ten kilometres might be difficult in the darkness, but if I kept the Forêt du Perche on my right, the road would take me to the Forêt de la Trappe and to the Abbey after leaving Mortagne. I might be able to get there in not much more than an hour, or an hour and a half.

I put down the map, and, glancing up at her window, I saw that she had pulled the curtains back once more. The light was shining from the window down to the canal and the footbridge. I backed the car, and turned and went up the avenue, and as I passed the hospital I saw the Renault drawn up beside the pavement. It was not outside the hospital entrance, but by the smaller gate, leading to the chapel. It was empty, and there was no sign of Gaston. Whoever had come in the car had gone in to pay tribute alone.

I drove to the network of roads at the top of the town, turned left, and took the road to Bellême and Mortagne.

The Moon and Sixpence

W. SOMERSET MAUGHAM

THE CLASSIC STORY OF A REBELLIOUS GENIUS
WHO SACRIFICED FAMILY AND FRIENDS
TO PURSUE HIS ARTISTIC DREAM

75198/75¢